Have a Little Faith

By: Zachary Hicks

Dedication

To my mother, Pa, Nana and aunts. I love you all. My
brother who I love more than he will ever know and is one of
my best friends.

Morgan, my beautiful wife. This book is only possible
because of you. You never gave up on me, you have
supported me through thick and thin. Words will never be
able to express to you how much I love you. You allowed me
to pursue my dream and I will never forget that. You are my
everything - best friend, wife, lover, partner, but most of all,
my soulmate. I love you.

Table of Contents

Chapter 1

October 19, 2017

Thursday

11:32a.m.

Jonathan was great at first impressions, he had everything someone needed to put people at ease. He was handsome with his green eyes that seem to look right through you. His strong jaw was covered by his perfectly trimmed beard. Jonathan felt that his best feature was his hair. He had brown hair with naturally white streaks that blended just right, giving him that distinguished looked. He loved to charm people, he secretly loved big events where he could dress his best and be the center of attention. Of course, women loved him and men envied him. Jonathan sat in his over-sized leather chair behind his expensive cocobolo desk, he took a sip of the coffee that his secretary made him. He picked up his phone from his desk, he was going to call her to gloat. He knew she wouldn't understand how that felt because she came from money, she had everything she ever wanted. But he came from nothing, he had fought for everything he ever got. Now is the time to start letting people know things are going to change, he is no longer at the mercy of others but they are at his. It's time he starts getting what he deserves in life, nothing but the best. He could think of no other person to share his wonderful news first with, than Faith. Jonathan dialed the number, he listened to it ring, finally on the fourth ring, she answered.

"Hello."

"Hey, how are you?" Jonathan asked.

"I'm fine, just got done with my yoga class. I'm going to the store for some items we need. Which reminds me, do you need more shirts? Because I'm- "

Jonathan interrupted her. "Faith."

"What?" she said, trying to think if she did something wrong.

"I got the stadium deal finalized. Everything is signed… I made it," he said, with an air of superiority in his voice.

The phone line was silent on both ends for a moment, until Faith's scream filled the receiver and Jonathan pulled the phone away from his ear. "Oh my gosh! We have to celebrate tonight. I will get dinner and call the nanny," Faith said.

Jonathan swiveled in his chair and took another sip of his coffee. "That sounds great Faith, but I have another meeting and I cannot reschedule it. Let's plan something for this weekend."

"Ok, that would be better for me. I am busy anyway," she said candidly.

Jonathan grinned and looked out his corner office wall of windows to the skyline of the city. "Have a good evening, babe, I will be home late," he said light-heartedly before hanging up. He sat staring out of the windows, he could feel his eye lids getting heavy. He was reminiscing about the day he asked Faith to marry him.

August 18, 2009

Tuesday

He remembered being so nervous that she would feel he was moving too fast. After all, they had only been dating for five months, but deep inside he knew Faith was the one for him. He could be himself around her and loved her more than anything in this world. She was young and beautiful; Faith could have had anyone she wanted. Jonathan knew what he had to do and he was ready to start a family. He

2

remembered how hot it was that August day. He went to pick up the ring from the jewelry store. The jeweler wrapped it up nice and wished Jonathan good luck.

He picked her up from work early that afternoon. He told her they needed to go by his warehouse because he forgot his wallet there. He pulled into the parking lot and parked his truck in the handicapped parking space. Faith looked at him and shook her head.

"Why can't you ever follow the rules?" she said.

"Rules are meant to be broken; live a little, beautiful".

They walked through the front glass doors and the woman behind the reception desk smiled and greeted them warmly. Jonathan smiled and led Faith down a long hallway. She noticed the big metal doors that swing open. Jonathan stopped just short of the doors and turned to face her.

"I have a surprise for you. You need to put this coat on first." He helped her slip into the coat, just as someone opened the doors.

Her eyes filled with tears and she had a look of amazement. She realized it was really cold and snowing. That's when she saw the snow machines. They walked through the open doors and stopped. He turned to her and said "Let me get this for you," zipping up her coat. Taking her hand, he led her to the waiting golf cart. He got behind the wheel and started it up.

"What is going on? What is all this?" she asked, smiling ear to ear.

"You will find out, just sit back and enjoy the ride" he leaned over and gave her a kiss.

As they drove up the makeshift road, he could see her expression changing on her face.

3

She said, "How did you do this?"

He looked at her and said, "I built this for you, so I could take you to a place you have never been before." He went all out on this experience for her, he had this construction crew build all the major buildings from her favorite television show.

"I'm so shocked by all of this, I can't believe you did all of this just for me".

"We aren't even finished babe" he told her.

He took her around the entire town, showing her the *Diner,* the *Market,* the church and of course the main characters' houses. He saved the best for last, the gazebo in the middle of town. When they reached that he stopped the cart and walked to the other side. Taking her hand in his hand they walked up the steps of the gazebo and stood in the center. He stared into her eyes.

"Do you like it?" he asked.

"I love it, it's amazing" she assured him.

He looked over her shoulder and said, "I believe you have something to give her."

She had a puzzled look on her face as she turned around. Her hands came up to cover her mouth and her eyes could not believe who she was seeing. Her parents were walking up the stairs of the gazebo, they handed her a small box. She held the box in her hand until Jonathan turned her around and took it from her. He got down on one knee.

"Faith, you are my best friend, the love of my life. I have never felt this way about anyone, ever. I want to spend the rest of my life with you. Will you marry me?" he said, with tears running down his face.

She was standing there, looking down at him, and realized she loved this man and wanted to be with him. "Yes!" she said ecstatically, bending down to kiss him. They held each other close and they both believed it would last forever.

October 19, 2017

Thursday

5:30p.m.

The phone ringing startled him. He must have fallen asleep. He reached for it on the fourth ring.

"Hello."

"Jonathan?"

"Yes."

"Have you been thinking about me?"

"I told you not to call me on this line." Jonathan said sharply.

"Well since you're not my daddy, I don't have to listen to you. Now do I."

"Yes, I've been thinking about you, be here at nine tonight. I will order us some dinner."

"I will. Maybe I'll wear something sexy."

"Just be here at nine."

"Would it kill you to be nice for once and treat me like a human being?"

"Please. Be here at nine."

"Whatever."

Jonathan is going to end it tonight, the relationship had run its course, he was moving up the socioeconomic ladder. He did not want to hurt his reputation over a fling. Jonathan hung up the phone and called for his secretary. She walked in a moment later, he handed her a piece of paper and she disappeared just as fast as she appeared. She looked at the list and began going about getting it done. First, she ordered the two steak dinners with baked potatoes and salads. Then she made sure to get Don

Perignon 2006 and to put it on ice. Lastly was to send Faith flowers and sign the card with *'Told you I would do it, Thanks for believing in me.'* She knew the drill about these meetings, once the door closes, she is to leave. She goes about her business, making phone calls and doing end of the day filing. Just as she finished the last few things, she hears the ding of the elevator doors. She gathers her things together and waits.

"Hello, how are you this evening?"

"I am good, good to see you again." She lied with a smile. "Follow me, please" she said, walking to Jonathan's office door. She knocked and waited for him to answer, "Yes?"

She opened his door, "Mr. Ross, your nine o'clock is here," Jonathan smiled as he looked his appointment up and down with lust burning in him.

"Thank you. That will be all, you can go home," Jonathan watched as his secretary closed the door.

They stood facing each other in silence, both feeling their sexual instincts growing with every passing second. They both want the other to succumb to the urges first. Jonathan walked closer, he could feel the blood rushing through his body, thrilling him like crazy.

"Would you like some wine?" Jonathan asked.

"That would be nice, thank you."

He poured the chilled wine into two wine glasses and thought to himself about how to break the news that this arrangement was finished. He was drawing a blank though, all that was coming to mind was the events of the day. He couldn't help but smile thinking about all of that money and the things he was going to do with it. He could do anything or anyone he wanted.

"Here, I got your favorite." Jonathan said, holding out a glass of wine.

"That's sweet, but we are celebrating for you, so I should have gotten something for you."

"Trust me, you have something that I want," he replied, touching their lips with his fingers.

"You don't get dessert until after we eat."

"You have something I'll eat." Jonathan felt himself getting hard already. He wanted it now.

"Nope. Not this time Mister, we are going to eat and have a little bit of conversation like normal humans do while they have dinner. This was not some booty call. I'm tired of being that for you, if that is what this was, sorry to disappoint you, Mr. Ross."

Jonathan scoffed, "No, then what the hell was it?"

"Date night, duh."

"Excuse me, date night? What exactly do you think this arrangement is?" Jonathan asked.

"Don't do this! You always get like this when you don't get what you want right away. Don't worry, I'm going to give you this ass. I would give you an appetizer, but we both know you can't handle that."

7

"Whatever, let's just eat." Jonathan said, visibly frustrated.

"Jesus Christ! Come here! I will give you a blow job. But that's it. Then, we will eat dinner and conversate like normal people. After that, if you're a good boy, I will let you have this. Ok?"

"Fair enough." Jonathan started to unfasten his belt.

"What are you doing?"

"Putting my pants down." Jonathan answered.

"You don't need to put your pants down for me to suck it. Unzip your pants and pull it out."

"I don't want to get come on my pants; I have to go home." Jonathan said, rolling his eyes.

"You won't. If I swallow it."

"Good point." Jonathan unzipped his pants and pulled his penis out. He walked over to them. "Get down on your knees."

"No. I'm going to sit in the chair, your carpet doesn't have much padding."

They sat in Jonathan's oversized chair. "God, you are excited."

He grabbed the back of their head and pushed himself into their mouth.

"Just suck it," he told them.

Jonathan loved being sucked off, it was almost better than sex. "That's it, holy shit that feels amazing." Jonathan started to thrust his hips.

"Listen, my clothes can't get messy either."

8

"Let me fuck your mouth." Jonathan said.

"Ok, but only soft thrusts, you can't be rough this time on me, understand?"

"Ok!" he said, as he started. He did it gently but it was getting hard to hold back. He was so close to exploding down their throat. "I'm close, baby. I'm going to come!"

He thrusted one more time then exploded.

"Feel better?"

"Yes… Can you clean it off, please?" Jonathan asked.

They ran their tongue around the tip, cleaning anything left on him, "Is that good?"

"Yes. Come here." Jonathan said. They stood up and Jonathan pulled them in, kissing them passionately. He thought about all of the good times they had together. He decided that maybe he will wait to end it.

"Thank you. What was that for?" They asked.

"For being so good at what you do. Let's eat, I'm starving."

"What did you get us?" They asked, walking over to the table on the other side of Jonathan's office.

"Our favorite. Steaks medium rare, baked potatoes with butter, sour cream and bacon bits on the side of course and Caesar salad. Oh, they sent dinner rolls, this time too."

"Sounds delicious."

They sat and ate dinner together, talked about Jonathan getting the stadium deal. Jonathan even asked how their job was going. Not that he cared about any of it, but he was being nice. They drank the rest of the wine and talked about the upcoming holidays. Jonathan told them he couldn't wait to get the hell out of Missouri, get some place warmer.

"That means you will be away from me, though."

"Then maybe you will have to come down a few times, I can charter a nice boat. Have you ever had sex on a boat?"

"You turn everything, into something sexual or about sex. Have you ever gone and gotten checked out?"

"For what?"

"Because I think you may be a sex addict."

"Whatever." They were both finished eating, Jonathan looked at his watch, it was 11:02 p.m. Jonathan hate wasting a couple of hours talking. He was focused on one thing and one thing only.

"Why are you looking at your watch, Jonathan?"

"Checking the time. We have to be out of here by the time the cleaning crew gets here at midnight."

"What is the big rush?"

"Well, I was told I would be getting some dessert and I would like to have it now." He told them.

"I literally sucked your dick two hours ago and you want more."

"You said…"

"I know what I said, son-of-bitch. Come on."

"Where the hell are you going?" Jonathan asked.

"Over by your desk, it smells like our dinner over here. I don't want my face in our food."

Jonathan nodded and followed them over to the desk. He wasted no time taking what he wanted from them. He grabbed and bent them over his desk and smacked their exposed ass. With each smack he gave, they let out a moan, each one louder than the last. Jonathan got down on his knees, kissing where he left hand prints. He stood up, he fumbled with his belt and zipper. Trying to get his pants down. Jonathan is so excited; he took a breath to try and calm himself down. He was going to enjoy this, he earned it.

"I'm going to use you like a whore." Jonathan said, rubbing himself.

"Is that all I am, your whore? I come here just so you can use me and send me on my way, master?"

Jonathan slid inside after some finessing, "Wow… that is tight!"

"Yeah, you love it… Why are you going easy on it? Fuck me like you mean it!"

Jonathan followed their demand, thrusting faster, enjoying the sounds of their flesh smacking together. He soon felt his body tense up for just a moment, "Shit! Don't move! Oh my God that's good" Jonathan said as he fell back into his chair and his legs went numb.

"Go clean yourself up in my bathroom."

"Why do you have to be a prick every time we finish?"

Jonathan rolled his eyes, "Just go."\

Jonathan sat in his chair thinking to himself about how to break the news that this arrangement was finished. He couldn't help but smile about all of the good things he has in his life.

Just as he starts to say something, the phone rings. "I have to take this Jonathan, in private it's a client".

11

"This is my office! Go answer it in the bathroom." Jonathan said.

"Ok, fine."

Jonathan looked at his watch. 11:30pm. Where did the time go, he thought to himself? He started to put himself together, he fixed the collar on his shirt.

"Where are you going?"

"Oh, I didn't hear you come out of the bathroom. It's getting late, I really have to get going" Jonathan replied.

"Ok, fine. I see how it is!"

Jonathan rolled his eyes, "What in the hell does that mean?"

"What I am supposed to feel like when you do this to me?"

"I'm sorry. It's getting late and I have to get home. Maybe we can do something this weekend?"

"Seriously, are you kidding? Just so you can cancel on me again?"

"Lower your voice, first of all. Second, you knew I had a family before all this started. It's no surprise."

"Yes, I knew. But to be fair, I thought you were going to leave your wife."

"Look, let's table this discussion for a later time, I have to get going."

Jonathan opened the door quietly, on the off chance that someone was still mulling around the office at this hour. "Coast is clear, everyone is gone," he said.

"I don't care who knows." They walked together to the bank of elevators; Jonathan pushed the button. The two of them stood there in an awkward silence. Things haven't been this awkward between them since the first time they had sex two years ago. The sound of the elevator reaching their floor was welcomed by the both of them.

"I know you don't like to discuss this but when are you going to leave her?"

"Shh. Wait until we get downstairs," Jonathan said as the elevator doors closed. They exit the elevator and walk towards Jonathan's truck. He stops halfway to his vehicle. "What makes you think I would ever leave my wife for *you*," he said indignantly.

"What? What did you just say to me?"

"You're not stupid. I am not going to repeat myself," Jonathan answered, his face becoming red.

"Because we are in love and we want to be together!"

Jonathan got inches away from their face. "Are you kidding me? Please tell me you're joking." He stared into their eyes and said, "You think because I fuck you, that I love you?"

"You told me that I was the best"

"I will never leave my wife for you! You are just a piece of ass."

"How can you say that to me?"

"Holy shit! I was going to wait to do this, but you have pushed me beyond my breaking point!"

"What are you talking about?"

"We are finished, I am done with you. Crazy bitch!" Jonathan said.

"I'm going to tell your wife!" Jonathan stopped cold in his tracks and turned to be face to face.

"Are you really threatening me? You of all people should know, just what I am capable of. Let me tell you a little secret. My wife knows all about your nasty ass. Tell me, does yours know about me?" Jonathan said.

Jonathan stood there waiting for a comeback, when they didn't say anything, he leaned in and said, "Now get the hell out of here and do not contact me again." He got into his truck and started to pull away.

"But I'm in love with you!" Douglas cried out.

October 19, 2017

Thursday

11:45p.m.

Claire clutched the robe tight around her as she opened the French doors to the resort-like backyard with its beautiful landscaping and stunning in ground pool. She took her physical appearance seriously, there was no way she was going to be caught dead not looking her best, even if it was just walking to the pool fifteen feet from the door. The crisp night air hit her face as she walked to the chase lounge, she took off her designer high-heels. She slid the robe off, tossing it on the lounger. Revealing her perfect Moroccan tan on her hour-glass body, her brown hair comes down to the small of her back and she is wearing a white two-piece designer bikini, that hugs her breasts and hips like it is an attachment of her body.

The pool is lit up with blue LED lights showing off the water magnificently. She pulls back her hair putting it into a

14

ponytail walking to the edge of the pool. She dipped her pedicured foot into the water, stirring it around to test the temperature. She giggled at herself because the pool is heated, this time of year the water temperature is kept at eighty-two degrees. There was no need to check the water, but Claire knew the old man next door was watching her from the window. She loves teasing him whenever possible. She pretended to look around making sure no one was watching her. She looked up at the window he was at and started to adjust her top, she was trying so hard not to smile while playing with her breasts. Then without hesitation Claire untied her bikini top and let it drop to the ground. She stood there a minute with bare breasts showing, the chilly air made her nipples instantly hard. It was hard for her to hold back her laughter, knowing this was the most action he's had in a long time. She smiled and dove into the pool head first and started doing her laps that she does every night. This is one of the few things that actually brings her enjoyment. Midway through her sixteenth lap she saw his head-light beams come into the backyard before disappearing into the garage. She took a deep breath and exhaled slowly.

She heard the back-yard gate open and she swam to the side of the pool just in time to get a glimpse of Douglas closing the gate.

"Hey, how was…" she was cut off mid-sentence.

"Claire, how many God-damn times have I told you not to lock the garage door?"

"I'm sorry. I forgot, my mistake." she said, turning her head, getting ready to finish her laps.

"Yeah. You. Are. The. Mistake." Douglas said. Something caught his eye and walked to the edge of the pool, "Are you topless?"

She smiled, "Yes, you like what you see?" as she twirled in the water.

15

"You are so pathetic; you're not getting enough attention that you have to show your tits to the whole neighborhood?"

Claire was confused, "Whole neighborhood?"

He turned around and as he was walking to the back door said, "If you want to start showing your tits, go work in a strip club. At least then, you might make a few bucks."

Claire shook her head as he went inside, she was use to his behavior but it was getting old. She didn't take it from him, like she did in the beginning. She climbed out of the pool, the night air hitting her body like a thousand needles. She quickly got over to her robe and put it on, grabbing her shoes she went inside. She closed the door behind her, she heard the ice clink into the glass and knew where he was.

Douglas was pouring himself a drink when she came into the lounge. He was not wanting to deal with her right now, he was still thinking about Jonathan; Douglas knew that Jonathan really didn't mean anything he said.

"Douglas!" she yelled.

"Son of a bitch! What is your problem now?"

She walked to the bar and sat down. "Really? What is my problem?"

He downed his drink and poured himself another one, "Claire I don't want to do this right now, I had a tough day at work. The keyword in that sentence WORK."

She shook her head, "You do this every time we have to have sex!"

"You really want to get into this?"

"I do because I'm tired of waiting around all day for you to fuck me!"

16

Douglas took a sip of his drink, "You done, Claire?". She started to walk away. "Whatever..." she muttered under her breath.

"Hey! We aren't finished yet. I have an answer for you."

She stopped, turning to face him. "I never asked a question; I said a statement."

"Regardless, let me tell you why Claire." He stepped out from behind the bar, "First, I work hard every day to provide all this shit: the house, the cars, the designer clothes and your Botox injections. Secondly, when is the last time you contributed any kind of money to this house? Lastly, how could I possibly enjoy having sex with you? You do nothing for me Claire, you don't even get me excited. You are all washed up as a model and have nothing to offer anymore. Things around here are going to change and it starts tonight."

Claire smiled, "I have been waiting for you to bring up money. I know that you are broke and have been living on your credit cards!" Claire let what she said sink in watching him stand there with his mouth open and nothing to say. "It's the talk amongst our friends. They know that without Jonathan, you would be out of business and you would have drowned in your debit already."

Douglas took a swig of his drink, "You think that bothers me? I don't give a shit what people think of me." She could see him turning red, trying to think of something to say.

"What's the matter honey? Did that hit a nerve?" She said with her eyes piercing him.

Douglas was about to come unhinged, he grabbed his car keys and was going to leave when Claire said, "What? Did you forget something at your boyfriend's office?"

The words hit Douglas like a freight train, "What did you say?"

Claire smiled and was basking in delight knowing that he was not expecting that to come out of her mouth.

"What I said was, did you forget something at your boyfriend's office?"

Douglas turned his back to her and lowered his head. Trying to recover from the words she said, he uttered "How long have you known?"

She didn't say a word; she was amazed at how quickly his attitude changed. Claire was going to leave him with that, as a last thought but seeing Douglas so vulnerable she found herself feeling sorry for him.

"Just for a few weeks, Faith told me." She said sitting on the arm of the chair against the wall.

"Like that whore has any room to talk, she is the town bicycle, everyone has ridden her."

Claire shot back at him, "It's ok for Jonathan to screw anything with two legs but when Faith does, she is a whore. Really?"

He stopped talking and sighed deeply, "Yeah, I guess it is a double standard. Listen Claire I have something to tell you...I'm Gay."

"Really! Tell me something I don't already know."

"I'm sorry but at least I told you."

"I have known you were gay for some time now."

"Ok, what's the problem?" he said with a confused look.

"That's it's with Jonathan."

He hung his head down and attempted to apologize to her. "Listen, Claire I am sorry for how you found out, but I am not sorry for liking men. Besides you knew when we got together that we both agreed to do want we wanted."

She exploded into him, "Are kidding me? We agreed that we would be discreet and have respect for each other. You broke both rules, when this comes out, we both will look like fools."

"It won't come out Claire, trust me" he explained to her that Jonathan wouldn't want any of this getting out.

She shouted, "Who cares what he wants, he may not have any control whether this gets out."

"What are you talking about it?" he asked.

"Faith. She knows and she is out for blood from the both of you. There is nothing stopping her from telling people."

"Faith will not tell anyone, she doesn't want anyone knowing, she just likes backing Jonathan into a corner," Douglas responded.

"What about a third party. Someone with a grudge against the almighty Jonathan Ross."

Chapter 2

October 20, 2017

Friday

12:15a.m.

Faith laid awake in the massive bed that she shares with her husband, when he comes home. He should be home soon, the drive from the city to their estate in Jefferson County is about a half hour. Faith got out of bed and looked out the huge arch windows in the bedroom. Looking towards the iron gates at the beginning of the driveway, she sees headlights on the road, but they pass by. She grabs her robe and goes to check on the children.

As she walks towards her two-year-old son Weston's room, she is happy they decided to put in the heated floors throughout the house it makes it so much cozier, on this chilly October night. She cracked open Weston's door and saw he was asleep. She walked across the hall to her daughter Pearl's room. She was laying in her bed, peacefully asleep. Faith closed the door and walked to the great room that over looked the main floor of the house. Maybe he was home already, normally he would have a drink in the living room. But he wasn't there.

The house is 4,679 square feet, it has six bedrooms and seven bathrooms. Along with a guest house, stables with four horses, a gigantic swimming pool with rock waterfall and all of this was sprawled across 200 acres. She thought about the cars, and all of the vacations too. She wanted for nothing and the children would be able to go to the best schools, even the Ivy league schools. Faith knew she was blessed with a life like this. She still could not fight the anger she had for her husband. She knew about the late-night meetings. They were in the process of discussing his activities this morning when he got a call and left her without finishing the conversation. Jonathan did not care; he was going to do whatever he wanted.

Faith saw his truck's headlights coming down the driveway. She quickly walked downstairs and went straight into the kitchen; she wanted to be in there when he walked in. She had it planned that they were going to continue their conversation from earlier, about ending the arrangement with the open marriage. He walked into the kitchen from the garage.

He saw her. "Close your eyes, I have a surprise for you," he told her.

"Jewelry is not going to fix this."

"Good, because it's not jewelry."

She closed her eyes and held out her hand, "Humor me, please." She felt the items in her hand and opened her eyes.

"Tacos? You got me tacos as a surprise?" she said, placing the tacos back into the bag.

"What?"

"First, I'm on a diet, I told you that yesterday if you would listen and care about anybody but yourself. Second, you walk in here like nothing happened."

"I'm sorry, I forgot," he said with a smile. She looked at him with a vexed look. She threw the bag of food at him.

"Piss off, Jonathan!" she said, walking back to their bedroom.

Jonathan left the food where it fell and followed her to the bedroom. Faith removed her robe and was getting ready to pick up the television remote when he slammed the bedroom door.

"What the hell are you doing? You are going to wake up the kids," she said.

"What's your problem? Sorry about the food, I forgot that you're dieting again,"

Faith looked at him with a resentful expression. "Do you *really* think this is about food?"

He stood there thinking about the question for a few seconds. "No. This is about the conversation we had this morning, right?"

"And what conversation would that be?" she asked sarcastically.

"The one where you want me to stop having late meetings and spending more time at home with you and the kids," he said while undressing and walking into the massive bathroom. He started the shower.

Faith came stomping behind him. "The late-night meetings, really? Let's call them what they are, you sticking your dick in somebody's ass" she yelled.

"We both agreed to this, Faith. I don't know why you're upset."

"Are you serious, John. I told you I did not want either of us sleeping with anyone else anymore! I'm done with the whole open marriage thing."

He stepped into the steaming shower and started washing up, ignoring her. She walked over to the shower and flung open the door. "Did you hear what I just said?"

He rinsed the soap off of his body as she stood there, waiting for a response. He turned and faced her, the hot water hitting his back. With no emotion on his face, he said, "Faith, I don't mind if we talk about this, but do not think for a moment that I will stand here and take orders from you, I'm

22

not one of your underlings. You better treat me with some respect".

She took a few steps back, so he could get out of the shower. "Respect? You want to talk about respect? You are the one fucking some guy instead of your wife. You have no respect for me, the kids, or this marriage. You are a repulsive husband and father."

Jonathan exhaled slowly trying to get control of his emotions. But it was no use, she had crossed the line. Jonathan reared his arm back and smacked her across the face, sending her to the floor.

Jonathan knelt down and looked her in the eyes. "Yes, I fucked some guy tonight. But what does that say about you? That I rather fuck a man in the ass, than you in either hole. That's how disgusted I am with you. I also ended it for good." He stood up to walk away, then stopped and turned.

"Since I pay all of the bills, make sure you and the kids have everything you need and want, I will do whatever I please. The next time you call someone repulsive, take a look in the mirror. You're the one spreading your legs for some uneducated trailer park trash! I use to think you were more than a twenty-dollar hooker, Faith. Guess I was wrong."

She laid on the bathroom floor shocked and in disbelief. In the eight years that Jonathan and she have been married, he has never hit her. But also, how in the hell did he know about Adam; the trailer park trash he was referring to.

"I have some papers to look over, I will be downstairs in the office for about a half hour, then I will be up," he told her, like nothing had happened. Jonathan put on a t-shirt and boxer briefs, then shut the bedroom door behind him.

She sat there in silence and thought about what she had said to him. How could she be upset with him when she did the same thing tonight. She curled up into the fetal position and began sobbing, thinking about her transgressions earlier this afternoon.

October 19, 2017

Thursday

11:35a.m.

Faith was getting ready to start her minivan when her phone rang. She looked and saw it was Jonathan calling. She debated answering, but then remembered the stadium big wigs were in town. She picked up and was shocked at the news, she did her best acting voice and pretended to be happy for him. She offered to celebrate with him by spending the whole evening with him but of course he turned her down.

He chose to be with Douglas over her. When he asked if they could just do something this weekend instead, of course she said it would work better for her too! When she got off of the phone, she was upset and her feelings were hurt. Without thinking, she immediately called Adam. He picked up on the second ring.

"Hello."

"Hey, can I come over?" she said in a quick tone.

"Yes, of course you can."

"Great, I'm on my way," she hung up before he could say anything.

She knew that this was wrong and it would not solve the way she was feeling, but she pushed that thought out of her head.

24

"Fuck him! He doesn't care anymore, why should I?" she said out loud.

As she got closer to his house, she began to lose her nerve. She pulled up to the mobile home park. She parked in the driveway next to his dented pick-up truck. She brushed her hair and looked at her face in the mirror. She has only been here one other time, when they did not have enough time to get a hotel room. It's like living in a tin can, she thought. It was small, stuffy, and nasty looking on the outside. She did not care about any of that today. She got out of the van and was walking up the three steep steps to the door. Adam opened the door before she could knock.

"Hey, come in beautiful," he said with a smile on his face. She walked inside and was in the living room. She glanced around and saw that it was a little cleaner than last time.

"You cleaned up," she said with a smirk on her face.

"Yes, I did just for you," he told her. He went and sat down on his broken-down couch. Adam motioned for her to come and sit next to him.

"I did not come here to sit and watch tv," she said, grinning while taking off her jacket. Adam stood up and walked toward her. He put his hands on her waist and pulled her up against his body. He gently kissed her on the lips while running his hands over her buttocks.

She grabbed his head and ran her fingers through his shoulder length brown hair, she pulled herself against him for a deeper kiss. She pulled his shirt up over his head, throwing it on the floor, exposing his large tanned chest, she kissed every inch of it. She loved rubbing her hands over his big biceps and broad shoulders. Adam picked her up and carried her to the bedroom.

He gently threw her on the bed and began disrobing her. He pulled off her pants exposing her beautiful fair skinned legs, with her yellow boy shorts underwear. Then he pulled off her shirt, she giggled as she asked,

"Do you like?"

"Hell yes! Yellow is my favorite color."

"I know. That's why I got them. I wanted you to think I'm sexy."

"You are too good to me, Faith. Matching bra and panties, they are amazing but they are still coming off." Adam said.

"So...What are you waiting for?" she said grinning.

Adam could not hold back any longer, "Faith, I love you."

"Yeah. Good." Faith whispered, looking into his eyes.

Kissing her stomach, he gazed upon her, realizing just how much he has fallen in love with her. Removing her remaining garments, he slowly got on top of her. He was so intoxicated by her beauty, that he forgot the reality of the situation. He hurried with his pants pulling them down, she pulled his boxers down, grabbing his semi-hard penis, she began rubbing it. She loved feeling him grow in her hands. She slid down off the bed, on her knees, on the floor. She put the tip in her mouth, sucking and licking it. She gradually put him deeper in her mouth, as much as she could. She started sucking harder and going deeper until she gagged. She loved gagging on him, it made her wet and ready for him. She looked at him, he could barely stand still.

"What's wrong?"

"I want inside of you."

"Take me, come on. Do it."

She stood up, he pushed her onto the bed. He pushed her legs open and got on top of her, she loved feeling his weight

26

on her, he kissed her neck and collar bone. He held her passionately in his arms, while he slowly slid inside of her, allowing her to feel him stretching her open with every gentle thrust. She kissed him pulling him deeper into her, wanting him more now than ever. As she became more comfortable with it, he thrusted faster. With each one going deeper than the last. He stopped to kiss her and said, "You are so beautiful. You know that?" He took his penis out and rubbed it up and down her lips. He remembered she told him she loved that. He put it back inside of her, "I want you to come on my cock. Please Faith, come on my cock." He went faster. Faith was lying beneath him taking everything he was giving her; when suddenly she felt her body tighten and she grabbed his biceps as she came apart. He followed right after her, falling on the bed next to her. They both laid there, gathering their thoughts about what just happened. They have had sex before, but this was not sex.

"Faith, I meant what I said. I truly love you with all of my heart, and I want to be with you." She sat up and began looking around for her bra and panties. Finally finding them she put them on and reached for her clothes.

"Hey, I said I love you Faith," Adam said, sitting up.

"Yes, I know. I care for you too," she said with her back towards him.

"Are you going to say it back?"

"Look, I'm running late. I don't have time to get into it with you, Adam," she said as she put her clothes on.

Adam got up and put on his boxers and his pants. "Why can't you say it?" he asked.

"Listen, if you're afraid of leaving him- "

She turned around to face him cutting him off mid-sentence, "Adam, if you really want to do this, fine! You knew what this

27

was when we started, I told you I would never leave my husband."

"That's got nothing to do with me telling you that I love you. Why can't you say it!" he yelled.

"Adam, I don't love you. You are a fun, caring, and good-looking guy, but you can't afford to buy yourself a decent couch. What makes you think you could afford my children and I?"

Not waiting for him to respond she turned and walked out of the front door, leaving him standing there in disbelief. She was sitting in her van when Adam came out of the trailer with her cell phone. She rolled down her window.

"You forgot this, I'm pretty sure you'll need it," he said, handing her the phone.

She took it and started the vehicle.

"Faith, why won't you say it?" he asked.

She cleared her throat "Adam, even if I did love you and wanted to spend the rest of my life with you, we would not be able to do it," she said.

"Why? Just because of money?" he shot back at her.

"Not only money, but look where I come from and look where you come from. Two totally different worlds, Adam."

Adam stood there, knowing deep down that she was right. But he wouldn't give up on them.

"I will not accept that as a reason, we could figure it out," he told her.

"Adam, you're not getting it. We are through, before anyone gets hurt," she said with a remorseful look on her face.

Adam leaned into the van window and told her, "Before someone gets hurt? I tell you I love you; you think it doesn't hurt when you won't say it back?"

"Adam, I didn't mean for this to happen. I do care about you," she said, wiping away tears.

"Just go! Go back to your fancy little life because it's clear my love and my feelings don't mean shit to you!" he told her as he turned and walked away.

October 20, 2017

Friday

2:45a.m.

Faith was sitting in bed still in disbelief that Jonathan hit her. She looked at the time and it had been well past the half hour Jonathan said he would be in his office. She put on her robe and went downstairs to find him. He was sitting at his desk when Faith walked in.

"Can I come in" she asked.

"Of course."

She sat across from him. He noticed that her face was bruised and that she had been crying.

"Faith, I don't want to fight, so if you came in here looking for that, it is not going to happen."

"Why did you marry me?" she asked, catching him off guard.

"Why do you ask? You should already know why."

"Can you answer the question, Jonathan?" she sighed.

He sat there for a minute looking at her. Faith saw his eyes filling with tears and then he answered her, "I married you because you're the one thing that I love unconditionally so much so, that it scares me."

She knew he was telling the truth because he never gets emotional. She got up from the chair she was sitting in and walked over to him. He swiveled to face her. Faith climbed onto him, straddling his lap, and gave him a passionate kiss.

"I want us to work this out, Jonathan. I want to be a family again."

Jonathan kissed her forehead and brushed his fingers through her hair. "I will do anything to make this work. I'm nothing without you," he reassured her.

For the first time, in a long time Faith and Jonathan were connecting and being honest. They talked for a few hours putting everything out on the table. They came to an agreement and promised each other they would try their hardest. If for no other reason, for the children. They knew changes were going to be made regarding their extracurricular activities. For starters, getting new phone numbers and having no contact with Adam or Douglas. Jonathan was going to take some time off and take a much-needed family vacation. They were going to work on their relationship. They agreed to go to do couples therapy, she wanted to make sure they learned how to communicate better.

There was one thing Faith demanded. He cut all ties with Douglas, including business dealings. He knew this one was going to cost him a lot of money, around $5 million, a small price to pay compared to if she left him.

"Faith, I just want to start fresh, do right by you and the kids."

"I really want that too! No more sleeping with other people. It's you and I in this marriage. No one else."

Jonathan smiled, "You and I all the way."

Jonathan wrapped his arms around her and stood up with her in his arms. He walked over to the large brown leather couch that was against the wall and set her down on the large arm of the couch.

"I love you." he said.

"I love you too" she answered, she knew what he wanted. She pulled his boxers down, Jonathan reciprocated by taking her panties off.

"Let me get a condom." He said, because it was a rule that Faith made; that as long as he was fooling around with other people, when they have sex, they use a condom.

She grabbed his hand, "No… this is a new beginning for both of us. You promise and swear it's done"

Jonathan looked directly into her eyes. "I swear. Just give me time, I will prove it to you."

October 26, 2017

Thursday

Claire and Faith are meeting for lunch to clear the air from their last encounter. Where Faith let the cat out of the bag about what their husbands were doing at those late-night meetings. Claire was shocked and unprepared to hear that. She always knew he slept around but never thought it would smack her in the face or come out that it was with a man. In their circle of friends this could ruin both their reputations. How could he be so selfish and risk everything that they have, she thought. Claire wanted to confront both of them, to see what they had to say about it. But Faith was having none of that.

Faith told her, "They can have each other for all I care because I'm seeing someone else anyway."

That was a few weeks ago and as she sits in the restaurant waiting for Faith to arrive, just thinking about it still gets her upset. Claire got the waiter's attention and asked for a glass of white wine. He nodded his head, rushing off to get it. Moments later he returned with her wine,

"Thank you" she said, taking a sip of it. Just as she was setting her glass down her phone started to buzz in her purse. She dug and finally found it, seeing that it was Faith calling.

"Hey, what's up?"

"Claire. Sorry, I'm running late. But I'm just around the corner, I didn't want you to think I forgot about you," she laughed.

"Oh please, I know. I'm unforgettable. I ordered a glass of wine; you want me to order you something?"

"Yes please, I will have whatever you're having"

After saying good-bye, they hung up. Claire lifted up her glass so the waiter knew she needed another one. She took another drink, hoping the wine would help her relax. She was nervous, she didn't want things to be weird between them. Faith walked in like she owned the place and she couldn't help but smile. She made her way to the booth where Claire was seated, when she got there, she embraced her with a genuine hug.

Claire returned her embrace tightly. "I missed you, Faith."

As the two of them sat down, the waiter came over with Faith's glass of wine.

"Would you like to start with an appetizer, ladies?"

Faith went ahead and ordered for the two of them, "No, we are going to do the sea-food salad for two and can we have some bread?"

"I will put that right in," he said with a smile, leaving the two of them.

Before Claire could start the conversation, Faith jumped right in saying, "Claire, I'm sorry for the way I handled the whole situation. I did not take your feelings into consideration and I was a real bitch. I want you to know I confronted Jonathan and gave him an ultimatum".

Claire could not hide the expression on her face, "First, I accept your apology. Really? What did he say?"

Faith took a drink, "Well it was not a pleasant discussion, but it's done between them."

Claire nodded. She was trying to wait as long as she could but it was no use, "I told Douglas as well, about everything: from the sleeping around all the way to the fact that I know he is damn near bankrupt."

"Holy shit, Claire! What did he say?"

"Screw him! What could he say? He is damn near broke; he definitely does not want it getting out that he was caught having an affair with a man because that would be the end of anyone doing any kind of business with him" she said finishing her wine.

"Yeah, you're right, Claire."

The waiter brought the food out and filled their glasses up again, they sat there eating while catching up on other gossip. It felt like old times, enjoying each other's company. Claire could see that Faith was wanting to say something.

"Will you just come out with it already, Faith?"

"What are you talking about?"

"How long have we been friends, I know when you have something on your mind. Like I said, come out with it."

Faith was grinning and shaking her head, "Claire, you know me better than my own husband. But this is a burden that I don't want to put on you."

"Faith, we are the only ones who would understand this fucked up situation we're in. Believe me, it can't be that bad."

"I can't help but feel responsible for all of this, especially since the kids have come along. I have not been able to spend as much time with Jonathan as he would like. I am just as bad as he is. I had an affair too, but I'm the one that let things go too far."

"Listen, I think we all have a part in this; so, what if you had an affair, Jonathan wasn't there for you. How many times did you try to fix things between the two of you?"

Faith was shaking her head, "You are not understanding Claire, if he finds out. He will… There is no telling what he will do."

Claire was not understanding what Faith was trying to tell her. "Faith, what is the big deal. Jonathan did what he did and you did what you did. Does that not even out?"

"No, it does not. I'm pregnant and before you ask. Jonathan is not the father."

The words smacked Claire in the face. She was not expecting that, it took her a minute to process what she had said. Claire took a drink of her wine and saw that Faith had begun to cry. Claire handed her a napkin and said the first thing to come to her, "How far along are you?"

"About eight weeks. I just found out the other day. I told you, I'm as bad if not worst."

Claire did not know how to word her next question, so she just said it. "What about an abortion, Faith?"

"No way! This happened for a reason and it is a part of me, no way I'm getting rid of this baby."

Claire nodded and accepted her decision. "When are you going to tell the real father?"

"I have not seen him since I found out and I'm not going to either. That is why I need a favor from you."

"Favor? Is that what this lunch is really about?"

"No! Of course not, but you are the only one I trust. You said it yourself; we are the only ones that understand our fucked-up lives." Faith leaned closer in whispering, "I need you to go talk to him and give him a letter from me."

"Are you serious! I don't even know the guy and you expect him to accept all that from me. You're crazy!"

Faith snickered. "Trust me, he will understand, you will too when you see him."

"I don't know, Faith. I have my own crazy ass shit to deal with."

"Come on, Claire! Please. Help me with this, I will do anything."

Claire sighed, drank the last bit of wine in her glass. "Ok, but this is the only time I'm going to talk with him. I will not be a messenger for the two of you."

They gathered their things together and paid the bill. They walked out, hugged, and went their separate ways to their vehicles before Claire realized that she didn't get the address from her. She was just opening her car door when she heard Claire calling her name.

"What's wrong?" she asked as Claire walked up to her.

"I can't talk to the mystery man, if I don't know where he lives."

Faith laughed, "Shit, where is my brain?" She reached into her glove compartment, got out an envelope and handed it to Claire.

Claire looked at it, it was already addressed. "Adam Lewis? Who the hell is that?"

"He is a nobody, just someone that was a distraction."

Claire tilted her head and raised her eye-brows at her. "Seriously… Don't play it off like that, you and I both know it's more than that."

Faith looked away from her. "It doesn't matter anymore."

Claire turned to walk away when Faith stopped her. "Hey, Claire!"

She turned around to see Faith walking towards her. "Yeah?"

"Thanks for being a great friend. I'm really happy that we have put the past behind us."

"What are you talking about?"

"I know the last few months have been rough on our friendship. I'm happy we have moved past all of that."

Claire stared at her.

"What is the matter?" Faith asks.

"Faith, sometimes you need to know when to keep your mouth shut and let sleeping dogs lie."

"Ok! I can see someone is touchy, let's not even bring it up again."

"I didn't bring it up, you did. Why, I don't know? See you later." Claire said as she walked away.

Claire started her car and entered the address into her navigation. She thought about what Faith said about "putting the past behind us." Claire thought that she did put everything in the past behind her, but she realized she hadn't.

Claire debated whether or not to deliver the letter. Claire drove off following her navigation, trying like hell to put the past behind her.

May 13, 2017

Saturday

5:45p.m.

Claire was getting ready for the evening that lay ahead. Douglas hired a stylist to do her hair and a makeup artist to have her looking perfect for tonight. She felt like a princess, he only does this for her on their anniversary but that is months away. She wondered why he was being so nice but she was not going to question it, instead she admired herself in the mirror. She really did not want to go but Douglas told her that they were obligated, if that was the case then she was going to wear her new dress and the new heels she got. Claire walked into the closet they shared, bigger than most New York City apartments. Douglas was getting dressed, when she noticed her red mini-skirt laying out.

"I got out what you're wearing, all you need to do is pick out some shoes."

Claire cleared her throat, "I can pick out my own clothes to wear." She said as she grabbed the new black dress.

"Listen, I need you looking perfect tonight, ok?"

She rolled her eyes, "Who am I supposed to be impressing?" Now she knew why he paid for her hair and makeup to be done professionally.

"Claire, I know you don't understand what it takes to keep us in this life style but we all have to do things we don't find enjoyable in order to keep what we have."

With a puzzled look on her face she asked, "What are you trying to say?"

Douglas stared at her, "I know you are not stupid. I have an investor that I need to land and would you believe that he fancies you."

She laughed, a little embarrassed, "Are you serious?"

Douglas nodded, "You bet."

"I'm only there to flirt and talk his arm off?"

By this time Douglas was putting on his shoes. "Claire, it's honestly simple. All you have to do is look perfect, put on that red skirt that you look semi-decent in and act as if you're into him. We will have some drinks, eat dinner, then come back here and if we all are having a good time, then whatever happens after that is what happens."

Claire put her hand up to stop him. "Whatever happens? What does that mean?" she said cautiously.

"Claire, come on. Let's turn on your brain and try to use it, please."

She hates when he talks this way towards her. "Douglas, I don't know why you have to talk to me like a child. First, I don't know this guy. Second, you spring this on me at the last moment. I'm not some whore you can pass around and use like the neighborhood bicycle!"

Douglas shook his head, "There is no need to worry because you already know them." He barely finished the sentence when Claire asked, "Them. Them who?"

"Jonathan and Faith are the investors, more so Jonathan. See nothing to worry about, we're all friends."

"What the hell do your mean, that's your best friend and my friends' husband, there is no way I'm doing that to her"

He rolled his eyes and shook his head, "Jesus, Claire. Whose idea do you think it was! They both came to me to see if you would be into it."

"And where do you get the right to agree to do this without talking about it with me?"

He tilted his head slightly and gave her a look as if she had a third eye. "I didn't agree to anything with them. I told them we would go to dinner, have drinks and come back here to hang out and see what happens. Secondly, I make the money, so I make the rules. I thought you would have understood that by now."

He chuckled, "You act as if you never slept with someone to get ahead. Act like you did before you met me, like when you had to screw around to get modeling jobs. At least this time it will be worth it."

"I did what needed to be done! What kind of husband uses their wife as a bargaining chip?"

"Jonathan is more than likely going to get the stadium deal. That means millions of dollars in contracts. We need that money; without it we are finished."

Claire shook her head, "Are we going into bankruptcy?"

"No, we are in bankruptcy. If I don't get a piece of this stadium, things are going to be different," he started walking away when he turned around, "Claire," he waited for her to look at him.

"Yes," she answered, waiting for insult.

"Be thankful that someone actually still finds something about you attractive."

6:57p.m.

They arrived to the restaurant early, the reservation is at 7:30p.m. The hostess greeted them warmly, "Good evening, we are happy you decided to join us. Name please?"

"Fulton" Douglas smiled.

"Yes, sir. We have you down for 7:30p.m. It will be about twenty minutes."

"That's fine, we are going to sit at the bar."

They walked up to the bar and ordered a couple of drinks. "Claire, I don't see why you are nervous?"

"Because this is not normal behavior."

"Do you not remember the agreement we made before we got married?"

"Yes, but this was not in the agreement."

Faith and Jonathan showed up midway through Claire's second drink.

"Good evening, how are you?" Jonathan asked.

"We're good! Having a drink until our table is ready," Douglas answered.

"You look so good in that Claire!" Faith said, leaning into hug her.

Claire reciprocated and whispered into her ear, "We need to talk."

"I have to use the restroom, order me a drink Jonathan."

Claire got up, "I have to go too. I'll walk with you," she said.

As soon as they got into the ladies' restroom, Claire made sure they were the only two in there. She locked the door so no one would interrupt them.

"Holy shit! What is so important?" Faith said, looking at Claire like she was crazy.

"What!? Don't look at me like that Faith! Not until you hear what I have to say."

"What the hell is it, Claire?"

"Alright, short version; Douglas said you and Jonathan came to him asking if I would be ok with all of us having sex."

Faith was looking at her like she was speaking a different language.

"Did you hear what I said?"

"Yes. To be fair I didn't ask shit, Jonathan mentioned it. I thought he wanted to get arise out of me by asking about it. Did Douglas say how all this was brought up?"

41

Claire took a breath, "Douglas told me I needed to look perfect tonight, for an investor. That I better put my charm on and if nothing else act like I'm into him. Come to find out, Jonathan is the investor. I pressed Douglas for a reason why, he told me that without the contracts that Jonathan will give him from the new stadium..."

Faith cut her off, "Wait! Jonathan got the new stadium?"

"Douglas seems to think that Jonathan will. Faith, you're missing the point."

"Yeah, you're right, sorry."

"Douglas needs the money because without he is going to be bankrupt and I'm being used as leverage!"

Faith started laughing.

"Your husband wants to sleep with me! Why are you laughing?" Claire asked.

"First, my husband does anything with a pulse. He thinks he is God's gift to the world. Secondly, I'm laughing because you think I can stop him. I have learned that Jonathan will do whatever he wants to do. The only one that can stop him from screwing you, is you, Claire. Think about it, those two morons came up with this scheme, without even including you. Nothing can happen, if you aren't willing to engage in it. Jonathan is a lot of things but a rapist is not one of them. Ok?"

After thinking about it, Claire started to laugh as well, realizing how ridiculous the idea was. "I guess you're right," Claire said.

"Listen, let's go out there have a fantastic dinner, order the best wine no matter how much it is and have fun. Don't think about later, ok? Let Jonathan get all worked up thinking he is about to get some. Then when it comes time that he thinks he has you right where he wants, hit him with the facts! That you don't like being treated like a trashy whore for hire," Faith said, looking at her with a determination.

"Sounds good to me."

Faith gave herself one last look in the mirror, "I look damn good for having two kids. Right, Claire?"

Without thinking about it she answered back, "You are totally a MILF!"

"Claire! You really think so?" They both started laughing uncontrollably. "Claire, you don't know how much your body changes after having kids, it's crazy." Claire didn't say a word, she stared at her until Faith realized what she said.

"Shit! Claire, I didn't mean anything by it. You know how sometimes my brain doesn't work."

"You know Faith, it seems like your brain doesn't work a lot here lately. Especially when it comes to sensitive remarks liked that," Claire said, holding back tears.

"No sweetie, I'm so sorry. Please don't cry!" Faith said giving her a hug.

"Forget it. I'm just stressed out and touchy," Claire said, catching the tears with a tissue before they ruined her makeup. Claire gathered herself, looking in the mirror to make sure there was no sign of running makeup.

"You look great," Faith told her.

"Thanks."

"I really am sorry, Claire."

"Forget about it. Let's go before they have hemorrhage."

Before making it back to the bar, the young hostess informed them that their party was seated now. Faith and Claire walked up to the table just as Jonathan and Douglas were ending a conversation.

"About time, we thought you two might have gotten lost," Jonathan said, looking at Claire.

She grinned bashfully and said, "If I knew there was a chance of you coming to find me, I would have stayed gone longer."

"I'm starving." Douglas motioned for them to sit down.

They ordered dinner and the best bottle of wine. It was just like old times; eating, drinking and having fun. They were having such a good time that they lost track of time; the waiter came over and informed them that the restaurant was closing in fifteen minutes.

"Oh wow, it's that late already? You can leave the check with me," Jonathan told him.

Claire and Faith were finishing the last of the wine and were immersed in a deep debate about which was better, beach vacation or mountain resort. Jonathan leaned close so only Douglas could hear him.

"Is everything good for tonight, then?"

"Don't worry. Everything is good." Douglas subtlety raised his eyebrow.

Jonathan sat back in his chair. The waiter brought the bill over and handed it to him.

"Damn, I didn't think we ordered that much!" The waiter stood there patiently for Jonathan to finish looking over the bill.

"Is everything correct sir?" The waiter asked timidly.

Jonathan reached into his pocket pulling out a clip full of money. "Here you go buddy, keep the extra for yourself."

"Yes sir, thank you. Have a good rest of the evening."

Getting up to leave, Douglas looked at Jonathan and said, "Come back to the house, I have some new bourbon you have to try."

"Bourbon! You know just what to say to a man," Jonathan said, smiling.

They pulled into the garage at about quarter till midnight. Claire was watching the clock the whole way home. Jonathan and Faith pulled into the empty space of the garage. Claire grabbed his arm.

"What?" he said, annoyed.

"Remember, I'm not going to do anything."

Douglas exhaled, "Yes, I know Claire! I want you to pack your shit and be out of the house by tomorrow night."

"Wait! What are you doing? You can't kick me out!"

He was out of the car, but leaned back in to say, "If you can't do this one little favor for me, then I want you out. You don't pay any of the bills and you definitely don't have any money; you can't afford this lifestyle without me." He slammed the car door and walked in the house.

Jonathan followed Douglas inside, while Faith waited for Claire to get out of the car. She finally opened the door and got out; she was physically drained from all the stress.

"What's wrong?" Faith asked.

"It doesn't matter."

"Jesus Claire! Go with the flow, you act as if we are in the 1800's."

She turned around looking at Faith, "Are you serious?"

"Listen, this life comes at a price and I think it's a small price to pay. Look at the house you live in and the cars you drive. Get serious, Claire."

Shocked, Claire answered, "Since you allow your husband to use you like a whore, I should do the same?"

Faith was caught off guard with that response, "I'm a big girl and I made my choice. I want my children to have the best and if that means I have to sacrifice myself or my marriage then so be it."

Claire was stunned, "What the hell happened to the woman that said, women can do whatever men can and a woman doesn't need a man for anything, Faith?"

Faith rolled her eyes, "I thought you would be all for this. Specially, since everyone knows Douglas doesn't fuck you. You act as if your vagina is trimmed in gold. You really need to get over yourself Claire."

Claire walked pass Faith to go inside. Faith turned to follow. Claire stopped at the door, turned around and said, "You may want to turn a blind eye when you go inside…"

They were standing by the bar, in the lounge. Douglas had just poured them drinks.

"Seriously, it is the best bourbon I have tasted," Douglas said, noticing Claire and Faith standing there.

"Hmm… It's good. I don't know about the best though."

"Jonathan, are you trying to annoy me?"

"When are you going to show me this hot tub so everyone can get relaxed," Jonathan said, winking at Claire.

Claire saw her opening and jumped through it, "I'm sure I could make you feel relaxed. Forget about the hot tub, let me show you the entertainment room and all the fun things we can do in there. Unless you boys are too tired."

Douglas's mouth dropped open and Jonathan's eyes got wide.

"Sounds like a great idea to me!" Jonathan said, clearing his throat.

Claire looked back at Faith, giving her a little wink. Then she looked at Jonathan, "What are you still sitting down for? Isn't this what you want?" she said seductively with her hand on her waist.

Jonathan got up and grabbed the bottle of bourbon out of Douglas's hand.

"I'm following you, Claire."

"Well come on you two. What are you waiting for?" Claire said, looking at Faith, as she and Jonathan walked downstairs.

Douglas followed them downstairs and started to sit down when Claire told him, "Put some music on and none of that easy listening shit." She went and turned the lights off and turned on the strobe lights. The music came through the speakers crisp and clear. The music moved Claire's body in ways Jonathan never imagined. He is fixated on her, his heart is about to pound out of his chest, he has to have her.

Claire touched and moved her body for Jonathan more in the past two minutes than she ever had in the past thirteen years for Douglas. She could see how much Jonathan is enjoying it, and for the first time in years she feels sexy, empowered, and most of all, alive.

Turning so that her back was to him, she slowly pushed off her shoulders the two straps that held the dress to her body, letting it fall casually to the floor. Jonathan stared at her like he had never seen anything like it before, when the dress fell it revealed her perfectly toned body.

"Holy shit, Douglas! I can't believe you got her. Claire your ass is amazing."

"Hmm… Thanks. You haven't seen anything yet, Jonathan."

She bent over and started to run her hand from her ankles, up her legs, over her calves, finishing with a good slap on her butt. She turned her head, looking behind her to see Jonathan almost hypnotized by her. Their eyes met and Claire brought her index finger up methodically to her mouth. She instinctively put it in her mouth, sucking it and twirling her tongue around it, so he could see what was in store for him.

She began rocking her hips from side to side, bending her knees as she went down toward the floor. She got on all four and crawled to where he was standing. She reached up grabbing his pants by the waist band to pull herself up. Enticing him every inch by having her breast rub against his body, he could feel them on his legs, then slowly over his groin, and against his chest by the time she was standing toe to toe with him.

"Is this what you wanted?"

"It's part of it," he said, grinning.

She pushed him down onto the oversized couch. She noticed his erection, "Looks like you have a big problem here."

Jonathan laughed and started to unfasten his belt. Claire smacked his hands away, "Not just yet. I'm going to build you up until you beg me to let you inside of me."

Claire straddled his lap, putting her hands on his chest to keep her balance, then started to grind against his groin. Feeling how hard he is through his pants was getting her excited. She has not done this to a man in a long time. The harder she grinds against him the wetter she gets, the sensation is almost more than she can take. When she finally lets go, it is like a volcanic eruption, Claire collapses on his chest like she finished running a marathon.

"If you think that felt good, just wait until it is inside," Jonathan said.

Claire was slowly getting her senses back, sitting back up she unhooked her bra and let Jonathan pull it off. His grasp was perfect, playing with one breast while exploring the other breast with his tongue. She felt her breathing quicken and her muscles start to tighten. *Not again so soon,* she thought to herself. Claire had to focus on something else to calm down, the eat shit and die expression on Faith's face was the first thing she noticed. This is her moment to get revenge, Claire realized. She shot a smile right back to Faith, that said it all.

"Tell me, how bad you want me," Claire whispered in Jonathan's ear.

"Aww… I want you so bad Claire. You feel that…." Taking her hand and putting it on his erection, "Grab it! You feel how hard that is, grab a hold of it good. That is all you."

Faith, tired of watching and wanting to prove a point, walked over and said, "Here let me show you." She started to nudge Claire off of his lap when Jonathan intervened.

"What are you doing, Faith? Take a tip from Claire, then maybe you could get me to fuck you. Oh…. I know what it is, someone has something and does something better than you. And the little princess can't handle it. What you're feeling is jealousy, Faith. Don't worry, you will get a turn."

Jonathan pushed Claire off and got undressed. He was fully naked when he ordered Claire to take off her underwear, as he sat back down on the couch. She slowly pushed them down around her ankles and stepped out of them. Jonathan grabbed Claire around her waist pulling her down to her knees while he told her, "You know what to do, show me how good your tongue can dance."

Claire chuckled. "Is that your best line? Surely you can do better than that," she grabbed and wrapped her fingers around him, looking him in the eyes and softly saying, "I'm going to show you how a real woman sucks cock, when I'm finished with you. I hope you have a better line."

Claire took him and put him in her mouth. Jonathan grabbed the back of her head and pushed her down deeper.

"Claire, you sure can suck a dick. Faith, get over here," he said in her direction. She walked over and sat next to him, she knew what he wanted, Faith pulled the ponytail band off her wrist and put her hair back and up.

"Come here, down on your knees. You are going to learn how to share tonight," Jonathan told her. Douglas is finishing what is left in the bottle of bourbon, when Jonathan called him from across the room.

"What is it?" he answered.

"Come over here and have a seat. I want you to watch me fuck your wife." Jonathan told him.

Douglas rolled his eyes and sat back on the couch, "Whatever... Good... Girl... Claire, fuck him like you mean it. You little trashy whore."

50

Jonathan was pushing Faith's head down for her to take him deeper into her mouth. Jonathan began to thrust his hips up as she went deeper making Faith choke each time. He looked at Claire each time he thrusted. He could not wait any longer.

"Get up on this cock and fuck me."

Claire looked at Douglas and shook her head. What a loser she thought. She could not wait to have Jonathan inside of her.

Claire stood up and straddled Johnathan, she glared at Douglas. "Take notes, this is how a real man fucks!" she told him.

Jonathan reached down and grabbed himself, and looking directly into her eyes he asks, "Are you ready," as he slides himself inside of her.

"Oh my god! That feels amazing, put it all the way in." she moaned. Jonathan started slow, giving her all 8 inches he had. She ran her fingers through his hair, pulling herself closer to him. She pushed her tongue inside of his mouth kissing him hard, then said "I've never been fucked this good before, I want you to use me to feel good." Jonathan wrapped his arms around her, holding her tight and started to thrust faster.

"Faith, take your shit off," he said forcefully, glancing at her as he penetrated Claire.

She began to undress as she watched her best friend have sex with her husband.

"Hurry up, Faith!" Jonathan said between thrusts.

Claire could feel herself getting close, "I'm close Jonathan. I want you to come inside me. That feels good, don't stop!

Deep in me, put it deep inside me. OH, SHIT I'M COMING!!" she screamed.

Jonathan, feeling Claire climax on him, suddenly felt himself getting close. Just as Faith pulled her panties down, she heard him finish, "God, you are tight." Jonathan said. He looked at Faith, "Come here, princess," he told her. Faith hesitated, watching Claire get off of Jonathan and sit next to him on the couch. Faith went to him and stood there staring at him.

"Now use your mouth and clean this off."

Faith was not expecting that, this was not what they had discussed, "Wait! What? This is not what we discussed…" before Faith could finish Claire said, "Jesus Faith, go with the flow, remember there is a price to pay for this life."

Seething, Faith looked at Claire. "I don't believe anyone was talking to you." Faith got down on her knees. She made sure to go nice and slow, getting from the tip, down to the base of his penis. She cleaned it better than she would have normally. She licked and sucked his balls dry; she knew he was enjoying it because he was getting hard again. That's when Claire leaned down and whispered to her, "How do I taste, Faith?"

"Fuck you! You're a nasty white-trash whore!" Faith screamed.

"You know what Jonathan!? It looks like you got all you could handle right there. Nice job not wearing a condom, you never know what she might have, asshole." Faith said while putting her clothes back on.

Chapter 3

November 20, 2017

Monday

Jonathan woke up to the sound of his phone ringing. He looked at the screen and it was his secretary. Shaking his head, he answered it. "This better be good," he said in a groggy voice.

"Good morning, Mr. Ross, This is your reminder that you have a meeting with the city inspectors at 9a.m."

"Thank you." he hissed.

He ended the call; he sat up and checked his email on his phone. He looked through them and noticed one from Douglas. He looked at Faith, who was still asleep. He opened it and his blood started to boil. Douglas could fly off the handle at times, but this was different. Douglas was threatening to expose him to the world unless Jonathan agreed to see him and discuss possible solutions regarding their business together. Jonathan closed the email and got into the shower. He wished he would have stayed in Galveston. Faith was right. They should move down there; he could find someone to run the company up here. He would be free and clear of this crazy drama. He knew deep down Douglas was bluffing but he was going to have to deal with him.

Faith walked in and got into the shower with him. He turned around to face her. She gave him a passionate kiss and bit his bottom lip.

Jonathan smiled. "What was that for?" he asked as he ran his tongue over where she bit.

"Because I can," she said with a smile. They finished their showers and were drying off when he finally told her about the email Douglas had sent. He assured her that he had a plan to deal with him, but that it involved him having to see Douglas one more time. Jonathan told her this was going to be the last meeting, after this Douglas would be out of their lives for good.

Jonathan grabbed his phone and pulled up Douglas's email, and hit reply.

'We need to meet and discuss a few things. Meet me at the Rosemont Hotel tonight, 9pm.'

- Jonathan

P.S. You and I both know you won't tell anyone anything but in case you try and grow a set of balls today, you need to look at the attachment I sent you. I hear a picture is worth a thousand words. Or maybe a million, in this case.'

He hit send and waited for a response. Jonathan did not have to wait long at all, his phone buzzed a few minutes later.

'I will see you tonight.'

Jonathan went downstairs where the kids were eating breakfast and Faith was drinking her morning energy smoothie. She handed him the morning paper as he sat down at the table.

"It's all set up for tonight," he told her. She nodded and smiled at him.

He looked at the time. 7:30am. He took a few more bites of his eggs and a couple of sips of his coffee. He kissed the children goodbye and gave Faith a kiss.

"I love you. I will keep you posted."

She smiled and fixed his tie. "Please be careful today," she told him. He smiled and walked out of the door.

Life has been good in the Ross home the last month. Jonathan's attitude and the way he treats her has completely changed. He has become more involved with the children, giving the baths and reading them bedtimes stories. He has been spending time with Faith. He has talked about going to their summer home in Galveston, Texas for Christmas and inviting the whole family. This was the new start they discussed. They were falling back in love. She was realistic though it was easier when they were on vacation and It was just them. She wished they would have stayed gone. Being back Faith knew that it would be a bumpy road.

Faith sat with the kids until they were finished eating breakfast. The nanny came and got the kids from the table, to get them ready for school. Since the kids were handled, Faith went upstairs and got dressed making sure to wear something warm because today is her flying lesson and she always gets cold in the plane.

She couldn't get Adam out of her mind. Since they had come back, she has been resisting her urge to go and see him. She did not think it would be this difficult to get him out of her mind.

"Pearl! Weston! We need to get going," she said walking down the steps.

Faith loaded the kids into the van and began her day. Dropping Pearl off at school, and then taking Weston to preschool. After dropping the kids off, she had a little bit of extra time. She drove to the coffee bistros to get an iced coffee for seven dollars, this was her secret vice. She knew how many calories were in it but she didn't care, it was her favorite. She was driving down the highway when she passed the exit for Adam's house. Faith felt guilty with the way she ended it. Adam has emailed her at least ten times since then, even driven by the front gates but after seeing Jonathan was home, he just drove off. Faith had told Jonathan all of this and he told her to talk with him, make sure he knows that it is over. She decided that after her flying lesson she would go by his house and clear the air. He deserved that much. She arrived to her lesson about twenty minutes early. She sat in her van and drank her iced coffee looking through her social media, when her cell phone rang. She did not recognize the number, but answered it anyway.

"Hello?"

"Hi, is this Mrs. Ross?" he asked.

"Yes, this is she."

"This is Captain Alex. Mrs. Ross, I'm sorry for the short notice, but I have to cancel your lesson today."

"I hope everything is, ok?"

"Everything is fine, there is a strong storm front coming in and I'd rather be on the safe side of things."

"I understand Captain. Thank you,"

"You have a good day Mrs. Ross."

"Thanks, you too," she said, and hung up.

56

She started the van and then hesitated for a moment. She picked up her phone to let the nanny know she would need to pick up Weston from preschool. Faith wanted enough time to explain herself to Adam. She needed to be honest with him. She went to call him but then decided not to. Maybe it will be a nice surprise for him. She was driving towards his house and trying to think of what to say to him and how to say it, but she was feeling guilty. Faith is not use to this; she never cares about how men feel. Adam is different though; she knows she hurt him and that hurts her. She turned into the mobile home park. She could either make the first left and be at Adam's house in thirty seconds, or she could go straight and go all of the way around for an extra two minutes.

She decided she needed that extra two minutes today. She drove around the park nearing his trailer when she made the decision not to stop.

That was until Faith made the slight turn onto the street where Adam lived and saw a car parked next to his. She drove slow past his trailer, but didn't recognize the car. It couldn't be his because its brand new and not his type. She parked up the street so he would not see her van. She sat there for twenty minutes watching, waiting. No one came out or went in.

She was growing impatient and wanted to know who was in there with Adam. She got out of her van and walked between two trailers to get to the back of Adam's, which is where his bedroom is. The blinds were open, but the window was too tall for her to look in. She looked around for something to stand on and found a wooden crate. She dragged it under the window and stepped up on it, placing her hands on the metal trailer to help get stability. She looked through the window. Adam was laying on his back naked in bed, smoking a joint. The windows were so dirty that she had to keep adjusting her position, so she could see what he was doing. A woman came into his room but she couldn't make out who it was. She could tell the woman was

57

undressing, Adam must like what he saw because he was fully erect. She adjusted her feet on the crate to get closer to the window, so she could get a better look inside. The woman was completely nude now, but she looked really good. Faith was a little jealous of how good she looked, she was surprised a woman with a body like that was with Adam. The woman walked toward him; she climbed on top of him, straddling him. The woman's face was covered by her hair, Faith watched as the woman grabbed Adam and slid him inside of her. Faith's eyes got big and her mouth dropped open, that's when the crate beneath her feet collapsed and she fell hard to the ground.

"Son of a bitch!" she said.

Faith got up to her feet and noticed she cut her leg, nothing too bad but it was bleeding enough.

Adam heard the crash outside and went to check it out.

She heard the front door swing open, Faith stumbled to her feet and fled back to where she left her van. When he got to the back of the trailer, he saw her running away. Her leg throbbing in pain from the running, she opened her door. Without warning it was slammed shut, she turned quickly to see Adam standing there, in his boxers, just as winded as she was.

"What the hell are you doing," he asked, trying to catch his breath.

"Coming to see you, which was a mistake!"

"What are you talking about?" He asked.

She opened her door but he shut it again. "You need to let me leave!" she yelled at him.

"No! Not until you tell me…"

Faith didn't let him finish. "Why… are… you with her," she asked, in between taking breaths.

Adam looked at her and the color on his face was gone. He was getting ready to speak but she held her hand up, stopping him. "Don't bother, I saw you two! How could you?"

"You have no right to tell me what I can or cannot do," Adam yelled.

"That's what you go and do," she said.

"It's none of your business what I do. You made your choice, remember?"

"To think I was coming here to give you an explanation," she said.

"You are pissed off because you made a decision and you thought I would be all broken up about you and I could give a shit less," Adam fired back.

"You're right Adam. That's the reason. I'm so happy I saw this because now I don't feel guilty," she said as tears fell from her face. "You better get back in there because that's all you got and you could have had a lot more!" She yelled at him as she got in her van and sped away.

Chapter 4

November 20, 2017

Monday

1:15 p.m.

Faith looked at her phone and saw he left a voicemail. "Fuck him and his lies. I can't believe how stupid I am," she said out loud. She grabbed her phone to listen to the voicemail.

Adam's voice came through. "Faith! Answer your phone! I'm sorry… That woman meant nothing to me, it's just…" after a long pause he said, "you left me high and dry with no explanation. I'm angry, confused and still in love with you. I know it is crazy because I have nothing to offer you financially but I would do anything to have you in my life. Call me back, please." She was about to erase it when she listened to it again, this time hanging on to every word he said; realizing that Adam means more to her then she ever intended. She longs for him and wants to be with him. Faith's heart is telling her to give it a chance but her brain is telling her that it will never workout. Several thoughts were running through her head; what would people think, what would she tell her children, how is Jonathan going to react. She decided to push all those questions out of her mind and focus on the here and now, as she called him back.

The phone rang once and Adam answered, "Faith! Listen, I…"

She cut him off, "Shut up! Don't say a word, only listen. First of all, I'm sorry for the way I left you, no one deserves that. The truth is Adam, I know you love me and I have feelings for you, more than I ever intended to have for you. I know I have fallen in love with you and it scares the hell out of me. I have two children to worry about, I have to think about what

60

is best for them. I am torn between trying to save my marriage for my children or us. I know you want me to make a decision right now but I can't and I need you to understand that."

Adam instantly said, "I do, but you deserve to be happy and we both know you're not with Jonathan."

"I know Jonathan is an asshole but I still have feelings for him," Faith said.

"I would never treat you the way he does," Adam snapped back.

"Come on Adam, be serious. Sleeping with her after the letter I wrote to you."

Adam interrupted her, "What letter? I never got a letter from you and the girl is nothing to me, I met her in a bar, she wanted to buy some weed from me and to be honest now she comes around all the time. I have been missing you and haven't been able to talk with you. I have been drinking and smoking more than normal because the past few weeks have been hard without you."

"Are you kidding? Are you trying to be funny?" she said insulted.

"Faith, I swear to God!"

There was silence on her end, she felt like a jealous teenager. She knew that she was being unreasonable and ridiculous. She is the one that told him they were finished, "Stop Adam, it's unfair for me to be upset with you. We aren't together and I hurt you. You don't owe me any kind of an explanation. I do have a question though; do you have feelings for her?"

"No! How many times do I have to say it? I love you and only you."

She began to cry, "Really?"

"Yes, I would do anything to have you."

"Ok, then I have something to tell you; but we first need to discuss what our intentions are going forward."

"Going forward, does that mean what I think it means Faith?"

"It means we have to discuss something before either of us make a decision because I will not leave a toxic relationship just to get into another one."

"Can't you just tell me now; it's not going to change my decision," Adam said.

The doorbell rang. "Look I have to go but I'll call you later, we can meet up to talk…. I love you, Adam."

"I love you too, Faith."

5:30p.m.

Jonathan had been looking at his watch all day. Time was flying by and he was dreading this confrontation he was going to have with Douglas. He has never been this nervous to see him, of course the two of them have never been in a fight either. Jonathan didn't understand why Douglas was so upset; he knew they could never have had a real relationship beyond what it was. He did not want it to come to this, Douglas is his only real friend but if it was between his family and him; well, he could live without Douglas. Besides, he threatened to expose him, he could no longer be trusted.

They have made a lot of money together and still have projects that are in the middle of completion. Jonathan told himself that he is thinking about this too much, but he could not help it. They have known each other since freshman year in college, Douglas even introduced Jonathan to Faith.

March 14, 2009

Saturday

Jonathan was working on a bid for a construction job, when his cell phone began ringing in the other room. He let it go to voicemail and continued working. He worked about ten minutes before getting up and going to make a mustard and cheese sandwich. Jonathan loved eating mustard and cheese sandwiches, ever since he was a kid. He remembered fixing them for lunch when he was in school. The phone rang again, so he went to see who was calling. Douglas's name was on the caller id. He rolled his eyes; he did not want to answer it, but he was not in a hurry to get back to work either.

"Hey, what's up man."

"Finally! Where in the hell have you been, I have called you like a hundred times," Douglas said.

"What! What is so pressing, that you are blowing up my phone?"

Douglas went on to explain about a benefit dinner that he and Claire had been invited to that evening. Douglas told Jonathan that Claire was sick and now he had an extra ticket and he wanted Jonathan to come with him.

"Doug, I can't. I have to get this bid done. I need this job or I am going to end up sleeping on your couch in the near future buddy."

"Come on man, you need to get out more," Douglas pressed him.

"I can't, I need to finish this."

"There will be good-looking women and free booze, how do you say no to that?"

"Free booze is a plus but I can get a good-looking woman any night of the week."

"Ok then smartass, let me hit you with this information; some of the biggest developers in Missouri are going to be there," Douglas said, knowing that would get his attention.

"What time are you picking me up?" Jonathan asked.

Jonathan was dressed and out the door an hour later. He had never really been to these types of dinners and he was nervous. When they pulled up to the Country Club, Douglas was rambling on about what not to say and who not to talk to. As they walked into the large banquet room, Jonathan was immediately handed a glass of champagne. He scanned the room looking at the crowd and getting more uncomfortable by the second. Douglas got his glass of liquid courage and turned to Jonathan "Get ready to sell yourself."

Douglas introduced him to everyone, telling them that Jonathan's construction company was the fastest growing company in St. Louis; building safer structures at half the cost. Douglas even told people that Jonathan and he were working together to help redevelop the inner-city housing development. Before dinner was served, Jonathan had shaken most of the high-roller's hands. Whatever Douglas had told people about Jonathan worked; he had three meetings setup for next week. Not bad for an hour of meet and greet, he thought to himself. Jonathan was sitting at the table they were assigned to when they checked in.

"Excuse me, if I could have everyone's attention, please. Dinner will be served shortly and don't forget to get your bids in for the silent auction," a woman said, standing in front at the podium. Jonathan looked up and was immediately hypnotized by her beauty. Jonathan could feel his heart rate quicken and was surprised it wasn't beating out of his chest. He knew he had to meet her.

"You look like a deer in head-lights, what's wrong with you," Douglas asked laughing.

"Who is that?"

"Who?"

"The woman at the podium?"

"Oh her, that's Faith Butler, her family owns a chain of hotels."

"Introduce me to her," Jonathan said.

Douglas laughed, just as the waiters placed the salads in front of them. "I think she is a little out of your league."

Jonathan watched as Faith went to each table, chatting and laughing with guests. Finally, she was walking towards their table. Jonathan took a deep breath to calm his nerves.

"And how is everything tasting over here?" she asked the table.

"Not as good as the hamburger joint down the street, but it will due," Douglas laughed, teasing her.

"Mr. Fulton, thanks for the compliment on the free food," Faith played along, giving him a playful smack on the arm. Jonathan kicked Douglas.

"Faith, I would like to introduce a friend of mine. Jonathan, this is Faith, her family is hosting this event."

"Well do you have a last name?" she asked.

Jonathan cleared his throat "Ross!"

"Please to meet you Jonathan Ross, I'm Faith Butler; welcome and please enjoy the evening."

"The pleasure is all mine, Ms. Butler."

Faith gave him an alluring smile, which made Jonathan blush.

"If you'll excuse me, I have a few more tables to welcome." she said, as she turned to walk away, but looking back to wink at the awestruck Jonathan Ross.

November 20, 2017

8:27p.m.

Jonathan pulled up to the entrance and was greeted by the friendly valet. He went to the front desk to check in. The woman sitting there was very attractive and he would have normally flirted with her but he had made a promise; his marriage and children were more important to him.

"Good evening, sir, welcome to the Rosemont Hotel. I'm Jessie, how can I help you?"

Trying not to stare at her perfectly sized breasts behind a too tight button up shirt, he told her that he was checking in. She was busy tapping away on the computer screen, when his phone started to ring. He did not recognize the number and sent it to voicemail.

"What name is the reservation under?"

"Ross."

"Mr. Ross. I have you in room 502 with a pool view," she smiled, glancing up at him.

"That's fine, thank you," he said.

"Just one checking-in?"

"Yes, it's only me."

"A king size bed all to yourself, at least."

"Hopefully I don't get too lonely," he said with a smile.

"If you get lonely up there Mr. Ross, I'm just a phone call away," she said, subtly biting her lower lip.

"I will keep that in mind." he said, turning to go to the elevators.

"Your keys sir," she held them outstretched over her desk.

"Thanks," Jonathan said with a smirk.

Jonathan got to his room and went straight to the mini-bar. He grabbed the first bottle he saw, tequila, and downed it. Jonathan took a deep breath, exhaled and went to use the restroom. He couldn't help but think about the woman's offer downstairs.

He decided to see what was on television, it would at least get his mind on something else. Grabbing the remote, he turned the television on and flipped through the stations until finding one that caught his attention. Jonathan stopped on one of those twenty-four-hour national news stations. The anchors were talking about the upcoming election and how they thought it was going to turn out. He was so tired of hearing about it and seeing all the ads, all the candidates wanted the same thing; to get people's money and get elected. He knew none of them actually cared for the "Normal Person," it

was a big racket. Jonathan chuckled to himself and thought who he was kidding, he didn't care about normal people either.

Jonathan changed the channel and stopped when he saw a good-looking woman wearing a bikini and smiling on a beach. It was a commercial for a vacation at one of those Mexican Resorts that look nice, until you get there; then it's overcrowded and the drinks are watered down. It got him thinking about that woman downstairs and he was sure she looked good in a bikini. Jonathan picked up the room phone and dialed to get to the front desk.

"Front Desk, this is Jessie; how can I help you", she said in her sweet and innocent voice. Jonathan hung up the phone, thinking about Faith. He pulled his cellphone out of his pocket and scrolled until he got to Faith's number. He swiped left to dial her phone; it went straight to voicemail. Jonathan shook his head; he hated leaving voicemails. He believes it is pointless because the person is going to see they have a missed call and every phone has caller-id so they would just call back. Tonight was different though, and he waited until he heard the beep.

"Hey babe, it's me, you know how I hate to leave these but I could not wait until I got home to tell you this; I really love you and I'm thankful we decided to give us another chance. I love you and will see you when I get home"

Jonathan sat there for a few moments, wondering why she didn't answer the phone. The insecure part of him was thinking she was with that piece of shit. He began to get angry and thought, *well two can play that game.*

Just then his phone started to ring. Jonathan did not recognize the number.

"Hello, Jonathan Ross."

"Hey it's me, I'm running late."

"Douglas! How in the hell did you get my new number?"

"Don't be stupid, we have many of the same friends."

"Look, I don't have all night. How long until you get here?"

"I don't know. Twenty minutes…. Have a drink and chill out."

"What the hell, you are never late and the one time I need you to be on time, you are late!" Jonathan yelled.

"Sounds like you have missed me." Douglas said.

Jonathan rolled his eyes.

"Listen, just get here so we can get this over with," he ended the conversation and tossed his phone on the bed.

"I need another drink," he said aloud. Jonathan got up from the bed and was almost to the mini-fridge to grab another drink, when his phone began to ring. *It must be Faith calling me back*, he thought. Picking up the phone put an end to that idea because it was a number he didn't know.

"Douglas?" he said looking at the number.

Jonathan answered the phone, "Just get your ass here, I would like to get this over with and be done with you," Jonathan yelled into the phone.

"Jonathan… This is Jonathan Ross, correct?"

"Yes, who is this?"

"Mr. Ross, this is Sheriff Bennett with the Jefferson County Sheriff's Department."

"Hey, Sheriff Bennett. I already donated to the re-election fund."

"This isn't about that. I have some news to tell you that is better said in person."

"What is this regarding?"

"Mr. Ross, there is no easy way to tell you this. I'm sorry to inform you that your wife was found dead this evening."

Chapter 5

November 20, 2017

Monday

11:17p.m.

Jonathan was sitting in Sheriff Thomas Bennett's office. A third-generation law enforcement officer who was up for re-election, the race was close already. The Sheriff didn't need a homicide investigation on his desk right now. The Sheriff stood outside his office door, looking inside at Jonathan. The Sheriff asked the deputy sitting there watching him, "Has he said anything?" the deputy shook his head no. "Give me a few minutes with him, come in when they are ready for the press conference" he told his deputy.

The Sheriff took a deep breath, walked into his office and sat in his chair behind his desk.

"Can I get you anything Mr. Ross?"

"No, thank you."

The Sheriff opened the file on his desk and looked at the preliminary report.

"I am very sorry for your loss; she was a wonderful person. I don't want you to worry because I'm going to find the person that did this and they're going to pay," the Sheriff

said.

"Thanks, Sheriff."

"With that being said, I have some questions I would like to ask you… Jonathan, do you understand that you don't have to answer them; we can wait to do this."

Jonathan looked at the Sheriff with tears in his eyes and a long blank stare. "Ask me whatever."

The Sheriff nodded his head and got out his cellphone to record the conversation, he put the phone close to Jonathan.

"When was the last time you saw your wife?"

"It was this morning before leaving for work."

"What time would you say that was?"

"I don't know, maybe around 7:30 a.m."

"Jonathan, we need an accurate time."

"It was eight this morning."

"Are you sure about that?"

"Yes," Jonathan said in a frustrated tone.

"I know this is a difficult time but this does help our investigation"

Jonathan nodded his head and cleared his throat. "I had a meeting at 9 a.m. and I wanted to make sure I was on time, so I left the house at 7:30 a.m."

"When was the last time you talked to her today"?

"This morning, I tried calling her this evening before a meeting I had, but she didn't answer her phone".

Jonathan broke down into tears for a moment, he could not believe this was happening to him. The Sheriff sat there trying to think of something to say. He was not an emotional man and was often accused of being unsympathetic. Sheriff Bennett was a no-nonsense type of guy. He was trying to get information to help solve this murder, he was not here to console families.

"What time did you try calling?"

"8:50p.m."

"Did your wife have any enemies that you know of or do you know of anyone that wanted to hurt your wife?"

"Faith doesn't have any enemies, Sheriff, my wife was a great person and she was a great mother; I don't know why anyone would want to hurt her."

"Did she owe anyone money?"

"No. Are you kidding me with that question? Do you know who I am?"

"Mr. Ross, these are standard questions, ok? And to tell you the truth I don't care who you are!"

"Ok. We will see about that. Keep asking your senseless questions!"

"Did she do any kind of illegal drugs or hang around with people that did or sold drugs?"

"Of course not."

"What about you Mr. Ross, you know anyone that would want to hurt you or your family?"

"No."

"These are questions that I have to ask, Jonathan. They are completely routine."

There was a knock on the office door and a deputy entered the room. "Sir, they are ready now," the deputy said.

"I will be right there," he replied as he and Jonathan both stood and walked towards the door.

"Mr. Ross when you answered your phone tonight you seemed to think it was someone else calling you."

"Your point," Jonathan said defensively.

"Well, who did you think was calling you?"

"A business associate"

"Can you be more specific Mr. Ross?"

Jonathan straightened his posture and looked Sheriff Bennett in his eyes. "Any other questions you have will have to wait until next time, I'm going home to be with my children."

"Yes of course," the Sheriff nodded.

With that, Jonathan walked out of the office and straight out the back door, where a deputy was waiting to drive him home.

The Sheriff has been standing at the podium for the last twenty minutes taking questions. This is one of the most important aspects of the case: the media. He knew having the media involved was both a blessing and a curse. Information would spread quickly and get to the people that possibly saw or knew something. On the other hand

the case could quickly get out of control. Not to mention, with all the media attention, everyone involved would be under a microscope.

"Just a few more questions," the Sheriff barked.

"Were there any illegal substances involved?" a voice from the back yelled out.

"We have not gotten any of the toxicology results back?"

"Do you have any suspects currently?" a female reporter asked in the front.

"Currently at this time… No," the Sheriff answered.

"Is Jonathan Ross a suspect?"

"We are still collecting evidence and it's early in the investigation. We have a lot of work that needs to be done."

"But you can't rule him out yet?"

"We aren't ruling anyone out yet!"

"So, is he a suspect or not?"

"Last question, folks!"

"Will we hear from the Ross family?" a reporter shouted/

"Listen folks, a young mother is gone and we have an investigation to conduct. We ask that you have respect for the family at this time and patience with us, let us do our job." He walked away from the podium and back to his office.

Sheriff Bennett looked at his watch, 12:45a.m. He decided to call it a day and go home to get a few hours of sleep. Tomorrow was going to be a busy day.

November 21, 2017

Tuesday

12:55 a.m.

Jonathan thanked the deputy for the ride home. The deputy assured him it was no problem and that he would be up at the gate if Jonathan needed anything. Jonathan got out of the squad car and walked inside the front door. He was happy to be home until reality hit him. Faith was gone. The house was quiet, the nanny had put the children to bed hours ago and had agreed to stay with them. Jonathan walked into the kitchen for a much-needed drink, opening the refrigerator he saw a plate covered in plastic wrap with a note on top addressed to him.

Jonathan,

Here is your dinner baby. I just wanted to tell you how much I love you.

He could feel his eyes filling with tears. Slamming the door close, he felt his legs go weak. He had to brace himself on the counter to stop from falling. The massive kitchen all of a sudden felt very small. Jonathan tried taking a breath but couldn't. The room began to spin, he was sweating and felt like he was having an out of body experience. Knowing he needed some air, he stumbled to the back door, which was on the other side of the kitchen. He flung the door open and felt the crisp cool night air hit his face and fell to the ground into the fetal position, and he finally was able to catch his breath. Jonathan let out an agonizing scream from the depths of his stomach. The pain was unlike anything he felt before; a crack of thunder exploded in the night sky and startled him. As Jonathan pushed himself up to his feet, the skies unleashed the powerful rain. He stood there in the pouring rain over-looking the beautiful garden that she loved so much. They had many wonderful times out here. They bought this house because Faith loved the surroundings and the kids would have plenty of room to play.

The children, how on earth was he going to explain to Pearl and Weston that their beautiful, loving mother was gone. How would they take it? What would they ask him? Are they even going to understand? His mind was racing and he could not shut it off.

"Jonathan!"

He heard through the roaring of the thunder and pounding rain. Turning around to his surprise to see Douglas standing there.

"I'm here as your friend," Douglas proclaimed. "I'm sorry... I rushed right over as soon as I heard the news".

Jonathan was staring at him, not sure what to do. "She's gone...what am I going to do," he said.

"I'm here for you and the kids, we can put all the other shit in the past".

Jonathan could see and hear Douglas talking, but his brain was not registering any of the words. The only thing he could do was look at Douglas with a vacant expression. Jonathan finally muttered, "She's gone..."

Douglas grabbed him by his arm to lead him back inside and out of the storm. Snapping out of the haze he was in; Jonathan pulled his arm away.

"Don't touch me!" he yelled at Douglas.

"What don't you understand, I chose her," Jonathan said, getting into Douglas' face.

"I understand," Douglas said.

"Wait. You told me I would regret it! Did you kill her?" Jonathan said with a dazed look on his face.

"What!? Are you stupid? I would never do that; I'm not even going to argue with you. You are wanting a fight." Douglas turned to go back inside the house.

"Don't walk away from me." Jonathan ran and tackled Douglas. They began to fight, both men exchanging punches. Jonathan got to his feet and immediately felt dizzy. He tried to steady himself, but by that time Douglas was up and ready.

"You couldn't handle that I wanted her and not you. You took her from me..." Jonathan yelled.

"I did not touch her. I have known Faith since we were kids, she was my friend... I loved her just as much as you did," Douglas yelled back at him. Both men stood there and let everything sink in until the silence between them was interrupted by the clapping of thunder.

"She's gone... she is dead; I should have treated her right," Jonathan screamed. Falling to his knees, he began sobbing uncontrollably. It was difficult for Douglas to see his best friend in this much pain. Douglas went over and got Jonathan to his feet. They reached the back door, Douglas grabbed the doorknob, just then the door opened. Standing there looking at them was Pearl. Jonathan's eyes locked with hers and the cobwebs began to clear.

Jonathan picked her up. "What are you doing out of bed, sweetie?"

"Mommy isn't in her room, so I looked down here." Jonathan held back his emotions. He wanted to wait to tell her, let her sleep one more night peacefully without the pain and

heartache he knew she would experience. Jonathan carried her upstairs avoiding what she said.

"Daddy, why are you all wet?" she asked halfway up the stairs.

Jonathan chuckled, "It's raining outside and I was outside talking with Uncle Douglas, silly. Now let's get back into bed." He laid her down and covered her up. "There, now you close those eyes and get your rest. I love you so much, my beautiful girl."

"Daddy, where's mommy? Will she be here when I get up?"

Jonathan didn't know what to say. He was still confused; how could he possibly explain what happened to a six-year-old. Pearl looked at him, waiting for an answer. He had to tell her, to prolong it would be unfair to her. Jonathan cleared his throat. "Pearl, do you remember last year when grandpa and grandma's dog Gus went to the place in the sky to wait for all of us until we got there?"

"Yes, I remember daddy."

The tears started to build in Jonathan's eyes, "Well sweetie, that is where mommy is now."

Pearl sat up. "Mommy left us? why would she want to leave us?" she asked.

"Sweetie, mommy didn't want to leave us, she had too. They needed her up there to help watch Gus and all those other dogs. But she loves you so much and she will always be in your heart," Jonathan said, trying to keep it together. She reached her arms out and he picked her up and embraced her.

She closed her eyes and put her head on his shoulder. "I miss mommy."

Jonathan no longer could control his emotions and let the tears flow down his face. "Me too, baby. Me too."

Chapter 6

Thanksgiving

November 23, 2017

It had been seventy-two hours since the Sheriff gave the first news conference. Now after standing here for the sixth time, he was becoming more comfortable.

"Sheriff, are there any suspects at this time?" someone shouted from the back.

"We are following up on several leads and making sure to be thorough with everything," the same answer he has given the last ten times.

"When can we expect some new information," a reporter from a national news organization asks. The Sheriff focused all his attention directly at the reporter.

"Listen, we are working around the clock and have given this top priority. When we get something, then you will, ok?" Sheriff Bennett kept his eyes on the reporter until he acknowledged that he understood.

The Sheriff thanked the reporters and walked away from the podium. He walked into the large briefing room where his deputies and detectives were all waiting for that day's assignments to be handed out. The room used to be large enough to accommodate everyone, but since the murder there have been several different agencies joining the investigation. Represented in the room was Lieutenant James Stephens from the Missouri State Trooper's and Special Agent Megan Brown from the Federal Bureau of Investigation, both of which brought a team of people with them. Needless to say, it was becoming harder to fit everyone in.

The Sheriff went over the daily incident report and told his deputies to continue with their daily assignments but to be ready if needed for anything. He told his detectives to follow any leads that deal with the Ross homicide. No matter how small or unlikely they are. If they reached a dead end, go back and work the hotline leads; and with that Sheriff Bennett concluded the meeting.

A deputy spoke up, "Sir?"

"Yes, what is it?" the Sheriff asked.

"We have run down every lead and the only thing coming through the hotline is crazies and pranksters, we aren't getting anything new."

"Then go back and re-examine the crime scene. I'm going to say this one time. We have all eyes watching us, this will not be some cold case file! There is something that got missed or overlooked, we need to find it!"

Doctor Lindsey King, Chief Medical Examiner for Jefferson County, was waiting in the Sheriff's office. She has turned in many autopsy reports, but none as horrific as this one in Jefferson County.

"Sorry to keep you waiting Dr. King, I know you have other cases."

"No problem, Sheriff, it's all hands-on deck until this is solved," she said, handing him a file packet.

"Dr. King, how bad is it?" he asked.

"Please call me Lindsey," she said.

"Well, let's just drop all the formalities," Sheriff Bennett said, smirking.

The Doctor smiled and nodded. They both looked like high school kids, not knowing what to say to each other.

Then doing a one-hundred and eighty degrees turn he asked, "What are we looking at as the cause of death?"

"C.O.D. is blunt force trauma to the head; victim has several abrasions and deep lacerations," Lindsey said.

The Sheriff tried to interrupt but she put her finger up to stop him. "The victim was badly beaten all over her body, but extensively to the head and face area," she paused. "I have never seen violence like this."

"You mean here? Have you seen violence like this here?" he asked.

"No. What I mean is that whoever did this had a lot of rage. They continued to beat her even after she was dead."

"Son of a bitch, are you kidding me?" he said in disbelief.

"No, it's the worst case of brutality I have ever seen," she responded.

The Sheriff buried his head in his hands. "So much for my day going smoothly".

Dr. King shifted in her chair. "There is something else, Thomas".

He looked up at her, the expression on her face told him it was serious.

"What is it?"

"She was also sodomized. She had rips and tears in her vaginal canal that were made by some kind of object that was repeatedly inserted into her. I'm guessing a tree branch or medium size stick."

"Why do you think it was a tree branch?"

"I found splinters of wood and particles of tree bark inside of her."

The Sheriff couldn't believe the amount of torment she went through.

"Do you know the time of death, Doc?"

"Yes, around 7 or 7:15p.m." she said.

"Please tell me, this animal left some DNA behind."

"He did. We found semen on her inner thigh and around the vaginal area, a few pubic hairs that were not the victim's and we found skin under her fingernails. She fought but didn't stand a chance. With all the DNA evidence that has been taken off the victim, when you find the person responsible, there will be no denying it," she said with a sense of accomplishment.

"Thank God."

"I know. It is pretty incredible that so much DNA was left at the crime scene. It was like he wasn't even worried about it. He is either the most confident killer or the dumbest." She said while trying to figure out how to bring the next subject up.

"What is it?" he asked.

"When you find the person responsible for this, you can tell the Prosecuting Attorney he can file two counts of murder."

Sheriff Bennett stared at her, confused.

"Thomas, she was pregnant, about thirteen weeks,"

November 27, 2017

Monday

9:00a.m.

Jonathan enjoyed drinking his morning coffee in the living room while looking out of the windows overlooking his estate. He has not had a quiet morning since Faith's murder. Everybody that he knows was coming over, bringing casseroles and their stories of "I can't believe this is happening." Jonathan was tired of everyone, he just wanted some time to himself.

Just when he thought he was going to get some time alone; his phone rang. It was his lawyer, Victor DeNoyer, telling Jonathan that he was on his way over and would need him dressed professionally. The Sheriff wanted them to come in so he could answer some questions.

"Can't we do this another day?" Jonathan asked.

"We need to do this now, so it doesn't look like we are hiding something."

"Ok… But I'm not stuck in a small room for six hours while they ask me the same damn question over and over," Jonathan said.

"I'll be at your house in fifteen minutes and we will go over everything."

Jonathan went to the kitchen to make another cup of coffee to help get his head straight. He went upstairs and got dressed while finishing his coffee. He fixed his hair, brushed his teeth and gave himself one last look in the mirror.

"Ok. Let's do this," he said out loud.

He was coming downstairs when the doorbell rang. He saw Victor standing there through the glass. He opened the door and greeted him like an old friend would.

"Let's get going. We can prepare in the car," Victor said.

Jonathan would normally like Victor to be so detailed in explaining how this interview will go, but he didn't want to hear any of it this morning. He could not wait to get out of this car, away from Victor DeNoyer. Victor is a high price and highly recommended criminal defense attorney. He was a seasoned litigator and had gotten his law degree from Saint Louis University School of Law in 1998. Before he was a lawyer, he had spent ten years working in Law enforcement as a police officer and narcotics agent. He was an active member of the St. Louis County Bar Association, Bar Association of Metropolitan St.Louis and the Missouri Bar. Jonathan gave him a $500,000 retainer fee, for that though Victor was putting this as his number one priority. Normally Victor does not have a case with this much positive publicity towards a client. The media loved Jonathan, the grieving husband and now single parent to those two beautiful children. Victor could easily work with that.

"Is there anything you need to tell me, before we get in there?" Victor said, putting his notes in his briefcase.

"I'm worried about how I will look," Jonathan said.

"How will you look?"

"Me showing up with a high-priced lawyer in front of the media and all their cameras!"

"First, you showing up with an attorney is smart because you are protecting your rights as an American citizen. Second, you get what you pay for, remember that I'm the best at what I do and that is why my services cost what they do. Third, we are going through the back of the building, not the front. No media and no cameras, that was the deal of this interview. Lastly, I am here to make sure you answer only the questions they need answered and nothing more. The police only need to know certain things and sometimes they like to try to be smart. I'm here to protect you, let me do my job," Victor reassured him.

"Alright."

"Trust me, what we are doing is the best decision right now. We talk to the police; it shows you have nothing to hide and that you are doing everything you can to help them find the person that did this," Victor said.

"I do want to find the person that did this, Victor," Jonathan said in a stern voice.

"Yes, of course. I didn't mean..."

"We are here Mr. DeNoyer," the driver said, interrupting the pair's conversation.

"Ok, thank you. Listen Jonathan, what I was trying to say..."

Jonathan cut him off, "Ok, let's get this over with... and Victor; don't ever imply that I don't want my wife's killer found."

Sheriff Bennett stood outside the interview room waiting for the Prosecutor to arrive. The Sheriff was looking forward to questioning Jonathan, he knew he was hiding

something. Bo Carver, the Prosecuting Attorney, arrived and looked as though he had been put through the gauntlet.

"What is wrong with you?" the Sheriff asked.

"I have gotten half a dozen phone calls from some of my wealthier constituents as well as both of our State Senators and the Governor," the young Prosecutor said.

"So what?" the Sheriff scuffed.

"They all insist that Mr. Ross is a pillar in the State of Missouri and will be treated with the utmost respect during this difficult time."

The Sheriff looked at him and realized that Bo was getting cold feet about Jonathan. They both thought that Jonathan knew more than he was telling. They worked up some hard questions for him and were going to show him the crime scene photos to shake him up.

"Listen Thomas, we need to be careful with this, we have no evidence against him."

"Are you getting cold feet?"

"No! But we will tread lightly. This is a routine interview and that is the way it will stay, I'm not committing career suicide," Bo fired back.

"Fine, get out of my way!"

The Sheriff opened the door and went in; he sat across from Jonathan and his attorney.

"Thank you for agreeing to come down and answer some questions for us. I know this is a difficult time for you and your family. We will try and keep this as short as possible"

Jonathan nodded his head, "I appreciate it, Sheriff. I want to do anything to help find justice for my wife."

"Ok, well let's get this started Mr. Ross" the Sheriff said.

"State your name for the record."

"Jonathan Ross."

"Date of birth?"

"July 15, 1980."

"You have decided to have an attorney present with you, do understand that this is being recorded."

"Yes."

"Where were you on the evening of November 20th between seven and nine?"

"I was still at my office at seven, I left around eight to go meet a friend for dinner."

"Where was this dinner at?"

"The Rosemont Hotel."

"At their restaurant or at the bar?"

Victor whispered something to Jonathan and then he answered the question.

"I checked into a room."

"Why did you get a room if it was just dinner with a friend?"

"The dinner was regarding sensitive business matters and I wanted privacy," Jonathan said.

"Does this business partner have a name?"

"Douglas Fulton," Jonathan said.

"Why would you need a private room to meet your business partner, you could've just met him at your office right?"

"I told you already."

"I don't remember you answering."

"Well, that sounds like your problem, Sheriff!" Jonathan said, getting irritated.

"Look, I'm doing my job, so can you answer it again," the Sheriff asked with a smirk on his face.

"So, we could have some privacy, what we were going to be discussing was not something I wanted everyone to hear."

"What was so important you needed all this privacy?" Sheriff Bennett asked.

"We were dissolving a partnership and all professional dealings," Jonathan was getting frustrated.

"Why?"

"We both wanted to go in different directions professionally."

"You got the room in case things went sour during this meeting?" the Sheriff asked.

"Listen, my partner and I have made a lot of money together, not that you would know what that is like, but emotions run high with things like this. We are good friends and I did not want anyone except for us to be in the conversation. Hence, I wanted to have some privacy, can you wrap your head around that?"

"How long were you there?"

Victor stopped Jonathan before he could even answer the question. "Please be more specific?"

"Of course, what time did you arrive at the Rosemont and what time did you leave?"

"I don't know what time I checked in, but the girl at the front desk might have a record of that. I left Rosemont right after I got off the phone with you, Sheriff."

"And what time would that have been?"

Jonathan laughed "Really… It was a little after nine."

"If you can take me through a normal day that Faith would have?"

Jonathan paused and took a drink of water, "She gets up around six or six-thirty, showers and gets herself together. Then around seven-thirty she gets the kids up, makes breakfast and then takes the kids to school. Depending on what day it is she takes flying lessons on Tuesdays and Thursdays... Oh she also does yoga every afternoon."

The Sheriff jotted down some notes. "When did you guys find out about the pregnancy?" the Sheriff asked.

Jonathan had a look of confusion on his face, he turned to Victor who also looked puzzled.

"Pregnancy?" Jonathan asked.

The Sheriff looked at both of them with contentment, "Oh... You didn't know, we thought you knew."

Jonathan sat straight up in the chair. "What are you talking about?"

"Faith was pregnant at the time of her death, about two and half months."

Jonathan was trying to process what he had just been told. Victor could see that his client had just been blind-sided.

"I need a moment alone with my client, please," Victor said.

"Sure, take all the time you need." The Sheriff stood and left the two of them alone in the room.

"I had no idea! Why wouldn't she tell me she was pregnant. You believe that? My own wife didn't tell me she was pregnant," Jonathan was devastated.

Victor had a theory why Faith did not tell him about it. "Jonathan, I have to ask this question. Is there a possibility that you are not the father and that is why Faith did not tell you, because she wasn't sure what she was going to do?"

Jonathan shook his head in defeat, "Yes there is a possibility but I don't know for sure."

Victor now had to figure out what to do. They needed a plan and they needed one fast. "Ok, well we are going to assume that Faith didn't tell you because she was keeping it a surprise until Christmas. We will say she told you she had a surprise for you," Victor said.

The Sheriff came back into the interview room. "Are we ready to continue?" he asked.

"Yes, we are," Victor answered.

The Sheriff sat back down at the table.

"Mr. Ross, when did you find out about the pregnancy?"

"Faith said she had a surprise for the family and wanted to wait until Christmas," he answered.

"So, you never knew she was pregnant? Is there a chance that it is not your child?" Sheriff Bennett asked.

Jonathan looked at Victor and said, "I need a break, I have to use the restroom."

"We just took a break, Jonathan!" the Sheriff said.

"Yeah, well that's because I just found out..." Jonathan was interrupted by Victor before he could finish the sentence.

"Listen, my client has sat here and answered every question you have asked. Mr. Ross is not under arrest, so he can use the restroom if needed too. If you have a problem with that, we can just walk out."

"Alright, that's fine. The restrooms are down the hall," the Sheriff said, shaking his head.

Jonathan locked the restroom's door to ensure that he and Victor were alone. "I'm tired of this shit, he keeps asking the same damn questions."

"They are getting you on the record with your answers. Then asking them again in different ways to see if your answers change. It's a tactic they use, Jonathan," Victor said.

"They are treating me like I killed her. I didn't do anything," Jonathan yelled.

"Lower your voice and get a hold of yourself. This is how they conduct their investigation, when someone is murdered, the first person the police look at is the spouse. They are ruling you out as a suspect and collecting as much information as they can. This whole process is time consuming but it is necessary because you may know something that can help them catch the person that did this," Victor was trying to reassure him when Jonathan finally exploded.

"No! Fuck this! I didn't do anything and I gave your ass $500,000 for what!? So, you can sit here and watch me answer the same fucking questions ten times…" Victor tried to interject but Jonathan was not having it. "You're just sitting in there watching him grill me like goddamn hamburger meat. What in the hell am I paying you for!?" Jonathan said, getting into Victor's face.

"You're paying me to make sure you aren't sitting in a 6 foot by 8-foot cell for the rest of your natural life, because right now at this moment, you are the only person that has the motive to commit the crime. Now get out of my face, get your shit together and let me do my job!" snapped Victor.

Jonathan stood there, stunned that Victor spoke to him like that. They were walking back to the interview room when they noticed the media setting up outside for a press conference.

"When we go back on the record in there, we are going to tell them," Victor said looking at Jonathan.

They were all back in the room and on record again. Before the Sheriff could start asking questions Victor said, "My client would like to offer some additional information regarding his personal relationship with his wife that could be beneficial. It's sensitive to my client and the memory of his late wife, it would be greatly appreciated if this did not end up in the press."

The Sheriff had an annoyed look on his face and took a breath before speaking. "I'm an investigator, I solve crimes and the current one that I'm trying to solve is your client's wife's murder. If you have something to add to this investigation, please say it."

"My wife and I had an open marriage," Jonathan said.

Chapter 7

November 27, 2017

Monday

11:35a.m.

The Sheriff's stomach dropped and he suddenly did not feel very well. He took a drink of his coffee and then replied, "You're telling me that you and Faith had an open marriage and you both knew each other were being unfaithful?"

"Yes, Sheriff."

"Did you two know who each other slept with?"

"Not all the time, we had an understanding and we both were fine with the way things were."

"Why didn't you tell us this earlier, Mr. Ross?"

"We have not been in an open marriage for a few months, I wasn't thinking about it."

"Your wife was murdered and you didn't think that maybe it could have been someone she slept with?"

"Listen, we have been in marriage counseling for a few months and she ended it months ago with him," Jonathan explained.

"You and your wife slept with other people, outside of your marriage, and you both know what the other was doing?"

"That is what I said," Jonathan smirked.

"What is so funny Mr. Ross?"

"How many times are you going to ask the same question?"

"Until I'm satisfied that it has been answered fully!"

"Yeah, ok Sheriff! Next question," Jonathan said, getting frustrated.

"Do you know any of her boyfriend's name?" the Sheriff asked in a disgusted tone.

"Sheriff, I do not expect you to understand our way of life, but they were not her boyfriends. They were just friends…Alright?"

"Mr. Ross, call it what you want, but these kinds of arrangements only create problems. I'm not here to judge your lifestyle, so like I asked before, what are the names of her 'friends' that you know," the Sheriff asked, sliding a piece of paper and pen to Jonathan.

Jonathan took the pen and paper; he wrote down something all while never breaking eye contact and he pushed it back across the table. The Sheriff picked it up and read it.

"What the hell is this, some kind of joke?" he said to Jonathan.

"No, it's no joke, Sheriff. What's wrong?" Jonathan was staring at him. The air in the room was becoming thick and uncomfortable.

The Sheriff broke the silence, "Are you sure this is the way, you want this to go down?"

"Sheriff, are you threatening my client?" Victor asked in a stern voice.

Victor was just about to rail into him when Jonathan held up his hand to stop him.

"Thomas, I think you have no idea what you're doing, but I know you have to have some common sense in that thick skull of yours. I would start looking for a new job"

The Sheriff stood up and was inches away from Jonathan's face. Victor grabbed Jonathan's arm to try and pull him away from the situation.

"You never loved her. It doesn't matter how much money you have, if I find out you were involved with this in any way, I'm going to personally walk you to the death chamber," the Sheriff said.

"That's it, we are done with this interview." Victor shouted.

"Enjoy wearing that badge while you still can, I don't think you will be wearing it much longer. Then what? You'll have nothing. No job. No friends, and no wealthy mistresses."

"You're crazy. You have no proof," the Sheriff snapped back.

"That's the great thing about being rich, I can afford to pay a private investigator to follow my wife. I hear a picture is worth a thousand words," the Sheriff's face went pale and he felt like he was going to be sick.

The door flew open and Bo Carver was standing there. Victor looked at him and said "We are done here Mr. Carver"

Victor and Jonathan walked out of the room and Bo closed the door behind them, leaving only him and the Sheriff in the room.

"Is it true, Thomas?"

The Sheriff was leaning on the table, trying to get his senses back.

"Thomas, is it true?"

"Yes."

"Are you serious? How do you not tell anyone that you knew the victim personally?"

95

"Are you kidding? In that case why didn't you tell anyone that you knew the victim and had known her on a personal level, Bo. I know they were at your fundraisers, too!?"

"Yeah, but I wasn't fucking her, Thomas."

"It was not like that."

"Yeah well, tell that to the Troopers and the F.B.I. They want to talk with you."

November 27, 2017

Monday

2:15p.m.

The Sheriff was in his office with the State Troopers, F.B.I. and the Prosecutor Attorney. The State Troopers were going to be taking over the investigation and handling the press releases as well. The Sheriff understood that he could no longer handle this investigation, due to his personal connection to the victim and the fact that he did not disclose it immediately to the other investigators. Sheriff Bennett handed-over all his files except for the press briefing packet.

"What are you doing?" Lieutenant Stephens asked.

"Getting my notes for the press release," he said.

The trooper looked at the Sheriff with disdain. "Are you joking? Because of your actions we now have to waste man hours on re-interviewing everyone and retracing everything

you have done. You aren't talking to any reporters on behalf of my investigation, you are finished with this whole case, as is this entire department. Now I have to treat you as a potential suspect in the investigation and you will go nowhere near Mr. Ross. If you interfere at all in any way, I will arrest your ass so fast it will make your head spin."

Thomas did not know what to say. The trooper grabbed the papers out of his hands.

"I expect every piece of evidence regarding this case to be boxed up and ready for us to take within the hour," Lieutenant Stephens ordered.

"Aren't you going to keep the investigation here, it would be easier," the Sheriff said.

"You have made that impossible with this investigation…" The Lieutenant stopped just before leaving the office. "I want you to come in tomorrow to give us a full statement regarding everything that happened between you and the victim. On the record."

The Sheriff nodded his head, "Yeah, you got it. I'm not a bad guy."

"Yeah. Tomorrow morning, 7a.m. my office," Stephens turned and walked out.

The Sheriff was left alone with his thoughts and replaying the events of the day in his head. He wanted to know how the hell he let things get this much out of hand, he gathered his things and left, knowing this would be the last time he would leave this office without everyone knowing the truth. He realized that his career as he knows it is now over. Everything he worked for down the drain. It bothered him that he would be remembered for being involved in a sex scandal where the woman he was involved with was murdered, and that that would be his legacy. There is only one thing left he can do, tell the truth and hope that the voters forgave him, then he would have a fighting chance at keeping his job.

Lieutenant James Stephens was fixing his uniform and straightening his hat before walking up to the podium.

"Ladies and gentlemen, if I could have your attention. I am Lieutenant James Stephens with the Missouri State Troopers; I have a brief statement and I won't be taking any questions afterward. Starting tomorrow all press releases will be made at the Missouri State Troopers headquarters, you can get the address from the cards that are being handed out. Effective immediately, the Missouri State Troopers are handling this investigation and will be the agency in charge. I will have more information for you tomorrow, thank you and goodnight."

Lieutenant Stephens kept the statement short and to the point. The reporters could only speculate why the troopers were now heading up the investigation.

November 28, 2017

Tuesday

7:00a.m.

Sheriff Bennett was ready to clear his name when he got to the Lieutenant's office that morning. He was led into an interview room where Lieutenant Stephens was already waiting for him.

"Sheriff, please have a seat. I got us some bagels and coffee."

"Thank you."

"I think we got off on the wrong foot, Sheriff. I would like this to be a conversion, let me start off by saying, we know that you have an alibi for the time of death. We know you were in a county council meeting but we are going to need the full story of everything that happened between you and the victim," Lieutenant Stephens said.

"What do you want to know?"

"First, let me give you this warning. If you lie to me about anything, no matter how small it is, I will charge you with obstruction of justice."

"I understand, I have nothing to hide."

"Ok, great! Let's start from the beginning, when the romantic relationship started and where I have questions, I will interject?" Lieutenant Stephens said.

"I first met Faith; I mean Mrs. Ross about three years ago after winning the election for Sheriff. Mr. and Mrs. Ross backed my campaign from the beginning, I only dealt with Mr. Ross."

The Lieutenant put his hand up. "Sheriff, when was the first time you met Mrs. Ross?"

"It was on the evening of November 4th, 2014 at her house."

"Why were you at her house that evening?" Lieutenant Stephens asked.

"They were having an election-night party. There were a bunch of people there drinking, eating and watching the results come in. After I found out that I won, everyone was

coming up shaking my hand and giving me congratulations. Faith walked up to me and told me to follow her," the Sheriff stopped and took another sip of his coffee.

November 4th, 2014

Election-Day

11:50p.m.

"Well, Congratulations Sheriff Bennett," Faith said with a grin.

"It does have a nice ring to it, thank you Mrs. Ross."

"Thomas, call me Faith; I feel like an old lady when you call me Mrs."

"Ok, thank you, Faith," he said grinning.

"You are welcome, Sheriff. Are you enjoying yourself?"

"Yes, this is great. I love your home, it's really nice."

Faith smiled. "Thank you, let me show you around." She grabbed him by the arm and began the tour, showing him the kitchen, dining room, family room and the wine cellar. Faith then took him outside and walked to what looked like a smaller house.

"Do you appreciate beautiful things, Sheriff?" she asked, unlocking the door.

"It depends on what it is," he said as he looked her up and down.

"Can I show you something then, but you can't tell anyone."

"You can trust me," he said as she opened the door and the lights flickered on.

"Holy shit!"

"You like it?" she asked.

"Hell yeah, it's a brand-new sports car, and who wouldn't love it?"

"I bought it for my husband and wanted a man's opinion"

He walked around the entire car admiring its beauty. Thomas popped the hood to get a look at the engine. He was checking everything out when she came over. She smelled

so good, and she was really close to him. He could feel himself getting warm, he was starting to sweat.

"It's a really nice car," he said, wiping the sweat off his forehead.

He closed the hood of the car and turned to walk out the door, Faith stepped in front of him.

"What is the hurry?"

"No hurry. I didn't want anyone wondering where you are and come looking for you and find your big surprise," he laughed nervously.

She walked toward him, backing him up against the car.

"Trust me, they are more concerned about drinking all my champagne and enjoying themselves, no one cares where I ran off too."

"I'm sure Jonathan does."

She laughed out loud. "Wow! You really don't know my husband."

"Trust me, he loves you; I mean what's not to love. You're beautiful, smart, and buy great gifts. C'mon, he would have to be crazy not to love you."

She smiled. "It's been a long time since I have heard that."

"Long time? What's the last ten minutes?"

"Sheriff, be serious."

"I am being serious; I know for a fact that every man here tonight has told you that you look amazing."

She looked at him with a slight grin.

"Alright. How do you know that every man here said that to me?"

Thomas stood there a moment, trying to come up with a better answer that did not make him look creepy.

"No answer I give you is going to make it not seem like I'm a weirdo. I haven't been able to take my eyes off you this evening."

"I don't think you're a weirdo. What if I told you that I saw you looking at me and that's the real reason I brought you out here."

"I think we need to get back to the party because if not we may do something we regret."

"Sheriff, life is too short for regrets or what ifs."

"I'm trying to restrain myself."

Faith grabbed him by the shirt and kissed him for what seemed like forever to him.

"See, was that so bad?" she asked. Before he could answer, she reached down and felt him.

"Oh! Yeah, you liked it," she said, rubbing him through his pants.

"We shouldn't do this Faith."

"Shhh... Relax Sheriff. Just go with it"

"But..."

"Be quiet. We wouldn't want to get caught like this," she said seductively, pushing him so he was leaning against the car. She slid down to her knees and was eye level with his belt. She unzipped his pants and maneuvered her hand through the opening of his boxers.

"Sheriff, remember what I said, you better be quiet. We don't want to get caught," she said smiling. She put him in her mouth and rolled her tongue over him ever inch that she could until she had to come back and take a breath. All while stroking it as she went along.

"You like that, Sheriff?"

"Yeah.... Don't stop!"

"Yeah, you like your prisoner sucking this cock?"

"You're my good little inmate."

"HMMM...."

"I'm...I'm..."

Thomas was so nervous someone was going to walk in on this. He could not believe this was happening, he was trying to think of something to say when he felt his body go numb.

"Oh, shit. Sorry," he said.

Faith took a hard swallow, smiled at him as she stood up and said, "No worries, let's get a drink, I need to wash the taste out of my mouth."

They started to walk to the door but before she opened it, she stopped and pulled up her dress and grabbed his hand.

"Push my panties to the side and feel it. Do you feel how wet I am?"

"Yes."

"That's from sucking your cock," she said, pushing his hand away as she fixed her dress and led them to get something to drink.

November 28, 2017

Tuesday

9:50 a.m.

Lieutenant Stephens returned with two cups of coffee, he handed the Sheriff a cup and jumped right into asking questions.

"Sheriff, why do you think Mrs. Ross would do that basically in her home with all those people there?"

"She was into it," he answered.

"How was she into it?"

"It was the thrill, she got off on it. You know, the possibility of getting caught by someone."

"Someone or her husband?"

"I don't know, honestly."

"Did Mrs. Ross say if she and her husband were having problems?"

"No, nothing like that. I think she felt that her husband did not care for or love her."

"Why do you say that, Sheriff?"

"She told me that night when I said we should get back because Jonathan would be missing her. She basically said that he doesn't care about her. She did not go into any details about it though."

"What happened when the two of you went back into the house?"

"We went into the kitchen where the caterers had the drinks and we each took a glass of champagne. Then Jonathan came into the kitchen and she went with him to talk with the other guests."

"So, to be clear, Mr. Ross found the both of you in the kitchen, correct?"

"Yes, but it's not like he caught us doing anything, there were like ten other people in there doing things, so it looked normal."

"Alright. Did you and Mrs. Ross had sex that night?"

"No. I did not see her the rest of the evening and I ended up going home about an hour later."

"Did you and Mrs. Ross only engage in oral sex that evening?"

"Correct."

"Sheriff, did you and Mrs. Ross ever have sex?"

"Yes."

"When was that?"

"It was about two weeks after our garage encounter, I'm not sure of the exact date."

"Ok, but you're sure it was two weeks after the first sexual encounter?"

"I'm not exactly sure of two weeks, but I think it was about two weeks. I know it was a Thursday night because I ordered a pizza and that's what I do every Thursday."

"Great. Continue," he said.

"I was sitting at home watching tv when I got a call from a number I didn't recognize."

November 19, 2014

Thursday

6:30p.m.

Thomas had just sat down to relax for the evening and was thinking about everything that has happened the past few weeks. There was so much to get done but he was exhausted and was not going to think about anything tonight. Then his cell phone rang.

"You've got to be shitting me."

He got up and went into the kitchen where it was plugged in. It was a number he didn't recognize.

"Hello?"

"Good-evening, Sheriff," a female voice said.

"Good-evening," he said hesitantly.

"This is Faith Ross... from the party..."

"Yes, Faith, how could I forget," he said in a boyish tone.

"Well, good. I was wondering if you wanted to get together and get started on planning the inaugural ball?"

"Sure, I have some free time tomorrow afternoon-"

She interrupted him. "Well, that's the thing, I have time now and I really need to get this done."

Thomas stood there debating, he knew he needed to tell her that things could not go that far again and that would be a conversation best kept out of public. But what if things happened again. He needed to be an adult and have self-control; this was his career and his family's legacy after all. No sooner than he thought that, he blurted out, "I'm not doing anything, come on by."

"I will be there," she said.

Before he could give her the address, she had already hung up. He was thinking about how in the hell did he get himself into this situation. He was an elected official now; this

was not going to end well for either of them, especially him. He did not want to have a scandal before or after he took office. He was going to have to make sure she understood that what happened the other night could not happen again.

"Damn!" he said, smelling his breath from the garlic bread he had with his pizza. He rushed into the bathroom to brush his teeth and use mouthwash. He finished and shoved a couple peppermints into his mouth when the doorbell rang.

"Here goes nothing," he said to himself.

He answered the door and was not prepared for the sight he saw. Faith was standing there in her tennis shoes, black yoga pants, a half-zipped sweat jacket, showing her work-out shirt, which the neck was cut out; exposing her amazing chest line. He didn't know what to say, she broke the awkward silence.

"Are you going to invite me in or should I stand here?"

His trance was broken and he managed to say, "Yes, please come in Mrs. Ross, sorry about that."

"Thomas, seriously you have to stop," she said as she laughed.

"Sorry. My mistake. Faith… Is that better?"

"Yes. But don't let it happen again," she said smiling.

He led her to the dining room and started to wipe the table off.

"Sorry, it is a little dusty."

"We can sit at the kitchen table," she said.

"Can I get you something to drink? Tea, water, coffee…"

"Do you have a beer?" she asked.

"Yes. Do you want a glass?"

"No," she said, making a face.

He got her a beer and one for himself. He took it over to her and took the seat next to her. He really didn't have a choice because she had a bunch of papers spread out on the table, except for the spot next to her.

"Hold on a second," he said.

"What is it, Sheriff?"

"I never told you where I lived. How did you find out?"

"Oh my god! Are you being serious right now? You're not the only one that has investigative powers around here Sheriff," she said smiling.

"Well ok, looks like I know the first deputy that I'm going to hire," he said while looking at her.

"We can work something out after I get what I need from you Sheriff."

"Ok, let's get this over with then."

"Ok, what I need from you Sheriff is decisions."

"Like what?" he asked.

"Food choices for the party."

"Ok."

"Do you like red or white pasta?"

"Red."

"Steak or fish?"

"Steak."

"Now here is the important question, beer or champagne?"

"Beer, no question."

Faith gathered the papers together and put them in the folder she had.

"Was that it?" he asked.

"Yes, sir."

"We could have done this over the phone, you didn't have to drive all the way over here."

"No, we couldn't. We have to discuss what happened a couple of weeks ago," she said.

"Yeah, I didn't know what was going on, Faith. I just don't want any hard feelings between us."

"Don't be silly. I know we both have a lot at stake and it's not like you're attracted to me."

"Whoa! Who said I wasn't attracted to you, look at you, you are beautiful!"

"You really think I'm beautiful?" she asked.

"Beautiful, smart and you like beer, looks like the complete package to me. That's sexy! Too bad you're taken already."

"Thanks. You are pretty sexy yourself," she said leaning in closer.

"We shouldn't do this," he said.

"I know, this is why it's the last time, Sheriff, so do what you want," she said, while biting her lower lip seductively. He could no longer take it, picking her up in his arms, he started to carry her to his bedroom.

"No. Right here" she said.

"In the kitchen, seriously?"

"Yes, treat me like a whore," she answered.

"What! Are you joking or being serious?" he said, setting her down.

"I'm serious. I am tired of being a good little housewife. Come on, think of this as my way of getting out of a future ticket......Please Sheriff."

He thought for a second and then answered, "Alright." He pushed her up against the kitchen island and started to kiss her neck and collar bone.

"You can't leave any marks. Sheriff…" she said, moaning from pure ecstasy.

"I can do whatever I want. I'm the Sheriff!"

He unzipped her sweat jacket and threw it on the floor. They were kissing when he turned her around and pushed her so she was face down laying on the island from the waist up. He pulled her black yoga pants down past her thighs and bent down to bury his face into her.

"Aww! You taste so good," he said, licking her and then slowly pushing his middle finger inside of her.

"Oh my god, don't stop!" she moaned.

"Yeah, has it been a while, you little whore?"

"Yes, Sheriff," she said, hiding her face.

"Don't you hide that face from me, there is no reason to be coy, we are way pass that!"

She looked back at him, "I have to be leaving soon."

"You will leave when I have finished with you and not before then."

He stood up and pulled his pants down. He began to rub his rock-hard penis up and down her, teasing her until she could barely take it anymore.

"Oh shit…Sheriff," she managed to get out before he penetrated her. He grabbed her shoulders and began thrusting into her, slow deep thrust at first gradually getting faster. He grabbed her ponytail and pulled it back.

"Ow… don't pull so hard," she said.

"This is what you wanted, you little whore! You're mine now, bitch!" He grabbed her by the waist and started to thrush with more force. She could feel him throbbing and stretching her.

"Tell me I better not tell anyone…Or else," she told him.

"You better keep your fucking mouth shut and not tell anyone about this! Or I'm going to come back and fuck you in the ass!"

"Oh shit, that's hot! I'm coming. Awwwww…..."

"That's right, come for me, I want your juices all over my dick. You trashy little whore… I'm going to come! Take it, you little come dumpster!"

"Wait, did you really just come inside of me?" she asked.

"What?"

"Don't worry about me! You heard what I asked."

"Yeah, so what?" he answered.

"So, what? I'm not on any birth control that's what!" she said pushing up off the island and looking for something to clean herself up with.

"What the hell do you mean you're not on birth control, why in the hell wouldn't you tell me that?"

"Do you have something I can clean up with at least?"

"Yeah, here use this it's clean" he said handing her a dish cloth.

"Thanks" she said, getting it wet at the kitchen sink.

"And by the way I would have no reason to be on birth control, I'm married. How would I explain that?" she said, pulling up her pants. She began to gather her things together when he noticed that his pants were still down.

She was on her way out the door, when he said, "Faith... I'm sorry."

She stopped and looked back at him, "It is what it is, I will deal with it. Goodbye, Thomas."

November 28, 2017

Tuesday

11:20a.m.

The Lieutenant drank the last bit of coffee in his cup.

"Did you see Mrs. Ross again after that evening?" Lieutenant Stephens asked.

The Sheriff took a drink of his coffee and answered, "Yes. The night I got sworn in as Sheriff, there was a big celebration for me getting elected."

"Did the two of you talk with each other that night?"

"We did. We exchanged hellos, that was it. They left the party early and it was a few weeks later that I found out she was pregnant."

"That is the pregnancy of her second child, correct?"

"Yes. Weston."

"How did you find out she was pregnant?"

"Well, it's a small town, people talk."

"Did Mrs. Ross ever talk with you about the pregnancy?"

The Sheriff shifted in his seat and took another drink of his coffee. "We never had an in-depth conversation about it."

The Lieutenant was looking at his notes, trying to think of the best way to ask his next question.

"Is there a possibility that you could be the father?"

"I don't know, if you're asking if we used protection, no we didn't."

"Sheriff, you never thought to ask whether or not the baby is yours?"

"I did ask her; I ran into her at a council meeting and pulled her to the side to ask her whether or not I was the father."

"What did she say?"

"She told me, " What did it matter, this baby is going to grow up a Ross and did I really want to ruin my career. I told her I needed a straight answer from her. Her reply was, "No, it's not yours."

The Sheriff drank the last of his coffee. He was tired and defeated. He told them everything that had happened between him and Faith. Now he had to deal with the repercussions of his actions.

The Lieutenant adjusted in his chair, finished writing his notes, and closed the file folder on the table.

"We are done here, I have no further questions at this point, but if I have questions at a later date you will need to make yourself available," the Lieutenant said.

"Of course."

"Sheriff, we both know it won't be long before the press finds out the reason, we took over the investigation. It would be better to notify the press ourselves, that way we can control what is said."

"I just want people to know I am not a suspect."

"They will," Lieutenant Stephens assured.

Press Conference

4:30p.m.

Lieutenant Stephens stepped up to the podium with his statement and waited for the room to quiet down.

"Good afternoon. I will make a brief statement and then take a few questions. Yesterday afternoon it was brought to our attention that Jefferson County Sheriff Thomas Bennett had a previous romantic relationship with Mrs. Ross. The Sheriff's Department, along with the Prosecuting Attorney's Office, the F.B.I., and the State Troopers all agreed that the Sheriff's Department would no longer handle the investigation to avoid any conflict of interest. The Sheriff asked the Missouri State Troopers to take over the investigation and we agreed. We immediately took possession of all case notes and evidence dealing with this case. We continue to gather evidence based on information given to us. Sheriff Bennett is not a suspect. Let me repeat that Sheriff Thomas Bennett is NOT a suspect. The Sheriff did come in this morning to answer some questions regarding the relationship that he and Mrs. Ross had. The Sheriff answered all the questions we asked and provided additional information. At this time, I would like to open it up for a few questions"

"Lieutenant, Lieutenant!" they shouted. Every reporter had their hand up. The Lieutenant just started picking at random and pointed to a reporter in the middle of the crowd.

"Lieutenant Stephens, was this relationship while she was married to Jonathan Ross?"

"Yes, it was."

They were shouting questions from all directions. "Listen! One at a time or I'm not taking any more questions."

"Did Sheriff Bennett admit to having an affair with Mrs. Ross?"

"Yes, he did. The Sheriff brought it to our attention."

"Was this the affair while in office?"

"Yes, the affair happened after the Sheriff was elected to office."

"Did Jonathan Ross know his wife was having an affair?"

"No comment," Stephens answered.

"Are you going to charge the Sheriff with obstruction of justice?"

"That's not my decision, the Sheriff answered all of our questions and there is no law making it illegal to have an affair with someone."

"Are we going to hear from Sheriff Bennett about all of this?" a reporter shouted.

"That's the Sheriff's choice on whether he speaks or not. But it won't be here."

"Lieutenant Stephens, where is the investigation standing right now?"

"We are actively following all leads and I'm confident that we will soon have the person responsible for this horrific crime in custody. We have spent a lot of man hours on this investigation so far and have a lot more ahead of us. We thank the public for all the helpful tips, there is nothing too small to report. I want to end this by saying that from here on out we will be giving one press release a day unless there is a major development in the investigation, then we can make the decision when to release that. Thank you." With that, Lieutenant Stephens walked back to his office. He was getting ready to call his commander when a trooper came running into his office.

The trooper's face was red, his eyes were big and you could tell he was excited about something.

"Tell me, you won the jackpot or something."

"Sir, we have an eyewitness report that must have been overlooked the first time. The witness says that Faith was running away from a trailer in the mobile home park and that a man was chasing her. She heard yelling from both of them and saw Faith drive off at a high rate of speed."

"When was this?"

"On the day she was murdered!"

"Well, that's a hell of a lead, do we know who it is?" Stephens asked.

"Adam Lewis."

Chapter 8

November 28, 2017

Tuesday

6:30p.m.

The Medical Examiner's office finally released Faith's body for burial. Jonathan made the arrangements with the funeral home. When Jonathan arrived at the funeral home there was a man waiting for him in the lobby. They exchanged pleasantries and the man expressed how sorry he was for the loss of his wife. The man led Jonathan to his office, then the nauseating process began. The man was giving him an overview of some of the questions he was going to need answered. He told Jonathan that they would get through these questions together and could take all the time that he needed. Jonathan began to feel overwhelmed and dizzy. He took a few deep breaths and asked the man for some water. The man went to grab a bottle of water, returning, he handed it to him.

"Do you need me to call someone?" the man asked.

"No… I'm ok, I just need a minute. All of this is so… I can't believe this is happening."

The man nodded in acknowledgement. "I know this is difficult," he told him, as he sat back down behind the desk.

"Sorry about that," Jonathan said. The man put his hand up, stopping Jonathan from saying another word.

"Mr. Ross, I am here to make this as easy as possible for you. Instead of asking you a bunch of questions we simply have packages to purchase that will include everything you need. All you do is tell us her favorite colors for the flowers and who she survived so we can put it in the paper."

"I don't want some cheap ass looking casket!"

"We have different burial packages with different levels, so it all depends on what price range you want to stay in, sir."

"The best. I want the best for her."

"Ok, what are her favorite colors, Mr. Ross?"

"Blue and yellow."

"Who is she survived by?"

"Her parents, Jim and Sherri Butler, our daughter Pearl, our son Weston, myself and too many friends to name." Jonathan began to cry.

The man handed him some tissues and tried his best to console him. "We will handle everything Mr. Ross. It will be done with the utmost dignity."

Jonathan pulled it together enough to ask one last question. He reached into his coat pocket and pulled out two-pictures that were hand drawn by the kids and a letter he wrote to Faith.

"Can you put these with her," he asked, handing the man the items.

"Mr. Ross, I will personally make sure these are with her."

"How much do I owe you?" Jonathan asked.

"We just ask for a deposit now and then we send you a final bill Mr. Ross."

Jonathan handed over his debit card and waited for the receipt. He could feel the tears coming and wanted to get out of there.

"Ok, Mr. Ross, everything is taken care of," the man was getting ready to say something else, Jonathan didn't give him the chance either. He grabbed his card and signed the receipt, then walked so fast to the door, it was almost a run. He got outside and the cool air hit his face, he took a few deep breaths trying to catch his breath but couldn't. He thought he was having a heart attack and was trying to get his phone out to call 911 but before he could, he collapsed to the ground.

November 29, 2017

Wednesday

4:15a.m.

Lieutenant Stephens and ten troopers were checking their gear and going over the plan again. The judge came through with the no-knock search warrant late last night. Stephens was taking no chances with this suspect. They have gone through all the possible scenarios and made the decision to make forced entry through the front door of the suspect's trailer. They are going to serve the warrant as quickly and safely as possible. Lieutenant Stephens looked at his men getting ready. "Alright, let's mount up."

The unmarked police vehicles made the short drive to the suspect's home two minutes away. Lieutenant Stephens has served countless felony arrest warrants and has gone on several raids; this is the part he loves the most. The rush of adrenaline that comes over him in the moments before and the not knowing what is going to happen.

"The suspect's house is on the right side, his truck is in the drive-way," Lieutenant Stephens said into the radio.

The troopers park their vehicles surrounding the trailer. Lieutenant Stephens and two troopers went to the front door as everyone else got into position.

"Is everyone ready?"

"We're all set, waiting for you to go."

Lieutenant Stephens took a breath, "Go!"

The troopers breached the front door and began searching methodically. They found Adam in the back bedroom asleep, he had no idea what was going on. Troopers cuffed and searched him. It was all over in twenty-five seconds.

"He's clean, sir," a trooper told Stephens.

"Mr. Lewis, I'm Lieutenant Stephens with the Missouri State Troopers. We have a warrant to search your home and vehicle. You are not under-arrest at this time; we are detaining you for questioning."

"What the hell for? I didn't do anything," Adam said.

"Take him to headquarters. Make sure you get him something to eat and some coffee," he told the trooper.

As soon as Adam was in the back of the car and on his way to the station, Stephens allowed himself to relax.

"Ok, let's get the technicians in here for the computer and cell phone, then we are going to search every inch of this trailer," Stephens said, while he started to search the living room.

They had been searching for an hour when a trooper shouted over the radio, "Lieutenant, you better come outside and have a look at this, sir." Stephens stopped what he was doing and went outside. He was being directed towards the back of the house, by the back bedroom.

"What is it?" he asked.

The trooper pointed to the back of the trailer, Stephens saw two hand marks on the siding just below the bedroom window, where someone had put their hands there.

"There is something else, sir." The trooper led them to the shed on the other side of the trailer. "There, on the floor", the trooper pointed.

Lieutenant Stephens walked in the shed and saw a broken-up crate. He didn't know what he was supposed to be looking at, then he noticed the broken-up crate in the corner of the shed and shined his light on it. That's when see noticed the blood, definitely enough to get some useable DNA

"Let's get forensic in here. Keep everyone else out of here. Good work!" Just as he was going back into the trailer his cell phone began to ring, it was Bo Carver. "Hello, Mr. Carver."

"Lieutenant, have you found anything?"

"Yes, we have. We are still searching the house. We need a warrant for a sample of Mr. Lewis's DNA."

"I will work on getting it. Just keep me informed, the more evidence I have the easier it will be to get a warrant," Bo ended the conversion without saying goodbye.

"What an asshole! It's not like I had anything else to say," he said as he put his phone away.

He looked at his watch, 5:30 A.M. They were making good time but he knew the media would find out, and he wanted to be gone before they showed up. He went back inside to get an update.

"Guys let's stop for a minute and gather around." All the troopers came into the living room.

"Where do we stand right now?" Stephens asked.

"Thankfully it's a small place, we have done the basic search of all the rooms. Not finding a whole lot of anything. Forensic just got here, they gathered the bed sheets and are working in the shed. We also found a laptop and got his cellphone; we are going to take them back to the lab and look through them."

"What about his truck - have we searched it?" Stephens asked.

"We searched it and did not find anything, but we have a tow truck on the way to take it back to headquarters so we can better process it."

"Ok, sounds good. We are going to have the Sheriffs' deputies secure the site."

Lieutenant Stephens looked at his men and then said, "Don't for any reason tell the deputies anything that we found here. When the truck is done, you guys get out and let forensics finish up. Alright?"

"Yes, sir!" the troopers answered.

Stephens headed back to the station, so he could start questioning Adam, hopefully he was feeling talkative and didn't lawyer up. He thought about what they have on Adam, nothing concrete, yet. Unless the DNA comes back with a match, they will need a confession.

November 28, 2017

Tuesday

6:47p.m.

"Sir! Sir! Can you open your eyes for me?" the voice said loudly.

Jonathan slowly opened his eyes, he had no idea where he was. He tried sitting up but soon realized he couldn't.

"Where the hell am I?"

"Sir, you're in an ambulance. Do you remember what happened?" the paramedic asked.

"I was walking to my car and after that I don't know what happened."

"Sir, did you take any kind of drugs or medication?"

"Are you kidding me?"

"Sir, I am just trying to figure out what happened."

"No, I did not," Jonathan answered.

"Any history of heart-attack or heart problems?"

"No, listen I feel fine, just let me out of here," Jonathan told him.

The paramedic shook his head, "No sir, I can't do that."

Jonathan became enraged, he was tired of everyone telling him what to do. Since Faith's death people have treated him like a child, as if he was a charity case. He reached his breaking point when the paramedic told him no. Jonathan began to struggle with the paramedic, trying to get unstrapped from the gurney.

"Let me the hell out of here… Do you know who the hell I am? I'm going to have you fired, you son-of-a-bitch!" Jonathan screamed.

The paramedic quickly gave him a shot to relax him, Jonathan closed his eyes and was still.

9:36 p.m.

Jonathan woke up in a hospital bed, he could hear Victor and the doctor talking, he felt groggy and his mouth was really dry, it felt like he had sand in it.

"Can I have some water?" he managed to get out. Victor and the doctor came walking in. They both reached for the cup of water on his tray. Victor reached it first and held the straw up to Jonathan's mouth. He drank almost the whole cup of water.

"My mouth is dry."

"That's a side effect of the tranquilizer," the doctor said.

"Tranquilizer?"

"Yes, Mr. Ross, in the ambulance you started to get aggressive towards the paramedic and trying to get out of the restraints; the paramedic administered a sleeping tranquilizer. It will wear off in a few hours."

Jonathan shook his head, "I don't remember any of that happening."

"That's normal Mr. Ross," the doctor said.

"What's wrong with me, Doc?"

"I believe you had a severe panic attack."

"Panic attack? I don't have panic attacks. How do you know it's that and not something else?"

"Mr. Ross all your blood work came back normal, we did an electrocardiogram which is an EKG and that came out clear as well. With the stress you have been under, I believe that's what it is."

"Now what? Is this going to happen again?" he asked.

"I am going to write you a prescription for Prozac, you should try to stay out of stressful situations and take it easy for a few days."

"Prozac! That's for depression," Jonathan said.

"Mr. Ross, Prozac is a selective serotonin reuptake inhibitor and it's used to treat depression, anxiety and obsessive-compulsive disorder."

"It makes me nervous taking those kinds of pills, Doc. I don't want to become addicted."

"Mr. Ross, the dosage I'm prescribing is very low and it is only a month supply."

"When can I get out of here?" Jonathan asked.

"Well as soon as we finish up the paperwork, you can go."

Victor interjected and asked the doctor a question about getting copies of everything. The doctor looked at Victor and then Jonathan, "That's up to the patient if he wants copies."

Victor looked at Jonathan, like a mother looks at her child when she wants them to do something.

"Can I get copies of all the paperwork regarding this today?"

"Of course, Mr. Ross," the doctor replied.

"Alright, I will get the car while you get dressed and you can meet me downstairs," Victor said, getting Jonathan's clothes.

"Thanks Victor."

Victor picked up Jonathan at the entrance where the nurse was waiting with him. He got into the car and put his seatbelt on.

"Can you drop me off at my car, please?" he asked Victor.

"I can take you home, you really should not be driving."

"I'm fine, just take me to my car, please."

"Alright, you're going straight home, right?" Victor asked.

"Yes! Who are you? My mother!"

It was nearly midnight when they arrived at his car.

"Thanks for the ride, I appreciate you coming to the hospital."

"It's no big deal, Jonathan."

"Faith's funeral is Thursday and I would like it if you would be there."

"I will be there."

"Thank you, Victor… It's sad isn't it?"

"What's sad?"

"That right now, you are the only friend I have and you are my attorney."

Jonathan got out of the car and got into his. Victor thought how can a man as successful, powerful, and wealthy as Jonathan is, not have friends. He thought it was sad because he never saw anything that would be a red flag from Jonathan, unless he was good at hiding it. He watched as Jonathan pulled away. Victor's phone started to ring, he looked at it but all it had was a private caller. Normally he would let it go to voicemail but he answered it instead.

"Hello?"

Chapter 9

November 29, 2017

Wednesday

7:35a.m.

Lieutenant Stephens is sitting at his desk with his morning drinking coffee, when Bo Carver comes bargaining in and startling Stephens.

"Excuse me, ever hear of knocking! Jesus! Give someone a heart attack!"

"Sorry Lieutenant, I thought you would like to hear this as soon as possible and I wanted to give you the good news," Bo said half laughing.

"Well then spit it out and let's hear it!"

"I got the warrant for Adam's DNA sample," Bo proclaimed victoriously.

Stephens's face had a look of shock. "Where did you find a judge this early?"

"Wouldn't you like to know my secrets?"

"Well good at least we can do that, we are waiting on the public defender," Stephens sighed.

Bo looked puzzled, "He asked for a lawyer?"

The young P.A. was anxious about this case. He wanted this to go perfectly, if he could be the prosecutor to put the murderer away in this case, he felt he could write his ticket to any public office in the state. Bo's first thought went to the Attorney General of Missouri, he could easily be elected to that if he could play his cards right if this case went the way he wanted it too. Stephens interrupted Bo's daydreaming by

128

giving him a rundown of all the evidence they collected from Adam's house.

"We found what might be blood on a section of broken scrap wood behind the house in a shed, along with some hand-prints on the back of the trailer, right below the back bedroom window that looks into the suspects bedroom. Someone was definitely looking into the window recently and the handprints are not large hands. If I had to guess, it was a woman or child. We found some women under garments and are processing those for DNA."

"What about the cellphone and laptop?" Bo asked.

"The technicians are going through them as we speak."

"Can they give us anything before you go in there to question him?" Bo asked.

Stephens smiled, "They already sent a few things, Bo. I think we will have plenty to ask of him."

A trooper knocked on the Lieutenant's door. "Sir, Mr. Lewis's attorney is here and is currently with him."

"Ok, thank you."

Stephens grabbed his file folder and Bo walked to the interview room.

"Let's hope this goes well, because the way I see it right now Lieutenant, we don't have anything physical to tie him to this murder," Bo said.

8:15a.m.

Adam has been sitting in the windowless interview room for about three and half hours. The trooper that brought him here did stop at a fast-food place and got Adam a breakfast

129

sandwich, a hash brown and an orange juice. He was thankful for that but since then he has been sitting here with his mind racing and stomach turning. The police were not telling him any information other than someone would be in shortly to talk with him after his lawyer got here. Adam is sure about one thing though; he doesn't trust anything the police have to say to him regarding everything. That's why he immediately told the trooper he wanted a lawyer and would not talk until he had one. As he sat waiting, he could not help but replay the events of earlier this morning. The sound of the cops breaking his door open, rushing in, throwing him on the floor and slapping handcuffs on him. Suddenly the door opened and a young guy walked in holding a briefcase, he sat down across from him and smiled.

"Hello, Mr. Lewis. I am with the public defender's office and I have been assigned your case. My name is Ronald Hartz, you can call me Ron if you like."

Adam looked at him with a puzzled expression, "You don't look like a lawyer, Ron."

Ronald smiled, "Thanks for the compliment. Let's get some basic information out of the way." He reached into his briefcase and pulled out a notepad.

"I don't even know why I'm here and I think that you might not be the right lawyer for me, no offense." Adam said.

Ronald studied him for a moment and then began his rebuttal, "Mr. Lewis, I am fully capable of handling this case. I have just the right amount of tenacity that is required for a case like this."

"Why do you say a case like this? What is so special about this case?" Adam asked.

"You really don't know why you are here, do you?"

"No! I don't!" Adam answered.

Ronald opened a file folder and pulled out some papers,

"Let me explain to you, Mr. Lewis. The police have an eyewitness that identified Faith Ross running from your trailer and saw you running after her. This eyewitness claims they saw the two of you getting into a heated argument, then saw Mrs. Ross speed away. On the same day as she was killed, making you a person of interest that the police would like to talk to and get any information you may have. They have conducted a search of your home and have your truck here and are searching through it with a comb. To answer your question, what is so special about this case, is the victim! She comes from a powerful family that has a lot of money and friends in high places.

"Ok, they pulled me out of bed this morning and brought me down here for that?" Adam asked.

"They exercised a search warrant and are looking for evidence that may connect you to the murder of Mrs. Ross. If they find evidence that supports that theory, they will come in here and ask you questions about what they found. They are going to ask you questions that have to deal with what this eye witness reported. They may ask you questions that you think have nothing to do with any of this. This is a tactic they use to try and catch you in a lie now, then use against you at a later time. Lucky for you though, you have an ace in the hole," Ronald said.

"What's that?"

"Me. I'm a great lawyer," Ronald smiled.

Adam sat back in his chair, letting what Ronald said process in his mind. He is overwhelmed and sick to his stomach.

"I'm screwed," Adam said.

"Tell me what happened."

Lieutenant Stephens sat across from Adam and his attorney.

"Mr. Lewis. Mr. Hartz. Would either of you like something to drink before we start?"

"No, thank you," Ronald answered.

Adam shook his head. He sat there with his arms crossed. Feeling like this was a complete waste of time.

"Mr. Lewis, I am Lieutenant Stephens with the Missouri State Troopers, I'm leading this investigation. I would like to ask you some questions. I believe your attorney has gone over why you are here. Is that correct?"

Adam looked at Ronald before he answered. Ronald leaned close to Adam and whispered something into his ear.

"Yes, that's correct," Adam said.

"Great. Before we get started, I have a warrant to get a DNA and hair sample." Stephens said as he handed it to Ronald to look at.

"Do what they say Adam, they got a warrant. I would like to know how you got one so fast," Ronald said.

"Everyone working together to try and close this case."

The lab technician came in, swabbed the inside of Adam's cheek and collected hairs from different parts of his head, arms, legs and pubic area. The whole process took about 10 minutes.

Lieutenant Stephens was writing in a notebook when the lab technician finished. He waited until they closed the door and he asked, "Did you know Faith Ross?"

"Yes."

"How did you know Mrs. Ross?"

"She had a lot of parties. I worked for a catering company that she always hired to do the event."

"It says here you're a waiter for a catering company, is that right?"

"Yeah."

"You must have made a good impression on her, for her to remember you and show up at your house one day."

"Yeah, I guess you could say that"

"Well, when was the last time you saw Mrs. Ross, Adam?"

He sat there a moment and thought about it, "Little over a week ago."

"Where was that at?"

"Outside my house."

"Why was she at your house, Adam?"

"I don't know why she was there; we hadn't talked lately."

"Why was that?" Stephens asked.

"She was trying to save her marriage, so she had to cut ties with me."

Stephens shifted in his chair before asking the next question, "Were Mrs. Ross and you in a relationship?"

"Yeah."

"Why didn't you say that earlier Adam?"

"You didn't ask me that, did you, Lieutenant?"

"Adam, you don't have to be disrespectful, I think I have treated you with respect, so I would appreciate it if you did the same."

"Yeah, well I don't trust any cops, I mean you already think I'm guilty."

"That is not true Adam, we are just having a conversation right now."

"Whatever, ask your questions, man!"

"We have an eyewitness that said they saw you chasing Mrs. Ross from your home. Is that correct?"

"I wasn't chasing her; I was running to catch up with her."

"Isn't that the same thing?" Stephens followed up with.

Ronald spoke up and said, "Lieutenant, he answered your question."

Stephens looked at Ronald, then back at Adam. "He actually didn't, counselor. It's up to him, but I have an eyewitness that states he was chasing Mrs. Ross from his trailer; then seen arguing with her out in the street."

Ronald adjusted in his chair and looked at Adam, "I would give him your explanation of what actually happened that day, Adam."

Adam sat up straight and put his hands on the table, "I was drunk and high that day, I don't remember a lot of what happened."

"What happened between Mrs. Ross and you? I don't care if you smoked some pot, I'm not concerned about that. I need the truth though, Adam."

134

"I was partying with a girl when all of a sudden, we heard a crashing sound outside my bedroom window. I got my boxers on and went outside to see what it was. That is when I saw Faith come running from behind the trailer. I ran after her, trying to get her to stop and talk to me. I finally caught up with her when she got to the van. That's when she started yelling at me about sleeping around and how I could do that. I got pissed off and told her she had no right yelling at me when she ended things between us. I went back to the trailer; Lexi was getting dressed. She asked me what was going on. I told her that Faith had seen what we were doing and was upset."

"Why was Lexi upset?"

"Lexi told me that I chose the wrong woman, that I was just as stupid as the rest of them. I asked her what she was talking about and she said that Faith was just using me as a toy and she would throw me away after she got tired of playing with me."

"How did Lexi know about Faith and your relationship?"

"That's a good question, I guess I told her about it when I was drunk and high, because I don't remember saying anything to her about it."

"What happened after that?"

"Lexi said she was done with me, if I ran after Faith, I clearly still had feelings for her. She said she wasn't going to allow me to disrespect her and then she stormed out. I haven't seen her since."

Lieutenant Stephens stopped him.

"Does Lexi have a last name?"

"I don't know."

"You don't know or you don't remember it?"

"I don't know! She never told me her last name."

"Ok. What about the kind of vehicle she drives?"

"An SUV of some kind."

Lieutenant Stephens sighed, "Make, color, any details about it?"

"I think it was dark blue or black. I don't know anything else."

"Do you at least remember where you met Lexi?"

"Yeah, it was at the Main Street Bar."

"Ok. Did you go up to her or did she come up to you?"

"She came up to me, she bought me a drink, then wanted to know if I had any weed we could smoke. I told her that we could go back to my place, she was all up for it. That's just what we did, smoked a little and then had sex. I woke up in the morning and she was gone."

"She didn't leave a number or any way to reach her?"

"No. She just drops by. Like I said, I don't know anything about her."

"What if you're not home and she drops by, how do you know?"

"Look man! I don't know who you buy your weed from but most of my clients don't give me their complete contact information, in case of situations like this!"

"Ok, ok. Calm down."

"Well shit man, you keep asking me the same Goddamn question over and over. My answer isn't going to change. If I had her phone number, I would give it to you!"

"Can you give me a description of Lexi?"

"She is taller, 5 '7-5' 9, she is thin but not too thin, more toned. She definitely works out; has a nice ass and the best tits I have seen."

"Any tattoos or scars that you remember?"

"No, nothing I can remember."

"Ok, we will work with that. Did you and Mrs. Ross have a romantic relationship?"

"You could say that."

"It's a yes or no question, Adam"

"Yeah, we had a romantic relationship. We were in love."

"In love? Was Mrs. Ross in love with you too?"

"Yes."

"How long were the two of you involved with one another, sexually," Stephens asked.

"Shit, I have no idea! We first hooked up at the New Year's Eve party."

"Was it consensual sex," Stephens asked.

Adam looked at him with confusion, "Yeah. Why wouldn't it have been consensual? What the hell are you trying to say?"

"It's a question I have to ask," Stephen answered.

"You're trying to make me look like some rapist or something, I don't like it!"

"I really don't care that you don't like it. This is my job and that's what I'm doing."

Adam looked at Ronald, "Aren't you going to do anything about this, man!"

"Adam, he is allowed to ask you any questions he wants, now you don't have to answer them. You can also end this questioning anytime you want. So, if the Lieutenant wants to keep asking inappropriate and ridiculous questions, in the hopes we end this interview, then by all means let him continue."

Stephens rolled his eyes as he flipped the page on his legal pad and finished writing his note, "You knew the Ross's socially?" he asked.

"Socially? What do you mean," Adam asked.

"Did they invite you to their party?"

"No. I was working the party, as a waiter," Adam answered.

Stephens looked back at his previous notes he had written. Stephens did the math in his head and asked, "Eleven months, then?"

Adam looked at him with a puzzled expression on his face. Stephens rolled his eyes and clarified.

"You were in a romantic relationship with Mrs. Ross for eleven months. From December 31, 2016. The New Year's Eve party until a month ago."

"Yes, that sounds about right," Adam said.

"How did you two meet each other?" Stephens asked.

Ronald sat up in his chair. "Listen, why are you concerned with how my client met the victim? He is trying to tell you what was really going on."

Lieutenant Stephens looked at Ronald with a matter-of-fact expression.

"I'm asking because your client was one of the last people to see Mrs. Ross alive. He also admits to chasing her down and having a heated altercation with her in the middle of the street, where an eyewitness saw the whole thing."

Ronald sat back in his seat, "Tell him that way it is put to rest."

"I told you already, we met at the party and hooked up that night," Adam said.

"Details Adam, I need the whole story, and names of people that can support it," Stephens stressed to him.

Adam exhaled and told them where it all began.

December 31, 2016

Saturday

11:15p.m.

Adam hated almost everything about his job, the one exception was the women that he met at these parties. The kind of women that need some excitement in their life because their husbands worked long hours or were always away on business trips. The only thing you have to tell them is they are pretty and listen to them talk about themselves. If you did that, they would give you anything you wanted. He has gotten many nice gifts

since starting this job: watches, clothes, trips, and his weed. The best thing about all of this is that he doesn't have to worry about them becoming too attached to him because he doesn't have that type of money. He provides them with a happy distraction while getting the things he wants in return. He didn't feel bad for these women because they knew what it was from the word go. But so far tonight the well is dry. He felt like he was wasting his time here and was thinking about walking out. He was on his way back to the kitchen to fill his tray with champagne when it happened.

The moment he saw Faith for the first time was like seeing the ocean for the first time, breathtaking. The silk red dress that she's wearing clung to her body in all the right places. He stood there for a moment and admired her beauty. The dress came down past her feet but he could see her open toed high-heels. The slit in the dress came up to her mid-thigh and showed off her stunning leg. His eyes moved past her curvy waist and slowly over her large breasts, coming to the small strap of silk fabric going around the back of her neck, holding the dress up, exposing her collarbone and smooth porcelain skin shoulders. Her lips are full and sat below her cute snub nose. What got his attention more than anything was her close-set eyes with an exotic emerald green color. He has never seen eyes this beautiful. Her eyebrows slanted sharply downward giving her a slight mischievous look and her beautiful dark rose colored hair is up off her shoulders. He'd never seen a woman this beautiful; he was speechless.

"Excuse me... Excuse me."

Adam quickly cleared his throat, "Yes, ma'am."

"I need some help getting some wine from the cellar, would you mind?"

"Of course," he said, trying to dazzle her with a grin. Then quickly realizing he didn't stand a chance with this woman.

They walked downstairs through the family room, past the huge bar with every kind of alcohol you can imagine and came to a wooden door. She opened the door and walked into a stone walled room with built-in wine racks. The room was circular in shape and big enough to hold a thousand bottles of wine and have a small table with two chairs. Adam chuckled a little and she turned around.

"What is so funny?" she asked, showing her perfectly white teeth.

"I thought it was going to be outside and underground because you said cellar," he chuckled.

She smiled and laughed. "It is silly to call it a wine cellar, when it's actually just a room."

She stared into his ice blue eyes, until the smile on his face disappeared.

"Sorry, I don't mean to be rude, you just have really pretty eyes," she said.

"Oh, well thank you. No one has ever said that to me."

She extended her hand to him, "I'm Faith."

Adam nodded his head, "I know, Mrs. Ross. I am Adam. Nice to meet you."

"Please, call me Faith."

Adam smiles at her. "Ok, Faith. Please call me Adam," he told her, laughing.

"Nice to meet you, Adam. Are you having a good time tonight?" she asked before realizing he was working. "Oh shit, sorry… It is out of habit. Of course, you're not having a good time, you're working."

Adam quickly came to her rescue, "It's good, my night has gotten a lot better in the past few minutes."

"Why is that?" she asked.

"I finally met someone decent, that didn't make me feel like the invisible man," he said, staring into her eyes.

"That is horrible if people are making you feel like that."

"It's not a big deal, I guess it is part of my job. Just bring the tray out and come back when it's emptied. But something I never understand about events like this, is they call them a party but nobody is actually partying. Where I come from when we have a party it's a party. Where people are dancing, having fun and dressed comfortably." he said, shrugging his shoulders.

Faith nodded in agreement, "Yeah, this party is depressing. I mean who wears dresses like this, I feel so uncomfortable, not to mention it looks terrible on me," she said, shaking her head in disappointment.

"I think you look really good in it, the most beautiful thing I have ever seen."

She smiled and turned a little red, "Thank you, but you don't have to say that."

"I know I don't have to, but I'm serious. You look stunning!"

Faith turned her back to him and didn't say anything. After a moment he heard her sniffling.

"I'm sorry, Mrs. Ross. I didn't mean to offend you," placing his hand on her shoulder, he noticed how smooth and baby-like her skin was. He could only imagine what the rest of her body felt like. Trying to think of what he could say to console her, he leaned closer so he could seem more genuine.

"I'm so sorry…" before he could finish the sentence, Faith turned around and without any warning grabbed his face and kissed him. All he could do was kiss her back, when she finally let his lips go, he was in awe.

"Shit I'm sorry, Adam. I don't know why I did that. I swear I don't normally do that."

"It's ok, you are a great kisser," he said smiling.

"I don't know what to say Adam. You are really easy to talk to and I definitely have had too much wine. I mean you probably have a girlfriend and I'm married. I am so sorry for doing that to you. I had no right to assume you would be ok with it."

"Mrs. Ross you are good, I'm fine. Besides, I don't have a girlfriend. If you want to know the truth, I would like to kiss you again," he said as he stepped closer to her.

Faith inhaled sharply. Before she could say a word, he grabbed her around her waist and pulled her against his body, kissing her with a passion that made her knees buckle.

"You smell so good," he said while kissing her neck, working his way to her collarbone.

"Oh my god!" she said as she ran her fingers through his brown wavy hair.

She grabbed him, unbuckling his belt with ease, his button and zipper came undone even easier. She reached into his boxers and tried to wrap her hand around him, she quickly realized that this was going to be interesting.

He turned her to face the wall and bent her over the little round table. He pushed up her dress, showing her matching red thong.

"Damn, those are sexy as hell. I'm going to take them with me as a souvenir," he said to her as he pulled his pants and boxers down around his knees. She was panting in anticipation of feeling him inside of her as he took off her panties.

"We have to be quick," she said.

He rubbed his rock-hard penis up and down, teasing her. She did not need to be teased for very long and he eased himself slowly inside of her. Faith's eyes opened wide and she let out half a moan and grunt.

"You have to be quiet, someone might hear us," Adam whispered to her, as he slowly pushed deeper, letting her get used to it.

"Holy shit, you're big!"

Faith grabbed his hips and started to pull him into her at a steadier pace. The wine cellar was fifty-five degrees, helping to keep them from sweating.

"Your juices feel amazing."

"Adam!" she managed to get out of her mouth.

"I want to feel you come on my cock."

She let out a moan, louder this time. She could not control them at this point, "You have to be quiet," he told her.

"I can't help it," she said as quietly as she could between moans.

"I can help keep you quiet if you'd like?" he asked. He reached for her panties that he put in his pocket. "Open your mouth," he said in a commanding tone.

She did what he said and he shoved them in her mouth.

"Now no one will hear you."

She said something that he could not make out, he took the panties out of her mouth.

"Fuck me like I owe you money!" She opened her mouth for Adam to put the panties back in and he shoved them back in.

He began to go deeper and harder with each thrust. He loved the sound of his balls hitting her and he could feel himself getting closer. He clutched her around the waist harder and started to pull her down at the same time pushing into her. Even with the panties in her mouth she was getting louder. He put his hand over her mouth as he felt her legs start to stiffen and her muscles tighten around him. She let out a long-muffled moan and her body began to shake as she climaxed on him. Just as her body started to relax, he felt his legs getting weak, he started to feel a little light-headed and then his whole body tightened up. He came inside of her and let himself fall on her as he caught his breath.

Taking her panties out of her mouth she said, "Goddamn! That was good!"

He started to pull out when she said, "Do it slow." He leaned down kissing her back and then slowly pulled out of her.

"Oh, God," she moaned when he pulled it out of her.

Smiling as he pulled his boxers and pants up, he looked at her and said, "Yes, it was for me too."

Faith stood up and cleaned herself off with her panties, then straightened her dress. She was still holding her underwear just as he was finishing tucking in his shirt, when she threw her balled up panties at him.

Catching them he asked, "What are these for?"

"I believe you said you were going to take them as a souvenir. There you go, I guess now I have to come and get them from you later," she told him, biting her lower lip.

"Don't worry. I'll keep them safe."

"I need to get back upstairs before my husband gets curious, grab that case of wine and bring it up."

"I thought you said he doesn't care," he said, picking up the case.

"He doesn't care what I do, but he does care who and where I do it. He would kill us both if he found out."

"Why?"

"Because the only thing my husband cares more about than his reputation is his ego."

"I don't get it."

"Jesus! Seriously? Look at him and what he has. Then look in the mirror. No offense. Close the door behind you," she walked out and left him standing there.

November 29, 2017

Wednesday

10:00a.m.

Lieutenant Stephens exhaled with a sigh. "Let me get this straight, all that happened the first time you two met each other?"

"Yes, sir."

Stephens pulled some papers out of the file that was sitting in front of him and looked them over. After studying them for a moment he asked, "Adam, did Mrs. Ross tell you that she and her husband had an open marriage?"

"Yes, but not in so many words."

"How did she tell you?" Stephens asked.

"Faith, told me that he does what he wants to do and she does whatever she wants too. Nobody gets their feelings hurt."

"Did she ever talk about how Mr. Ross treated her?"

"She said that he was a good provider and he loved the children, but that he liked having sex with other people and their relationship was one of convenience rather than love."

"Did Mrs. Ross ever bring her children around you?" Stephens asked.

"No way, she never brought them with her when we met."

"Did you and Mrs. Ross meet a lot?"

"We would meet two or three times a week, sometimes less," Adam said, shrugging.

"How would you describe your and Mrs. Ross's relationship?"

"We were in love, Faith and I had something special."

Lieutenant Stephens looked at him. "Love. That is a pretty strong word to use, don't you think Adam?"

"No, I don't. She was going to leave that arrogant asshole. We talked about it all the time; she just wanted the time to be right. Faith was trying to think of a way to tell him about us falling in love."

Stephens finished what he was noting and then focused his attention on Ronald. "Mr. Hartz, did you explain to your client that lying only makes things worse," Stephens cautioned him.

Before Ronald could say anything, Adam spoke up in a raised voice, "I'm not lying about anything!"

"I have text messages between Mrs. Ross and yourself, that would lead people to think the complete opposite of everything you say about the nature of the relationship Mrs. Ross and you had."

"What are you talking about?" Adam said, looking at Ronald.

Ronald looked at Adam and then back at Stephens. "I would like to get a copy of these texts."

"No worry counselor, here you go," Stephens said, handing him copies of the messages.

Ronald looked them over and showed them to Adam, "Are you kidding me with this, come on!"

"It looks like Faith ended things with you in October, Adam." Stephens said.

"No, it wasn't like that."

"Let's look at the text message Adam."

October 20th

Faith 1:34 p.m.: Hey Adam, you are a great guy and we have had a lot of fun; but like all great things it must come to an end. I hope you understand.

Adam 1:36 p.m.: What is going on? What's wrong? What about everything we have talked about, are you going to throw that away?

October 21st

Adam 12:24 a.m.: Faith?

Adam 12:45 a.m.: Seriously, you can't even answer me!

Adam 2:42 a.m.: You know how I feel about you baby. I know you HATE him! Please message me back.

Adam 3:48 a.m.: WTF I know you're getting these.

Faith 6:02 a.m.: OMG!! Can you not take a hint! I'm on vacation with my family and working things out with my HUSBAND! Who by the way I'm still in love with. Read my words very slowly and clearly. It is over, finished, no more… Get that through your head. Do Not Text Me!

Adam 6:05 a.m.: Faith, just give me a chance. You are not happy with him, I love you!

Faith 6:10 a.m.: What part of do not text me did you not understand? Do it again and we are going to have a problem.

October 22nd

Adam 10:43 a.m.: I have some of your items here, thought you could use them. LOL (with a picture of Faith's underwear)

Faith 10:50 a.m.: Are you kidding me? Why would you send that? If Jonathan would see this, he would kill me, I'm sorry but I'm done! I hope you find everything you're looking for but it's not me!!

"Ok. So what?" Adam said, pushing the paper away.

"Why did you continue to contact Mrs. Ross after she told you it was over?"

"We were always breaking up and getting back together, that was our relationship. We both have issues."

"You mean other than the fact that she was married?

Adam chuckled, "That wasn't an issue, Faith was popular, everyone wanted to be around her and do the things she did. She was tired of the fake ass people that tried to be her friend when they didn't care about her. Especially that douche bag she was married to."

"It seems like you were harassing Mrs. Ross."

"I was not harassing her, after she sent me that last text on the 21ˢᵗ she called me, alright?" Adam said, pointing to the text.

Stephens looked at the message, "Why did she call you?"

Adam sighed, "She told me that Jonathan checks her phone and that's the reason she texted me that. She said it needed to be believable and that she would get ahold of me when they got back in a few weeks. But she sounded off, like she wanted to tell me something and couldn't because the kids were around."

"What do you mean she sounded off?"

"Like she was afraid to tell me something."

"What do you think she was afraid to tell you?"

Just then Ronald interrupted, "I need a moment with my client, please."

Lieutenant Stephens gathered his things and left the two of them to have the room. As he shut the door behind him, Special Agent Megan Brown, who was representing the F.B.I., was standing against the wall.

"I need to talk with you Lieutenant, in private," she said.

He could tell something was up by the tone of her voice.

"We'll go to my office," Stephens said.

Lieutenant Stephens gestured for S.A. Brown to have a seat as he shut the door. "Is everything alright, Agent Brown?" He asked as he sat down behind his desk.

"We got a match!"

Stephen's eyes got wide as he sat up in his chair. "A match. Who?"

S.A. Brown stood up, handing him the folder.

Chapter 10

November 28, 2017

Tuesday

11:45p.m.

His phone began to ring and an unknown caller came across the screen. "Hello?"

"Victor DeNoyer?" a baritone voice asked.

"Speaking."

"Is it the same one representing the rich closet homosexual?" they asked in a calm and calculated tone.

"Who the hell is this?"

"We will get to that, first I have a question. Has Mr. Ross tried anything with you? Ha. Ha."

"It's late and I'm tired. You sound like you need to get a life and move out of your mother's basement you dickhead! Don't call me again."

"Don't raise your voice to me counselor, I'm trying to save you. Without me you will never get the truth out of that asshole you're representing."

"What are you talking about," Victor asked.

"He is another disgustingly wealthy person that will never have to pay for all the pain he has inflicted because he can afford people like you."

Shaking his head Victor snapped back at him, "You know what, why don't you take that social justice attitude and shove it up your ass! I don't care what you think. Fact of the matter; if you had the money to hire me, you would. The only thing this tells me is you don't have shit."

"I want Jonathan Ross to suffer just as much disgrace as his wife has in her death."

"Disgrace, what the hell is this?"

"You watch the news, Victor! Faith has been dragged through the mud, made to look like a whore. No one is telling the truth." They belligerently said.

"The truth?"

"Yes, the truth, Victor! Jonathan Ross has a secret that he does not want anyone to know. But I know and I have undeniable proof."

Victor was confused and was trying to make sense of what he was being told.

"What kind of proof?"

There was a long pause.

"Hello?" Victor said.

"The kind that is worth a thousand words."

"Why should I believe anything you say," Victor asked.

"Make sure you're with your client tomorrow at 9:30a.m. Tell him that it is going to cost him to keep my mouth shut. Until then, counselor."

"Wait! How am I supposed to contact you?"

"Don't worry Victor, I have your number."

Victor was analyzing the conversation, trying to determine his next move. His mind was racing with questions. Who was this person, what did they want and why were they doing this? He couldn't worry about those questions right now, he needed to have a talk with Jonathan. Victor called him right away.

Jonathan looked at his phone and rolled his eyes, "What could possibly be the reason for calling me, when you just saw me?" he answered, without saying hello.

Victor instantly became annoyed with the tone that Jonathan was using, "Jonathan, listen to me. I received a phone call from someone claiming to have information on you. They said they have proof and that they want some money for it." Victor waited for Jonathan's response.

"Is that it?" Jonathan asked.

"No. They said to make sure that I'm with you tomorrow at nine-thirty in the morning because they are going to call with more instructions," Victor exclaimed.

"They are probably some pieces of shit, trying to get money out of me."

"Does that happen a lot to you?"

"When you're at the top of the mountain, everyone wants to knock you off. Price of doing business," Jonathan said.

Victor shook his head and was trying not to lose his temper. "Listen to me carefully, I need to know everything right now, no matter how bad or how small you think it is. Any skeletons that are in the closet need to come out. The last thing we want is a photo of you in a compromising situation getting leaked to the media."

Jonathan immediately felt nauseated and started to sweat.

"Photo! What photo are you talking about?"

"They said they have proof and when I asked what kind, they said the kind that is worth a thousand words. I am assuming it is a picture or pictures," Victor explained.

"Victor, get over here and I will explain a few things. We can talk about a plan to deal with this."

"I'm on my way."

Victor arrived and Jonathan was waiting for him at the front door. Jonathan led him to his office. Victor sat down on a large leather couch.

"Would you like a drink," Jonathan asked.

"Yes, please." Victor knew it had to be something big if Jonathan offered him a drink.

Jonathan sat in the chair that was across from him and handed him his drink.

"I don't know where to begin, to be honest with you."

Victor set his drink down on the side table.

"Let's start this way, anything you tell me is confidential. I can't say anything unless you say I can."

"I know," Jonathan answered.

"Good. Start at the beginning and don't leave anything out."

"You already know that Faith and I had an open marriage, but what you don't know is, we had that arrangement because of me."

Victor didn't say a word, he was wishing that Jonathan would just spit it out already.

"I'm sick, I have one weakness! Not being able to keep my dick in my pants."

Victor breathed a sigh of relief, "Women? That's it? Shit I can deal with women…"

Jonathan cut him off, "It's a man! But don't get the wrong idea, I never took it up…"

"Jonathan! I get it," Victor said, putting his hand up for him to stop.

"I'm not gay!" Jonathan stressed.

"I don't care, Jonathan! I don't give a rat's ass about your sexual orientation; my job is to keep you out of jail and out of police cross-hairs. Having an affair is not a crime and who cares if it was with a man. This isn't the 1950's anymore. But you hiding all of this doesn't help you with public perception."

"What are people thinking?' Jonathan asked.

"That you killed your wife or you paid someone to kill her," Victor shouted.

Jonathan stood up and started pacing the room. "This is bullshit, I didn't hurt her. Fuck them and fuck you if you think that!"

"You pay me to put on the best defense for you! With that comes honesty between the two of us. I'm not here to kiss your ass, Jonathan! Let me think for a minute!" Victor snapped.

"Victor, I know you're here to help me, but I don't know what I'm doing. I feel like a dog chasing my own fucking tail." Jonathan sat back down in the chair in exhaustion.

They had been sitting in silence for about ten minutes, Victor was trying to think of ways to spin this in the media.

"Hey!... Say something." Jonathan said.

Victor sighed, "How many extramarital affairs have you had with men?"

"Just the one! You think I want something like this to get out?" Jonathan answered.

"We have to assume the man you have been sleeping with is a suspect in all of this."

Jonathan smiled and started shaking his head, "No, way! It's not him, trust me."

"How can you be sure, Jonathan?"

Jonathan got up from the chair and walked to his desk. Opening a drawer, he brought out a manila envelope. Jonathan handed it to Victor, who hesitated at first then reluctantly took it.

"It's proof that the guy I was sleeping with is not trying to blackmail me," Jonathan said.

Victor opened the envelope and pulled some pictures out. He was surprised by the content of the pictures. It was a man performing various sexual acts on another man. The pictures only showed one of the men's faces. The other man was only shown from below the abdomen. The man's face looked familiar to Victor, but he couldn't place it. Victor looked at Jonathan and asked, "Who is this? I know I have seen him before."

Jonathan sat back down in the chair. "Douglas Fulton."

It was the moment after Jonathan said his name, Victor realized who it was. Victor flipped through the pictures again.

"Jonathan, how did you get these?" he asked.

Jonathan looked puzzled, "How did I get them? Like, how did I get them developed or how did I take them?"

Victor was confused. "Who took the photos?" he asked.

"I did."

"How?" Victor asked.

Jonathan gave Victor a crooked grin and realized that Victor was not understanding what he was looking at. Jonathan let him in on the secret, "Victor, that is Douglas and I in those pictures, I made sure that none of them have my face in them. I was going to use these to convince him to back off."

"Back off, what do you mean," Victor asked.

Jonathan rolled his eyes.

"I need the whole story." Victor said.

"Alright, Douglas and I were fucking and I say fucking because that is all we did. Faith decided in October that she wanted us to stop having an open marriage. I agreed because my family is what's most important to me. It was October 19; I remember that because it was the day, I finalized the stadium deal. Douglas came to my office later that night, we had sex and then I told him we would no longer continue with our

arrangement. Douglas became upset and threatened to tell Faith. When I told him she already knew and to fuck off, he did not handle it well. I took my family on a much-needed vacation and because I thought time away would give Douglas time to calm down and think things through. Faith and I started to reconnect with one another in ways that I thought were long gone. We started going to marriage counseling and were making progress. I always loved Faith but I was falling back in love with her and she with me. We came back home and about a month later I got an email from him. He threatened to expose the affair if I didn't talk with him. I told him to meet me later that night and we would discuss it. We were supposed to meet at the Rosemont

Hotel. I was in the room waiting for him when I got the call from the Sheriff that Faith had been killed. Everything changed after that, things that once were important just aren't anymore," he poured himself a drink and downed it.

Victor was digesting all the information, he rubbed his eyes and let out a yawn, "Did you tell the Sheriff this when he questioned you that night?"

Jonathan scuffed at him, "Hell no! Why would I have done that?"

Shaking his head, Victor said, "That would have given the police a suspect and it looks better for you because then you're not hiding anything."

Looking at Victor with raised eye-brows he said, "Are you done?"

Victor threw his hands up.

"I know how Douglas thinks and this is far beneath what he would do. We need to wait until we are contacted again," Jonathan said, pouring them both another drink.

Victor looked at his watch. "It's 3:20 a.m. now, we have about six hours before they call. We need to come up with a plan."

"We are going to pay them whatever they want, then we are going to put it behind us," Jonathan said, taking a sip of his drink.

They began to formulate a plan; Victor would do all the talking and handle all the details of the exchange. Jonathan wanted to make sure they would not come back for more money or that they would not leak anything to the media after they were paid. Victor was explaining to Jonathan that there was no guarantee that they would not leak it to the media. That is why he wanted to contact the police and let them handle it because then it does not look like you are trying to cover anything up.

"The police will use that against me. Let's just stick to the plan and leave it at that."

"It's your call," Victor sat back on the sofa, rubbing his head. He felt the onset of a headache. "Jonathan, do you have some aspirin?"

Jonathan handed him two pills and refilled his drink.

"Let's have one more drink, then call it a night, everything will work out. Just have a little faith."

Victor looked at Jonathan, noticing that there were tears building in his eyes. Victor asked, "Are you alright?"

"She would always tell me that, I used to think it was so stupid because she would laugh after saying it then look at me and say, *'Oh never mind, you already have Faith!'* I wish she was still here to say it."

Victor didn't know what to do, other than offer him some words of wisdom, "I can't imagine what you're going through, no words will make it better. You cannot give up though, because those beautiful kids just lost their mother and they are going to have a lot of questions. They need their father there to answer those difficult questions, because you know the truth, and that will help them get through all the hard times." The two of them sat there and drank in silence until they drifted off to sleep.

November 29, 2017

Wednesday

9:45 a.m.

160

Victor woke up in a daze, head throbbing and the sound of his cell phone ringing. He was trying to open his eyes but the bright rays from the morning sunlight coming through the massive window was blinding. He was feeling around in his pockets for his phone but was having no luck finding it.

"Son of a bitch! Where the hell is it?" he shouted. Victor shifted on the couch trying to sit up, when he heard something drop on the floor. He managed to sit up, letting his eyes adjust to the light in the room. When he could finally see, he noticed his phone on the floor. Rubbing his eyes, trying to clear the sleep out of them, he reached for his phone. Victor looked at the screen, five missed calls. He noticed the time, 9:45 a.m., he was instantly hit with panic and fear, thinking that they missed the call. He went to the call logs and breathed a sigh of relief when he saw all the missed calls were from his office. Victor dialed his office number and his secretary answered.

"Victor DeNoyer's office."

"Jan, it's me. What is going on?" he said, clearing his throat.

"Jesus, where have you been? Are you ok?" she asked in a frantic tone.

Victor got up and walked out of the room, he walked down the hall and into the large bathroom, "I'm fine, I am at Jonathan's house. We got an unexpected development in the case last night."

"So, you already know about the police carrying out a search warrant this morning."

"Hold on," Victor told her as he set the phone down and turned on the cold water. Victor splashed water on his face, his mouth and throat were bone dry from the drinking last night; he put his mouth under the facet. Sucking up the water like a sponge, finally feeling like he could talk with ease, he asked, "Search warrant, against who?"

"It was early this morning in a mobile home park. The trailer is rented by Adam Lewis. We had one of our men in blue call in the heads up. I have the local news on and it is not on there but they also haven't given their press conference."

Victor was dumb founded, "Who is Adam Lewis and what the hell does he have to do with this case?"

The secretary was silent for a moment and then asked, "I can put in a couple of calls to the private investigators to check into it?"

Victor thought about it for a moment, then agreed the private investigators should start looking into it.

"I will ask Jonathan if he knows anything about this Lewis fellow. Listen, Jan, has anyone called the office looking for me?"

"No Vic, is everything ok?"

Victor hesitated for a moment. "Yes, just let me know, I'm expecting one." There was nothing but silence on the other end. "Jan? Jan?"

"I'm here Victor, are you close to a television?" she asked.

"Yeah, why?"

"Get to it quick and turn on the news," she said with a tone of urgency.

Victor ran back into the office and turned on the television. When the picture came up, it showed police at a trailer bringing boxes and bags out marked evidence.

Chapter 11

November 29, 2017

Wednesday

10:18 A.M.

Lieutenant Stephens opened it and read the name. Adam Lewis. "Son of a bitch! Was he already in the system? They took his samples this morning."

"Mr. Lewis was arrested a few years ago at a national park for trespassing, when the officer did a search, they found some weed and Mr. Lewis started to resist arrest. He was charged and pleaded out, paid a fine and did some drug program. They started to collect DNA samples to store in their database and we got lucky enough that he was there at that time. It takes some time for samples to come back because the database is so large, but the important thing is, it's a match and there is no denying it," Agent Brown said.

"This is wonderful news! It's an open and shut case now!"

"That is up to the Prosecutor, Lieutenant. I have seen a lot less evidence get convictions. You know how the game is played, the best thing to do, get that confession."

Stephens knew she was right; these cases are never airtight. A defense attorney only needs to convince one juror of reasonable doubt and the trial could end in a hung jury. Nobody wanted that to happen. He went to the coffee maker in the corner of his office, pouring himself another cup and decided to go back in there.

"Let's go in there and get that confession," Stephens said.

She smiled at him, "No. I was sent here to assist the local investigative agencies and that is what I will do. This is the State Troopers case and you should finish it. Good luck."

"It has been a pleasure working with you," Stephens said, extending his hand to her.

"Likewise, Lieutenant. I like to leave on positive vibes, with the hope that I represented the Bureau in the best way possible. I wish you the best of luck," Agent Brown said, shaking his hand.

"Thanks for your help."

Lieutenant Stephens went to his Sergeants and told them about the new evidence that he just received. He told them to focus on Adam Lewis, gathering as much information about him from anyone that knew him or had any dealings with him. Also, to check if anyone could back his story up about having an affair with Mrs. Ross.

"I have to get back in there before they smarten up," he told his Sergeants. He walked back to the interview room and took a deep breath before going in. "Ready to continue?" he asked entering the room.

"Yes, we are."

Lieutenant Stephens sat down. "Adam, when were you and Faith last together sexually?"

"I don't know the exact day, but probably about a month ago"

"Today is November 29, then October 29 is the last time you two had sex," Stephens asked.

"No, it has to be longer because Faith was on vacation with the kids at the end of October, and it was before that. Somewhere in the middle of October," he said, putting his head down.

"What's wrong, Adam," Stephens asked.

"It's hard to believe that she is gone. I just talked with her."

164

"You talked to Faith a few times that day, according to her phone records. What was the nature of those conversations?" Stephens asked.

"I called her because when we were out in the street, she would not listen to anything I had to say. She wasn't answering her phone to me, I probably tried to call her a few times. When she refused to answer my calls, I left a voicemail."

"What did you say to her on the voicemail?"

"I told her I was sorry and that Lexi meant nothing to me. I told her she was the one who left me first, what was I supposed to do. But I still love her and want to be with her."

"Did she call you back?" Stephens asked.

"Yes."

"And how did that go?"

Adam was becoming irritated with the questions, but he decided to answer. "She said she was sorry for leaving me because I did not deserve that. She told me she loved me and had feelings for me, but she needed some time to think because she has two kids with him. Then she said something about a letter she wrote me but I never got it. She told me that we had to discuss something important before we made any decisions about being together and then she said she would call me later to meet up and talk. Then she had to go because someone was at the door."

"Did she say who was at the door?"

"No."

"You were the last phone call she made."

"I was?"

"Yes. What was that conversation about?"

"She called to tell me she was on her way but that she only had an hour. Then she told me she loved me and hung up." Adam held back tears as he answered.

"You are obviously upset, why?"

"I didn't know that would be the last time I would ever talk to her. It's tough to love someone and have to hide it."

"After Faith didn't show up, what did you do?"

"Her house is about 5 minutes from mine, I waited for about 30 minutes. After that I started drinking and smoking because I thought something came up or she decided not to come over."

"Why didn't you try to call or text her to make sure she was alright?"

"I wasn't worried because she did that sometimes. Faith would be on her way then show up a couple hours later or not at all."

"Did you just wait at your trailer for her the whole night or did you go anywhere?"

"I waited at home."

"Can anyone verify that?"

"I was alone."

"Were you home alone between 4:20 p.m. and 5:30 p.m.?"

"Yes."

Stephens shifts in his chair and looks at Adam's face with his next question. "Did Faith tell you she was pregnant?"

Adam's heart sunk to the pit of his stomach. "What?"

"Yes. She was about thirteen weeks along."

Adam sank back in his chair and put his head in his hands. Stephens could tell that he had no idea about the pregnancy. Stephens is having a difficult time watching Adam react to the news. He could not wait to hit him with the DNA evidence and watch his story fall apart.

"Is there a chance that you are the father?"

Adam lifted his head out of his hands. "I assumed Faith was on the pill or something, she never made me wear anything."

"You said that you thought Faith wanted to tell you something but didn't, maybe she wanted to tell you about the pregnancy."

"Yeah, maybe," Adam said in a cold tone.

Seeing the toll the questions had on Adam, Ronald spoke up, "Lieutenant, what is all of this coming to? My client has answered all of your questions, I think this is enough for today."

Stephens was not about to let him go anywhere. "I just have a few more questions, it won't be long," he said with a smile.

Ronald looked at Adam. "Alright, a few more questions," Adam said.

Stephens scooted closer to the table. "Adam, is there any reason your DNA would be at the crime scene?"

Adam, with a confused look on his face said, "My DNA at the crime scene?"

"Yes."

"No! Why would it be?!" Adam answered.

"Where in the hell are you going with this?" Ronald asked.

"We got DNA off of Mrs. Ross at the scene that the killer left. It's an exact match to your client's DNA," Stephens said, handing them copies of the results.

"Bullshit! I never hurt her; I knew better than to talk with you bastards!" Adam said as he jumped up out of his chair and went after Stephens.

Stephens grabbed him and began to fight, trying to take him to the ground but was having some difficulties. Ten seconds later the room was filled with troopers tackling Adam and cuffing him. He was led away, screaming his innocence.

"Looks like I have my work cut out for me on this one," Ronald said to Stephens.

"How can you defend that piece shit? It's clear with undeniable proof that he killed her."

"That's your opinion, Lieutenant. We don't know everything yet, not all the evidence has been precedent."

"You go ahead, believe that bullshit that he is saying. I'm going to believe the evidence."

November 29

9:50 a.m.

Victor was watching the television intently. The newscaster was recapping the story of the raid at the home of the suspect in the brutal murder of socialite Faith Ross. The police have taken someone into custody and are continuing to search the property at this hour. Victor was trying to clear the haziness out of his mind when he remembered that he still had Jan on the phone.

"Jan, clear my schedule. Lock up the office and come over to the Ross's house. We will be working from there today."

"Alright. Is everything ok?" she asked.

"Yes. It will be less hectic here than our office. Can you bring the spare suit I have in the office closet with you?"

"Of course, I will get that now and be on my way, Vic."

"And Jan, do me a favor. Don't tell anybody, please, I will explain later. Alright?"

"Yes, sir."

Victor hung up and went looking for Jonathan. He saw a maid in the kitchen cleaning up.

"Excuse me, Miss?"

"Good morning Mr. DeNoyer, I have some breakfast for you," she said as she put a plate of food on the table for him.

"Thank you, that's great, but I need to talk with Mr. Ross. Can you get him or tell me where he is?"

"Mr. Ross is upstairs getting ready; he should be down shortly. Eat your food before it gets cold."

"May I at least get your name, Miss…?"

"Hailee."

"Thank you, Miss Hailee, this looks delicious."

Victor smiled and sat down, he was hungry and it smelled wonderful. He picked up the fork and cut a bite size pancake and took a bite. "Wow, these are really good! Did you make these?" he asked.

"Yes sir, they were Mrs. Ross's favorite," she said with tears in her eyes.

"I'm sorry. Were you and Mrs. Ross close?"

"I have worked for the Ross family for four years and in that time, Mrs. Ross and I have become friends, I would say. We understood each other."

"What do you mean by understanding each other?"

"Nothing. It was a bad choice of words"

Victor interrupted her. "Please, I'm not going to tell anyone. It's just us having a conservation."

She was hesitant at first but then opened up to Victor. "I'm a single mother and with the way Mr. Ross works, Mrs. Ross felt like she was alone. I remember telling her that I had finally gotten the courage to leave an abusive relationship and her comment back to me

was that she wished she had the courage to do the same. I have never seen Mr. Ross be physically abusive to her but the way she put it, not all abuse is physical."

Victor was listening and making mental notes in his head. He knew there was more than what Jonathan was telling him. He needed to know everything and if Jonathan wasn't going to be honest with him, then he was going to have to talk with Hailee and anyone else who worked for the Ross family.

"Did Mrs. Ross ever have any male visitors over when Mr. Ross wasn't home?"

"I know what you're asking, she never had anyone like that here, to my knowledge. Actually, neither one of them, they wouldn't do that to the children."

"Then you already know that they had an open marriage?"

Hailee did not want to answer but Victor assured her it was alright.

"Yes. It was evident that they did whatever they wanted."

"Did Mrs. Ross and you talk about it or any of her friends she may have been involved with?"

"We were friends but not that close. I would ask Skyler, the nanny. She spent the most time with the Ross's."

"Skyler? When you say she spent the most time with them, you mean she worked a lot of hours?"

Hailee shrugged and rolled her eyes, "I don't know if people would call it working but she is basically a live-in nanny."

Victor found that a little suspicious. "Really? Live-in… Did Mrs. Ross work that much outside of the house?"

"No, but apparently Skyler is useful for other reasons."

That caught Victor's attention. "Other reasons?"

"She told me once that she had been involved in a sexual relationship with the Ross's."

"Ross's? Like she was having affairs with both of them separately or together?"

"Together," she answered right away.

"Do you believe that," Victor said, taking a drink of his coffee.

Hailee stopped wiping down the counter and looked Victor in the eyes. "I do. There were plenty of times that Faith's parents would have the kids for the weekend or overnight. Skyler would still stay here, when there was no reason for her to be here. They gave her a brand-new car for a gift. I have worked here longer; they never gave me a car. Skyler is untouchable, everyone knows it; she is allowed to do whatever she wants."

Victor was skeptical about the story. "Hailee, did you ever see anything happen first hand?"

"The only thing I saw was the looks that would be exchanged between Mr. and Mrs. Ross when she would catch him being too friendly with Skyler when the kids were around."

"Was that recently or was that a while ago?"

"It was a while ago, more recently the Ross's seemed to be doing better in their relationship."

He thought it was interesting that Hailee would say that about the Ross's relationship. "What makes you say that?" Victor asked with a smile.

"I'm sorry sir, I was putting these pans away and they are so noisy. What did you ask?" Hailee said, closing the cabinet door.

"My question was, what makes you say that the Ross's relationship was doing better?"

"Well, Mrs. Ross was excited about how much attention Mr. Ross was giving her and the fact he was home more often. At least that's what she said."

"I thought Mrs. Ross and you were not that close, that seems like something friends would talk about," Victor asked, pressing her to explain.

"It's not like that, she always asked me how I'm doing, and on this particular morning I told her about a date I went on the night before and how much of a disaster it was. I remember her telling me she was happy that Mr. Ross and her had decided to work together to build their relationship foundation back up. The reason why I remember is because

172

she used relationship foundation, who uses that?" she said, giggling.

Victor chuckled and agreed with her. "In your opinion, would you say they were a couple in love and were working through whatever issues that they had?"

Hailee thought about it for a second, "Yes. They were working things out; I could tell by the way they acted with each other that they were in a good place with their relationship."

"If it came to it, would you be willing to testify in court regarding that," Victor asked her.

Without hesitating Hailee answered, "Of course! Anything I can do to help the Ross's I will. Would you like some more coffee?"

"Thanks. That would be great."

Jonathan walked into the kitchen, "Good morning, Hailee. How are you this morning?"

Hailee jumped not seeing him come into the kitchen. "Good morning, Mr. Ross. I have some coffee ready for you."

"Thank you," he said, sitting down at the opposite end of the table from Victor. "Good morning, Victor," he said laughing.

Victor smiled and looked away from him trying to hide his embarrassment for getting drunk. "Good morning. Listen, there has been some developments since last night. We have a few things to go over and discuss-"

Jonathan cut him off. "Victor, we can do all that after I drink my coffee. I tell you what, why don't you use the guest suite, it has everything you need for a nice shower and we can send out for some clothes."

"Ok. Thank you. My secretary Jan is on her way over with some clothes. We have a lot of things to discuss."

"Yeah, yeah" he said, taking a sip of his coffee.

"I thought it would be best to work from here today if that's alright with you?"

"It's fine by me Victor. Tell you the truth I really wasn't planning on going out today anyway," he said, drinking his coffee.

"I will take you up on the offer of the shower though."

"Absolutely. Hailee, if you don't mind."

Victor left him to finish his coffee in peace and went to get a shower. Hailee showed him to the guest suite, she told him anything he would need is in the linen closet and if he didn't see something just let her know. Victor nodded at her and asked, "I have a bit of a headache, would you happen to have something for it?"

She smiled. "Second shelf in the linen closet, that is where the medicine is."

"Thank you, Hailee. For everything," Victor said as he closed the door behind him. Just as he was getting out of the shower and drying off there was a knock on the door.

"Vic, it's Jan. I'm going to put your clothes on the bed, is there anything else you need?"

"No. Thanks for doing that for me, I will be down in a few minutes."

"Alright, is there a certain area I should set-up in," she asked him.

"Yeah, set-up in the dining room, there's plenty of room and no one is going to bother us."

Jan went downstairs and set up their work space. When she finished, she made her way into the kitchen to make some fresh coffee. She was amazed at how large and beautiful it is. *This is a kitchen you would see on one of those cooking shows*, she thought to herself. She started looking through the cabinets for coffee to make.

"Excuse me, can I help you find something?" Hailee asked.

"Ooh, you startled me! I was just looking for some coffee to make."

"That's my job, Mr. Ross doesn't want his guests to do anything. All you have to do is ask me and I will get it for you. Alright?" Hailee told her.

"I just don't like to bother people for something I can do myself, I figured you had more important things to do, I apologize."

Hailee went to the pantry and got the coffee, she handed it to Jan. "The coffee pot is in the bottom cabinet over there. If Mr. Ross asks though, I will tell him you prefer to do things your way."

Jan chuckled. "That's fine, just consider me another employee of Mr. Ross's in a way; I work for Mr. DeNoyer and he works for Mr. Ross."

Hailee smiled at her. "I don't think Mr. Ross will look at it like that, he likes things done his way and doesn't like it when people don't follow the rules."

Jan was now getting irritated with this exchange; she was doing her best not to snap on Hailee. "Thank you for the warning but I think it will be fine, I'm making coffee for Mr. DeNoyer, not Mr. Ross."

"Yes, but you're in Mr. Ross's house and you really should follow his rules until he tells us otherwise." Hailee said walking out of the kitchen.

When Victor got done dressing, he came downstairs to find Jan visibly frustrated. "What's wrong, Jan?"

"I don't like that maid or whatever she is called."

"Who?" he asked genuinely surprised.

"The one who insists on making the coffee because that's her job and Mr. Ross doesn't want his guests having to lift a finger to do anything while in his house. Seriously!"

"Alright, just calm down. Think of it this way, that is one less thing you have to worry about," he said.

She rolled her eyes at his statement. "Just forget it, I'm making a bigger deal out of this than what it needs to be. You're right, it is one less thing I have to do."

Jonathan walked in the dining room. "Is it alright if I come in?"

Victor chuckled. "This is your house; you don't have to ask me. Have a seat."

Jonathan sat down. "Ok, hit me with it. What's going on?"

"There were some developments early this morning, it seems the state troopers executed a search warrant not too far from here. It's a private resident, a man named Adam Lewis. Do you by chance know him?"

Jonathan shifted in his chair, clearly being caught off guard. "Do they think he killed her?"

"To be honest, they don't conduct search warrants on people's homes unless they have enough evidence to convince a judge to allow it. I would say they have something on him. But I ask again, do you know him, Jonathan?"

"Yes. I know who he is. Faith was sleeping with him."

Victor's mouth dropped wide open and he stared at Jonathan for a moment before turning to his secretary. "Jan, give us a minute alone." He waited until she was out of the room. "Goddamn it, Jonathan, why didn't you tell me about this sooner?" He shouted as he slammed his hand on the table.

Jonathan jumped and almost spilled his coffee that was in front of him. He was slightly embarrassed for jumping and laughed.

"I don't think this is funny, why are you laughing?"

"Take it easy Vic, I'm not laughing at you. When you slammed your hand down it made me jump. What's the problem?"

Victor stood up and started to pace around the table. "The problem is, I feel like I'm always playing catch up with you. You seem to only tell me what you think you need to and when something happens that is when you finally tell me. I cannot adequately represent you if you don't trust me, Jonathan. Now the police are going to ask you why you didn't tell them about it; what the hell are we going to tell them?"

Jonathan looked at him with a stone face. "I will tell them exactly what I am going to tell you. I don't have to tell you every person that my wife slept with, Vic!"

"Alright, alright!" Victor said, throwing up his hands as he sat back down in his chair. "I have some questions."

"What do you want to know?"

Victor took a drink of coffee. "How long was Faith sleeping with Adam?"

Jonathan sighed, "Look I don't know when it started, but I found out about it a few months ago."

"And how did you find out?"

"Our vehicles have GPS; I downloaded an app and was able to see wherever she went and for how long the vehicle was not moving. I saw this address keep popping up, I looked it up and found that the trailer was in the name of Adam Lewis. After that, I went on social media and looked him up. Other than me, she had a thing for losers. Why would you want to be with someone like that when she could have had a lot better. She did that shit just to piss me off," Jonathan said, becoming angry.

"Could the baby be Adam's and maybe that's why she didn't tell you about it," Victor asked.

Jonathan sat there a moment, visibly distraught. Tears pooled in his eyes and he cleared his throat before answering. "I have asked myself that question a hundred times since I found out. I have no idea, but I hope like hell she wouldn't do that to me."

"Did you confront her about Adam?"

Jonathan went on to explain what happened the night he came home late after finding out he got the new stadium deal and ending things with Douglas. He told Victor about the fight Faith and him had that night. He told him that they had talked about working their problems out and going to counseling. They both needed to get away and have a fresh start, so they went on a vacation to reconnect as a family. Things were going great, they agreed they could not have an open marriage anymore. Faith ended things with him and was trying to start fresh in their relationship. Then they came back home and things continued to progress in a positive way when his world was turned upside down.

Victor made some notes while listening to Jonathan and was about to ask him a question when Hailee walked in, "Mr. Ross, Douglas and Claire are here and would like to speak with you."

"Ok, I will be right there. Thank you."

Victor gave him a look. "What are they doing here?"

"Well, they are my friends. They probably came to see how I'm doing."

Victor leaned in and whispered, "Even after everything that has gone on between you and Douglas?"

Rolling his eyes, Jonathan said, "Victor, please!" He walked out of the dining room, leaving Victor to ponder why someone would still be friends with their ex-lover and who is still angry at the fact that the relationship has ended.

Jan walked back in, and after seeing the expression on Victor's face asked, "Everything alright, Vic? You look confused."

"Yeah, it's confusing. On the other hand, if I tried to understand everything about my client's lives, I could never focus on the real reason they attained my services. It's not our problem, until it is our problem."

Jan wrinkled up her nose. "Is that one of those phases only you understand?' she said, laughing.

"Yeah, just roll with it, Jan," he said, rolling his eyes.

Jonathan walked into the main living room where Hailee asked them to wait. He greeted them and led them into his office.

"Hailee?"

"Yes, Mr. Ross?"

"Could you tell Skyler to come to my office, she doesn't need to bring the children."

"Yes, sir."

Jonathan closed the door. "You are early according to my watch," he told them.

"We aren't here for that; we saw they arrested someone early this morning; We wanted to make sure you're alright," Claire said.

"I'm alright, but they didn't arrest him. They took him in for questioning," Jonathan said, staring intently at her.

Douglas scoffed, "Jeez."

Jonathan turned his attention to him. "What is it?" he asked.

"I'm standing right here; you can't acknowledge me at all?" Douglas said.

"What more do you want?"

"Well, it seems like you are only happy to see her. I have feelings too, you know!"

"Douglas, I'm going to say this as nicely as I can. Shut. The. Fuck. Up. I don't want to hear shit from you."

"You can be so rude and hurtful at times, I'm still your friend, Jonathan. I'm over all that other bullshit. You two can have each other; I will keep my mouth shut but I want my money and the future work contracts as promised," Douglas said looking at him.

Jonathan went to his desk; he pulled a folder out of his top drawer and handed it to him. Douglas opened it and saw the check on top.

"Don't worry, the amount is correct," Jonathan said sarcastically.

"This isn't the contract!" Douglas said.

"No, it's not. Those are the bids of everyone else's, that way you can submit the lowest bid." Jonathan said, starting to lose his patience.

"Are you kidding me with this shit, Jonathan?"

Jonathan had finally had enough. "Look! I have a lot of people watching me right now, I just gave you a $3 million check, you are now debt free. Be happy, submit your fucking bid and move on. After a year Claire will file for divorce and leave. You will not contest it; she will leave and you keep everything. You keep your mouth shut about everything and all will be good."

Douglas had a puzzled look on his face. "Everything? Like what?"

"I mean that Claire will be spending time here with me and you will need to not mention anything about it." Jonathan said.

"I get it, she can stay here all the time as far as I'm concerned."

"No, we do it this way, but you need to sign that non-disclosure agreement, if you want that check!"

"How do I know if it's a good check," Douglas asked, smiling.

"Look at it closer, it's a cashier's check, you moron!"

Douglas chuckled, "You have a pen that I can use?"

Jonathan reached into his pocket and tossed him the pen. Douglas signed it and handed it back; he looked it over and put it in his desk.

"I will get you a copy tomorrow. Now since that's handled, tonight both of you will stay here for appearances sake."

"Our bags are in the car," Claire said with a school girl smile.

"Put them in the guest suite for now. I have a feeling you aren't going to need much anyway," he told her, grinning.

There was a knock at the door, Jonathan motioned for Claire to open it.

"Hello Mrs. Fulton!"

"Skyler, please don't call me that. Claire is fine, seriously."

"Come in, Sky," Jonathan said.

She was wearing skin tight work-out pants, furry snow boots and an oversized hoodie. Claire looked her up and down as she walked in. "Where is the blizzard?" she asked.

"Blizzard?" Skyler asked.

"Because of your snow boots!" Claire laughed.

"Yeah, I think they are so cute," she said, turning her foot from side to side. Claire closed the door and Douglas had a seat on the sofa. Jonathan gestured for her to sit in the chair in front of his desk.

"Is everything alright, Mr. Ross?"

"It's safe to talk in front of them, Sky. Claire is going to be here tonight and will be joining us."

"We may have an issue with that, I started my period today. It's not a lot, but enough to have a tampon in," Skyler said.

Jonathan smirked, "We can handle that."

Claire walked over and sat on the edge of the desk, directly in front of the chair Skyler was sitting in. "Is that going to stop you from going down on me?"

Skyler's eyes widened and her face turned red from embarrassment. Douglas rolled his eyes and laughed. "Jesus, Claire. You act like you are a professional dominatrix. Don't worry honey, the only experience she has is from being a model. You know they all either suck dick or fuck someone to get where they are."

Claire stood up from desk facing him and said, "Sit there and keep your opinion to yourself. In fact, why are you even here? I don't believe anyone here invited here to join tonight's activities"

"Whatever," Douglas muttered. Claire looked back at Skyler and raised her eyebrows waiting for her response to the question.

"No, it will not stop me."

"Then great. We are going to have so much fun. I can't wait to see your body," she said, winking at her. Skyler smirked, "Who said you had to wait for tonight, Claire?" as she started to lift up her hoodie. But before it could go too far Jonathan slammed on the brakes.

"Calm down. Tonight, everyone will be gone; we will have the entire house to ourselves. We can make as much noise as we want."

Skyler smiled and crossed her legs. "I'm looking forward to it, but if I can have a moment of your time Mr. Ross?"

"Of course, what's up?" he asked, walking behind his desk and sitting in his chair.

"In private?" she asked.

Jonathan smiled, "Claire, Douglas. Why don't you go up and put your things away in one of the guest suites while I speak with Skyler."

Claire hesitated until Jonathan gave her a look. As they were walking out Skyler glanced at her and saw the look of jealousy on her face. She couldn't help but smile a little. As the door closed Jonathan asked, "What's going on Skyler?"

She uncrossed her legs and scooted the chair closer and put her hands flat on the desk.

"I'm getting my nails done later and I remember you telling me you like when my nails are done. But I can be so forgetful sometimes because I cannot recall what color you said would look good."

Jonathan was not expecting this, but he did love it when she would tease him. "Yellow. Or something bright. No dark colors, definitely bright and fun. Like you."

Skyler grinned, "Mr. Ross… Stop it. You are going to make me blush."

Jonathan leaned back in his chair. "I have a question for you now."

"Alright."

"Why did you wear that outfit?"

Skyler took her hands off the desk and sat back. "What? This? Mr. Ross, I was in a hurry this morning and threw this on," she said with a seductive smile.

He leaned forward, "I have told you about that outfit before Skyler, this is nothing new. You know exactly what it does to me and you still wear it."

"Yes, I do know. I know exactly what it does to you."

Jonathan got up and walked over to her. "Be a good girl, help me with this problem."

"Mr. Ross, you like this outfit that much!" As she ran her hand over the bulge in his pants. He started to undo his belt, she slapped his hand away, "Be patient, don't you know that good things come to those that wait."

"What are you a philosopher; I don't wait for anything!"

"You know the deal; how much is it worth to you?"

She began to rub him through his pants, she watched him reach into his pocket and pull out a wad of money.

"Here, take it all," he said, handing it to her. She put it in the pocket of her hoodie.

She unfastened his belt, unbuttoned and pulled down his zipper on his trousers, letting them fall to the floor around his ankles. She pulled him out and began stroking.

"Is that what you wanted?"

He was standing with his head back, groaning with pleasure. He looked down at Skyler who was still sitting in the chair. "That feels good Sky, but you know what to do. "Suck that cock!"

Skyler was growing impatient, after what seemed like forever he finally came. Of course he wasn't nice about it, letting it go anywhere he wanted.

"You know, I would prefer to just swallow it then you get it all over me!"

"I will put it anywhere I want too, as long as I'm paying for it." He snapped back.

"Jonathan. You're an asshole. You make people hate you."

He took a step back from her. "Let's get a few things straight: this fucking attitude and tone you have with me needs to stop. I will not let you disrespect me. Secondly, I paid good money that you took from me. Trust me when I tell you that your pussy is good but it's not trimmed in gold. Lastly, little girl, don't you ever forget who is in charge. You signed a non-disclosure agreement, don't even fuck with me. I think you're overreacting because of your period. I know how sensitive and emotional you get, use my bathroom to clean up and get yourself together."

She didn't know what to say to him. She went into the bathroom, closed and locked the door. She burst into tears, she put her face into a towel so he wouldn't hear her.

She sat down on the toilet, thinking about how she could get out of staying here tonight. She grabbed the wet wipes on the counter. Shaking her head and thinking, how thoughtful of him leaving wet wipes on the counter for me to clean up with.

She finished washing her hands and cleaned her face. She took a deep breath and opened the bathroom door.

"What took you so long?" Claire asked, startling her.

"Where's Jonathan," Skyler asked.

"You know him, once he is finished that's all that matters. To be fair, I told him to leave us alone, that I wanted to talk with you."

"About what," Skyler asked with a side-eyed look.

Claire sat down in Jonathan's chair behind his desk. "Tonight, going forward, and what our relationship is going to look like."

Skyler didn't know what to say to her. "I will be honest with you, I don't want to see Jonathan, as far as tonight, that's a no go for me. I'm not even sure I'm going to continue working here."

Claire was shocked to hear this, the way Jonathan had talked about Skyler, it sounded like this was going to be a regular thing between the three of them. Claire couldn't believe she was about to do this because she really wanted Skyler gone, but she knew Jonathan liked her.

"Skyler, he is going through a tough time, he is lashing out at anyone he can. I know he can be a real asshole at times, but I know for a fact that he cares about you. He just doesn't think things through. What changed your mind, if you don't mind me asking," she asked with a slight grin.

"I don't want to do this anymore. He used to know what limits were, now he has none and the only person he would semi-listen to is gone," Skyler told her.

Claire stared at her. "Well, if that is how you feel then you should follow your gut sweetie, and I say that from the bottom of my heart. I know Jonathan will be disappointed to hear this, but don't worry, there are lots of pretty girls looking for jobs."

Skyler scoffed at her remark. "Whatever. I don't care, to be honest." And with that, she walked out.

Jonathan returned to check on how Victor was getting along and if he needed anything. Victor started to talk with him about getting things in order for the possibility of the police coming here to search the property. Jonathan took issue with that. "Why would they need to search my house, I didn't do anything!"

"Jonathan, I said it's a possibility, nothing is set in stone."

Claire came out to the dining room and was getting ready to sit down when the doorbell rang. They all looked at each other, none of them moved a muscle. Hailee came into the dining room, "Excuse me, Mr. Ross?"

"Yes, Hailee?"

"Lieutenant Stephens is here, asking to speak with you. He said it's urgent."

"Is it just the Lieutenant?" Victor asked.

"Yes, sir"

Victor looked at Jonathan. "It's alright, they don't just send one person to serve a search warrant."

"I will be right there, Hailee." He looked at Victor, motioned for him to follow him. They walked out to the living room and greeted the Lieutenant. He wasted no time getting right to the point.

"I know you have probably seen the news this morning."

"Yes, we have," they said in unison.

"We received a tip from an eyewitness that places your wife outside of a mobile home, having a verbal argument with a man hours before her death. We began to gather information on this individual, Adam Lewis. Does that name ring a bell?"

Jonathan glanced at Victor, "Mr. Ross's wife and Mr. Lewis was engaging in a sexual relationship," Victor said.

Stephens had a perplexed look on his face. "Why didn't you inform law enforcement, Mr. Ross?"

Victor spoke up, "Mr. Ross was protecting his wife's dignity, after all he believed the relationship was over. He did not want to air their dirty laundry out for everyone to see, he believed the matter between Mr. Lewis and his wife was over and held no significance."

"Yes, I understand that, but that could have helped us. I know you want to protect your wife and her memory but if that eyewitness hadn't called in, we may not have connected Mr. Lewis to her," Stephens said looking at Jonathan.

"I understand, Lieutenant, but I have the utmost faith in your abilities to do your job, without me having to tell the world that she was having an extra-marital affair."

Stephens was getting aggravated with his attitude. "Didn't you already tell the Sheriff that you and your wife had an open marriage?"

Victor put his hand up, motioning to Jonathan to not reply. Jonathan grinned at Stephens with contempt.

"Listen Lieutenant, I think we are getting off topic. The reason you came to the house is what?" Victor asked. He did not take his eyes off of Jonathan the whole time Victor was speaking.

"Excuse me, Lieutenant Stephens?" Victor tried getting his attention off of Jonathan.

Finally, he broke his stare from him and looked at Victor. "As I was saying, we took a man in for questioning. During our interview with him, we got back DNA results from semen left at the crime scene. It came back as a match to Mr. Lewis. Now with this evidence coming to light, we are going to hold a press conference letting the public know we have arrested him for the rape and murder of Mrs. Ross."

"I'm sure I speak for Mr. Ross as well when I say we are relieved to hear that news, but we are still in a state of shock."

Stephens nodded. "Are there any questions you have for me before I go?"

"Yes, how did you get the results back so fast if you just brought him in for questioning this morning?" Jonathan asked him.

"The DNA evidence we collected was from the crime scene. We sent that to the F.B.I.'s lab and put a rush on it - normally high-profile cases get priority. It helped that Mr. Lewis was already in the system because of a prior arrest and conviction. The F.B.I. started collecting DNA profiles of all federal inmates and individuals convicted of a federal crime as a condition of their parole."

"Federal crime! What kind of federal crime?" Victor asked.

He turned his focus to Victor. "Well, that's a matter of public record, go and look it up."

Victor was taken back by his comment, "I'm sorry, but why don't you just tell us, since it is public record?"

"That would make it easier if I told you, wouldn't it?" he asked Victor.

Victor smiled, "Yes it would."

He nodded, "I know it would, like it would have been easier if you and your client would have given us Mr. Lewis, instead of hiding it," Stephens said.

"Lieutenant, that is not an accurate statement." Victor was about to say more until Jonathan spoke up, "Thank you, Lieutenant. I appreciate you doing your job and finding the monster that did this to my family."

Stephens glared at him, then turned to Victor. "We are submitting everything to the Prosecuting Attorney, going forward you will be updated from their office. Unless you have any new information you would like to share, don't bother to contact us."

"Lieutenant, you seem upset, why do I get the feeling it is with me?" Jonathan asked, grinning.

He was annoyed by his comment. "Mr. Ross, I would like to give you some advice. Police ask questions for a reason, it's to find out the truth and facts. Those truths and facts help us solve the crime. We were trying to solve the crime of your wife's rape and murder. You didn't want to tell us everything, why? The only people that lie, are either stupid or guilty. I'll let you decide which one you are."

"Hailee, would you please show Lieutenant Stephens to the door," Jonathan said.

"No need, I can let myself out."

Victor's and Jonathan's phones were blowing up with calls and text messages from news outlets and reporters wanting to get a statement regarding the police handing the case to the Prosecuting Attorney Office, as well as a statement about Faith's and Mr. Lewis's sexual relationship. It somehow got leaked that Faith and Adam were in a romantic affair.

"Jonathan, I'm giving you Jan's phone number if you need to get a hold of me tonight."

"Victor, you worry too much. I'm going to relax and have a peaceful dinner with my friends. Douglas and Claire will be here, stop worrying about me. I will come to your office tomorrow and we can make a statement."

Victor gave him a hesitant look. "Alright, I will see you tomorrow morning around 10am; we will have the press conference at noon."

Jonathan nodded in agreement. "I'll be there, Vic."

Victor helped Jan gather her things, Jonathan and Hailee walked them to the door. After they left, he noticed it was quiet, which was odd, because there was always something going on in this house.

"Hailee, are the kids upstairs?"

"No sir, Mrs. Ross's mother picked them up earlier. She said Skyler set it up with her a few days ago. Is that alright, Mr. Ross?"

"Yes, of course," he told her. She started to walk away when he said, "Thank you for everything, I know things have been difficult and stressful around here lately."

"It's my pleasure, Mr. Ross. I enjoy working for your family and have no plans on leaving any time soon. That is assuming my services are still wanted."

"Hailee, you are important to this family. I trust you and my children are crazy about you; we definitely want you to stay working with us. We need you more than ever right now."

She smiled with tears in her eyes. "It's nice to be appreciated. There is no other place I would rather be than here for all of you. If I can be so bold as to say, I cared a great deal for Mrs. Ross. Everyone is feeling lost without her, not as much as you and the children are. But you are not alone and we are all here to help you in any way."

Jonathan shook his head in acknowledgement, "Thank you, Hailee. I know it has been a long week for you, don't worry about dinner tonight. I am going to order a pizza; you and everyone else take off early."

"Ok, Mr. Ross. Have a good evening."

"You as well, Hailee," he said, walking away.

Jonathan saw Douglas sitting in the dining room. He went in and had a seat next to him. Douglas put his phone down,

"What's up," Douglas said hesitantly.

192

"Listen, I'm sorry for earlier today and how I have treated you lately. No matter what has happened between us, we have always been great friends. You have helped me out many times, when no one else would lift a finger for me. With everything going on I have been extremely stressed out. I know that is no excuse to be an asshole but that's all I know how to be. I can't grieve the way I want to grieve because that's not normal. At least in the public's eye. But you have always been there. I'm sorry."

Douglas was shocked at what he was hearing from him. "Thanks, I appreciate that. I know we will never be together like before, but I don't want to lose our friendship or our business partnership for that matter. Everything else is good, too," he sighed.

Jonathan raised his left eyebrow at him. "Everything else?"

"Yes, I don't care about it."

"The contracts?"

"Damn Jonathan, I said it was good. I just want to move on with life."

"What about Claire?"

He shook his head in disappointment. "It's been over between us for a long time. Honestly, we should have never gotten married. I have never found women to be desirable but that is what was expected of me; marry a beautiful woman, have kids, have this picture-perfect life. I never wanted any of that, my parents would have disowned me if they knew the truth about me. I met Claire, we both needed something from the other, it was a lie from the beginning. We found out she could not have children, all that did was make an already bad marriage worse. I feel responsible for Claire's bitterness towards the world. I could have done right by her; she deserves to be loved and treated right. If you two are happy, then I'm happy for you."

"Really?"

"Yes," Douglas said, relieved they were finally having this discussion.

"If you don't mind me asking, what in the hell changed your mind?"

"I'm tired of living a lie. Every time I look into the mirror, I feel disgusted by the reflection staring back at me. What good is a big ass house, fancy cars and money, if you can't be the true person, you are? Truthfully, I want to get as much work as possible out of this stadium, make my money and get the hell out of this place."

Jonathan laughed, "You are going to run away? Where are you going to go?"

"Somewhere warm year-round, on the beach where I can open a tiki bar. Jonathan, I'm not as strong as you. You would have no difficulties standing up to people, I'm not built that way. It's easier for me to run away." Douglas said, half grinning.

"Well, you let me know when you find the place, maybe I will get a spot next to you." He got up, extending his hand to Douglas, "You know, one day you are not going to be able to run away from a problem. You will have two choices: stand up and fight or lay down and die. As your friend, I hope when that day comes you make the right choice. You're a good person Douglas, a great friend." They buried the hatchet; Jonathan knew he had a true friend; Douglas was able to be honest about himself to Jonathan.

"Why don't you order all of us some food, pizza. Pick out a few bottles of wine, let them start chilling," he told Douglas.

"Ok. But once it gets here, I'm not waiting for you all," he said laughing at him, knowing full well what he was going to do.

"Yeah, yeah," Jonathan said, walking away.

Jonathan walked in the guest suite without knocking to find Claire standing by the bed wrapped in a towel with her hair in a bun. She looked at him, while he stared at her. "You coming in or just going to stand there with your mouth open," she said, winking at him. He smiled and walked in, leaving the door open. She dropped the towel to the floor, exposing her body. He was instantly excited.

"I don't care if people see me."

He walked past her looking around the bed at first, then scanned the room. She thought he was going to come over to her but instead was paying no attention to her. She became frustrated with him and couldn't take it any longer.

"What are you looking for, Jonathan?"

"What are you going to wear tonight?"

She grabbed the lotion out of her bag, putting some in her hand, "Wouldn't you love to know," she said.

"No, seriously, what are you wearing tonight?"

She was rubbing lotion on her legs when he walked towards her. "Don't even try that bullshit with me," she said, facing him. He was caught off guard with her comment, he stopped and looked at her, confused. "Don't act like you don't know what I'm talking about!"

"What are you talking about?"

"You and the nanny, earlier today. I'm not her, I have no problem standing up to you!"

"Skyler? What about her?"

Claire grabbed a pair of neon blue leggings out of her suitcase, holding them up for him to see. He nodded his approval as she put them on. She dug in her suitcase and from the bottom pulled out a plain white t-shirt, she put it on without showing him.

"I found her in your office crying her eyes out, she was tight lipped about what happened, but I have an idea of what did. I will not take that shit from you; I will be treated with respect. Now what we do behind closed doors is different. But I will not be treated like some paid piece of ass."

Jonathan was grinning and looked to be holding back laughter. "Claire Fulton, are you jealous?"

She turned around, giving him a smirk. "We can play games; I assumed you would have been tired of doing that. Especially since that's what you and Faith did."

"Claire, I'm not hiding the fact that I was with Skyler. This is who I am. If I want something I take it."

"I understand, you know it works both ways," she said as she pulled her hair out of a bun and into a ponytail.

"You knew what this was when we started it." He was becoming irritated with her. She started laughing for no apparent reason.

"What's funny?"

"The fact you think this is the same as when we started," she said, crossing her arms.

Jonathan had a seat on the bed and motioned for her. She went over and he put his arms around her waist, pulling her close to him. "I need to tell you something because it's important and I believe in being honest with people, no matter how hard it is."

She smiled and rolled her eyes at him. "Ok, I'm listening."

"Claire, you are a beautiful woman and I always have a great time with you but if you mention Faith again to me; I won't think twice about smacking. This is the only warning you will get from me. Are we understood?" Before she could answer him, a voice came from the open door., "Well look at that, two peas in a pod."

"Skyler!" Jonathan exclaimed, letting go of Claire.

"Safe to come in or do you two need a minute?"

"Oh please, come in," he said.

"I really didn't expect to see you tonight," Claire said, genuinely surprised.

"Surprise! I'm here."

"Yes, I can see that," Claire responded.

Jonathan, wanting to release the tension in the air, clapped his hands and said, "Ok, ladies, let's drop all this nonsense and focus on having a great evening."

Claire paid no attention to him. Keeping her eye contact with Skyler she asked, "Are you sure this is what you want to do."

Jonathan started to walk to Skyler when out of nowhere Claire said sternly, "Don't even think about it! Sit your ass down in that chair. It's time for her and I to get to know each other better."

He scoffed at her, "You know how hard that's going to be?"

"At least you are getting to watch me with her," she said, never looking away from Skyler. He took off his pants and boxers before sitting in the chair; he was already semi-hard and couldn't resist the urge to start rubbing himself. Claire walked over to her, taking her by the hands and leading her to the bed. Skyler started to take off her hoodie, when Claire stopped her.

"I will undress you; you will undress me. Start with my shirt, then my leggings, and be sure to put that mouth to work on me."

Skyler grabbed the bottom of the t-shirt and pulled it over Claire's head, throwing it to the foot of the bed. She noticed Claire's beautiful skin tone, the way her stomach was perfectly flat. She could tell that she spent a lot of time in the gym and worked hard to keep her physique. She couldn't believe how perfect her natural breasts were; Claire was the perfect specimen for what men look for in a woman. Skyler was a little intimidated by how perfect she was, she didn't want to disappoint her sexually. This was a new feeling for Skyler. She could no longer resist, putting her hands on Claire's body, feeling how soft and smooth her skin was. Taking Claire's right breast in her hand, she brought it to her mouth, using her tongue to lick and suck on her nipple. Claire pressed Skyler's head down harder on her breast, desperately wanting more. Skyler then took her left breast and did the same. This time Claire was verbally telling her what to do.

"Bite my nipple."

Jonathan watched every moment as he sat, sulking.

Claire wanted more, "Take my pants off, now," she said. She slid Claire's pants down, then pushed her onto the bed. Claire grabbed a pillow, laying her head on it; she wanted to be comfortable. Skyler put her hands on Claire's knees and gently pushed her legs apart, exposing a perfectly manicured strip of pubic hair.

"Wait. Let's get you out of those clothes," Claire said. She sat up, grabbing both sleeves of Skyler's hoodie and pulled it up and over her head, exposing her small perky breasts. Claire looked at her and said, "I don't think I have ever seen a more perky set of titties like yours. They are so sexy!"

She laughed. "Thanks. Yours are perfect, Claire."

"They hurt my back sometimes, but I guess I will keep them. Take off your boots and socks," she said, smiling at her.

She pulled off her boots, setting them aside and put her socks in them, making sure that Jonathan could see that her toenails were painted yellow like he wanted them. He smiled and winked at her.

"I love them," he said, winking and flashing her a smile.

Claire cleared her throat to get her attention. "Is it a heavy or light day," she asked.

Embarrassed, Skyler whispered "Light."

Claire nodded and scooted closer to Skyler, grabbed her around the waist and pulled her in to kiss her stomach. She slid her hands down from her waist under Skyler's underwear band, slowly pulling them down until she stepped out of them. Claire ran her hands up and down her thighs and ass, caressing her. "You are absolutely stunning."

Skyler blushed at the compliment, adjusting the way she stood, widening her stance to make it easier for Claire to explore her body. Claire ran her fingers over Skyler's smooth lips, grabbing the tampon string.

"Is it alright if I take this out?"

"Yes," Skyler answered. She gently pulled it out and inspected it.

"It's a very light day, nothing on it," Claire smiled as she lay back on the bed.

Skyler kissed her way up Claire's legs, gently exploring her toned and muscular thighs with her tongue. She kissed her stomach, between her perfectly round breasts, swirling her tongue around each of Claire's hard nipples, working her way to her collar bone and kissed the nape of her neck, positioning herself so that their breasts were touching. Claire put her hands on each side of Skyler's face and pulled her lips to her mouth, pressing her tongue against Skyler's lips, testing her. Skyler opened her mouth, letting Claire explore her mouth with her tongue. She loved how gentle Claire was. She felt comfortable with Claire, unlike how she now felt with Jonathan.

She moved her mouth to Claire's cheek, and made her way back to her neck. She kissed and softly licked her neck, feeling Claire's hands run up and down her back and she slightly panted. Skyler started moving towards her breasts, Claire grabbed her face and pulled her back up.

"Get back up here, I'm not done with those lips," Claire smiled.

When Claire grabbed her face and pulled her back up, "Get back up here. I'm not done with those lips."

Skyler smiled, "Oh, really?"

"Yes, you're an amazing kisser," Claire told her.

She started laughing and turned red. "Well, I could say the same about you."

Jonathan watched from the chair; it was becoming difficult not to join them or at least tell them what to do with every passing moment. He was hard as a rock and his balls swollen from excitement; he wanted his release now. He got up from the chair thinking he was going to be welcomed to join.

Claire noticed him getting up. "Sit down! No one invited you to this party!"

Jonathan stopped; he sat back down in the chair frustrated; this is not what he wanted to happen tonight. Claire saw he was upset. "Stop pouting. You will get your turn too but I want your balls so full they are hurting, before you join us."

Jonathan perked up and started rubbing his penis; watching the two of them touch and kiss was making it difficult for him not to come. He watched as Skyler kissed her lips and pushed her back down on the bed. She straddled Claire kissing her deeper. Claire slid her hand down between Skyler's legs and started to rub her. Skyler moaned and broke the kiss off, "Don't put any fingers in yet, just rub it a little harder."

"You like that sweetie?"

"Don't you feel how wet I am?"

"I want you to say it, tell me it feels good to you."

"That feels amazing, please don't stop!"

"How do you want to come for me?"

Skyler was confused. "What do you mean?"

"I want you to tell me how you would like me to make you come."

"Seriously?"

"Yes, it turns me on."

Skyler moaned with delight. She wanted to come. "Eat my pussy a little, then turn me on my stomach and…" Skyler hesitated to say the last part but Claire gave her a look. "Then finger me and eat me from behind."

"Lay back. Spread those legs." Skyler did as she was told. Claire kissed the top of her foot, then worked her way up to Skyler's inner thigh kissing every inch of her.

"Are you ready, beautiful?"

"Yes!" Skyler's legs were shaking with anticipation.

Claire teased her with small wet kisses around her vagina. She inhaled her musky odor; she spread Skyler's lips and took her first taste of her. Using her tongue she started at the bottom, gliding up and twirling around her clit, sucking on her little hood. She continued, listening to Skyler's moans get louder and feeling her getting wetter. She felt her getting closer to climax and slowed down. Claire was letting nothing go to waste, as she cleaned up all of her juices before telling her to turn over. Claire turned to see Jonathan stroking himself and watching them intently. This was the moment she was waiting for, now was the time to show him how it feels to be humiliated.

"Jonathan!"

Startling him out of his enjoyment, he looked at her and started to get up.

"I want you to watch and listen; this is how you make a woman come."

Jonathan glared at her, "I'm definitely watching and listening, but don't make the mistake of thinking I ever give a shit whether whores come."

Claire turned her attention to Skyler. "Are you another one of his whores?"

"I'm only his whore."

Jonathan smiled. "That's a good girl. See Claire, she understands exactly where she stands."

Claire rolled her eyes. "Really? I bet I make her come better than you."

"You talk a lot of shit Claire, make her come already."

Claire ignored him; she slid two fingers inside of her. She was warm, wet, and tight; she felt amazing. Skyler moved her body back and forth, keeping rhythm with Claire. It was

202

becoming too much for her, and she buried her face into the pillow. She felt Skyler quivering, knowing she was close to exploding on her fingers. Claire put her tongue on her asshole, eating it like an ice cream cone. Tonguing on and around it until Skyler screamed into the pillow.

"How was that?"

"I could come again, that's how turned on I am," she said, still panting.

"You weren't expecting you would be into it?"

"Not really, I mean you're attractive but I'm not into women."

"Alright, but you clearly did enjoy it."

"Yes, I did. Do you always ask someone you're with what makes them come?"

"I do. Everyone involved should have fun and orgasm as many times as possible!"

Skyler laughed, "I have never heard of someone doing that, but more people definitely should."

"Well Skyler, there are still some of us that aren't selfish around here." Claire said looking at Jonathan, who was visibly frustrated.

"When I'm paying for the pussy, I will be and do whatever the hell I want Claire."

"It doesn't mean you have to be a bastard to her, Jonathan."

Skyler started to become uncomfortable. "It's not a big deal, whatever is between Jonathan and I is between us."

"Listen, say what you want but take it from one who knows, don't trade yourself for a little money. It's not worth it!"

Jonathan grinned watching Claire get jealous, "I know what you are doing to her Claire, I don't like it."

She got off the bed smiling. She knew he was at his limit and wasn't going to push her luck.

"Ok, ok. I have teased you long enough. Let me help you with that." She grabbed him by his penis as if it were a leash and led him out of the bedroom, down the hall to where she could look down into the living room and out the windows overlooking the back half of the property so that she could catch a glimpse of the river between the tree tops.

"I want you to fuck me here!"

"Why here?"

"The view from here is spectacular, anyone out there would be able to see us and that makes me wet!"

"What about Skyler? All of us-"

"Just you and I, she is welcome to watch us, but that's it."

"Skyler!" Jonathan yelled.

She came walking out in her hoodie, "Yes?"

"Go downstairs in the living room, watch me fuck her. Tell me how good it looks from your point of view."

"Alright…" she answered, rolling her eyes.

"And take that hoodie off!"

She took the hoodie off, throwing it over the banister. She smacked Claire on her ass as she walked by them and down the stairs. She walked into the living room and sat down on the sofa, giving her the perfect vantage point and gave them the thumbs up.

"You're getting soft, what's the matter?"

"I'm excited, sometimes it happens," he said sharply.

"I have never heard of a man going soft because he is excited."

"It happens! Just give me a minute!"

"Do you need me to grab you a pill?"

"No, I don't Claire!"

"Alright, I'm trying to help."

"Then shut up!"

"I mean if you think that will help," she said, rolling her eyes.

Jonathan grabbed a handful of her hair and pulled her down to her knees.

"What the hell are you doing?" She raised her voice as she struggled with him.

"Go with it, you said you like it rough. That's what I'm doing," he told her, loosening his grip on her hair.

She instantly felt herself get wet, hearing him say those words, she has been wanting this from him for some time now. She started to sweat and her pulse quickened, it has been a while since she has felt like this. Claire was going to take this as far as she could. "Do your worst. I can take anything you have!"

He looked at her with a slight side grin. "What's off limits?"

She looked up at him while biting her lower lip. "Nothing, except you have to stop if I say GRAPE. That's our safe word, understand?"

"Understood. Grape is the word."

Out of nowhere Claire shoved him, hard enough he let go of her hair and had to catch himself from falling. She wasted no time getting to her feet, she took off running downstairs. Jonathan stood at the balcony and watched her run to Skyler. He yelled down at them, "Now it's on!" and took off down the stairs. Claire grabbed Skyler's hand, "Let's go… By the way, our safe word is grape."

Jonathan bolted into the living room. "Make it easy on yourselves and give up."

"And if we don't!?" Claire asked.

"I will tear you and that pussy up."

"Promise?" Claire asked, while Skyler stood there silently.

He went to Claire, putting his hands around her neck, pulling her in close to him. "I promise I am going to fuck you in all your holes, until you beg me to stop." He looked at Skyler. "And you're going to hold her down while I do it, understand?"

"Yes. Make sure you save some for me," Skyler answered.

Claire butted in. "I bet he won't have enough for the both of us. He is all talk and no action," she smiled at him.

He tightened his grip around her neck, she tried to pull his hand off and he squeezed harder.

"You never know when to stop running that mouth. You will by the time I'm done with you," he said, forcing her to sit on the couch. He let go of her neck, grasping a fist full of her hair. He rubbed and squeezed her breast, until catching her off guard, he slapped both of them hard. The sound made Skyler jump.

"Skyler, get behind her and hold her hands behind her back."

She got behind her, wrapping her legs around Claire's waist holding on to her.

Claire turned her head to try and look back at her. "You can hold them tighter; you won't hurt me."

"That better?" she asked using more strength. Claire nodded.

Jonathan let go of her hair and stepped forward rubbing his penis down her entire face, taunting her with it.

"I'm going to put this in every hole you have and when I'm done, you're going to clean it with your mouth."

"A lot of talk and no action," Claire said.

He stared at her for a moment, then smacked her across the face, forcing a gasp to escape her. Before she could say anything, he backhanded her on the other side of her face.

She cried out, "That's too hard!"

"Unless you're screaming the safe word, keep your mouth shut whore!" he said, spitting in her face.

"I never agreed to spitting-"

He thrusted himself in her mouth, he went as deep as he could go until he could hear her gag on it. He took it out, giving her a few breaths before forcing it back in. Only this time, he held her head with both hands making sure she took the whole thing down to his balls. She choked and gagged, almost vomiting. He stopped and withdrew himself. He let go of her, while she tried to regain her breath and some sense of composure. His focus turned to Skyler, "Let go of her hands." She obeyed his command but didn't know how long she was going to participate in this kink.

"Skyler, lay back on the sofa and spread your legs."

Jonathan pulled Claire up off the sofa by her hair and turned her around to face Skyler, "Take a good look at that pussy, Claire. You see how perfect it is? You are going to eat it, until I tell you otherwise!" Then without warning he pushed her face down into Skyler.

"I did already!" Claire shouted out.

"Bitch! You are a glutton for punishment!" Grabbing her by the back of the neck and pulling her up to face him, he smacked her hard enough for her to fall to the floor. Skyler instinctively started to get up to help her. "Don't move, she put herself down there, she can pick herself up."

He locked eyes with Claire, "Do what you are told and this won't happen!" She nodded in agreement and got back up on the sofa.

Claire put her mouth on Skyler, moving her tongue over the same places she had moments ago in the bedroom. But this time Claire sensed how stiff and uncomfortable Skyler was, she looked up and whispered to her, "Loosen up, it's alright."

Skyler exhaled a sigh of relief and allowed her body to relax. Somehow, she knew that Claire was enjoying this and was clueing her in on it. Claire's tongue followed Skyler's pelvic movements, up and down. Skyler didn't think she was horny enough to come twice, but she felt herself building up again. No longer able to lay still, she grabbed Claire's head and pulled her up for a kiss. She wanted to taste how good she was. Jonathan loved watching the two of them together, the way their bodies moved, how they touched one another; he could not deny the chemistry they seemed to have. A man would be lucky to have one of them but to be able to have them both at the same time, that would be Heaven on Earth.

"My pussy quivers every time you kiss me," Skyler said.

Claire slid her hand down from Skyler's face to between her legs, rubbing her clit. Her fingers were like laser guided missiles, hitting every target with precision. Skyler could barely contain herself; she was on the precipice of exploding.

"STOP!" he yelled out. Claire stopped instantly, Skyler on the other hand was so close she failed to register what he said for a split second.

"I need to come! I'm right there!" she said, while resisting the urge to finish the job herself.

"I will make you come, but you have to tell her you want me too."

"Are you kidding?" Skyler asked.

"I'm serious, so that way she can't get mad at me. You have to tell her you want me to make you come."

Skyler, still not understanding what the hell is going on between them, said, "I want you to make me come!"

"Are you sure that is what you want, Skyler?"

"Yes! Please. Fuck me until I come!" she said, becoming agitated.

Jonathan smiled at Claire, "You heard her, let me in there to finish the job." Claire got up and he positioned himself between her legs. He grabbed himself and rubbed the head up and down on Skyler's sensitive lips.

"Are you ready for it, baby?"

"Yes."

"Claire, stay right here. After she comes, I want you to finish me off by riding me." She nodded with a smirk. He slid inside Skyler with ease, he grabbed her waist and held her in one place so she could move with him. He went slow and methodical, making a point not to finish her fast. Skyler couldn't take it; she had held off this orgasm for long enough and it was starting to become frustrating, to the point she started to cry.

"Why are you crying?" Jonathan asked.

"Because you both are teasing me, not letting me come and it's not fair!"

He laughed, "I'm sorry baby. You want it faster?"

"Do it, like you used to!"

Jonathan knew exactly what she was talking about. They used to sneak off to one of the other spare bedrooms and have a quickie in the bathroom. He would always have to cover her mouth because she would always come loud. They almost got caught one night by Hailee.

"Ok. You want it like that, alright." He got closer to her, putting her arms around his neck. It was like throwing gasoline on a fire, he pushed deeper, harder, and faster into her. Every thrust is harder than the last. Kissing, licking and biting her neck, he made certain that she enjoyed what he was giving her. He felt her body get heavy and her legs stiffen. He covered her mouth with his hand and whispered in her ear, "Come for me like the little whore you are. Come for daddy!" The earth stood still for Skyler, for what seemed like an hour. Her head is hurting, she is exhausted and yet she is so content at that moment. Feeling as though she just conquered a major accomplishment. She has never had an orgasm like that in her life.

"That was amazing!" She felt him pull out, still rock hard. He stood up and motioned for Claire to come to him. She got on top of him, straddling him. He spit on his fingers, reached down, and rubbed around her lips and inside of her. Making sure she was wet enough for him. She did like how his fingers felt inside of her, she began to press herself deeper on them until he took them out.

She was primed and ready to go. Wanting to wait no more, she grabbed him and was about to put it inside of her.

He stopped her and whispered, "I want you to ride this cock just like the first time. I know you remember making Faith so jealous. That's how hard I want to come!"

She had no idea why that turned her on so much, but she almost exploded that moment as he uttered those words to her. She put him inside of her; the moment he entered her she started to come.

"Claire, I knew you needed this," he whispered.

She collapsed on his chest. "Jonathan! You have always had a good cock!" She was ready for round two, she put her hands on his chest and started thrusting her pelvis up and down as hard and fast as she could go. She lasted about two minutes before losing herself again on his throbbing member. She felt like she had run a marathon.

"I love how easy you come for me. How your lips wrap around me, but what I love the most, is putting every inch of me inside you. Does it feel good?" he whispered. She did not understand how he had this power over her, they were just words but they hit in all the right ways.

"Oh God, yes!" she said, trying not to come again.

He was going so fast and hard she had to grab the top of the sofa to stop from looking like a rag doll being thrown about. Having zero control, she couldn't hold back, feeling the pressure build to a point she has not felt in a long time. She had no other choice but to let it take over, all she can do is warn him.

"JONATHAN... I'M. COM...ING!" He felt her juices shoot on him and pulled himself out of her, to let her have her release. Claire collapsed on to his chest again; he slid back in, continuing his rampage.

"Claire, that's good! I'm going to empty these balls in you! Are you ready for this, you little slut?"

Claire started to regain her wits when she heard this. "Yes! Please come inside of me!"

"I'm close, Claire…!"

"Come inside me! Come inside me!"

"I'm going to come!" he shouted.

"Jonathan. I'm going to come again. Please come. I'm… COM…ING!" she moaned at the exact moment he exploded inside of her.

Neither one of them said anything. The only sound is their breathing, lowering their heart rate back to a normal range, coming down from the high of great sex. Jonathan sat, holding her, in no rush to pull out. She is completely exhausted and yet still wants more of him, they have both forgotten that Skyler is still laying on the sofa. They are too much into each other, both feeling that she is a toy they shared for amusement, nothing more. Because what they have is something special, a connection that Jonathan has had with only one other person, Faith.

For Claire it's a different story, she has never had this with anyone, ever. She never felt this with Douglas, not even in the beginning. She felt more of a business relationship with him, they both did what they had to do, but still respected one another. This was her first relationship in which she was actually attracted to the man and she wasn't trying to get something from him. She wasn't proud of it but in her life, she did a lot of things she wished she hadn't. She always told herself that she did what needed to be done, in order for her to reach the top where she wanted to be. Once she got there, she was making enough money modeling that she didn't need anyone. Then Douglas came along, he was nice, charming, and said all the right things. The best part was he never pressured her about sex. The first time they had sex she just thought he was really bad at it, but the more time she spent with him, the more obvious it became that he wasn't interested in women. She brought it up to him one evening and he didn't deny it.

That was the night he offered a partnership. He needed to marry and have the appearance of being stable; she needed financial security. His offer was this; he would buy her any house she wanted in the St. Louis, Missouri area, she never had to pay for a thing, no bills, cars, clothes, vacations, nothing. She would get a monthly allowance and any money she made was hers. In return, she would do everything that a wife would do for a husband whenever they were around people or out in public. Whatever they did away from each other, needed to be done quietly and lowkey. They needed to respect each other and each other's reputations. Claire at the time thought that was a great deal, she got everything a wife would get, but did not have to sleep with him or lie to his face about loving him. She agreed to marry him, it worked out in the beginning but like with everything, things got complicated, feelings got hurt, which led to anger, and anger led to resentment. The only thing they have in common now is Jonathan. The marriage is done, the partnership is done and respect flew out the widow a long time ago.

Chapter 12

November 30, 2017

Thursday

9:45a.m.

When Jonathan arrived at Victor's office at 9:45 a.m., he was greeted warmly by Jan. She explained that Victor would be with him shortly, he was on a phone call with the Prosecuting Attorney. She led Jonathan into a small conference room with a wall of windows overlooking the city. He walked over to the windows and looked at the view.

"Mr. Ross, is there anything you would like to drink?"

"Coffee and water, if it's not too much trouble."

"I will bring that right in, if there is anything else, please let me know."

He stood looking at the city, watching everyone go about their lives. He secretly wished that he was one of them right now. He wondered how long all this was going to go on for; he worried that his children would still be dealing with this when they were adults. He loved this place, but everything was different now. No matter where he goes, people are going to know him; he will always be the guy whose wife was murdered. There will be people that will always think he had something to do with her death. He knew this was going to be the new normal for a while. He couldn't help but think how this was going to be a never-ending story in his life. He started to feel tears come down his face, he hasn't cried since the night he passed out in the funeral home parking lot. The tears were coming down more steadily; he had to sit down, his legs felt weak. The conference door opened, Jan came in with the coffee and water.

"Here you go… Mr. Ross are you alright?"

"Yes, I'm sorry."

She set the drinks down and ran out to her desk to get some tissues. "Don't you apologize, Mr. Ross," she said, handing him some tissues.

"I'm just tired and under a lot of stress. That's what it is."

She sat down in the chair next to him. "May I tell you something Mr. Ross? Without you thinking differently of me?"

"Are you kidding me, you just walked in on me crying like a baby. I need to be worried that you will think differently about me. Please go ahead," he said, blowing his nose.

"With everything you and your family have been through these past few weeks, you have been nothing short of stoic. You have watched as everyone else around you mourn, but have you mourn your loss? You are allowed to have emotions, Mr. Ross; you have those two beautiful babies that are going to need you. Let them see you mourn too; nothing is going to change what happened. Take it from one who knows, that you can't run from grief."

"Thank you for your kind words, it's ironic, what you're saying, not running from grief."

"Why is that Mr. Ross?"

"I was sitting here thinking, when all this is over, I'm moving, starting fresh somewhere else."

Jan smiled, rubbed his arm, and asked, "Mr. Ross, can I give you a hug, you look like you could use one."

"I most certainly could" he said standing up and giving her one back. Just as they ended their embrace Victor walked in.

"Is everything alright?" Victor asked, feeling a bit awkward.

"Yes, just pouring my soul out to Jan here. Victor, you need to give this woman a pay increase."

"I pay her just fine, thank you."

The phone out front started to ring, giving her the perfect excuse to leave. She closed the door as she left, Victor put his things on the table and sat down.

"Well, I just got done talking to Bo Carver the Prosecuting Attorney, I have some information."

"Come on Vic, don't leave me in suspense," he said, sitting down. He took a drink of his coffee.

"Jonathan, Bo assured me that he never thought for a moment that you were involved with this violent crime, he apologized for how the Sheriff's Department and Lieutenant Stephens treated you. He wanted to reach out to see how you felt about a plea bargain. That way it saves everyone from a trial, where the defense will drag you and Faith through the mud. They will hold back nothing, everything that is said during the trial would become public record. We have time to think about it and talk it through, in these kinds of cases the family has a big part in whether or not the defendant gets offered a deal."

Jonathan took another drink of his coffee. "Vic, I'm going to tell you the truth. I want this to be over. I would be grateful for a plea deal; I don't want my children reading about the horrific acts that their mother went through during her last moments."

Victor nodded; he couldn't imagine having to make a decision like that. On one hand wanting justice for your loved one, but also wanting to protect the rest of your family from finding out the horrors of what happened. It was a double-edged sword, either way someone was going to disagree with Jonathan's decision. Victor felt sorry for him.

"Jonathan, are you still alright with doing this press conference?"

"Does it matter?"

Victor was confused by his question. "Of course, it matters. If you don't want to do it, we won't."

"Really, after everything you said to me yesterday. What people think about me and how it would look."

"Jonathan, I-"

"No. I can't run from this anymore, I'm going to put it all out there and tell them the truth. Faith would like that the truth was out. She tried telling me, it doesn't matter what people think. It's our lives, we only answer to each other. She wanted to stay in Galveston, I should have listened to her. The only thing I can do now is be honest going forward."

Victor was astonished at what he just heard him say. He wondered what had changed from the previous day. He sat there with Jonathan for a little bit, listening to him talk about the things he had done, things Faith had done. Jonathan told him about all the affairs with women and men, the times he used his money and power to get whatever he wanted, including the time he talked Douglas into letting him sleep with Claire, and how Faith had gotten mad and stormed off. He admitted he threw Faith away, treated her like property. How he mentally abused her, and he backhanded her not too long before her death, the first and only time he had ever physically hit her. They would not have had an open marriage if Faith would have been a little more willing to try new things in the bedroom. He resented her for not being willing to try new things, take risks, have some fun and adventures, "Faith did not understand me; she was unwilling to try and make an effort."

Victor realized that the more Jonathan talked, the more he started to think he wasn't that upset by Faith being gone.

Victor interjected, "Jonathan if you don't mind being asked, if you felt like that in your marriage, why not get a divorce? There is no sense being unhappy."

Jonathan looked at him like he was crazy. "Are you joking? She would have taken all my money."

Victor didn't understand why people stayed in unhappy situations when they had all the means to get out. He did understand that money can control people, he was just figuring out that money definitely controlled Jonathan in every aspect. He looked at his watch. 11:30 a.m. "I'm going to let them in here to set up, why don't you go into my office and sit in there until everything is ready."

He felt like Victor was upset with him. "Listen Vic, I didn't have anything to do with her being killed. I'll swear on anything, somewhere in my heart I loved that woman, God knows I did. But things work out the way they are meant to work out. I told her that he was a piece of shit, trailer trash and nothing but trouble. Look how it turned out - he killed her. How I rationalize it, you reap what you sow." Jonathan felt better, and surprised himself had finally spoken those words out loud.

Victor was feeling conflicted, thinking that Jonathan was heartbroken by the loss of Faith, when he was actually relieved by her death. He felt like he was being used. He has had clients in the past that he knew were guilty and still defended them. This time was different, he truly thought Jonathan was being mistreated by the police. But they saw something in Jonathan that Victor was blind to. He knew Jonathan didn't actually kill Faith but maybe he did have something to do with it. He always stayed professional with his clients, even when they made it hard for him. He believed that the justice system worked best when the prosecutors did their job, he did his, and the jury decided who won. That is not going to happen though, Jonathan is not being charged. According to the evidence, the only thing Jonathan Ross is guilty of, is being a bad husband. That's not a crime; now the police and public did not know how Jonathan felt, nor would they ever find out because Victor would never break attorney-client privilege. Victor did give his clients advice though, after all, it is part of his job.

"Jonathan, do you think of me as a friend?"

Jonathan was surprised by his question. "Yeah Vic, I see you as a friend."

"Then is it alright if I tell you something as a friend?"

"Vic, just say it already, please."

"There is another old saying, it goes like this; there's a natural law of karma that vindictive people, who go out of their way to hurt others, will end up broke and alone." Victor was trying to gauge how he took it, when Jonathan stood and walked to Victor's office.

As Victor opened the door and let the reporters into the conference room he told, "Come on in and get set up, we will get started shortly."

Jonathan pondered it, while walking to Victor's office. When Victor came in, he asked. "Vic, where did you hear that from? If you don't mind my asking."

Victor smiled, knowing he hit a nerve with him. "I have an app on my phone that gives me a quote a day. The good ones I write down and try to use sometimes. That quote comes from Sylvester Stallone."

"Interesting," he said. Jonathan was trying not to lose his temper. This was not the time nor the place for that. But he was not going to let him talk down to him, after all, he is paying him. "Vic, what did you mean by that comment?"

Victor certainly didn't want to give the dozen reporters in the next room anything negative to write about, so he played it cool, "I didn't mean anything by it, you said an old saying, I thought I would tell you one that I knew."

"You sure? It sounded like you think I'm a bad person or I'm going to end up broke and alone."

Victor now felt like Jonathan was trying to be a bully. "Jonathan with those sayings, they are open to interpretation. If that's what you got out of it, that's on you. You have to quit thinking about things all the time. It will make you go crazy," he smiled, then added, "I'm going to make sure everything is ready and go over the rules with them. When you are ready, come out and we will get started, alright?"

Jonathan smiled, "Sounds like a plan, Vic." Victor was just about to walk out when he asked, "Vic, can I use your restroom man. I had too much coffee this morning," he laughed.

"Sure, go ahead use my personal one, that door there," he pointed towards the door. He then shut the office door and went to check on the reporters. Jonathan went into the bathroom and was trying to get his temper under control.

"I know what he meant. That weasel doesn't want to say anything when I question him," he yelled, looking at himself in the mirror. He took a few deep breaths, turned on the cold water, gathered some cold water in his hands, and splashed his face. He dried his face off, unzipped his pants and began to urinate on the floor, the walls and all over the toilet seat. "I feel better now, have fun cleaning that up, you cocksucker." He said under his breath as he closed the bathroom door behind him.

"Ladies and gentlemen, we would like to get this press conference started. My name is Victor DeNoyer, I represent Mr. Jonathan Ross. Mr. Ross has agreed to make a statement regarding recent developments with his wife's untimely death and share some insight into their lives together. He will take a few questions at the end; I would just like to remind everyone that he is still dealing with all the emotions that come with a tragic event. Please be patient and be respectful. With that, Mr. Jonathan Ross."

Jonathan walked to the front of the podium, took a sip of water, and pulled out a piece of paper from his pocket. "First, let me thank all of you for coming here today and hearing what I have to say. I have had to be patient and not make any public statements because of the ongoing police investigation. My attorney, Mr. DeNoyer, and myself have been in contact with the Prosecuting Attorney Mr. Bo Carver, everything I say here today has been cleared with his office. First, I would like to thank everyone for their hard work, dedication, respect, love and support for my family at this difficult time. This includes: The Deputies of the Sheriff's Department, the Missouri State Highway Patrol, Special Agent Megan Brown of the Federal Bureau of Investigation, Dr. Lindsey King Chief Medical Examiner, Prosecuting Attorney Carver, our friends and family, the countless volunteers and our community. Without all of you, today would not be possible. Thank you." Jonathan took another drink of water, then continued, "Anyone who knows me, knows that I like my privacy. I believe that no matter who you are, everyone has that right. I understand that when you are in the limelight or you're a public figure that you give up some privacy, but that is not the case with my family or I. We were thrown into the public eye by a devastating event, put under a microscope and had our lives judged. Any talks about Faith or I having an affair, is out of the question. Neither of us did anything outside of our marriage, without the other one knowing about it. We had an agreement that our marriage would be open and we would be honest with each other. I know many of you do not agree with it, but it worked for Faith and I. She did at one point have a sexual relationship with the man that is in custody. But Faith had ended that relationship about a month before her death. That was about the time that we decided to go to couples therapy, end our open marriage and have a marriage with just the two of us. We were happy, looking forward to spending our lives together with our children." Tears were coming down his face, he took a moment to wipe them away. He cleared his throat, "Let me reiterate Faith and I both participated in the open marriage; we, like everyone else, had ups and downs in our relationship but always knew we loved each other. I won't go any further into this, going forward from today, I would appreciate privacy in this matter.

Mr. DeNoyer received a phone call earlier this week from an individual who used a threatening tone and tried to blackmail me for money. I want that person to know, whoever you are, I will never pay you a dime! I filed a police report and the ball is in their hands now. My hope for the future is that the killer does what is right; confess to the terrible acts you committed. If you have an ounce of compassion left inside of you, you will save my children all the heart-breaking details of how their beautiful mother was brutally beaten, viciously raped, and savagely mutilated." He folded the paper back up, putting it back in his pocket.

He took another drink of water. "I want to describe the true Faith, not what has been portrayed here recently. Faith was the best person I knew, she loved horseback riding, hosting fundraising events for every charity, she was learning how to fly, spending time with her friends and family. But the thing she loved the most was being a mom and a wife. Faith was a great wife, but she was an awesome mom. Faith adored our children, she loved spending time out in the garden with them, teaching them about plants and animals. Faith used every moment to teach them about something. She taught them how to be caring, thoughtful, respectful, loving, and unselfish. Faith, believe it or not, taught me those same qualities as well. I'm a better man since having her in my life. Faith took our children every Sunday to church and did her best to follow what is right, we all fall short because we are human and she would be the first to tell you that she is not perfect. But Faith believed people deserve second chances. I know she would want me, all of us, to forgive the person who did this. She would want us to use this situation for something good, that's why I hope everyone will follow in my lead. I plan on donating a combined $1 million to the charities that were Faith's passions. I would request that anyone wanting to honor Faith or wanting to do something to make a difference in her name, please donate to any charity. I don't care if it's a dollar or hundred thousand dollars, anything helps and everything makes a difference. That's what she would have wanted. Thank you." Jonathan stepped away from the podium to let Victor up.

"Mr. Ross will take a few questions now."

The reporters that have been sitting and listening patiently. They now came alive, shouting questions.

Victor pointed to a young woman. "Did you know the Sheriff and Mrs. Ross were having a sexual relationship at the time they were having it?"

Jonathan stood back behind the podium. "Yes, I did," he answered.

"Were there ever political favors that Mrs. Ross or you received because they were in a sexual relationship?" She immediately followed up with.

"No. To my knowledge I never received any kind of favors or special treatment because of the relationship that Faith had with the Sheriff." Victor pointed to the next reporter.

"Did you, Mr. Ross, ever personally talk with Mr. Lewis?"

"No, I have never met with or talked to Mr. Lewis personally. I do know that he was a waiter for a company that Faith hired to cater events or parties that we had, but to my knowledge I never had any run-ins with him." Victor nodded to the next reporter.

"Did you and Mrs. Ross ever have a sexual relationship with the same person?"

"Yes, we did. No, I will not name anyone, nor tell you whether it was a male or female."

"Were you two involved in swinging, sharing or orgies?"

"Yes. Does anyone have a question that doesn't involve our sex life?"

A woman in the back raised her hand.

Jonathan pointed to her, "Yes, Ma'am."

"Do you hope for the death penalty in this case?"

"Good question!" he answered. He rubbed the bridge of his nose, "I would rather see him waste away in a prison cell, then fall asleep strapped to a table and not wake up. Now, if I knew he would suffer the same way Faith did, absolutely I would support the death penalty. But seeing how that's not going to happen, let him rot inside that cell."

Someone shouted the next question, "What was the demand the blackmailer made?"

"I'm not going to comment on that, the police are handling that."

"Was it a male or female caller?"

"Again, that is a matter that the police are handling."

"Do you feel your wife's case was given special treatment, given your socioeconomic status in the community and the State, for that matter?"

Jonathan didn't know how to answer this question. "I will be honest with you; I hope that had nothing to do with it. I would like to think, if this happened to anyone, the police would work just as hard as they did for my wife."

"Last question," Victor shouted.

"Are you willing to talk with Mr. Lewis to try and convince him to confess to the murder?"

"I would be willing to do anything, if that meant he did the right thing and confessed. Thank you again everyone."

Victor led Jonathan out to the waiting room.

Jonathan shook Victor's hand. "Thank you, Victor. I guess this will be the last time we see each other."

Victor was a bit confused, "Why do you say that Jonathan, the case isn't closed yet. Plus, they still have to get his confession or there is going to be a trial."

Jonathan smiled at him, "Vic, they have the right guy. Everyone knows it, now it is just a matter of time until he confesses or we go to trial. Either way, the police know I committed no crime, so I don't need a big expense lawyer like you, to waste my money on."

"It's not about whether you committed a crime or not, you did withhold information from the police. We may need to deal with that later on down the road," Victor answered him.

"Vic. You're fired. Oh, by the way, sorry about the bathroom. Sometimes I can't control myself." Jonathan patted him on the arm and walked out of his office.

Prosecuting Attorney Bo Carver was waiting patiently with Adam's lawyer, Mr. Hartz, for the guards to bring Adam down to the interview room. Bo wanted to talk with him and discuss a possible deal that can be made. They waited for what seemed like an hour, when they finally brought Adam into the room.

"Can the restraints be removed, please?" Ronald asked.

Bo looked at the guard, "Can you release his restraints?" The guard shook his head, "I can only remove the handcuffs, the ankles have to stay on, it's protocol." Bo gave the guard the go-ahead nod to release his hands.

"My client has not been convicted of any crime, yet he is still treated like a criminal!"

Bo rolled his eyes and sat down. Adam and Ronald sat down; Ronald picked Adam up a soda from the vending machine. Adam opened it and took a drink.

"Oh my God, that is good."

"Adam, P.A. Carver requested this meeting with you, I'm here as your legal counsel. You can stop this at any time you want, ok?"

"Ok… What would you like to talk about Mr. Carver?"

"You're charged with First-degree murder. Now I'm sure Mr. Hartz has told you the penalty if convicted."

"Yes, he has explained it in detail."

"Good, I'm here to offer you a deal. If you plead guilty to First-degree murder, then we will drop the death penalty. You will get life imprisonment without possibility of parole."

Adam laughed, looking at Ronald, "Are you serious? I'm innocent. There is no way I'm taking that deal!"

"Maybe you want to discuss it with your attorney before you turn it down." Adam shook his head, holding his frustration back.

Ronald spoke up, "My client has made it clear to myself and to you, that he will not plead guilty to a crime he did not commit."

Bo opened his briefcase, he pulled a thick folder out, setting it down on the table, "Adam, let me be honest with you. The evidence against you is overwhelming. We have eyewitness testimony, blood evidence, the text messages between Faith and you… you don't have a credible alibi for the time period of her death and the cherry on the top is I have undeniable DNA proof that puts your semen and pubic hairs on the victim and at the crime scene. That's what we call a slam dunk case."

"Mr. Lewis already said no to your deal, unless there is something else you would like to discuss or another offer you would like to make. This conversation is over."

"As you wish, Mr. Hartz. You may want to convey to your client that here in Missouri we actually use the death penalty." Bo gathered his things and stormed out of the interview room. *This is ridiculous,* he thought, *all the evidence they have on him and he still is proclaiming that he is innocent.* Bo knows that Jonathan doesn't want a trial, but the way things are looking, they will be going to trial.

Ronald sat across from Adam, since Bo left. Adam is sweating and almost in tears. "Ron, what the hell are we going to do! I know all the evidence they have against me, but I swear, I didn't have anything to do with her death."

"I know Adam, we are going to have to take it one step at a time. I will poke holes in their evidence where I can, and you wait until I get Jonathan Ross on the stand. By the time I'm done with him, the whole world will see the real Faith Ross."

"What do you mean by that, Ron?" Adam asked.

"She slept with a lot of people Adam, not just you and Mr. Ross. Faith got around; the police never looked into all the people she had an affair with. I want to know how far they looked into the former Sheriff Bennett."

"Ron, I don't want to drag Faith through the mud."

"Adam, we will be fighting for your life. My job is to create reasonable doubt in everything the prosecution presents, including the fact that there are a lot of men out there that are suspects. That's the cold hard truth, Adam."

Adam felt hopeless, realizing he would die in prison one way or the other. He wished that he never had gotten drunk and high that night. He wished that Faith never saw him with Lexi, maybe none of this would have happened. This felt like a horrible nightmare, one that he could not wake up from.

"What is going through your mind, Adam?" Ronald asked.

"I was wishing I never got drunk, high and ending up passing out that night. Shit, I wish Faith never would have seen me and Lexi. Then none of this would have happened."

"I have gone to that bar, asked dozens of people if they remember seeing a woman like you described no one remembers seeing her. They have security cameras but the only one that works is the one watching the cash register. I haven't given up and I won't. But we may have to consider some options."

"I'm not pleading guilty to first-degree murder! That's life imprisonment with no chance of getting out! I will go to trial, just to see Jonathan and that asshole Sheriff Bennett tell the jury everything they knew and did!"

Ronald paid attention to details, he had to correct Adam, "He is actually former Sheriff Bennett."

"You know what I mean, Ron."

"Listen, let's take the next couple of days to think. I know they have substantial evidence against you. But P.A. Carver watched Jonathan's press conference, just like I did. Jonathan does not want this going to trial because he knows the flood gates will open and the media will bring every dirty

228

little secret to light. Let's wait and see what the next couple of days bring us."

"Ok. What choice do I have?"

"Don't give up, that's half the battle."

P.A. Carver has been trying to contact Jonathan for a few days. He called Victor DeNoyer's office and was told that he no longer represented Mr. Ross. He was shocked by that news; Victor was the best lawyer money could buy in St. Louis, he waited for a day because he thought that Jonathan's new lawyer would call him, and when the call never came, he tried calling him on his cell phone, nothing. The number had been disconnected; he tried calling his office, his secretary took a message and promised to give it to Mr. Ross. He was getting nowhere; it's been three days now. He could wait no longer.

He phoned his assistant telling her he would be late this morning; he was going to take a drive out to Jonathan's house and see if he was there. He pulled up to the gate, and an armed guard was standing in front of it. The guard held his hand up like a stop sign, Bo stopped, rolled down his window.

"Yes, I'm Prosecuting Attorney Bo Carver, I need to see Mr. Jonathan Ross please. Tell him it is an urgent matter."

The guard pulled his radio out of his waistband and spoke into it. Bo could not hear what he was saying but whatever he said it worked because the gate opened and he was waved through. Bo parked; he has never been to the Ross's house. The home is stunning and the property even better. Bo refocuses and tells himself to remain professional. As he is walking up to the door, a young woman opens it and greets him.

"Hello, Mr. Carver. Please come in. I'm Hailee."

"Good morning, Hailee."

"Can I take your coat for you?"

"Please, thank you" Bo handed her his coat, watching her hang it up in the closet. He took a moment to get a quick glance of the beautiful spiral-like staircase; he wished he could get a tour of the house and grounds but that was not what today is about.

"Follow me, Mr. Carver," Hailee led him to the dining room. "Please have a seat, Mr. Ross will be down in a few minutes."

"Ok, thank you Hailee."

"Mr. Carver, what would you like to drink? I have water, coffee, tea and orange juice."

"Coffee would be great."

He was sitting patiently alone when Jonathan entered the room. Bo stood up and greeted him. "Mr. Ross, thank you for seeing me, I didn't want to barge in on you but I haven't been able to get a hold of you for a few days."

"It's no bother, I disconnected my old number and got a new one. I was going to call you and… I won't lie to you Mr. Carver; I needed a few days to myself. I don't know if you are aware but I fired Victor DeNoyer as my representative."

"I called him to try and set up a meeting with you, I was informed that you were no longer his client."

"I hope you don't think this is impolite, but do you care if we are a little less formal today?" Jonathan asked.

"Not at all, Mr. Ross."

"Great, let's eat out in the sun room, don't worry it is heated, we will be comfortable."

230

They walked into the kitchen where Hailee was preparing breakfast. "Don't mind us Hailee, change of plans though, we are going to sit out in the sun room," Jonathan said.

"Smells great," Bo said as he followed Jonathan out to the sun room. He wasn't hungry until he smelled her cooking. They sat at a little table, this was more Bo's style, he was glad Jonathan suggested this.

"Mr. Ross, you have a beautiful home."

"Thank you. Tell you the truth, I feel like it is a prison here lately, I had to hire armed guards just so reporters can't come onto my property; they call every day, all day. My daughter can't even go school without at least two news vans following her. That's why I just want all of this to be over so we can be left in peace and properly mourn our loss."

Hailee brought the coffee in and told them it would be just a few more minutes for the food.

"Sorry Mr. Carver, you didn't come here to listen to my problems."

"Mr. Ross, I don't mind listening to you. I can only imagine what you and your family are going through. It is hard enough suffering this kind of loss, but given your and Mrs. Ross's status in the community makes it ten times more difficult."

"Thank you, Mr. Carver," Jonathan said, taking a sip of his coffee.

Hailee brought out the food; big fluffy pancakes, scrambled eggs, sausage patties, bacon, biscuits and country gravy. Hailee looked at them both. "No business talk until after you have eaten." She looked at Bo, "Mr. Carver, that goes for you too."

"Yes, Ma'am," he said, taking a bite of bacon. They sat there eating and discussing the upcoming holidays. Jonathan talked about going to Galveston, Texas for Christmas, that Faith loved going there. They fell in love with it on their honeymoon, he talked about how that was their last trip together before she was killed. Bo listened and ate his breakfast, trying to remember the last time he had a meal like this that wasn't at a restaurant. They got done eating; Hailee returned to clear the mess.

"Ok, Mr. Carver. I have sat through enough board meetings to know when its bad news. Give it to me straight."

Bo smiled, "Mr. Ross, it's not bad news, I know you said you don't want this to go to trial. I need to warn you, I believe that is where we will end up. Mr. Lewis is unwilling to take the plea deal that I offered."

"What was the deal?"

"That he pleads guilty to first-degree murder and I take the death penalty off. He would get life imprisonment without possibility of parole."

"Why wouldn't he take that deal?" Jonathan genuinely asked.

"He maintains that he did not kill your wife."

"Maybe he just needs time to think about it."

"Mr. Lewis has had enough time to think it over, every moment that goes by I don't hear from his attorney, I feel stronger that we are going to trial."

Jonathan shook his head, "Mr. Carver, that's unacceptable to me. I don't want my children to know the details of how their mother was murdered."

"Mr. Ross, I appreciate the fact that you want to save your children this pain, but I can't make him take a deal. I'm confident that I have more than enough evidence to convince any jury that he is guilty." Bo opened his briefcase and pulled out a large binder. "Mr. Ross, we have eyewitness testimony from one of Mr. Lewis's neighbors, who saw Mrs. Ross and him arguing the day of her death. I have DNA evidence from the crime scene that matches Mr. Lewis, as well as hairs that match him. We have his side of the story that doesn't add up with any of the text messages between him and Mrs. Ross. I have had cases that don't have this much evidence and I have gotten convictions; I have no worries about this case."

Jonathan was getting frustrated; he wanted no part of a courtroom. That meant more time, more media and a lot more information coming out. "Mr. Carver, try to see it from my point of view. Faith was brutally raped and beaten once already, a trial would be like doing it again to her, only this time the media has a front row seat!"

Bo could tell he was getting upset. "Mr. Ross, I know trials can be hard for the families to go through, but we have a tremendous amount of physical evidence which you don't always have in cases like this. Try not to get hung up on him not confessing, he is only walking himself closer to the death chamber," he said, trying to reassure him that no matter what, Adam was going to prison.

Jonathan tried a new approach with Bo, "Let me ask you a question, Mr. Carver. What if you offer him a different deal? Let's say second-degree murder, he would receive the maximum penalty of thirty years and after that parole, do you think he would go for that deal?"

Bo was stunned. He never had a victim's family fight so hard for a confession, for the sole reason of not wanting a trial. Especially when there is a high probability that the accused would get the death penalty. This situation is like nothing he has dealt with before; he felt Jonathan was trying to rush the process. Bo wanted to make sure he wasn't misunderstanding.

"Mr. Ross, I want to make sure I'm understanding you correctly. You don't want this case to go to trial, would you be alright if Mr. Lewis was offered a deal for a lesser crime and would make it possible for him to possibly get out of prison?"

Jonathan didn't like the way it sounded when repeated back to him. "When you say it like that, it sounds like I'm heartless!"

"Mr. Ross, people would be outraged. They would throw me out of office if I did not stand by the principles and morals that got me elected. I always try to take into consideration what the victim's family wants. But you have to understand that there are a lot of people emotionally involved with this crime. People look at your family and think, if it can happen to them, it can happen to me. Everyone wants justice, including the State of Missouri. I'm sorry Mr. Ross, but this was a violent act, justice needs to be swift, certain, and severe."

Jonathan nodded in agreement with him. "I understand, Mr. Carver. But if he pleads guilty, everyone wins."

"Mr. Ross, I cannot appear to be soft on crime, it goes against everything that I campaigned for," Bo said, sticking to his guns.

Jonathan straightened up in his chair. "It should be my decision Bo, it's my wife and family that has to run through the gauntlet. Let's be honest with one another, that defense attorney is going to crucify me if I get on that stand. Then after me, you got that piece of shit former Sheriff Bennett who will no doubt tell every detail of how he and my wife were together. But he will do it just because he hates me, it will be a circus!"

Bo was surprised by two things: the first being that Jonathan called him by his first name. Secondly, Jonathan was finally being honest, when he said that he and the former Sheriff

234

will decimate the Prosecution case. In Bo's opinion that's the only two people the defense would have to call, they would cast doubt in some of the juror's minds. Bo put his binder back into his briefcase, "Jonathan, are you absolutely sure, this is what you want?"

"Yes!" he said without hesitation.

"Alright, I will need you to come into my office the day we make the announcement. I want you there standing right beside me and I want you to give a brief statement, telling them you came to me with this deal. Those are my terms; I will reach out to Mr. Lewis's attorney today to tell them. If they don't take this deal, then we go to trial."

Jonathan stood up and extended his hand. Bo shook his hand as he stood up.

"It's a deal! Mr. Carver."

Jonathan walked Bo to the door, Hailee helped him put his coat on. "Hailee, thank you for the wonderful meal. Mr. Ross is lucky to have someone with your talent in the kitchen, working for him. If something ever happens, I will hire you in a minute."

"Thank you, sir. Be careful out there Mr. Carver."

Bo turned to Jonathan, "I will call you as soon as I know something."

Jonathan nodded, "Thank you, Mr. Carver. You are one of the last truly good men left."

Bo got into his car, driving slowly away from the house, realizing the old adage was true; don't judge a book by its cover. Jonathan had a beautiful house, good looking wife, tons of money, seemingly the perfect life. All of it was just a cover. When you looked just below the surface of his life, it was a complete disaster. Jonathan didn't want this case going to trial because he knew secrets were going to come out.

When Bo arrived at his office, his secretary gave him his messages. "Anything from Mr. Hartz?"

"No sir."

"Can you get his number and bring it to me, please?"

"Right away, Mr. Carver."

Bo was mentally exhausted, feeling deflated. Nothing has been routine about this case, it has been craziness throughout the whole investigation. He wants no foolishness with regards to the Prosecution side. With that in mind, he dialed Mr. Hartz's number.

Ronald picks up on the second ring, "Hello?"

"Ron, it's Bo Carver. How are you doing?"

Ronald was surprised to be hearing from him. This must be something of importance. "Yes, hi. I'm doing good, and you?"

"Doing just fine, thank you."

"What can I do for you, Bo?"

"I was wondering if you could spare a few minutes to talk?"

"Of course, what's up?"

"Ron, I have a new deal on the table, before I tell you, you need to know that this deal comes with an expiration date. Forty-eight hours your client has to decide if he wants it or not. At the end of forty-eight hours, the deal is void and we go to trial. Understand?"

Ronald was taken back by how direct Bo was being and that the deal came with an expiration date, "Ok, I understand. Why the sense of urgency, Bo? That's not a lot of time to let my client think about it."

"Because I'm not messing around with this deal. This is the final offer for him and it's a better offer than I want to give."

"I see, Jonathan Ross breathing down your neck?"

Bo was beginning to get irritated. "I will email it to you, discuss it with your client. The timer starts when I push send, Ron. Have a good day." He hung up the receiver. He felt sick to his stomach, guilty even. He was mad at himself for even offering that kind of deal, he felt like he was betraying his oath of office. Bo knew that he would have never offered anyone else this kind of deal, he would rather go to trial and risk it all. He was hoping that Adam didn't take the deal, because he would go after him with extreme prejudice, he would ask for the death penalty and watch as they put this monster down.

Ronald was at the gym when Bo called. He rushed back to his office to check his email, opened it, and was completely shocked by the offer. They never offer something like this in these situations, he thought to himself. He changed into a suit and rushed to give Adam the news. He sped all the way to the county jail, making it there in record time; it felt like everyone was going in slow motion today. They took twenty minutes to check him in and another fifteen minutes to get Adam from his cell.

Adam walked into the interview room to find Ronald pacing the room. The guard undid his handcuffs, but left the shackles on as always. Adam took a seat at the table.

"Adam, I have news," he told him as he sat across from him.

"Ok, what the hell is it?"

Ronald pulled the papers from the file folder, "Alright, they sent a new deal. I was told this is the final offer, if you don't take this, we're going to trial."

"Ok. What is the offer?"

"First, you only have 44 hours to decide whether to take the offer or not, they gave you 48 hours from the time it was sent to me. Time is critical and we have to be smart about this. I have never seen them offer this kind of deal when they have the amount of physical evidence that they do."

Adam was losing his patience. "What is the goddamn offer, Ron!"

"Plead guilty to second-degree murder, sentence of twenty-five to thirty years, and then paroled."

"What! That's a lifetime!"

"Adam, I advise you as your attorney to strongly consider this offer. They have enough evidence to put you away for the rest of your life. They are only offering this to you because the family does not want this to go to trial. This is a sweetheart deal, Adam."

"Not for me it isn't! I get to spend the next twenty-five to thirty years in a cell!"

Ronald was normally very patient with his clients, but he could only take so much. "Adam! I know this is not the deal or outcome you want. But this deal is the best you are going to get. If you don't take this deal, all bullshit aside, you are going to die in prison. Whether it's by lethal injection or old age, you will die there. This deal makes sure you get to see the light of day outside of prison in the future. It's your decision."

They sat in silence for ten minutes, when Adam spoke. "Ron, I know it may not mean much to you, but I have to say it. I will take this deal, I don't want to die in here, but I never killed anyone. I did a lot of stupid shit in my life but I swear I never hurt her; they have the wrong person."

Ron didn't know exactly what to say to him. "Adam, I'm sorry. I know you don't see any silver lining in this, but in prison you can get a free education in anything you want. You have access to all the evidence that the police have."

Adam thought about it. "How do I go about getting all of it?"

"I will help you, I will go a step further, if you find anything that looks interesting you let me know and I will look into it."

Adam nodded. Ronald slid the offer over to him and handed him a pen. "I need you to sign that, I will fax it over to them and that will be it."

Adam picked up the pen, it was the heaviest pen he ever held. "Damn Ron, this is a heavy pen." As Adam signed his name on the line, he chuckled, "Signing my life away for real."

Ron took the paper and pen back. "Adam, I have no idea what you're going through, but I can tell you this. You can handle being locked in prison, but don't get locked in your mind. Don't let them beat you like that. I will get you all the files from your case, if you're not the killer, then the real one is in that file. You just have to find them."

"Thanks Ron, I will see you around."

Adam was escorted back to his cell. He felt defeated taking that deal, he was innocent. What choice did he have, he didn't want to die in prison. It was the only rational choice he could make. Adam laid in his bunk the rest of the day thinking about what had led him to this moment - the night he met Faith. He cared for her, he knew that, but did she feel the same way? Was she really going to leave Jonathan? Did

239

Faith and he really have any chance at all? That was the first of many nights that he cried himself to sleep.

Bo called Jonathan, telling him that Mr. Lewis took the deal and he would be making the announcement in the morning when everything was finalized. Jonathan was overjoyed that it was over. It wouldn't be long and he would have his life back, to be able to hop a plane and go be on a beach with Claire, maybe Skyler too, he thought. Jonathan was going to use this as a fresh start. He was going to focus more on him and the things he wanted. Jonathan was not going to waste any more time. He picked up his phone and called Claire.

"Yes, Jonathan," she answered.

"How would you like to get away from here for a few weeks?"

"Are you serious? Do not even joke with me."

"Tomorrow be ready and of course Douglas. You can meet me at the airport and we will fly down to Galveston. I already got a beautiful penthouse, it's close to everything, all you have to bring is clothes."

"Jonathan, are you sure this is the right time to be going on vacation?"

"Can you keep a secret, until after tomorrow?"

"Yes," she answered.

"Adam has pleaded guilty, no trial. Thank God!"

"Oh my God. Really?"

"Yeah, Bo and I sat down the other day and talked. I talked him into giving him a better offer and told him I would support him publicly on it. They are going to announce it tomorrow afternoon, all of this is behind us and we can start our journey."

"What did he say about the plea deal?"

"He asked me if I was sure I wanted to make this offer because he normally never gives that kind of deal, when they have the amount of evidence they have."

"No, Jonathan. I mean what did Adam say about the deal?"

"How the hell should I know, he took it, I assume he liked it enough. What is with the twenty questions, Claire!"

"I don't know, I'm curious."

"Don't worry your pretty little self about matters that don't concern you. Pack a bag, tell Douglas to pack one as well, meet me at the airport tomorrow. Easy enough for you?"

"How do you go from being sweet, to an asshole in the blink of an eye?"

"Well Claire, I would have to say, it's a gift."

"Yeah, here is another gift for you, Jonathan," Claire hung up on him.

Jonathan hated being hung up on. It drove him crazy; he called her again. Went straight to voicemail. He called again, straight to voicemail. Angrily, he called Douglas's phone.

"Hey, Jonathan! What's up?"

"Am I on speaker phone?"

"No."

"Are you home with Claire?"

"Yes, is everything ok?"

"Put her on the phone, please."

"Sure, let me go get her." He walked upstairs to where she was. Jonathan heard Douglas tell her he was on the phone for her.

"Nice try asshole!" She hung up on him again.

Jonathan was fuming at this point. "This bitch, who does she think she is dealing with!" He shouted out loud. He was about to text her when he realized he had his phone and he stopped. He opened his desk drawer, pulled out one of the prepaid phones that wasn't in his name, nor could be traced back to him. He began his message.

Claire was sitting in her closet, trying to choose what to bring with her on this trip with Jonathan. She knew he was pissed off, but she didn't care. He needed to know that the way he talked to Faith was not going to fly with her. She was letting him stew for a little bit, she would call him after she got done packing. Her phone dinged; she knew it was Jonathan. It was from an unknown number.

Unknown 3:43pm: Claire, you better answer your phone when I call!

Claire 3:45pm: Really?? You are too chicken shit to text me from your own phone! Don't tell me what to do!

Unknown 3:46pm: Why do you insist on being a bitch? When I'm just trying to do something nice with you.

Claire 3:48pm: Don't act like this trip is for me. You mean to tell me you're not going to want anything that's between my legs?

Unknown 3:49pm: STOP!!

Claire 3:50pm: What is it? Is it getting hard, thinking about how tight and wet I'm getting?

Unknown 3:52pm: I'm sorry. Alright, I'm sorry. The stress is going to kill me! I want to be with you more than anything. I am tired of hiding from the world. I'm in love with you, Claire.

Claire 3:53pm: Thank you for apologizing. My bag is packed, I'm so ready to get away with you. I love you too, Jonathan. You deserve the best and I want to be the best, but you have to be the best for me as well.

Unknown 3:55pm: I promise, I will do better.

Claire 3:57pm: You should invite our friend from last time to join us! Make things interesting.

Unknown 3:59pm: I will call her and see if she is available.

Claire 4:02pm: Call me later. Going to work out.

Jonathan arrived at Bo's office about ten minutes before the announcement. Bo had just gotten back from finalizing the deal, he had just sat down in his chair when he was informed Jonathan had arrived. Bo went out to greet him, "Mr. Ross, good afternoon. How are you doing today?"

"Good afternoon, Mr. Carver. I'm actually doing rather good today. I am happy to be putting all of this behind us, start to move forward."

Bo smiled and led him into his office. "Mr. Ross, we only have a few minutes until we go out, are there any questions you have for me regarding anything?"

Jonathan did have a question. "Yes. Is it officially done with? He will be going to prison?"

"Please, come into my office. We can talk more freely there." Jonathan walked past Bo, into his office, taking a sit on the sofa.

Bo closed the door and sat down. "To answer your question, yes. It is officially a closed case as far as the police investigation is concerned. Mr. Lewis's attorney and I spoke with the judge that will preside over the hearing tomorrow. He looked over the plea deal and seemed ok with it, as long as you have not changed your mind regarding it."

"No, I'm happy with what is in place. But I do have a question about this hearing, what is that about?"

"The hearing tomorrow is so the judge can read the plea deal for the record, make sure the defendant understands his rights, understands that he is pleading guilty to second-degree murder and that he is happy with the way his lawyer has represented him. When he tells the judge yes to all three of those questions, the judge will then decide his sentence. The penalty for second-degree murder is between ten to thirty years. In the deal we offered we put the sentence at twenty-five to thirty years. Now the judge can honor that or give his own sentence, but having talked with him this morning, I feel the judge is going to honor the deal, giving Mr. Lewis twenty-five years."

"Is there any chance of the judge not accepting his guilty plea?"

"As long as Mr. Lewis doesn't answer no to any of those questions we just talked about, the judge will accept the deal. It's up to Mr. Lewis to keep his end of the deal, but let me assure you Mr. Ross, if he doesn't hold his end up. I will take his ass to trial and walk him myself to death row."

Jonathan smiled, "Mr. Carver, you have gone above and beyond for my family and I. I will never forget this. You are true to your word and I appreciate that." Jonathan stood up and shook Bo's hand, "Are you ready to go and get this done?" he asked Bo.

"Let's go do this!"

They walked out of the office, both relieved that all of this was coming to a conclusion. Bo walked into the large press conference room, he stood in front of the podium, Jonathan was on his right and some of Bo's colleagues that helped with the case were on his left. The room got quiet.

"Ladies and gentlemen, I have a brief statement and Mr. Ross will then make a statement. I will take questions at the end; Mr. Ross will not be taking questions. First, I would like to thank all the men and women that worked hundreds of hours on this case; without your help we would not be here today. I would like to thank Mr. Ross and his family for allowing the investigators and my team to do our jobs. It is never easy when a family has to go through this but they have gone above and beyond, by their words of encouragement and always being available to us. Adam Lewis has signed a full confession for the brutal rape and murder of Faith Ross on the twentieth of November. This was a plea deal that was worked out between both sides and agreed upon. The people of this county can sleep well tonight, knowing the perpetrator is and will remain behind bars for a long time. At this time, I would like to pass it over to Mr. Jonathan Ross."

Jonathan shook Bo's hand and everyone else's hand that was standing next to Bo, thanking them all in front of the cameras. He finally stepped up to the podium. "Thank you everyone for all your hard work, dedication and respect for my family and Faith. I would like to thank Prosecuting Attorney Bo Carver, for his kindness and compassion. I know many of you don't see the work that goes on behind the scenes, but I did and I want to thank you Mr. Carver for being a true man of your craft. You came to my home when I was at a low point, just to check in on me and my family. From the bottom of my heart, I appreciate that. You have walked with us through this whole process, offering explanation whenever needed. I am very pleased with the outcome. When Mr. Carver and I met, we talked about what justice we wanted. I told Mr. Carver that I wanted a deal to be made. I wanted to spare my children and my wife's memory from the traumatic experience of a trial. Mr. Carver explained to me that there is a plethora of evidence against

245

Mr. Lewis, that I should rethink my decision. I told Mr. Carver that justice needs to be swift, certain and severe. I believe that this plea deal covers all of that, as well as honors the memory of Faith. It punishes the guilty, allows for healing and forgiveness, but gives a second chance to someone who needs it. In closing, I would like to ask for continued privacy in this difficult time and your continued prayers for my family. Thank you."

Bo stepped back to the podium. "Thank you, Mr. Ross, for your kind words. With that, we will take questions now, in an orderly fashion. We will go around the room starting here."

"What is the charge Mr. Lewis is pleading guilty to?"

Bo was dreading this question, as much as he was dreading answering it. "Mr. Lewis pled guilty to second-degree murder."

The room erupted with shouting, "Are you kidding me…", "What is wrong with you?", "Where is justice for Faith!"

Bo slammed his hand down. "QUIET!! Now, I said this was going to be conducted in an orderly fashion and I intend on keeping it that way. I don't mind answering all of your questions, but I will not stand up here, being disrespected or second guessed. You all better conduct yourselves in a matter that is professional or we will end this right now!" The room got quiet. Bo made sure to make eye contact with every person he could. "Ok. Next question"

"Mr. Carver, what is the maximum sentence?"

"The sentencing guidelines for second-degree murder is between ten and thirty years. Mr. Lewis's deal is for twenty-five to thirty years."

"Why second-degree and not first-degree murder?"

"After taking time, consideration and talking with Mr. Ross and his family, second-degree was decided to be justice."

"Were you afraid of going to trial Mr. Carver?"

"No. Like I said before, we felt like this deal was justice and that's what we wanted."

"Mr. Ross, are you upset that Mr. Lewis could possibly walk the streets again?"

"Mr. Ross is not answering any questions…" Bo felt a hand on his shoulder, then heard Jonathan whisper in his ear, "Let me answer some questions, put this shit to bed." Bo gave him a nod and let him have the floor.

Jonathan adjusted the microphone. "You guys are brutal. To answer your question, no; I'm not upset. When I spoke with Mr. Carver, he told the facts of the case and walked me through the possible outcomes. He shared his opinions with me, as well as listened to my concerns. I told him that my family and I agree that we would like to see a deal be made that gives us justice without going through a trial. I had no choice in the matter of looking at the pictures, finding out the graphic details of Faith's final moments on earth and knowing the amount of pain she suffered at the hands of that monster. That son of a bitch took my wife! He is not getting my children. They will remain innocent, I'm not ready for them to see the evil that is in the world. I know one day they will have questions about their mother. When that day comes, I will talk with them. I will explain what happened, but I will also tell them that Mr. Carver, along with all the other heroes involved in this investigation, gave us justice!"

Chapter 13

10 Years Later

Adam is sitting in the chair across from Samantha González, a young investigative reporter from New York. She works for the big national news agency that Adam agreed to do an interview with for the ten-year anniversary of Faith's death. They are doing a special about the crime, and they are getting Adam's story for the first time. They were setting up the lights and making sure they had the correct camera angles when Adam noticed that Samantha looked nervous.

"Aren't I the one that should be nervous," he said to her, trying to break the ice.

She laughed, "Is it that noticeable?"

Adam nodded his head.

"Mr. Lewis, forgive me this is my first-time interviewing someone that I have followed and had a big interest in since the beginning."

"Please, call me Adam. Since the beginning, you can't be that old, Ms. González"

She giggled. "I will call you Adam if you call me Samantha. It's true, I was in high school when Mrs. Ross was killed, I have all the press clippings and my notes from back then."

Adam was confused; he didn't think Faith's killing got national coverage back then. Samantha was smiling because she could tell he was confused about how she would have heard about this crime in New York. "I'm originally from St Louis, I moved when I started college. But I grew up and went to school in St. Louis City."

"Ok, that makes more sense. I was wondering how you would have heard about it up in New York, because back then Faith's killing didn't get national coverage. This must be exciting for you then to do a story so close to your home. Adds a little pressure," he said, smiling at her.

"It does, Adam. But I'm confident in us both that we will do great. If there is a question that you're not comfortable with answering, just say the next question. If you want to elaborate on something that I said, please feel free to."

"Yes, Ma'am. I think we are going to kick a hornet's nest with this interview. A few people are going to be surprised, that's all I can say."

The two sat there a few more minutes until a gentleman told them they were ready. Samantha took a drink of water. "Adam, are you ready?"

"Yes, I am, Samantha."

"Adam, what has the last ten years been like for you?"

He took a breath, and exhaled. "The first year was the most difficult; I was angry, hurt, and depressed. Believe it or not I met some good people here that took me under their wing and helped me adjust to this world. Prison is a completely different world than outside of these walls. Once I was adjusted, I started to take college classes. I earned my Bachelor degree in Criminology and Criminal Justice. I went on to get my Juris Doctorate degree two years ago. Sense then I have been working on my case, along with Ronald Hartz, my attorney through all of this and my best friend."

"That's impressive. Is that why your attorney isn't here today with us, because you are representing yourself?"

"Yes, that is one reason."

"What is the other reason?"

"Ron, currently at the time of this interview, is meeting with police regarding new evidence that has come to surface. I'm sorry that is incorrect, it is not new evidence, it has always been there, but someone dropped the ball and did not follow through with proper procedure and get it analyzed."

"Adam, you signed a confession letter, stating that you killed Mrs. Faith Ross. What does new evidence matter?"

"I recanted my confession. I signed a plea deal to second-degree murder; I didn't want to spend the rest of my life behind bars for a crime I did not commit. It was the only option I had at the time."

Samantha stayed professional, keeping her personal opinion out of it. "What kind of evidence, Adam?"

"DNA evidence, Samantha." She remained stone faced, even though she was thinking what does it matter. Adam could feel her vibes and knew what she was thinking. "I know what you're thinking Samantha. What is the big deal about new DNA evidence, right?" She was reluctant to answer his question, until Adam said, "It's alright."

"Yes, that is exactly what I'm thinking, because they found your semen on the victim and at the crime scene."

"You are absolutely right, they did. But we will talk about that in a moment. Are you familiar with the facts of this case?"

"Yes I am."

"When I was arrested, they checked my entire body from head to toe, correct?"

"Yes."

"Do you know why they did that?"

"Yes. They were checking for marks or bruises you may have gotten in a struggle, or that you may have gotten from someone."

"Yes, that is correct. Did they photograph my entire body?"

Samantha was growing tired of this exchange, she wanted to get back to her asking the questions. "Yes, they took photographs. What does this have to do with anything, Adam?"

"Hold your horses, I'm getting there. What was the conclusion they made after examining my body and photographing it?"

"That you had no marks or bruises of any kind." She answered with a bored look on her face.

"Are you one-hundred percent sure with that answer?"

"Yes, Adam."

"The DNA evidence that is in question, was found underneath the victim's fingernails. That means Faith fought her attacker and scratched them. The police did not find any marks, scratches, or bruises on me because it says that right here in the evidence and shows it in the photographs they took. The only logical answer is that I'm not Faith's killer. Because it is skin, they were found under her nails and I did not have a scratch on my body."

Samantha's eyes lit up like a Christmas tree, she was not expecting that. Adam smiled, "I told you we were going to kick a hornet's nest with this interview today."

"Is this true, Adam? How did you find this out?" She was now on this roller coaster ride that she was excited to be on. *This is the kind interview that wins awards,* she thought to herself.

"We have been going through every piece of evidence and we came across a document stating all the evidence that was found at the crime scene and the victim. There was this DNA sample that they had from underneath her fingernails, that they never sent off to get analyzed."

"Is that what they are doing today?"

"Ronald went to them weeks ago; they finally sent it off and today they got the results back. I asked Ron if he would give us a call with the results."

"Alright. We will keep our fingers crossed for that phone call. What about all the other evidence against you? How do you explain all of that?"

Adam nodded his head in agreement with her. "I know it looks bad, but when you take the evidence piece by piece, it is all explainable."

They were two and half hours into the interview, when a guard knocked on the door. "Mr. Lewis, your attorney called and wanted a message passed on to you."

"Alright" The guard came in, leaned into Adam's ear and whispered something.

"Thank you, Carl."

"No problem, Mr. Lewis"

Samantha was on pins and needles as the guard walked out, closing the door behind him. She looked at Adam with anticipation. He was saying nothing, not being able to take it anymore she asked, "Is everything alright?"

"Yes, Ma'am."

"What was that about?"

"That was Ron, saying he is coming here to tell me in person."

"Are you nervous to find out?"

"There is some level of anxiety to learn the results"

252

"Why is that, Adam?"

"A lot is riding on this not being my DNA."

Samantha didn't say a word, she let the cameras capture the expression on his face realizing that it was all coming down to this one piece of evidence. When she finally broke the silence she asked, "Would you like to break until Ronald gets here?"

"Thank you, but I'm alright. Ronald is about two hours away, we can continue."

She smiled at him, "Ok, you know my next question then, explain it to us."

Adam cleared his throat and repositioned in his chair, "Let me start with the blatant circumstantial evidence, that they blew out of proportion."

This is what Samantha has been waiting for, she waited to hear what Adam had to say about all of this, how was he going to wiggle out of this mountain of evidence. *There is no way he has an explanation for every piece of evidence,* she thought to herself, but she sat there and listened, with as much of an open mind as she could.

"The police said that I lied in my interview with them, they are basing that off of me telling them Faith and I were in love, and that she was thinking of leaving her husband. The police said they had text messages between Faith and I that proved otherwise. They said if anything, it proved Faith had moved on from our affair and that she was repairing her relationship with her husband. I told them that Jonathan would check her phone, of course she is not going to say she is leaving him through a text message. I never lied during my interview; the police are using text messages to prove I lied. That doesn't prove a damn thing, except that two people were having problems in their relationship. Then, it doesn't look good that the police cannot verify my alibi for the night Faith was killed."

Samantha interrupted him, "Can you remind us, what was your alibi for that night?"

"I got drunk and high, then passed out. I don't remember anything. The police asked if anybody was with me or could have seen me, but I was by myself. Soaking up my sorrows."

"Why were you soaking up your sorrows," she asked.

"I thought my life could not get any worse than what it was at that moment."

"Were you wrong about that?"

Adam laughed, "Yes, totally wrong. If I knew then what I know now."

"Now I will move on to the solid physical evidence and the witness they had. The eyewitness they had was my neighbor, she lived two doors down from me, Alyssa Lopez. I have nothing against her, the police went door to door asking people if they saw or heard anything. She did what any good citizen would do, she told the police what she saw. They took a statement from her the day they arrested me. Her statement reads: I saw my neighbor running after a female with dark hair. They argued in the street for a few minutes before she drove off." Adam paused to get Samantha's reaction.

"What?" she asked him.

"The eyewitness's statement doesn't make sense; I will tell you why. When the police told me about their eyewitness and read me the statement, I said I caught Faith at the van and we had words. According to the eyewitness we were in the street arguing, then Faith drove off. How can we be arguing in the street one second, then Faith driving off another second."

"Maybe she wrote it down wrong, Adam," Samantha answered.

"Ok, then they should have gone and gotten that corrected. That's sloppy police work!"

"Adam, some may say it does not matter in the grand scheme of things."

Adam's voice was raising with each sentence he spoke, "If it's sloppy police work once, then who's to say it's not sloppy police work throughout this whole damn investigation and other cases! I mean this is my life, I'm an innocent man and have rotted in this prison for the last ten years of my life!" Adam yelled.

The guard flung open the door, "Mr. Lewis!" catching Adam and everyone else by surprise, "Is there a problem?"

Adam sat there a moment realizing that he was just shouting that last statement, "No, Carl. Sorry about that."

"There's no problem." Samantha said, coming to Adam's aid.

"Alright, Mr. Lewis, if you need to take a break to compose yourself that's fine."

Adam smiled at him, "Thank you. I'm fine, it won't happen again." Carl backed out, closing the door.

"You know, he's right. If you need a break we can," she told him.

"Thank you, Samantha. Obviously, this subject gets me emotional."

"Understandable. Anyone in your situation would be emotional."

255

"Let's move on to the blood evidence that they have. First, it's misleading. It is blood evidence, but they found only a few pin droplets on a piece of splintered wood in my shed and they knew exactly how it got there because I told them."

"Whose blood, was it?" Samantha asked for context.

"It was Faith's blood. How it got there is simple, the police knew she was at my trailer. I had an old wooden crate outside of my house that was trash. It had been sitting there for a few months because I never threw it away. On the day that she and I got into that argument, she came by my trailer unexpectedly. I was with a woman in my bedroom, Faith used the crate to stand up on it and look in. The reason why we know that happened is because police found her prints on my trailer. The crate broke, Faith fell down knocking other stuff over, that's the crash sound I heard outside. I got up to go check what it was, I saw Faith running away. I put shorts on and ran after her, that is what my neighbor saw unfolding at that time. Faith had cut her leg, that is where the blood came from. But when the police say they have blood evidence, it sounds like there were buckets of blood. When in reality, the amount of Faith's blood they found at my home was about the size of your pinky fingernail."

Samantha instinctively looked at her pinky fingernail for a moment. She then said, "Ok, Adam. What about the-"

Adam cut her off before she could even finish the sentence, "The semen and pubic hair, right?"

"How do you explain those, because those both definitely matched your DNA profile. The odds of any two unrelated samples having the same patterns are what? One in hundreds of billions. Is it safe to say that the semen and pubic hair found at the crime scene and on Faith are yours?" she asked.

Adam sat there in silence. This was the question he has been waiting for all along. This was the reason he decided to do the interview, it's the reason he and Ron had planned so carefully. This is the moment that Adam gets to fight back.

"YES. The semen and pubic hairs found at the crime scene and on Faith are 100 percent mine," he said.

Samantha was surprised by his response. "I suppose you have an explanation."

"Not an explanation, but a theory and like every theory; it can be tested to see if it's correct."

"What is your theory, Adam?"

"I first have to give you some back story, before I get into the theory. Right before Faith's death I had been seeing a woman named Lexi. I met her in a bar, she wanted to buy some weed off of me or at least smoke some. One thing led to another and we ended up sleeping together. Lexi kept coming over, almost every day. Faith was on vacation with her family and supposedly working on her marriage with Jonathan. I had not seen or talked with her and I allowed myself to move on, or at least try. I told the police about Lexi, they thought that maybe she came over when I passed out and could corroborate my story; but I told them I didn't have her number, I didn't know her last name or where she lived. Literally, she would pop up at my door and let herself in. They were going to have a hard time finding her. The argument between Faith and I was about Lexi, because Faith caught us sleeping together. That is when I ran after Faith. After she drove off, I walked back to my trailer, by the time I got back Lexi was finished dressing. She asked me what the hell was going on. I told her that it was Faith and that she is upset because she caught us and that she never wants to see me again. By that point, Lexi had heard enough, she told me that I chose the wrong woman, that I was stupid to run after her, when Faith clearly did not give a shit about me because she was still with her husband. She then stormed out of my trailer."

Samantha was captivated thus far. "What happened next?"

"I called Faith, probably six or seven times. I finally left a voicemail, I don't remember word for word what I said, but it was something along the lines of, I'm sorry, she meant nothing to me, I love you and I want to be with you. You get the point."

"Yes."

"I think it was maybe an hour later when she called me back. I remember I was overjoyed that she called me. I answered the phone, instantly started apologizing for everything. She cut me off, told me to basically shut up; she then asked me if I had feelings for Lexi. I assured her I didn't, I told her that she was the only woman I have ever been in love with. She said that she had no right to tell me what to do with my life or who to see, especially since she was still married. She asked me about some letter, I guess she thought she gave me, because like I told her I never got any letter from her. It must have not been that important, because the next thing she said to me was, we needed to talk but before that, she wanted to know what our intentions are with this arrangement we have."

Samantha wasted no time asking him, "What did Faith want to talk about and what were your intentions with the arrangement?"

Adam took a drink. "I never got the chance to find out. I heard the doorbell ring in the background; she had to go. She called me back a few hours later, she said she was coming over and she only had an hour. My last words to her were ok, I will see you soon." Adam stopped. He was visibly upset with tears trickling down his face. Samantha sat there, letting him take his time getting through this, she knew this was going to make great television.

Adam regained his composure. "We hung up from one another, I hurried to try and clean the place up for her. I waited for a few hours, but she never showed up. I assumed she got cold feet, that she decided she didn't want anything to do with me. That's when I started drinking, smoking, and ended up passing out."

"Adam, what do you think Faith wanted to tell you?"

"I found out later that Faith was pregnant and the baby was mine. I believe Faith was coming to tell me she was pregnant, she wanted to see if I was ready for a family, because she was going to leave that son-of-bitch."

"Forgive me if I am being rude; what does all that have to do with your semen and pubic hairs found at the crime scene and on Faith?"

He acknowledged her point by nodding. "I had to give you background information before dropping the big one." He smiled. "I'm in prison, I have nothing but time on my hands. I read a lot of books, magazines and newspapers. Seven years ago, I opened the Sunday paper to page 4 and saw that Jonathan Ross got remarried to a beautiful woman named Claire Fulton, and it showed a picture of the couple. I realized that the woman in the picture with Jonathan, I knew her as Lexi."

Samantha was confused, "What do you mean it was Lexi?"

Adam held his hand up and said, "Please hold all questions until the end."

Samantha made a note of it.

Adam continued, "When I saw that I was stunned, I couldn't sleep for three days. Finally, I went to our prison library to use the computer. I did some digging; Claire Fulton used to be married to Douglas Fulton. He was Jonathan's best friend and business partner for a long time. A few months after they built the new stadium, Douglas packed up and moved to Florida, with an extra $10 million in his account from the construction contracts he got from Jonathan. Douglas Fulton was damn near bankrupt before December 2017. Then out of nowhere, he is able to pay off all of his debts, and submits winning bids that are worth $10 million in profit. Gets a quick and quiet divorce from his wife, relocates to Florida. Claire Fulton didn't fight for a dime of money or property from the marriage. More interesting, is the new Mrs. Ross was best friends with the former Mrs. Ross. You can ask anyone; it was common knowledge. After finding all of this out, everything fell into place for me. That day at my trailer, Faith recognized Claire when she looked into my window and saw us together. It became clear why she was upset, that was her so-called best friend and I having sex. Now at the time I did not know Lexi… I'm sorry. Claire was Faith's best friend; she never said anything to me. The police said they could never find anyone named Lexi; I told them what bar I met her in, they went there, asked around about her, but no one remembered. The bar's security cameras didn't work at the time, so no help there. It was like she was a ghost. The police did take DNA samples from my bed sheets, most of the samples belonged to Faith and I. There were a couple unknown samples from another person. I told the police that it had to be Lexi's DNA because I had only been with Faith and her. They ran it through their system but nothing came back. But all that tells you is the person has never committed a crime. To cap this off, Lexi is the only person that could have gotten my semen from a condom, she probably got the pubic hairs from the bed. My theory is that either she planted my DNA there or gave it to the killer and they planted it. Framing me, making it the perfect crime."

Samantha was processing everything that Adam had told her. To say she was apprehensive was the understatement of the year. If everything Adam said is true, those are startling facts that could point this case in an entirely different direction. She felt overwhelmed and slightly nauseous. There was a knock on the door, Samantha turned to see who it was. Ron came walking into the room.

"Hello, Samantha," Ronald said.

"Hello, Mr. Hartz."

"Are you guys at a point where you can take a break?" he asked.

"Of course, I was going to ask Adam if we could break for lunch. Is half an hour alright?"

"That would be perfect," Ron answered. Samantha and the camera crew were going outside to discuss the material already covered and to outline the second half of the day.

"Samantha, can I bother you to turn off the mics and cameras? We would go to another room but they already are bending the rules for us by doing this."

She smiled at him, "Of course. Hey guys, before we go can you cut the equipment?" The crew power down the cameras and turned the mics off.

Ronald passed Adam his lunch. "Nothing special I'm afraid. Bologna and cheese."

Adam grabbed the brown paper lunch bag smiling, "That's alright, it's better than some of the shit they serve in here."

Ronald sat there watching Adam eat his sandwich for about a minute. "Aren't you going to ask me how it went?"

Adam started grinning. "Ron, you gave yourself away when you walked into the room. I knew it was good news by the way you were acting."

"I call bullshit on that!" Ron laughed.

Adam put his sandwich down and took a drink of water. "Ok. Come on, my poker face is only good for so long! Tell me already, man!"

"The DNA taken from underneath Faith's fingernails does not match yours."

"Ok, that's good news; why are you not more excited about that?"

Ronald looked down at the floor, trying to avoid looking Adam in the eyes. "Ron, what the hell is it, you're making me nervous!"

"But it did match the unknown DNA taken from your bedroom sheet."

Adam's mouth dropped open, "Are you being serious with me?"

"Yes. It was a perfect match!" Adam exhaled a large breath not believing what he was hearing.

"What happens now, Ron? Where do we go from here? You turned over that deposition with Douglas to them, they have that. When are they going to get a sample from her?"

"Adam. Breath, it's going to take some time. They can't march up to their door, demanding a DNA sample from her. The Ross's have lawyers in their pockets, like I am carrying quarters in mine. It will happen though; the police will have to talk with Douglas first."

"I know. I need to be patient," Adam said.

"Shit, Adam, I don't blame you for being impatient. You have had ten years to think about this; now freedom is closer than it has ever been in the past decade, you can almost touch it with your fingers. Do you want to know what I would do?"

"Ron, why do you even ask me that? Tell me already."

"I would put it out there for everyone to see, this is a nationally televised primetime show. Let's put some pressure on these people. They haven't given a shit about you, let's throw some mud at people."

Adam was surprised at how Ronald was reacting, normally he is the cooler of the two heads. *He's right, nobody gave a shit about me*, Adam thought. He finished his lunch and was ready to get started. Adam wanted Ron to sit in during the interview, "Ron."

"Yeah, what's up?"

"Thank you, without you none of this would be possible."

"Don't thank me until I'm walking you out of here. That's when we have won."

Samantha asked as she walked in and sat back in her chair, "Ok. Is everyone ready?"

"Yes, Ma'am." Ronald and Adam said simultaneously. Samantha laughed and nodded at the crew to start recording again.

"Adam, that was a lot of information, I want to make sure that I understood you correctly. Is Lexi, the woman you were having sex with, the day Faith was killed, and Claire Ross the same person?"

"Yes. She used a fake name with me."

"How can you be sure that they are the same person?"

"I know she is the woman I was with; the only difference is her hair."

"She wore a wig or she had different colored hair?"

"I don't know, if I had to take a guess. She wore a wig."

Samantha decided to address another issue. "Adam, what's the significance of Douglas Fulton paying off his debts, having $10 million profits with his company, getting a divorce from his wife and moving to Florida?"

"If you look at photos from right after Faith's murder, anytime Jonathan is photographed, either right by him or a few feet away from him is Claire Fulton. Days after Faith's death, Douglas paid off his house, credit cards and all other personal debts. Tax records show that Douglas claimed he was gifted around $3 million. Who do you know that has that kind of money to give someone? Jonathan Ross. After Faith's death, you see Claire spending a lot of time with Jonathan, going on vacation and staying at his home. Douglas submitted a winning bid for work on the stadium, which netted him $10 million in profits that he never would have gotten before Faith's death. Jonathan made it known to everyone that he had cut ties with Douglas; they had a falling out. Douglas was going bankrupt and would have lost everything but Jonathan gives him a $3 million gift, changes his mind and begins working with him again? Then marries his best friend's ex-wife?"

"Are you saying that Douglas had something to do with Faith's death?"

"No. What I'm saying is, Jonathan Ross basically paid Douglas for Claire!"

Samantha didn't understand what he was getting at. "Adam, I'm sorry. I'm having a difficult time seeing a connection to Faith's death?"

"Samantha, Jonathan was quick to replace his wife. The woman he replaced her with, was her best friend and who just happened to be sleeping with me, the man who got Faith pregnant. Who now sits in prison for killing his wife. I would say it's pretty significant."

"Have you told the police all of this? At least what you have told me?"

"Yes."

"Have they taken any action?"

Ronald interjected, "We have conducted a deposition with a person that we turned over to the police. They have been in contact with them to get an official statement. After that I would assume with this person's statement and this interview; a few heads are going to roll."

"Can you tell us who this person is that came forward with the new information?"

"No, we will let the police comment on that, if and when they decide to."

"Are the police reopening the investigation, Mr. Hartz?"

Ronald smiled, "That's not up to Adam or I to decide. We have handed over everything we have regarding this case that we came across. We did what the police should have done ten years ago."

Adam butted in, "Samantha, let's be honest; did the police really investigate this case to the fullest? Jonathan admitted that he and Faith had an open marriage. Did the police investigate thoroughly? Did they question every person that the Ross' had affairs with? I mean maybe you should talk with Sheriff Bennett, see what he has to say about reopening the case. The police had tunnel vision back then; now they are trying to cover up their mistakes. The evidence was overwhelming against me; they should have still done their jobs. They didn't put much effort into finding Lexi. If they would have talked with Claire; they may have been able to see if she had marks and bruises, or a limp and maybe a black eye. Now, I'm not a police officer, but that would suggest to me someone got into a fight! Not to mention, this being the victim's best friend. The things that she said to me when I got back to the trailer that day make sense, how she told me I was stupid, that Faith would get tired of me, how she was just using me. Claire was upset about me choosing Faith over her, I feel." He felt himself getting angry again, he took a moment. "None of that matters now, we have to go forward working together, to bring the real murderer to justice."

"Adam, this is a serious allegation against Claire Ross, who is an upstanding member of society. Do you have any evidence to support your claims?"

Adam sat straight in his chair. "I'm willing to fill out an affidavit about everything that I have said. I stand by what I said. There is an easy way for her to prove me wrong. Let Lexi, I'm sorry, let Claire give a DNA sample to the police and have them get it analyzed. That would solve the mystery, but I know she won't willingly give a sample."

"Why do you say that?"

He let her question hang in the air for a minute then answered, "She is the real monster that killed the love of my life, the mother of my unborn child, the mother of two other children, and not to mention Faith was supposedly her best friend."

"Adam if it comes out that someone else was involved or responsible for Faith's death, what should be the punishment?"

"I don't know if you want my honest answer for that question," he said laughing.

Samantha wanted to know. She asked again, "Seriously, what should be the punishment?"

"I have two answers: my politically correct answer, is they should be punished to the fullest extent of the law, for both crimes; first for the murder of Faith. Second, for framing an innocent man and taking away ten years of my life, thus far! My honest answer: put them in a cell for the rest of their life, let them live like an animal."

"If you could take back getting involved with Faith Ross, take back everything that has led to this moment, right here and now, would you?"

"No. Taking all that back means I never would have known what true love is, I don't care who says what, Faith and I were in love with one another. But Faith would have still been killed with or without me in her life, the only difference is someone else would have been framed. I have learned that I'm strong enough to deal with the outcome no matter what it is and be alright."

Samantha smiled and told the crew, "That's it. We are done." She turned to Adam and Ronald, watching them shake each other's hand, smiling.

Ronald told Adam, "You did a great job, Adam."

Samantha interrupted them, "Mr. Hartz, thank you for sitting in with us, you added great insight, I know it made Adam feel more comfortable." She shook his hand and focused on Adam. Ronald walked outside in the hallway to make room for the camera crew to get their equipment.

"Adam, I would like to thank you for the wonderful opportunity to come speak with you, get your side of the story. I can only hope that everything you told us is correct, maybe the next time I see you will be outside these walls."

Adam grinned at her, "Samantha, it was a pleasure talking with you. I cannot express the gratitude I have for you. Thank you for having an open mind about this. A lot of people have written this case off and believe I'm guilty. But I have something to tell you, but this is completely off the record. Agreed?"

Samantha was taken aback. "Agreed. Off the record."

"This interview is incredibly important; you asked who the person is that came forward with the new information."

Samantha felt her heart starting to race, "Yes, I did. I was told you were not going to say who it was."

"Ronald told you that, I didn't." Adam said.

"Ok. Who is it, Adam?"

"Douglas Fulton"

Samantha gave a less than impressed look, "Claire's ex-husband? Adam-"

"Before you say anything, this is not a revenge or spiteful situation for him. He is actually telling the truth."

"He has everything to lose and nothing to gain by talking."

"Is it enough to legit have a shot at you getting your confession thrown out?"

"I would not be doing all of this, if that was not a possibility."

"What do you want?" Samantha asked.

"I want everything we talked about dealing with Claire, aired for sure."

"What do I get out of it?"

"I will give you exclusive access to me when I walk out of this prison and an acknowledgement in my book," he said smiling at her, hoping she knew that last part was a joke.

She laughed, "Ok, Adam. You have a deal."

Chapter 14

One Month Before Adam's Interview

Prosecuting Attorney Rachel Meadows didn't sleep a wink last night. She was worrying about a case that happened over ten years ago, when she wasn't even elected yet. Now she is sitting in the waiting room of the Missouri State Highway Patrol Troop C office waiting to see Major James Stephens, who had been promoted from Lieutenant in the years after the Ross case. She talked with him yesterday, filling him in on what was going on and asked to meet with him.

"Ma'am, if you want to follow me, I can take you back now." Rachel followed the young trooper, he led her to a small meeting room, "You can have a seat in here, Major Stephens will be right in. Help yourself to some water in the fridge."

"Thank you." Rachel sat down; she was a little nervous this morning. It was the case; she remembers how much media attention it got back then and everything that happened. This was the most horrific crime that had ever happened in Jefferson County. Rachel thought this was a closed case, but in light of everything that has happened, it needed to be re-examined.

Major Stephens came walking into the room, "Prosecuting Attorney Rachel Meadows, I do not believe I have had the pleasure of meeting you, I'm Major James Stephens. How are you doing this morning," he said, shaking her hand.

"I'm good, it's nice to meet you, Major Stephens. Congratulations on your promotion."

"It's been about four years now, but thank you." They both took a seat at a small table. "Do you mind if we use first names?"

Rachel smiled at him, "Of course not."

"I know we talked yesterday about what's going on, but can you fill me in again?"

"I brought the video for you to watch, this is a deposition done by Mr. Lewis's attorney Ronald Hartz. He is interviewing Douglas Fulton. Mr. Fulton says many things that if they are true, it changes this case completely. You add his interview, the DNA not getting sent to the lab when it should have been, and it not coming back a match to Mr. Lewis. This could be bad for everyone involved."

"Ok, I know it looks bad about the DNA not getting sent off, but that is the Sheriff's department problem. They handled that entire scene, collected everything and handled most of the investigation until the whole affair thing came out. The Highway Patrol took it over and we ran with what we had, arrested Mr. Lewis and he confessed. I don't know what you want me to do about it, Rachel."

"Major Stephens, I would like this case to be re-examined. I want someone from the MHSP to go get an official statement from Mr. Fulton and follow up any new leads."

"Rachel, I'm confused. Why is this a big deal now, what is the interest with this case? Mr. Lewis's DNA is still at the crime scene, it's still on the victim. Nothing regarding these new developments' changes that. I mean how many times have guys confessed to a crime, then later down the road recants their confession. We don't reopen all those cases."

"Major Stephens, I understand that it's going to be a pain in the ass, as well as eat into your budget. Mr. Lewis will be getting interviewed about his side of things by a national television news show that focuses on true crime stories, about a month from now. I want to give them a statement that we are looking into the allegations."

"Rachel what kind of allegations? And please call me James."

"Mr. Lewis claims he knows who Lexi is."

"Lexi? The woman no one could find? He magically finds her, while sitting in prison? Yeah, right!"

"James, he claims it's Claire Ross. Saw her picture in the newspaper. His attorney reached out to Douglas Fulton. I assume that is how we now have this deposition."

His mouth hung open. "Are you serious? You're not messing with me?" Rachel shook her head and let it sink in.

"James, watch the deposition, listen to what Mr. Fulton says, get someone down there to take his official statement. We have to investigate this; that means questioning Claire Ross too. I came to you because the MSHP took authority over this case. I wanted you to be ready, not blindsided by any of this. Use this time to get a head start on the media. Get some new blood in here with fresh eyes and a new perspective, someone who doesn't mind getting dirty. Make sure they have thick skin, too, they are going to need it. But you are fair warned, when that film crew gets here and wants a statement, I'm sending them your way."

He smiled at her. "You know, I like you a lot better than Bo Carver."

She grinned, "Thank you, James. I just don't want to fumble the ball and I definitely don't want the MSHP looking bad. I want to be able to work together to get this done. Anything you need from me or my office, just call or visit."

"Alright Rachel, I will watch this and call you later today with an update. If you get anything else that could be helpful, call me." They shook on it and the meeting was over. James walked her out, he went back to his office and watched the deposition. *She was right,* he thought, *if just half of what Mr.*

Fulton says it is true, this whole case could be blown wide open.

Lieutenant Nicole Walker was the youngest and brightest up and coming star for the MSHP. She is 30 years old, never been married and has no children. She puts in sixty-five hours a week and hasn't taken a vacation in two years. In the last year she has been on one date, if you can call it that. They met for coffee; Nicole got about five words in the whole two hours she was there. All this girl did was talk about her ex, how she didn't understand what she needed, how she wasn't supportive enough in growing her brand. If she was being honest, Nicole didn't understand it, but she pretended to be interested because the sex that they had was amazing. The only thing Nicole did for herself was meet up with this girl once-a-month and have sex. Nicole wasn't leading her on, she made sure she knew what it was, strictly sex, no relationship. She was not about having drama in her life, she was married to the job and had dreams of going further. This morning, she was reviewing her cases and filing reports, when her phone rang.

"Lieutenant Walker."

"Lieutenant, this is Major Stephens. Would you come to my office?"

"Yes, sir. On my way."

She was wondering when this was going to happen. Nicole had some words with one of her peers in the cafeteria. They were giving her shit about being so young and how she rose so fast to Lieutenant. Normally she can take it and not say anything, but she was not having a good day on that particular day. She went over to the one doing all the talking, leaned down and said to him, "You don't want to get into a dick measuring contest with me, I have a drawer full of them, and every one of them is bigger than yours!" Then she dropped her water in his lap. Looking back, she may have gone too far with it, but they still told her, now she must face the punishment, she thought.

Major Stephens' door was open, she knocked anyway. "You wanted to see me, Major."

"Yes. Please, come in Lieutenant. Close the door behind you." Nicole closed the door and stood there waiting for it. Major Stephens looked at her with a raised eyebrow, "You can sit down Walker."

"I would rather stand for this Major; I will accept my punishment."

Major Stephens looked at her. "Walker, I have no idea what you're talking about. I didn't call you in here to reprimand you. Should I be?"

"No, sir. I will take a seat."

"I had a meeting with Prosecuting Attorney Rachel Meadows earlier this morning. It appears there have been some new developments with a closed case that I originally worked on. I'm going to reopen the case; I want fresh eyes and new perspectives. You are also pretty open-minded and you think outside of the box. You are going to need that with this case. I will tell you this, new DNA evidence has come to light, the samples from the defendant's bed sheets, match samples taken from under the victim's fingernails. But it is not the defendant's DNA, it's from an unknown suspect."

"Have we run it through CODIS?"

"Yes. They are not in the system. The only lead we have, regarding whom it may be, is the defendant claims he was involved with a woman named Lexi."

Nicole was intrigued, "What case is this regarding, Major?"

He sighed, "It's the rape and murder of Faith Ross."

Nicole's eyes widened, "Are you serious? That's a huge case!"

"I know it is, that's why I want you on it and leading the investigation. But it needs to be done quietly for right now."

"I understand, Major. Do you want me to talk with Mr. Lewis?"

"Not yet, we have his original statement regarding the matter. We never found this Lexi woman that he claimed to be fooling around with. To be fair, we didn't have a lot to go on; we only had a first name and where he met her. We went to the Main Street Bar where he said he met her, but no one remembers Lexi being there. We asked about the security cameras, but the only one that worked was the one above the cash register. That only showed employees."

Nicole was making mental notes. "You didn't have shit to go on then."

"Exactly! When we took this case from the Sheriff's Department, it was not on the best of terms, we looked through everything. The Sheriff's deputies handled the crime scene, collected all the evidence, and gave it to the F.B.I. for analyzing and running it through CODIS. Bang! It came back a match to Adam Lewis. His DNA is at the crime scene and on the victim. In my view, this does nothing to prove he is innocent, only to prove there is possibly a second killer."

"I understand, Major. I need to ask; how far do you want me to take this?"

"What do you mean?"

"I mean, if I find something that is leading somewhere else, do you want me to chase it down or is this… make sure we are not liable for anything?"

"Walker, I want you to treat this case like any other case, go where you have to, talk with whoever you need to talk with. Only two things I ask; Do it quietly and I need to be kept in the loop regarding everything. I will need a debrief every day."

Nicole was surprised by that statement. "Is there something I did wrong, Major?"

"Lieutenant Walker, it has nothing to do with you or your abilities in the field. I will tell you why it must remain between us. The only other person that knows what I'm about to tell you is P.A. Meadows."

"I understand."

"Mr. Lewis will be doing an interview in a month, a true crime television news show. He and his attorney are planning on exposing all of this in that interview. There's going to be a media shit storm around here. Especially with him naming Claire Ross as this Lexi girl. We don't want to raise any suspicions to the Ross's about any of this. Like it or not, we will have to talk with them and they have the money and the power to make life hell for us."

"Absolutely Major, I will go home to read over the case and hit the ground running tomorrow."

"Actually, I need you to read over it on the plane ride."

"Plane! What plane?"

"The plane you're taking to Florida. When you get down there you are going to get an official statement from Douglas Fulton. After that we will discuss what the next step forward is. Alright?"

Nicole got up grabbing the box of files. "Are there more boxes?"

"Oh, hell yeah, but this will give you the overview. This also contains Adam's interview, all the stuff that will get you started. We can go through the other boxes if necessary."

"Ok. When does the plane leave, Major?"

"As soon as you get there."

Nicole went home, packed a few things and headed to the airport. She didn't realize that she was taking the MSHP jet all alone. The pilot told her to sit anywhere, they would land in Tampa in about two hours. Nicole was fine with that; it gave her enough time to read through the facts of the case. They took off and she settled in. She opened the box, pulled the first file out. It was the crime scene pictures; she was not new to the atrocities people were capable of. But this sort of crime to happen to an affluent woman like Faith Ross, was out of the ordinary. She was a high-profile target, the person that committed this crime had to know they were going to get caught. Nicole also noticed there was no attempt at hiding evidence or trying to clean up at the crime scene or on the victim. Everyone knew about DNA back then, if you watched television of any kind, all the crime shows had it on. So why wouldn't Adam try to clean up or wear a condom? Why was he so confident he wouldn't be caught, especially since he knew he was already in the system? It did not make sense to her. The pictures showed how badly beaten Faith was, she was unrecognizable. It was overkill to the max; the autopsy report said that Faith was beaten for a period of time after she was dead. That's an immense amount of anger someone had against her. But the worst was pictures of the tree branch that was shoved inside of her. That was to degrade her, knowing that she would be found like that, the killer/killers were telling everyone they didn't care. Nicole finished with looking through the pictures, she pulled the next file out, it was notes from the interview of Jonathan Ross. She skimmed through it, on to the next file. She skimmed through most of the box's contents until she got to the interview with Adam. She read every word of it, trying to catch him saying something that would give a hint or clue to the truth. She read through the text messages he and Faith had sent to each other. Nicole knew that the physical evidence was there, but if Adam's semen wasn't there, what else could they have used to convict him? She wrote that in her notebook, underlining it.

She has seen killers before have no empathy, compassion or remorse for what they have done. But this was on a different level; Faith did not have the normal high-risk factors that women of violent sexual crimes normally have. She did not live in a big city, she was not a prostitute, no signs of mental illness, and she had stable relationships with family. The only risk factor she had was multiple sexual partners. Nicole was puzzled to say the least, she didn't fit the profile for a victim of a crime like this, Adam did not seem like the kind of person that could have pulled it off. Nicole thought this was a very smart offender, they would have to be able to blend in with the area, and had to know Faith's routine. The offender would have had visible marks on their body: bruises, scratches or scrapes. They would have to be at least a little bit in shape because of the terrain they walked through. There was one thing Nicole couldn't get out of her mind. Faith was beaten with an expandable police baton, at least that's what the Medical Examiner thought it could be. Adam could have easily overpowered Faith with no trouble, why would he resort to using a baton. The police never found the weapon anywhere in Adam's home or vehicle. She was pulling out the last file in the box when they said over the speaker that they were making their approach.

They landed in Tampa in just over two hours, when she stepped off the plane there was a car and a gentleman waiting for her. "Are you Lieutenant Walker, Ma'am?"

"Yes."

"I'm Corporal Ray Mellor, from the Florida State Highway Patrol Troop C. I was sent to pick you up and bring you to the office, Major Stephens called and got it all setup."

"Ok, Corporal. You pass the test, I believe you," she said laughing. He chuckled and offered to take her bag. She normally didn't let anyone do that for her, but she knew he was being nice, so she let him. He opened the car door for her and closed it too. He threw her bag in the backseat. *Ok be nice, Nicole*, she thought to herself. She wasn't used to all this pampering from a man. She normally told them to back off, but she could see he had good intentions with it.

"How far is it to the office?" she asked when he got in.

"Not far, about ten minutes."

She hated these kinds of rides, so let me get to know you and your whole life story. She just wanted to get back home and be able to do her job there. It was about half way into the ride before he said anything, "Lieutenant, if you need anything while you're here, let me know and I will be more than happy to help."

"Actually, I haven't eaten and I'm hungry, could you run through a drive thru, I can pick something quick?"

"I can do that. Do you like fish tacos?"

"I do."

"Lieutenant, we have a wonderful food truck at the office that has the best fish tacos of all time. The fish is caught fresh every day and they use this secret sauce that is great. I myself was going to stop and get some when we got back."

"Sounds great, thank you."

She sat on a picnic table in the parking lot and ate. Nicole was surprised by how good they were, so she went and got another order of them. She was eating her second order when her phone rang.

"Hello?"

"Walker, did you make it down there alright?" Major Stephens asked.

"Yes, sir. Sorry, I was eating lunch."

"That's alright. Listen, Mr. Fulton called and asked if he could come in today to give his statement. Will that work for you?"

"Yes. I'm ready."

"Great! He will be there at 3pm. That gives you two hours to prepare, if you need anything while you're down there be sure to ask them."

"Yes, Major."

She went to find Corporal Mellor, who was eating at a different table.

"Corporal Mellor?"

"Yes, Lieutenant Walker?"

"My interview just got pushed up to today at 3pm, will you have a room I can conduct that in?"

"Absolutely, Lieutenant. Let me finish this taco real fast, I will go and get you set up."

"Take your time, it's no rush."

While she waited for him to finish, she started to think about some of the questions she wanted to ask. The more detailed the question, the better the answer was going to be. She felt like this was a brand-new case, she was going to be as detailed as she could, she sat down and started writing them down.

"Lieutenant, if you're ready I can get you set up inside."

"Thanks" she said, gathering her things and following him.

Douglas walked into the building promptly, he hated being late. He would rather not show up at all than be five minutes late. Corporal Mellor was waiting at the front desk for him. Douglas walked up to the desk. "Excuse me, I'm here to see a Lieutenant Walker"

Corporal Mellor asked before the trooper sitting behind the desk, "What is your name, sir?"

"Douglas Fulton?"

"Right this way, Mr. Fulton." Corporal Mellor led him to the interview room. He knocked on the door, "Mr. Fulton is here, Lieutenant Walker."

Nicole stood as Douglas entered the room. "Mr. Fulton, I'm Lieutenant Nicole Walker with the Missouri State Highway Patrol, thank you for taking the time out of your day to come down here and answer some questions." They shook hands and Douglas sat down.

"It's nice to meet you as well, Lieutenant Walker. I answered a bunch of questions for Ronald Hartz, he asked me everything under the sun."

"These are different kinds of questions and this is going to help determine what direction we need to go. Before we get started, do you want anything other than water to drink."

"No. Thank you."

"Ok. I'm going to record this. This is Lieutenant Nicole Walker interviewing. State your full name."

"Douglas Fulton"

"Mr. Fulton you can stop this at any time, if you want to or you change your mind. Ok?"

"I understand."

"When was the last time you saw Jonathan and Claire Ross?"

"2018. It was the day we signed the divorce papers."

"How long were you two married?"

"Fourteen years, from 2004-2018"

"What was the reason for the divorce?"

Douglas exhaled and shifted in his seat. "Several things, but if I'm being honest with myself, we never should have gotten married. Our marriage started off as a lie; I am gay. I have always liked men but I was afraid to come out. I come from a wealthy, conservative family that I thought would not support my decision and was afraid they would disown me. She was a struggling model and needed someone to take care of her financially. It worked out great for a while, until her career started to decline and we spent more time together. We grew to resent one another."

"Was there any infidelity in the marriage?"

"Yes, there was, both parties were guilty of that. Actually, with the same person, too."

"Who was the person?"

Douglas waited a moment thinking before he said it, because once he said it, there was no going back. "Jonathan Ross."

Nicole was flabbergasted by his omission. "I know that the Ross's had an open marriage, did you and Claire have that arrangement, too?"

"We had an understanding; I would do my thing and she would do hers. There was a fine line we walked because it wasn't supposed to be anybody that was in our circle of friends. We both broke that rule."

"Did Faith know about you and Claire having sexual relations with Jonathan?"

"Yes. She and Jonathan came to me, I don't know the exact date but Claire was not home. They came over and the topic got brought up, they asked me straight up if Claire would be willing to have a threesome. At the time my business was hurting and I needed an investor; Jonathan knew that - he told me that he wanted to set up a business partnership. I was excited, because the well was running dry. I told him I would get the paperwork together and bring it over for him to sign. That's when he basically told me, let's see how Claire does. I knew that he wanted her and if he didn't get her, I didn't get any investment money. I set up this whole evening, I paid for Claire to get her hair and makeup done professionally, I picked out a sexy outfit and told her I needed her to at least flirt with my potential investor. She was rightfully upset about the situation; I was using her to get money. Anyway, Claire was against the whole idea, but something changed when we got home. I assume she tried talking to Faith about it and Faith didn't give her the answer she wanted to hear, because when Jonathan walked in the house, Claire was on him like white on rice! To a point where she was making Faith jealous. Jonathan and Claire ended up having sex while Faith and I watched. Jonathan wanted Faith to join in but she was pissed off and stormed out. That was the last time we did anything with them."

"Did Jonathan ever tell you what happened between Faith and him?"

"Not really, he didn't have to, from that point on, it was just Jonathan and me, or Claire and Jonathan. Faith didn't come around anymore; Faith and Claire were close friends but after that night everything changed. Claire and Faith didn't talk until just a few short weeks before Faith was killed."

"You had a sexual relationship with Jonathan Ross?"

"Yes. We were meeting every week, up until about a month before Faith's death. I was actually meeting him the night she was killed at a hotel to talk. I was running late, I got there and he was gone."

"Mr. Fulton, when you say meeting every week, meeting and doing what?"

"Having sex. Jonathan likes having rough sex, he likes being in control."

"Is Mr. Ross bi-sexual or gay in your opinion?"

"Jonathan... I guess if you had to put a label on it, you would call it bi-sexual. But it's never about the person or feelings because he doesn't have feelings for people, he is all about himself. He puts on a great act but he doesn't give a shit about anyone. He wants money, power, control and sex, in that order, and doesn't care who it hurts or who it's with."

"Why were you meeting with Mr. Ross the night Faith was killed?"

"Jonathan had broken things off with our arrangement because Faith was pissed about him still seeing both Claire and myself behind her back. He was ending our personal and professional relationships all together. I can admit, I was blinded because I thought I was in love with him. It was my first steady male partner sexually, that I had. When he ended it, that hurt, but him cutting our professional relationship was going to ruin me. I would have been bankrupt. I was angry, I tried calling him to discuss it, I tried calling Faith. No one was answering my calls, I wrote him an email and threatened to go public about everything unless he met up with me to talk and iron things out. We did have signed contracts and I needed that money. He responded back to my email telling me he would meet with me but this would be the last time, and I agreed. He told me to meet him at the Rosemont Hotel. I was running late. I called him to tell him, and he became angry because he wanted to get home. He was frustrated but nothing out of the ordinary. I got there, went up to the room, and he was nowhere to be found. Then my phone started blowing up with text messages asking me if I knew anything and asking me how Jonathan was doing? I had to finally ask someone what the hell was going on, that's when I was told that they found Faith's body in the woods. I was shocked, to say the least."

"I know I'm going back and forth with these questions Mr. Fulton, but you said Claire and Jonathan were having an affair behind Faith's back?"

"Yes, Claire and Jonathan were having an affair that Faith did not know about."

"Do you know if Faith was having an affair with anyone at that time?"

"I mean, I know now that she was sleeping with Adam Lewis, but back then I had no idea what Faith did."

Nicole took a drink of water as she shifted in her chair. "Do you need to use the restroom or anything Mr. Fulton?"

"I'm good, I just want to get this over with."

"Understandable. Not too much longer. What did you do after you found out Faith had been killed?"

"I stayed at the hotel watching the news. Claire and I were not getting along, it was easier to stay there until I thought Claire was in bed, that way we did not have to see or speak with each other. I guess it was about 11:45 p.m. I was on my way home. I have known Jonathan for a long time, we were still friends regardless of what was going on between us. I drove over to his house. When I got there, there was a police car at the gate. They stopped me but I told them who I was and that I was a family friend coming by to check on

284

them. They let me pass, I got up to the house and knocked on the door for at least 5 minutes. When no one answered, I opened the door, I went to Jonathan's office because that's where he spends most of his time when he is home. He wasn't there. I went to the kitchen and saw him standing outside on the patio. I went outside, tried to talk with him. The moment he saw me, he was pissed off. He told me that he loved Faith and why couldn't I get the point. I asked him what the hell he was talking about. I didn't do anything to her, I told him I came by to check on him. Not as a lover or anything but a friend, he ran at me and we fought… if that's what you could even call it, I would say it was more of an aggressive hug, the ones where you're trying to console someone. But it was pouring down rain and storming like crazy. Jonathan snapped out of it when Pearl opened the back door and asked what was going on. He picked her up and put her back to bed. I waited for him to come down. We talked for a little bit and he said he wanted some space to think. I gave him a hug, then drove home."

Douglas was becoming more comfortable with Nicole. "Can I get a cup of coffee, by chance?"

"Of course, I'll grab you a cup." Nicole went to use the bathroom first; she sat in the stall thinking how different wealthy people were. They have all the money and resources to do anything they want and all they do is sit around trying to screw each other. She grabbed two cups of coffee. "I didn't ask how you liked it, but I did grab two sugars and a creamer."

Douglas grabbed the cup from her, "Thank you so much. I drink my coffee regular with nothing in it."

Nicole sat down, taking a few sips from her coffee. "When you got home, was Claire there?"

"Yes. But it was odd because I didn't get home until after 1 a.m. and she was still up. I felt like she was waiting for me, which she never did."

285

"What happened when you went inside, where was she?"

"I walked in and heard her in the bar area, which I also found to be odd because she only drinks at social events and that's always wine, never the hard stuff. But I remember she was drinking whiskey that night, or I guess you would say that morning because it was earlier in the morning by then."

Nicole wrote a note down. "What happened next, Mr. Fulton?"

"When she saw me, she immediately asked me where I had been. Before I could answer her, she noticed that my clothes were all wet. She asked me why. I told her that I went to see Jonathan, to check on him and the kids. I told her she should have been there, too; Faith was her friend. She rolled her eyes; she told me she thought Jonathan would need space. I remember thinking that was bullshit, she never missed an opportunity to see him or she had already talked with him. She had finished her drink and was pouring another one, when I noticed her face. I walked in the room to look at her closer and I asked her what the hell happened to her."

Nicole stopped him there, "Sorry, Mr. Fulton. Describe what you saw in detail."

"I went into the bar room, that's when I noticed she had a black eye on the right side, she had some bruises around her right cheek, she looked like she had been in a fight. I asked her what had happened. She told me that she was jogging and she fell, hitting her face. I asked her if she went to urgent care to get checked out, and she looked at me like I was stupid, and told me no. I poured myself a drink and asked her if she wanted to sit and talk. She agreed, that's when I noticed a slight limp in her step. I know you probably think I'm making more out of this than I should, but you have to understand Claire. She is a machine when it comes to working out and taking care of yourself. She works out and does yoga, she could probably kick both our asses. Back then she would take those self-defense classes. She could handle herself, so if she looked like that I could only imagine what the other person looked like."

"What did the two of you talk about?"

"We talked about what happened, I told her I couldn't believe Faith was actually gone. It was shocking to me. I remember her response to the situation vividly. She said, 'There is only so much a person can take before they snap. That bitch deserved a lot more than just a beating.' I remember being upset that she said something like that. I told her to explain what she meant. She told me, 'Faith plays with people's hearts and emotion's too much, someone obviously got tired of it.' I was pissed. I asked her how she could say that, no matter what Faith and her were going through, that was still her friend. Claire saw I was upset and backpedaled, telling me that Faith was her friend but that we needed to be honest, Faith used a lot of people. At that point I was done with her, I didn't want to hear it. I told her I was going to bed. As I was walking away, she told me that she hoped they had some physical evidence; if they had to start rounding up people that had issues with Faith, they didn't have enough time in the world to interview everyone. I asked her 'What people had issues with Faith?' She told me about every woman with a husband that smiled at her. I defended her, I said 'Faith did what she did and Jonathan did what he did. It doesn't make her a whore because more people liked her.' Claire told me to keep living in denial, but that she was going to be realistic. I told her that if that's the case then she will be a suspect for a couple of reasons: first, she slept with Jonathan while Faith watched, that is being involved with Faith in a sexual manner. Secondly, she had that huge falling out with her over having sex with her husband, like that's not a huge red flag."

Nicole was intently listening to every word Douglas let out. "What did she say to that?"

"When I say Claire got angry, I mean I have never seen this woman want to physically hurt me but if she could have

287

gotten away with it, I think she would have definitely hit me that night. Claire started screaming at me, that they made up, they worked out their issues and everything was great between the two of them. Faith and her went to lunch and Faith told her a secret and wanted her help with something. I told her she is crazy, I asked her why would Faith need her help? That's when she told me she was supposed to deliver some letter for Faith. Claire followed me upstairs to my bedroom and told me that I was a bigger suspect than her."

"Why would she think you were a suspect?" Nicole asked him.

"Like I mentioned before, I was having money problems, I was going to be bankrupt in the next two months. When Jonathan cut professional ties with me, everyone followed him, no one would work with me and I had made some bad investment decisions. I did not have any cash; I was living on credit and that was running out. Jonathan didn't want to cut ties with me, he knew when it came to business, he could count on me. But Faith found out Jonathan was sleeping with me, that was hard for her to accept. I get it... You know your husband isn't having sex with you but he will have sex with a man. Faith knew Jonathan wasn't gay, he liked having sex and it didn't matter who it was with. Of course, she would be upset, she gave him an ultimatum: his family and continued respect in the community or me. Not a hard decision for Jonathan, that's when everything ended between us. I wrote that email and was meeting him that night to talk some sense into him. But Claire said, if Faith was out of the picture, Jonathan would not cut ties with me. So, I had a motive to kill Faith or at least want her dead."

"Did she say anything else to you?"

"Claire told me to keep my mouth shut and mind my own business. Don't create problems where there is none."

288

Nicole was going back through her notes. "Did you see any other marks, scratches, bumps or bruises on Claire, besides the ones you already mentioned?"

"Yes, the next morning while she was taking a shower, I went in to ask if she was going to see Jonathan. I saw through the glass doors that she had a large scratch by her collar bone. I asked her about it, but she claimed it was from the fall. She had a couple large bruises on arm and one on her thigh. She was still angry from the night before; she told me unless I was going to get in there and fuck her like a real man, I needed to get out and stay away from her."

Nicole was writing more notes, "Mr. Fulton, when did Claire start seeing Jonathan exclusively?"

He laughed, "Days after Faith was killed, she was going over to check on him. Then both of us would go over and stay the night, I went just to help protect their affair from the media. I would sleep in a different room and they would sleep in Jonathan's room."

"Jonathan's room?"

"Yes."

"Is that the same room Faith and he had together?"

"Yes, it is. Lieutenant he gets what he wants. Plain and simple. We worked out a deal that I would come over with Claire, we would tell people and the media that we were helping him out during his time of need. The only thing that was going on was sex. Jonathan, Claire and sometimes his children's nanny. I don't remember her name but she was a beautiful young girl."

"Do you know how young?"

"She was over the age of 18, if that's what you're asking."

"What was the deal you all worked out?"

"Jonathan gave me $3 million in cash. That paid off every debit I had with some leftover. Jonathan told me to submit my bids for jobs at the stadium and he would make sure they went with me. All I had to do was keep coming over with Claire, to make everything look on the up and up, don't make any waves regarding the relationship between Claire and him. I would also let Claire file for divorce and I would get everything."

"What do you mean you would get everything?"

"Claire wouldn't fight for the house or cars, but at the end all I wanted was my car. I told them to do whatever they wanted with the rest of the stuff and I got the hell out of there."

"Mr. Fulton, you mention a letter Faith gave to Claire, do you know if she ever delivered that letter?"

"I asked her about it a few days later when she calmed down, she said she was going to but then decided not to. I asked her why; she told me that I would never believe what kind of person Faith goes for. I was still confused; she went on to tell me that Faith was fooling around with some trailer trash guy."

"Why did she call him trailer trash?"

Douglas smiled, "You don't know?"

"Know what Mr. Fulton?"

"Adam lived in a trailer. That's why she called him trailer trash."

"Then that means she had to go over there at least once, right?"

Douglas chuckled, "Damn, see I lived with her for fourteen years, I didn't even catch that, but yeah, I would have to assume she at least drove by the place."

"Mr. Fulton, is there anything else you would like to add to your statement today?"

"No, ma'am."

"Mr. Fulton, do you swear that everything you said here is true and accurate to the best of your knowledge?"

"Yes."

"Ok. Thank you, Mr. Fulton." Nicole stood up, gathering her notes. Douglas stood up and extended his hand to her, "Thank you, Lieutenant," he said, shaking her hand.

"For what, Mr. Fulton?"

"For being respectful, you treated me like a human being and not like I have a disease."

Nicole knew what he was saying, "Mr. Fulton, a lot has changed since you left Missouri, I think you would be pleasantly surprised."

"Maybe."

Nicole was exhausted after that, but she promised to call the Major with all updates. She looked at her watch, it was 7 p.m. She dialed his office number; it rang once and he picked it up.

"Major Stephens."

"Major, it's Walker."

"Lieutenant, how did it go?"

"Sir, there is a lot more information that I got. I feel we need to talk about it with everyone involved, to decide how much dust you want me to kick up." The phone was silent, to the point where Nicole thought maybe they got disconnected.

"Ok, Walker. Get back up here, I'm going to call P.A. Meadows, get us a meeting for tomorrow morning. Will you be ready to present your findings?"

"Yes."

Nicole was exhausted from the flight home; she got in late last night. Once she got home, she read through her notes again making her presentation for the morning. The last time she looked at the clock it was 3:37 a.m. Her alarm was set for 5:30 a.m. By the time she was sitting next to Major Stephens she was on her fourth cup of coffee this morning. They are in the waiting room of the Prosecuting Attorney's office.
 "You know Lieutenant, you should drink tea, it is much better for you."

"Major, if tea would do for me what coffee does, I would gladly switch."

"I'm just trying to make you be more health conscious, Walker," Major Stephens said.

Nicole did not want this lecture today. "Well, Major. I know for a fact you get two king size candy bars from the vending machine every day. When you break your vice, let me know."

Major Stephens looked at her, "How do you know it's twice a day?"

"Please, you go in the morning, then at around 3pm you have the rookie go to get the other one for you," she said smiling.

"Did he talk?"

"Are you kidding, he would drink water out of his shoe if you told him too. I'm just that damn good."

"See why I chose you for this case."

292

P.A. Meadows walked through the office door. "Sorry Major, I hit some wicked traffic, please come in. Let me put my things away and I will be right over."

Nicole followed him into her office, closing the door behind her. They sat at the round table in the corner of her office. As Rachel finished putting her things away, she finally noticed Nicole, "I'm so sorry Lieutenant, I'm a little lost this morning."

Nicole adjusted in her seat, "It's no problem, ma'am."

Rachel grabbed a notepad and took a seat at the table with them. Her assistant came in with coffee and freshly sliced fruit. "Please take some, I'm trying to start my day off with fruit." Rachel waited until her assistant shut the door.

"Ok, Lieutenant. I hear you have some information for us," Rachel said as she took a bite of a pineapple chunk.

Nicole opened her notes. "I sat with Mr. Fulton for four hours yesterday and in those four hours got an enormous amount of information that could possibly open another case for fraud against Jonathan Ross. I needed this meeting to discuss with you and Major Stephens to what extent you want to go. I ask because what we have isn't dust, we have fire that could burn them. Let me tell you what we learned." Nicole spent the next forty-five minutes laying everything out for them.

"I saved the most damaging things for the end. Claire had a motive, she was having an affair with Jonathan; she had a black eye, a massive scratch below her collar bone, bumps and bruises as well. She told Douglas and I'm quoting, 'that bitch deserved a lot more than just a beating.' She said that hours after her death, but before anything came out regarding how Faith was killed. How did Claire know that Faith had been beaten?"

293

Rachel sat back in her chair, stunned from everything Nicole told them. They all sat there thinking about it until Rachel said, "How in the hell did this get missed? This is how convictions get overturned and how I get my ass handed to me for shit I didn't even do!"

Major Stephens spoke up, "Rachel, this was before you were even working here. This doesn't have your name anywhere on it. You are trying to correct a mistake, if they need to blame someone let them blame me. The only one at fault, is the killer or killers. We didn't talk with a lot of people back then because Adam Lewis pleaded guilty! Not to mention, we have his DNA at the crime scene and on the victim!"

The room was silent before Nicole said, "We need to keep digging and turning stones over. I'm going to go one step further; we need to talk with Claire Ross. If we are treating this like any other case, we would bring her down here and have a conversation."

Everyone knew that needed to be done, they were trying to hold off for as long as possible. "Ok, let's do it. But we need to tread very lightly with this. They can make life difficult for all of us."

Nicole looked at Major Stephens. "Ok, let me put it this way, how much heat do you want me to put on her?"

Before Rachel could answer, Major Stephens said, "Deal with it like you would someone that lawyer up and you don't have any physical evidence on them. It's just a conversation, until you can find holes in her story."

Nicole nodded, "Alright I will reach out to Claire Ross and see if she will come in."

"Lieutenant, try to get that interview done before Adam's television debut, because once all this gets out, it will be a circus."

"Yes, ma'am. I will certainly try," Nicole said. "What about getting a warrant for a DNA sample?" Nicole asked.

"Not a chance, no judge will give us that at this point, bring her in for questioning and see how that goes."

It's been a few days since they all sat down. Rachel received a call yesterday from Ronald Hartz wanting to speak with her, that was her first meeting on her agenda. Her assistant came in and let her know Mr. Hartz was there. *Here we go*, Rachel thought.

"Send him in, please." A moment later Ronald walked into her office.

"Good morning, Ronald. How are you?"

"I'm good. How are you, Rachel?"

"I'm good. Please have a seat." He took a seat, in front of her desk. "What is it that you wanted to speak about?" she asked.

"Rachel, I want to know where we stand with the information I gave you a few weeks ago?"

"Ronald, you know how this works, we are looking into it. I can't give you much more than that."

"Rachel, I came to you first with our findings, you can at least be straight with me."

Rachel got up from her chair, she put on her coat. "Come on Ronald, let's go for a walk."

The two of them went across the street to the park.

"Are you going to tell me why we are out here walking around the lake when it's cold as shit?" Ronald asked.

"Listen, I know you did us a favor by coming to us first before the media. I thank you for that. You wanted straight, I'm going to give it to you. We spoke with Douglas. We are trying to talk with Jonathan and Claire, but they are dodging us. Just before you arrived, I got a call from their attorney, telling me the only way they are going to meet with us is if we arrest them. I have no physical evidence, Ron; they would sue me and win."

"Come on, Rachel. You and I know there are ways around that! You could get them in here for questioning, no problem."

"This case is already messed up, I will not continue the cycle of dysfunction, Ronald. Now if you have anything else, give it to me and I will run with it. If not, let us do our job." They were frustrated, both of them knowing that for right now everyone had to play the waiting game with the Ross's.

"Ronald, even if everything that Douglas said is true, your client's DNA is still there and you have no explanation. What is your plan for that?"

"Our plan is to put our faith in your hands; we know the only way Adam's DNA gets explained is by Claire. We are hoping that she cracks under all the pressure."

Rachel's mouth dropped open.

"What?" Ronald asked.

"What is your plan? What if she doesn't? Then what?"

"Hey, I didn't say it was a good plan, but we have no other way to explain it. My client admits to being with a woman before Faith was killed, he used a condom with her. He tells the police about her but they can't find her. I couldn't find her, and while he is in prison, he opens up the newspaper to see the woman he knows as Lexi, getting married to, of all people, Jonathan Ross, and that her name is actually Claire

Fulton? He knew then that the only way out of all this was getting her to confess. He feels strongly that when she is finally confronted with the truth, she will want to tell the world about it."

Rachel felt guilty for snapping on him. "Ronald, I'm sorry. I know you're doing your job; this is all I can tell you. We are looking into everything, ok? That's all I'm going to say Ronald."

"Does that mean what I think it does?" he asked.

"Like I said, that's all I'm saying about that. But I think you should totally let nothing go unsaid in that interview." They walked about ten more minutes before Ronald left, he had to get to court for a different client. Rachel walked back to her office, feeling better than when she left. It was short lived.

"Mrs. Meadows, Major Stephens called, he said it's urgent that you call him back," her assistant informed her.

She put her head down. "Why is this case consuming my life right now? We have other cases, right?" she said out loud. She dialed Major Stephens' number.

"Major Stephens."

"James. This is Rachel returning your call."

"Hey, Rachel. I have an update; I don't think you will be surprised but the Ross's are not willing to come in and talk with us."

"Yeah, I was going to call you, but I had a meeting this morning. The Ross's attorney called me and told me the only way they are coming down to talk is if they are arrested."

"I can do that, no problem!" he exclaimed.

"No, they will sue us. We have to find evidence. If we keep digging and wait until Adam's interview comes out, then we can issue a statement telling the media and community that the Ross's have nothing to do with this and are unwilling to help with the investigation. We make it clear that the case goes nowhere without their cooperation. That's the only thing left I can think of."

"I agree. Let the media and public know exactly what is going on. Let the pressure build around them like a pressure cooker."

"Sorry for the no-good news update James."

"Stop beating yourself up, besides I feel like this is some good news."

"What good news?"

"Lieutenant Walker is a machine, when it comes to investigative work. When she could not get a hold of Jonathan or Claire, she started tracking down people that work for them. She caught up with the housekeeper/cook. A woman named Hailee; she has worked for the Ross's since they were married in 2006. She was hesitant to talk because she filled out a Non-Disclosure Agreement, but Lieutenant Walker let her know that if it had anything to do with Faith, then she was safe to talk about it."

"James, tell me she is going to talk with us," Rachel said, almost begging him.

"Lieutenant Walker is meeting with her tomorrow morning. Apparently, she overheard an argument that Faith and Claire had hours before Faith's death."

"James, I don't need to tell you how important every detail is."

"Rachel, Lieutenant Walker is the best at getting people to talk, trust me, she has this."

"Ok, let me know how it goes. This could make things a lot easier."

They hung up. Major Stephens called Lieutenant Walker into his office.

"Lieutenant, have you heard back from Claire or Jonathan?

"No, sir. I have called them every day, leaving voicemails, they go unanswered."

"Have any other people come forward to talk other than the housekeeper?"

 "Yes, but nothing they had to say wasn't of any use. A lot of hearsay."

"Lieutenant, do you need anything from me for tomorrow?"

"I'm all set, Major. Is there anything that you need from me?"

"Yes. Keep doing what you're doing," Major Stephens told her.

"Thank you, Major."

Chapter 15

It was the next day and Hailee is sitting in her car debating on whether or not to go inside. She is nervous; she can't help but feel like she is doing something wrong by being here. Nicole saw her from the lobby, she walked outside and knocked on her window, accidentally scaring her.

"OH SHIT!!" Hailee shouted.

"Sorry, Hailee," Nicole said, putting up her hands, showing her, she was no threat.

Hailee rolled down her window, "I'm sorry, Nicole. I don't think I can do this." Nicole had dealt with reluctant witnesses before, for the most part they are afraid of being hurt. But Nicole could sense this was different. Hailee was trying to protect someone.

"At least come inside for some coffee, I bought it from that expensive coffee shop." Nicole said to her. "Come on, it's chilly out here and I don't have my coat." Hailee opened the door; she followed Nicole inside and they sat at her desk drinking coffee. Nicole offered her a pastry.

"No thanks, I really shouldn't." Nicole looked at her disapprovingly. "Ok, fine I will have one. Is this what you do to criminals, wear them down with kindness?"

Nicole laughed, "Are you kidding, I don't think anyone has ever accused me of being nice."

"I'm sorry. I know I am being difficult about this; I don't want anyone to get hurt," Hailee said.

"Who are you afraid of getting hurt by talking with me?"

"The children. They have been through so much, they don't deserve anymore pain."

"You care for them, like they are your own children," Nicole said.

"I wouldn't have it any other way. I only stayed on with Jonathan after he married Claire for the children."

"How old are they now?" Nicole asked.

"Pearl is Sixteen and Weston is Twelve."

"I know you think by not talking you're saving them. But one day soon, they are going to want to know the truth. Whatever the truth is, they deserve to know."

"Ok. Let's talk," Hailee said. Nicole grabbed the pastries and her coffee; they went to an interview room.

Nicole grabbed a Danish out of the box. "Do you need anything before we get started?" Nicole asked.

"No, I'm alright. Thank you."

"I'm going to be recording this today. This is Lieutenant Nicole Walker taking the statement of state your name for the record."

"Hailee Wilson."

"Ms. Wilson, is here today of her own free will and you can stop at any time you want. Do you understand?"

"Yes."

"Ms. Wilson, why don't you tell me what you heard? If I have questions, I can ask them afterward."

"Alright. It was November 20th, 2017. I was washing up the lunch dishes when the doorbell rang. I turned off the water and was on my way to open the door, when Faith told me she would get it. But she had a tone to her voice like she was angry, I stood about five feet from the door when she answered it and said, 'What the hell do you want?' I had never seen her act like that. I went to the dining room window because I wanted to see who it was and opened it so I could hear what was being said. I couldn't believe it when I saw it was Claire Fulton; I thought they were friends. I heard Claire trying to explain why she hadn't given him the letter. I heard Faith yell, 'That makes it alright to sleep with him?!' At that point I thought she was talking about Mr. Ross. Faith stepped outside and closed the door behind her, I continued watching and listening from the window, just in case she needed anything. I remember she asked Claire, 'Do you know what women were called if they slept with their best friend's boyfriend?' Claire didn't answer and that's when Faith said, 'sluts and whores.' I remember Claire got enraged with her. She got into Faith's face and said, 'What do they call married women that get knocked up by someone other than their husband?' Faith looked like a deer in the headlights, she yelled, 'That's none of your business' to Claire. The last thing I remember clearly is Claire told Faith, 'I came over here because you are messing with Adam's head. We both know you will never leave Jonathan.' That is when Faith heard enough, she told Claire, 'Fuck you' and came back inside. She closed and locked the door."

"What time did this exchange happen?" Nicole asked.

"A little after 1 p.m."

"You seem pretty sure about that time."

"Yes, Faith and the kids were on a strict schedule. They ate lunch at 12:30 p.m. every day on the dot, Faith allotted thirty minutes for lunch. I was to clean up the lunch dishes promptly at 1 p.m. I was just about finished doing the dishes when the doorbell rang."

"Do you remember what Claire was wearing that day?"

"Yes, she was wearing yellow yoga pants, tennis shoes, yellow undershirt and a black jacket zipped up half way. I remember because they were very bright and tight on her and you could read everything, if you catch my drift."

"Yes, Ma'am, I get it. Do you know who Claire was supposed to give the letter to?"

"No. But, if I had to guess, I would think Adam."

"Why would you say Adam?" Nicole asked.

"Because of what Claire told Faith about messing with Adam's head. I would compare the two of them to two high school girls fighting over the same boy, and the boy wasn't Jonathan."

"Hailee, you have worked for the Ross's for how many years?"

"Seven years. I started with them in 2010."

"Wow, that's a long time. Is it safe to say you have seen the Ross's at their best and worst times?"

"Yes, I have."

"At the time of Faith's death, how was the Ross's relationship?"

"They had returned from Texas and seemed like they were working on things. I know Faith did not want to come back. She wanted a fresh start for the family."

"Why didn't she just stay down there with the kids?"

"Jonathan had some business meetings. I remember them talking about that. They were only going to be in town for a few weeks. Christmas they were going back down to Texas. I was asked if I wanted to go because they were going to stay down there for a while."

"Why is that?"

"Faith hated the winters here, she loved when everything was green and warm. She could get through the holidays up here for her family, but once Christmas was over, they were gone until March or April. Jonathan would work from wherever they were."

"Do you know who Faith meant when she yelled, 'That makes it alright to sleep with him'?

"I don't know for a fact, but my guess again would be Adam. I say that because again, it was like they were fighting over a boy."

Nicole finished making her notes. "Hailee, is there anything else you would like to tell us, that you can remember?"

"I'm not trying to make trouble for anyone, but when you came to me and asked me if I wanted to talk or if I could remember anything out of the normal, I definitely remembered that exchange between those two. But something else came to my mind too."

"What is it, Hailee?"

"I would say about less than a month after Faith's death, Jonathan came to me and told me to go home early, it was on a Friday. The kids were at Faith's parents' house for the weekend. Jonathan had all the staff leave early. I did, but I realized I had forgotten my purse when I was halfway home, so I turned around to go back and get it. When I arrived back there, I walked in through the side door like I always do. But when I went into the kitchen to grab my purse, I heard a commotion in the living room. I peeked in to see what was going on. I saw Jonathan, Claire, and Skyler having sex on the couch. But it wasn't normal sex, it was very rough sex."

Nicole thought she could not be surprised by anything else, but she was wrong. "Rough sex. What do you mean by rough sex? Can you describe it?"

"Jonathan was smacking Claire on the face and her breasts. He pulled her hair; he had Skyler holding her arms behind her. I couldn't believe what I was seeing, at first, I really thought he was hurting her, but the longer I stood there the more I realized they all were enjoying it. I ran out of the house, got in my car and drove right home."

Nicole had to keep herself from jumping up and down with excitement, this was all new information. "Hailee, who is Skyler?"

"She was the children's nanny."

Nicole had a confused look on her face. "I thought you took care of the kids?"

"I did, but it looked better if her title was nanny, because then she could be there at the house at all hours, day or night."

"You said 'was'. Is she not with the Ross's anymore?"

Hailee laughed, "No way! Claire got rid of her not too long after her and Jonathan made it official by getting married."

"Do you happen to know where Skyler is now?"

"The last I heard she had gotten married and was living out in California."

"Did you ever tell the Ross's what you saw?"

"No way! I never told anyone that. You are the only other person that knows."

"I have to be honest with you, Hailee. The Ross's will never know that you told us, unless we go to court. How are you going to be if it does come out and they find out it was you?"

"Like you said, the children deserve to know the whole truth."

"Hailee, thank you for coming in and talking with me. You have no idea how much I appreciate it. If you remember anything else, please give me a call. Here is my card." She handed her a business card and shook her hand; she walked her to the lobby, making sure she got to her car alright and ran back upstairs.

Nicole went to Major Stephens office, she noticed he was on the phone.

"Lieutenant Walker, come in. P.A. Meadows is on the line." Major Stephens put the phone on speaker. She closed the door and took a seat.

"Lieutenant Walker, how did it go?" Rachel asked.

"It was definitely eye opening, Hailee would make a good witness, she can provide a detailed description of what Claire was wearing that day. I think we need to talk with Mr. Lewis, check if he remembers what Lexi was wearing that day, too?"

"Ok, please tell me you got more than that," Rachel asked.

"Hailee saw and heard Faith and Claire have a verbal argument hours before Faith's death. I will send you the notes but this is a very heated exchange between the two of them. It would be enough to bring Claire in for questioning."

Rachel chimed in, "It's that bad?"

"I'll read it to you. Faith asked Claire, 'if she knew what women were called if they slept with their best friend's boyfriend? Sluts and Whores.'"

"Holy shit!" Rachel said.

"I'm not finished… Then Claire got angry and told Faith, 'Faith, what do they call married women that get knocked up by someone other than their husband?' Then later in the conversation Hailee heard Claire tell Faith, 'I came over here because you are messing with Adam's head. We both know you are never going to leave Jonathan.'" Major Stephens and Rachel were silent, Nicole let this piece of information hang in the air for a minute.

"There is something else that Hailee saw."

Chapter 16

Major Stephens was hanging on to every word Nicole spoke, he was having regrets about wrapping the investigation up when he did ten years ago. On the other end of the phone was Rachel, not having anything to do with this case up until a month ago. She was hoping this was not going to backfire on her office, this needed to be done right this time.

"What did she see, Lieutenant?" Major Stephens asked.

"Yeah," Rachel added.

"I need to tell you that she saw this first hand, a few weeks after Faith's death. Jonathan told all the estate workers to leave early, I mean everyone but the security guard at the front gate. Hailee left and got halfway home when she realized that she forgot her purse. She came back and of course the guard let her in. Hailee went in through the side door and grabbed her purse off of the counter. She heard some commotion coming from the living room, just off the kitchen. She peeked her head around the corner to see Jonathan, Claire and a woman named Skyler having sex. Not just sex, but rough sex. According to Hailee, Skyler was holding Claire's arms behind her back. Jonathan was smacking Claire's face and breasts. At that point, Hailee ran out of the house."

"That is a goldmine; this goes against Jonathan's 'I love my wife and I'm so broken up about it.' Who is this Skyler woman?" Rachel asked.

"Skyler was at least on paper Ross's nanny, apparently sometimes a live-in nanny. Hailee told me Skyler did not do much for the kids, she was mostly around for Jonathan's enjoyment."

"Great work, Lieutenant!" Rachel said.

"When are we getting Claire to come in?" Major Stephens asked her.

"Well, that is something I wanted to talk with P.A. Meadows, I would like to bring in both Claire and Jonathan right now."

Rachel shot that idea down right away. "We need to take our time with this. We have no evidence against them."

Nicole was frustrated. "How am I supposed to get evidence against them, if I can't talk with them?"

"We will have to keep at it, Lieutenant," Rachel told her. Nicole was about to burst with anger, Major Stephens could see it.

"What if we put them under surveillance, see where they go. Maybe we get lucky and they go to a restaurant. Then we can get their glasses or silverware," Major Stephens said.

Nicole knew he was trying to compromise with her. "Major, if this was anybody else, we would have arrested them already."

Rachel spoke up, "I know that! Do you want to arrest them, then two hours later watch them walk out? That is the type of money and power they have; they can get a judge out of bed at 2 a.m. to come down and walk them right out!"

"She's right, Lieutenant. As much as we all want to nail these bastards, we have to do it right," Major Stephens said.

"I know it looks like I'm on their side, but we have to get our ducks in a row, that way all those high-powered friends they have won't even come to their rescue," Rachel explained.

Nicole understood what Rachel was saying. It was hard sitting back and letting people hang themselves. Nicole was used to rattling people's cages and getting in their face. But the Ross's are a different kind, their money gives them power and the power gives them more time than others.

Major Stephens asked Nicole, "What do we have on Jonathan? The way I'm seeing and hearing it, none of this points to him."

"None of it points to him directly, but indirectly is a different story. I think the fact that he made everyone go home early, to hide the fact that Claire, Skyler, and himself were having the threesome is a big deal. For one, it was just weeks after her death. He then ends up marrying the woman who is supposedly her best friend? I know at first, we all were thinking Adam's story was bogus, but maybe it's truer than we would like to think. Everything I have right now points to Claire knowing something, I feel like she is a person of interest."

"Do you want to talk with Jonathan?" Rachel asked Nicole.

"Absolutely I do."

"We are going to talk with everyone, but for now I feel we put all of our attention on Claire. That's where things are pointing, that's where we go. Whether they want to admit it or not, if she would have given us a DNA sample all of this would have been cleared up. There is a reason she doesn't want to give one," Major Stephens said.

"Agreed," Rachel said.

"Sounds good to me, Major," Nicole answered.

Chapter 17

After Interview Aired

Jonathan and Claire are having breakfast. He is having his sausage, egg and cheese burrito, while she is having her customary shake. They are sitting in silence, until Claire breaks the ice.

"How is your breakfast burrito?"

Jonathan makes a face of disgust. "It's definitely not how Hailee made it."

Claire was tired of talking about this. "Jonathan I'm sure if you talk with Eric, he can make them even better than Hailee. I bet they taste different because he actually uses fresh ingredients."

"You never answered me about firing Hailee?"

"I told you, she wasn't making healthy meals, with healthy ingredients. Not to mention, she was always having to leave early to go do something with her kid. Sorry but it's not my problem."

"Claire, her kid has health issues. We knew that, it's never been a problem."

"The amount of severance you so graciously gave her, should pay for her child's needs for the rest of his life!"

He was getting annoyed with this conversation. He picked up his morning paper and started to read it, but he quickly regretted that. All of the headlines were about Adam's interview, "Reopen the case!", "Two Killers?", and "What is Ross's Hiding?" He threw the newspaper in the air out of frustration; it's been three days since the interview aired on television. It has been hell every minute since then. Jonathan had to turn his phone off, he hadn't left the house, and he sent Pearl and Weston to stay with Faith's parents

311

until things calmed down. Faith's parents were being very supportive considering everything that was said in that interview.

"What the hell is wrong with you?" Claire asked.

"Seriously? Are you blind, Claire? Are you not living in the same world I am?"

"I don't know why you're mad, the police haven't been up your ass!"

"Claire, I have had several calls from business partners, asking what the hell is going on. This looks bad for business. The last three days, I have lost five deals because they walked away from the table. They don't want to be associated with a scandal!"

"Well, I'm upset too, I didn't see why we had to postpone our vacation, the police could have waited!" Claire said.

Jonathan looked at her with contempt. "Claire, the police have been hounding us for weeks to come down and talk with them. We could have had all this cleared up and been able to go on vacation. But because of some reason, you don't want to cooperate with them. Now we have pressure coming from all sides of us and you don't see it."

Claire threw her shake against the wall, shattering glass everywhere. "You think you're the only one going through this, how do you think I feel everyone is taking his word over mine!"

"Claire, everyone is taking his word over yours because you are not saying anything! I mean I'm your husband and we haven't talked about it!"

"What do you want to know?"

"Have you ever been with him?"

"Are you kidding me? You actually believe him over me! I can see everyone else thinking I'm a monster. But how could you think I'm capable of those things?"

"Stop being dramatic! I don't think you did anything. But you have to admit, we look as if we're hiding something by not cooperating with the investigation."

"What about innocent until proven guilty? Does that not matter anymore?" Claire yelled.

"Claire, please don't say that out in public. The only reason why you were not dragged down there already is because of who you are. I feel they have been more than patient with us, and if I'm being truthful, you're the reason I haven't gone to talk with them." Jonathan got up from the table and walked toward his office.

"Are you fucking kidding, you are going to walk away from me!" she screamed at him.

"Yeah, watch. It's really easy." He was almost to his office when a plate whipped by his head, hitting the wall. He turned around to see her glaring at him, "You are a crazy bitch! I would slap the shit out of you if I knew you wouldn't get off on it."

"You pick on people you know you can get away with. When someone fights back it's no fun for you. You're a coward!" Claire yelled at him.

"Claire, I have had about enough of your crazy ass. It's no wonder Douglas didn't want to fuck you; wish I had listened back then."

She started to walk towards him when the doorbell rang. She instantly snapped out of it, putting on a smile. She opened the door; standing there was Matthew Davis, their family attorney. He was here today because he was going with Claire down to talk with Lieutenant Walker.

"Good morning, Claire," He greeted her.

"Is it really?" she asked.

"We both woke up this morning, didn't we?"

"Ok, listen. If you are going to be up in the clouds today, stay outside until it's time to leave. If you're going to live in the real world, come inside."

Matthew stopped smiling; he walked inside to see Jonathan standing in the foyer.

"Hello, Jonathan."

"Oh, Matt. Don't let her bother you, she is pissed off because everyone thinks she is a psycho killer," Jonathan laughed.

"Fuck you, Jonathan!" Claire said.

"I would like to go through some things with Claire in private, if that's alright?" Matthew asked.

"Yeah, that is fine Matt," Jonathan answered him.

"This has nothing to do with you Jonathan, this is between me and Matt" Claire said, looking at Matthew.

"I'm afraid she is right, Jonathan. Confidentiality," Matthew told him.

"I will remember that when the bill comes in and I have to pay it."

Claire led Matthew to the dining room.

"Ok, Claire. We will be talking with Lieutenant Nicole Walker today; she is a young and bright investigator. She will definitely have some difficult questions for you, she will ask you questions that you feel she has no right to ask you but they are doing this to gauge your reaction. They will try to use your words against you. The best advice I can give you is if you don't know an answer, simply say I don't know. If there is a question you don't want to answer, then don't. But saying that, if there is anything you need to tell me or let me know, now is the time to do that. Remember that this is their job and they have to prove everything and they don't have shit on you. Ok?"

"I understand," Claire answered.

"When I spoke with them, I knew they wanted to get a DNA sample of yours to rule you out."

"No way in hell! They are not getting shit from me, not after everything they have put me through."

"What do you mean to put you through?"

"Making me postpone my vacation for this!"

"To be fair Claire, they have been trying for weeks to get you to come in. The reason why I was so adamant about today, they told me if we didn't come in, they would come here and arrest you."

"Does that mean I'm getting arrested today!?"

"No, you're not getting arrested today. I'm telling you this because I need you to know how seriously they are taking this. If it was me, I would answer all their questions, as long as I'm not incriminating myself."

"What evidence do they have, anyway?" She asked.

"I honestly have no idea what they have. I would assume that they are wanting you to answer questions about the allegations that Adam made against you in the interview."

Claire started to feel sick to her stomach, "Excuse me, I need to use the restroom."

"Alright. We'll leave when you are finished." Claire came downstairs in a different outfit.

Matthew asked, "Everything alright, Mrs. Ross?"

"Yes, why do you ask, Matt?"

"You changed your outfit."

"I'm fine, you just make sure they don't try and screw me with no lube, ok?"

"Yes, ma'am."

"Jonathan! We are leaving now!" Claire shouted. Jonathan came out of his office and gave her a kiss on the cheek.

"Matthew, keep her in line and get this shit dealt with."

"I will do my best, Jonathan. Claire, I will be out in the car." Matthew could feel the tension between them.

"Claire, don't worry about it. Answer their questions and put all this to bed. I love you."

"I love you, too. What are you going to be doing while I'm gone?"

"I am going to make a few calls, see if I can smooth things over with some of the investors and get them back to the table."

"Ok. Matt said we would be late, probably about five or six tonight. I will see you then?"

"You already know."

Jonathan walked her to Matthew's car and watched them drive away.

They arrived at the Highway Patrol office about 10 minutes early. Matt wanted to make sure Claire didn't have any last-minute questions or concerns. Claire was feeling better, to her surprise, maybe she was over thinking all of this. They walked into the lobby; Lieutenant Walker was there to greet them.

They exchanged pleasantries. "Follow me, I will take you upstairs." They followed Nicole to the elevators, going up to the third floor, they passed a coffee pot. "Would either of you like some coffee?"

"I would love a cup, thank you," Matthew said. They waited for him to get his cup and continued to the interview room.

They all sat down.

"I'm Lieutenant Nicole Walker, I will be conducting this interview today. Do you have any questions before we go on record."

"I don't understand why I am here, is it just because of what Adam said in that interview?" Claire answered.

"We asked you to come down because we thought you could add insight into why Adam said those things. We have to look into all possibilities, no matter how crazy they sound. Does that answer your question?"

"Yes, thank you. I thought you all were taking his word over mine. That's why I was upset."

"We have to look into all claims made no matter how unlikely they are. If it's alright with you, I'm going to get started?"

"Of course," Claire answered.

"This is Lieutenant Nicole Walker with the Missouri State Highway Patrol. I will be interviewing, please state your name for the record."

"Claire Ross."

"Thank you. Mrs. Ross's attorney is present as well, state your name for the record, please."

"Matthew Davis. I would like to add that Mrs. Ross is here out of courtesy."

Lieutenant Walker smiled, "Yes, thank you for being willing to come down and answer some questions for us. We appreciate it. Mrs. Ross, I'm going to be asking you questions that may or may not have happened ten or more years ago, but please understand I have to ask them. You are also free to go at any time during the interview, if you need a break or something to drink, please let me know."

"I am fine for right now, thank you," Claire answered.

"Ok. Then I will jump right into it, if that's alright?"

Claire nodded her head, Lieutenant Walker opened her notepad, flipping to the next blank page, which was somewhere in the middle and began.

"Do you know Mr. Lewis?"

"Yes. He is the man who killed my best friend."

"I meant; did you know Mr. Lewis before Faith's death?"

"No."

"Were you ever in a romantic relationship with Mr. Lewis?"

"No."

"Have you ever talked with or had any kind of communication with Mr. Lewis?"

"No."

"You never talked with Mr. Lewis on the phone, texted or social media?"

"No."

"Did Faith ever mention Mr. Lewis?"

"Yes, she mentioned him at a lunch we had together."

"What did she say about him?"

"She told me that she had been seeing someone and his name was Adam." Claire kept her answers short and simple. Not giving anything more then she needed too, just like Mr. Davis told her.

"That's it, she didn't say anything else about him?"

"No."

Nicole could feel how cold Claire was being, she was going to have to walk on eggshells through this interview so Claire wouldn't walk away.

"No girl talks about him?"

"No, Lieutenant. We are grown women, she told me what she wanted too. Nothing more."

This was going to be harder than she thought, but Nicole didn't get to where she was by giving up. She continued, "Did Faith give you something to give or send to Mr. Lewis?"

"Yes, she gave me a letter to give to him, but I never did."

"Why didn't you give it to him?"

"I thought about it, realized it was none of my business and wanted nothing to do with the matter."

"What did you do with the letter Mrs. Ross?"

"I threw it away."

"Did you ever open and read it?"

"I told you; I threw it away."

"Dang! See I'm nosey, I would have had to open it to find out what it was regarding."

Claire sat there, unimpressed, and getting annoyed.

"Why didn't you give it back to Faith?"

"I didn't think about it to be honest."

"Have you ever been to Mr. Lewis's home?"

"No."

"Ever driven by it or seen it?"

"No."

"Have you ever gone by the name, Lexi?"

"No," She answered as she shifted in the chair.

"Mrs. Ross, just to be clear, you have never gone by the name Lexi?"

"No, I have not."

"Do you know of any reason Mr. Lewis would make these kinds of allegations against you?"

"How would I know; he is trailer trash! Mr. Lewis wanted his five minutes of fame and he's getting it."

"Trailer trash? Why trailer trash, Mrs. Ross?"

"Because that's what he is, trailer trash," she said confidently.

320

"How did you know Mr. Lewis lived in a trailer?"

Claire was stunned, she had no idea what to say, "Excuse me?"

"How did you know Mr. Lewis lived in a trailer?"

Claire was visibly nervous. "I didn't know. I just assumed..." Matthew whispered something into her ear, and then she said, "I believe I saw on the news that he lived in a trailer." She smiled, "Like I said he is trailer trash."

"You just remembered seeing it on the news, that he lived in a trailer?"

"Yes."

Nicole decided to change up the questions. "Were Faith and you close friends?"

"Yes. Faith was my best friend."

"How did Faith and you meet?"

"We met through my ex-husband; their families were friends and they grew up together."

"Who is your ex-husband?"

Claire rolled her eyes, "Douglas Fulton."

"Why does that name sound familiar?"

"His family owns Fulton Farms and he used to be in business with my husband Fulton/Ross construction."

"That's right, I used to go pumpkin picking at Fulton Farm every year. It was always a good time."

If looks could kill, Nicole would have been dead. Claire was staring a hole through her, "Listen, Nicole. I'm not here for a new friend, I have enough of those, ok sweetie?"

"It's Lieutenant Walker, Mrs. Ross. I'm glad you have enough friends. Speaking of friends, being Faith's best friend, did you know about their open marriage?"

"Yes, I knew about it."

"Were you ever sexually involved with either one of them at any time during the marriage?"

Claire looked annoyed, "Yes, I was."

"With who?"

"Jonathan," Claire answered sharply.

"Did Faith know this?"

"Yes."

"How did she find out?"

"Find out? She didn't need to find out, she was there with us!"

"Oh, ok. Was this a threesome or a foursome?"

"I don't think that is any of your business! What the hell does that situation have to do with anything said in that interview?"

"Lieutenant Walker, what is the importance of this," Matthew asked.

Nicole has grown tired of the attitude that Claire has, acting like she hasn't been dodging them for weeks. "Mr. Davis, we have statements from witnesses' saying that the former Mrs. Ross and Claire had a falling out over several sexual encounters that your client and Jonathan Ross had during his marriage to Faith Ross."

"Individuals other than Adam Lewis?" Matthew asked.

"Mr. Davis, come on."

Claire popped in, "It was Jonathan and I having sex in the entertainment room of my old house, while my ex-husband and Faith watched. Ok!"

"Claire, you don't have to say anything, we are done here," Matthew said.

"No! Let her ask these bullshit questions. I'm not afraid."

"Claire, as your attorney, I'm advising you to not answer another question."

"Sit down! My husband and I paid you a hefty retainer, you work for me, I say what goes," Claire said, raising her voice at him. He turned quiet and motioned for Nicole to continue with her questions.

"To be clear, you never had an affair with Jonathan behind Faith's back?

"No."

"Were you married at the time to Douglas Fulton?"

"Yes."

"Douglas was there that night during the sexual encounter with Jonathan, correct?"

"Yes. He and Faith were both there."

"Was that a spur of the moment decision or did you all plan to do that?"

"Jonathan and my ex-husband had it planned, I did not find out until later. I was fully against the idea."

"What made you change your mind?"

"What can I say, my husband is very attractive and persuasive," Claire said, smiling.

"To be clear, Douglas Fulton is attractive and persuasive, because he was your husband at the time?"

Claire looked insulted. "No! I mean my husband now."

"Oh, see I got confused because he was not your husband back then. Faith was married to Jonathan."

Claire could feel her blood boiling, she wanted out of this room and away from this bitch.

Nicole smiled at her, trying to hide the contempt she has for her. "Did you ever have a sexual encounter with Jonathan that Faith was not there for?"

"No. How many times are you going to ask the same damn question? Is this why these always take forever?"

Nicole ignored her question and asked, "Were Jonathan and Faith happy in their marriage?"

"I don't know if they were happy in their marriage, I only knew about my marriage."

"How would you describe your marriage to Mr. Fulton?"

"A symbiotic relationship."

"That's interesting. Why would you use that term?"

"Because that's exactly what it was, we helped each other. He got to stay in the closet for fourteen more years and I got stability and security."

"Do you mean that Mr. Fulton is gay?"

Claire laughed, "Yes. Gay as gay comes."

"What's funny about that?"

"You are the first person I have ever told and it feels good."

"Nobody knows that Mr. Fulton is gay?"

"He came out a few years ago, but I won't talk about it."
Claire is sweating and trying to not explode with anger.

"What kind of stability and security did you get from Mr. Fulton?"

"I was a model at the time Douglas and I met. With modeling you're only as good as your last job. It's a highly competitive career. There will be times you work every day for three months and then won't get a call back for six months. It can be very hard. With marrying Douglas, I didn't have to worry about money, I could focus solely on my career."

"When was the last time you saw or spoke with Mr. Fulton?"

Claire thought about it for a second. "Gosh, it has to be probably 2018. The year we got our divorce."

"How did the divorce go?"

"It was a breeze, no one was upset or hurt. Douglas and I both knew it was a long time coming. We each took what we wanted, sold the rest and donated it to a charity."

"That's great. There is no reason why Mr. Fulton would be angry with you or Mr. Ross?"

"No. I would not think so."

"There would be no reason for Mr. Fulton to lie?"

"I don't know, people change, Lieutenant Walker. You being in law enforcement, I thought would know that better than anyone else."

"Fair enough, Mrs. Ross."

"Did you and Faith have a disagreement about your sexual involvement with her husband?"

"I wouldn't call it a disagreement, but we had words about it and worked through our issues and Faith's insecurities."

"If that's not a disagreement, what would you call it?"

"Faith was insecure about how she looked vs how I looked. She needed to work through that and deal with it, she did and we were fine."

"Did Faith and you ever have a fight or argument about you sleeping with Jonathan?"

"I just told you, we discussed it and worked through it."

"Is it true that Faith and you had a heated verbal discussion at her house on the day she was murdered?"

"Do you know how long ago that was, I don't remember."

This is what Nicole has been waiting for, to see how Claire reacts to this. "You don't remember having a discussion with Faith, where she called you: a whore, slut and said fuck you?"

Claire instantly became enraged and she shouted, "Who said that happened? This is bullshit!"

"Mrs. Ross, we have an eyewitness that claims they were there at the time of this encounter, between Faith and you."

At this point Matthew was trying to calm her down and keep her from saying anything else that would make things worse.

Claire shouted, "Let me guess. Hailee! She is a liar; she's pissed off at me because I fired her two weeks ago! She is a terrible person, always trying to stick her nose somewhere that it does not belong."

Nicole was loving this, seeing her come unhinged like that was worth the wait. "Mrs. Ross, we got Hailee's signed affidavit four weeks ago."

Claire could not take it anymore. "I would like to take a break!"

"Absolutely Mrs. Ross. I will leave you and your attorney, does a ten-minute break sound alright?"

"Sounds good," Matthew said.

Claire was furious, the nerve that bitch Hailee had to come after her, she thought. Wait until she tells Jonathan what that bitch did, now he will agree with her for firing her. Her mind was racing, she couldn't think straight, she felt like she was in a haze.

Suddenly Matthew held a cup of coffee in front of her. "Here drink this, it's strong but it will do the trick." He sat down next to her, "Listen, you are doing great, try to keep your emotions in check. They are doing this to try, to get you to slip up and say something. Unless they have physical proof, all this is a he said, she said deal. I don't believe people will take his word over yours. Do yourself a favor, relax. Answer her question and that's it. Nothing else. I got you, trust me."

She felt better after hearing him say that. She just wanted this to be over. There was a knock at the interview door, "Are we ready to continue, in here?" Nicole asked.

"Yes, we are," Matthew answered. Claire took a sip of the coffee; boy was it strong. If this coffee didn't clear the haze, nothing would.

"Alright, let's get started. Did you go see Faith the day she was killed?

Claire rolled her eyes, "I don't remember."

"Ok, do you remember what you were wearing that day?"

"No, how would I remember that!"

Nicole was going to switch it up. "Do you know Skyler?"

"Who?" Claire answered with a slight pitch difference in her voice.

"Skyler, she was the children's nanny for a few years. At least I believe that was her job title."

Claire looked uncomfortable. "Yes, I remember her vaguely."

"Have you ever been involved in a threesome with Skyler?"

Matthew stopped her before she answered, "Lieutenant, what does this have to do with anything?"

"It has to deal with certain facts of this case. I'm asking questions to determine whether or not any of the allegations made against her are true. I'm trying to help clear her name by asking her these questions. If she would have come down early to answer our questions, all this might have been avoidable. But here we are."

"Mrs. Ross, have you ever been involved in a threesome?"

"Yes."

"With Jonathan?

"Yes."

"Before you two were married?"

"Yes."

"Did you and Jonathan have a threesome with Skyler, his children's nanny, just weeks after Faith's death?"

Claire didn't answer right away. Nicole looked at her, knowing that Claire could feel the walls closing in on her with each passing question.

"Yes, we did. The last time I checked it wasn't against the law."

"Have you ever been involved with rough sex?"

"Yes. You should try it sometime."

Nicole paid no attention to her comment, "Have you ever been involved with rough sex with Jonathan?"

"Yes. All the time, any other way is no fun."

"Ever been involved with rough sex with Jonathan, while being held down by Skyler?"

"Yes. That was one of the first times we all had fun together! Are you getting off on this Lieutenant? Are you going to use this when you go home and rub yourself asleep?"

Matthew interrupted Claire, "Lieutenant! I will not put up with this, if you don't start treating my client with some respect, we will walk out of here!"

Nicole sat there a moment. "Alright, we can come back to that." Nicole knew she had Claire right where she wanted her.

"On the early morning of November 21, 2017 between 1:30 am. and 2 am. do you remember where you were Mrs. Ross?"

"Yes. I was at my home with my then husband Douglas Fulton."

"Do you remember what the two of you discussed that morning?"

"I had been trying to reach him all night and couldn't. I was getting worried about him, when he finally got home, his clothes were soaking wet. I asked him why; he told me he had gone to see Jonathan and they had a fight outside in the rain."

"Do you remember how you hurt yourself earlier that day?"

"Hurt myself? I never hurt myself."

"Really? Mr. Fulton said that he remembers you having a black eye, bumps, a couple of big bruises and a bad limp from an injured ankle."

Claire sat there a moment thinking back. "Yes, come to think of it. I do remember slipping on the concrete out by our pool. It's pretty embarrassing, isn't."

"You fell on the concrete out by your pool?"

"Yes."

"Because Mr. Fulton told us, you told him you fell while jogging that day."

Claire was silent. "It was a long time ago, it's hard to remember."

Nicole kept pushing, "What about the scratch marks by your collar bone you had?"

"Like I said, it was a long time ago. I don't remember."

"Do you remember how you fell, flat on your face, on your side or on your back?"

"No. I don't, it was a long time ago."

Nicole wasn't sure if she would get another chance to question her. "Because if you had bruises and a black eye on the right side of your face, then all your injuries should be on your right side. But that wouldn't explain the scratch marks below your collarbone or the bruise on your left thigh or your left arm."

Claire just sat there and didn't say a word. Nicole waited for a response for a few seconds. "Nothing to say about Mrs. Ross?"

"I did not hear a question; I heard a statement and I don't care what you think."

"Did you ever discuss what happened to Faith that morning with Douglas?"

"I don't remember, I could have."

"Just to be clear, you don't remember talking about it, or you don't know if you talked about it?"

Claire was confused, "I don't remember talking about it."

"Claire, do you think Faith deserved to die?"

"Are you fucking kidding me, how could you even ask me a question like that?"

Before she could say anything else, Nicole fired another question at her, "Do you remember telling Douglas, 'that bitch deserved a lot more than just a beating'?"

"Hell no!"

"Claire, think about it, are you sure?"

"I don't have to think about it, I'm sure!"

"Then how did you know she was beaten, before any of that came out to the public?"

Claire was in a haze; she was seeing red and about ready to explode."No answer for that either, huh? You think about it and we can come back to that one." Nicole just kept going right along, she was going to keep asking questions until they got up and left.

"Do you remember telling Mr. Fulton, he was going to be a prime suspect?"

"No."

"Do you recall Mr. Fulton telling you because of the falling out Faith and you had, that the police should look at you, especially because of your injuries that you sustained earlier that day?"

"I remember us joking around about being suspects, but neither one of us actually meant it."

"Joking around, Mrs. Ross I don't believe Mr. Fulton thought it was a joke. I certainly don't think this is a joke! Your answers don't add up and your story has more holes than Swiss cheese!"

Matthew butted in, "That is enough Lieutenant, this interview is over. My client will not sit here and be verbally assaulted by you!"

Nicole had one more question to hit her with. "Claire, let's clear this up, give us a DNA sample! What do you say?"

Claire didn't know what to say, she was just sitting there. Matthew jumped in, "Not a chance in hell is she helping you after what you have done here today. This will not be tolerated; I will have your badge, Lieutenant!" They stood up and stormed out of the interview room, Matthew practically dragging Claire out of the station. As they were walking out, Nicole shouted, "Get in line, Matt!"

The car ride was silent until Claire spoke. "I'm going to need to be alone with Jonathan when we get back. You can come over later or tomorrow and we can talk."

"Listen, Claire. I can deal with anything; we just have to get out in front of it. We don't want to lose leverage."

Claire looked at Matthew, "I appreciate it, but I need to talk with Jonathan."

They pulled up to the gate and were waved through. He drove up to the house and dropped her off. She decided to walk around the back of the house, she wanted to sit on the back patio. She wasn't ready to talk with him yet, she needed a glass of wine. She went inside, downstairs to the wine cellar. Before making it to the wine cellar door, she heard something. At first, she wasn't sure what it was, but then it dawned on her. "That son of a bitch!" she said out loud. It was coming from the salon room, she opened the door slowly, their backs were facing the door. She opened it all the way, stood there and watched for a moment to see how long it took them to realize someone was there. After a couple of minutes Claire got tired of standing there.

Chapter 18

"Brandy! Can you take my husband's dick out of your ass?" she said in a stern voice.

They jumped and Brandy screamed, "Oh my God, Claire. I'm sorry, it just-"

Claire cut her off, "Shut up!" She focused her attention on Jonathan, who was standing there swaying back and forth. He rolled his eyes, "Claire, don't even start with me, you knew who I was when you and I started."

"Yes, but we made an agreement. We do this together! Not without one another!" Brandy started to put on her underwear. "Bitch, no one told you to get dressed! Stand there, keep your mouth shut and don't move!" Claire told her. Brandy did as she was told. She started to shake, as tears came down her face. Claire hasn't felt this way in a long time, Jonathan had sat down in the barber chair. Claire kicked the chair to spin him around to face her, "Look at her. Who does she remind you of?" Jonathan was confused, he looked at Claire like she was crazy.

"I don't know, who?"

"Come on, take a good look at her and think about it. Who was another person you were with that was a spinless, scared, little bitch?"

"Claire, I'm not playing this game with you. Get out and let us finish."

"Ok." Claire walked out, went upstairs to their bedroom, got her .38 revolver and a stun gun out of her bedside table. She barged into the salon room, Brandy was dressed, Jonathan was getting dressed. They did not see the stun gun by her side.

"Claire, get the hell out of here. It's not enough, you already ruined a good time, now you are going to make a fool of yourself," he told her.

She went straight to him; she got within arm's reach and hit him with a stun gun. He dropped to the floor; Brandy screamed. "Bitch, shut up or I hit you with it too! He's fine. Give him a few minutes, he'll wake up. But until he does, make yourself useful, follow me." Brandy followed Claire out to the bar area. "You see that door?" Claire asked, pointing to it.

"Yes"

"I want you to go open that door and there should be a black duffle bag on the top shelf. Get it and bring it here."

Brandy did as she was told, the bag wasn't heavy but it had enough weight to it. They went back to check on Jonathan and he was waking up, Claire rolled him over to his stomach.

"Hand me those zip ties in there." She told Brandy. Claire zip tied Jonathan's hands behind his back. She unbuttoned and unzipped the pants he had on, she pulled them off him and threw them across the room.

"Brandy, get over here, help me get him to his feet and take him out by the bar. We will sit him on the couch out there."

Brandy came over and helped her. He was coming out of it, but pissed himself because of the stun gun.

"Before we sit him down, slide his underwear off him." They sat him down on the couch. Claire grabbed the bag from Brandy and found the duct tape, she put his feet together and began duct taping his ankles together.

"There. I don't think you will be going anywhere. Brandy, normally this stuff is used for our kink when we invite someone over to share. We fuck them together! That's the key word, together! You dumb bastard!" she yelled at Jonathan.

Claire reached into her pocket, pulled out his little helper pill. She shoved it down his throat, then held his nose and mouth shut. "Swallow prick!" Jonathan choked, but got it down. "Now we wait. Don't worry Brandy, it shouldn't be long. Come over here, have a seat next to Jonathan." Claire sat on the coffee table in front of them. "Jonathan, have you ever cared about anyone, other than yourself?"

"Yes, Claire I do. My children are my world."

"Bullshit! You can't even be truthful with yourself! Face it, you are a piece of shit! Your own children don't want to be with you!"

"Fuck you, Claire!"

"No. Not anymore Jonathan. That ship has sailed. The shame of it is that you used to be a really nice guy. I remember Faith telling me many stories of how wonderful, romantic and caring you were to her. I was jealous of her, I thought she was the fucked up one in that relationship. Turns out, I was wrong. I thought she was being a complete bitch, that she wasn't taking care of your needs, and that she was selfish and a brat. If I only knew then, what I know now. You had a good woman with Faith, you took advantage of her family's name, money and connections. Without her, you would have been nothing! No one cared about some low-life piece of shit that was trying to build something from the ground up. You are pathetic!"

Jonathan was sitting there, she could tell he was getting angry because his ears were turning red, he was trying not to say anything but he was about to explode.

"Truth be told, you couldn't even keep her happy."

"You are a slimy piece of shit! What makes you better, you were sucking dick for food before you met Douglas. What does that make you!" he yelled at her.

She started to laugh, "I sucked dick because I had to, you sucked it because you wanted too. You have had so many beautiful women and none of them can please you like a man can, maybe you need to stop living in the closet."

"Keep talking bitch, you know you will never get away with this, Claire! You are a psycho bitch!"

Claire leaned forward. She pulled the gun from her waist band, showing it to him. "Listen to you, talking tough in your position. Jonathan, did it ever occur to you, I have already planned to get caught. I want to make sure you get your punishment first."

Jonathan didn't know what to say. "Listen, Claire, let's talk about this."

"Jonathan, please do us both a favor; shut the fuck up." Claire grabbed the ball gag without Jonathan noticing. She got behind him. "Open your mouth," she told him.

"Please, Claire."

"Jonathan Ross, are you begging? Holy shit, who knew you would beg. Listen, you made a lot of women wear this. I think it is only fair if you wear it."

"You promise, you're not going to hurt me?"

"I promise. Come on, open up." Jonathan opened his mouth, she put the gag in and buckled it, making sure it was tight. Now that he was set, she turned to Brandy, "Stand up. Let's get you undressed. Take off everything too, I want to see that body my husband had to have." As Brandy took off her clothes, she started to cry.

"Brandy? I need you to listen to what I'm about to say. If you start that crying bullshit, I will use this stun gun on your ass. Do you understand?" Claire said, staring at her with contempt.

"Yes."

"Good, I will be nice and tell you. I have no plans on hurting you, I understand why you did what you did. You need the money, but you need to realize that if you don't do what I say, I will shoot you in the head."

"I understand, Claire." Brandy finished undressing; she stood waiting for instructions.

"Damn, alright Brandy. I see what he was seeing, you have nice tits, a fat ass and what is that?" Claire pointed to Brandy's inner thigh.

"It's a tattoo," Brandy answered, her voice shaking.

Claire looked surprised, "No shit? What does it say?" Brandy started to speak, but Claire cut her off. "I know what it says! It's a caution sign 'Slippery When Wet' please tell me you got that because you lost a bet."

"I was in high school; I was young and dumb."

"Wow! Jonathan. Is it true? Is she 'Slippery When Wet'?"

Jonathan said something under the ball gag.

"Brandy, show me how you sucked his dick!"

Brandy stared at her for a moment, then got down on her knees in front of him.

"Wait! Did you already suck it today?" Claire asked.

"Yes, I did."

"Well, then he doesn't get that again. Brandy, I think you two did everything already right?"

"Yes."

Claire stood up and took off her clothes, "Brandy come over here and eat my ass for me, please."

Brandy started to cry.

"Stop!" Claire shouted. She turned around to see tears coming down from Brandy's face. "Brandy, what did I tell you about crying? I mean I warned you, right?" Claire brought the revolver up, putting it against Brandy's head. She pulled the trigger. *Click.* Claire let out a laugh. "Damn, it's your lucky day. No bullet in that cylinder."

Brandy was trying not to cry; she was holding it back as long as she could. Claire watched as Brandy struggled. "Brandy, what is a lesson you have learned here today?"

"Not to get involved with stuff like this."

Claire nodded, "Good answer. Where is your phone? Get it."

Brandy got her phone out of her purse; she tried handing it to Claire.

"No, do a live stream video." Brandy started a live stream. "Leave the phone on you, tell everyone what you did today," Claire said.

Brandy was trying to cover her breast, "Show them your tits, show them my husband." Brandy did what Claire said. "Now tell them what you did."

"I had sex with a married man."

"In detail."

"I sucked him off, he ate me, and he fucked me in both holes."

"Did you come on him or did you come when he ate you out?"

"On him."

"Are you ever going to do this again?"

"No!"

"Are you sorry for what you did?"

"Yes, I am."

Claire smiled at her, "One more question, then I'm going to let you go because you definitely aren't worth a bullet. Brandy, have you ever had sex so good that you felt like you had an out of body experience?"

"Yes, I know exactly what that feels like."

"Did it feel good or great?"

Brandy started to smile, "It was amazing, it felt wonderful."

"Good, hopefully this will feel just like that!" Claire shot Brandy in the head at point-blank range. The video continued to play, Claire picked the phone up, she panned down to Brandy's life-less body and then put it on her face. "People say men are the violent ones. That's because they have never met a woman as strong as me. Let me show you who is responsible for Brandy's death. This man, right there! Jonathan Ross!" She had panned it over to Jonathan who was trying to get out of his restraints.

"Jonathan, tell the world that this is not the first woman you have killed, is it?" Claire went behind him and unbuckled the strap on the ball gag.

"I never killed anyone! You're crazy! Help me!"

"Yes, you have. Jonathan, you may not have physically killed Faith, but you might as well have. You kill everything good, decent and pure that you come into contact with. Your own children want nothing to do with you. What does that tell you? You all are the same; as long as you get to eat, sleep and get off, everything is fine. That stops today, Jonathan. How many women do you think you have taken advantage of? They won't call it what it is because you had the money and you tore them down, making them believe they were nothing but a sex toy; that because they accepted your money, they wanted it."

"I never did anything to anyone! It was always consensual!"

"Consensual? Ha! Right! You piece of shit. How many times did we sleep with some innocent eighteen-year-old right here on this couch and pay her several thousands of dollars to keep her mouth shut or make her sign one of your non-disclosure agreements. You are a predator, preying on people weaker than you. You make me sick; you think you're God's gift to women in bed. Please we both know that ship sailed long ago, now you need help before doing anything. I can't believe how far you have fallen from who you used to be. I fell in love with that Jonathan, now I have this shell of a man that used to be something. You caused all of this on yourself."

Jonathan started to cry.

"Oh. My. God. Are you crying?"

"Help me! Please! Anyone listening I'm Jonathan Ross, I live at 7700 Yacht Club Drive-"

Before he could say anything else, Claire walked up to him and emptied the gun in his head. She inhaled and exhaled a big breath of air. She forgot she was holding the phone. "Oh, shit. Sorry everyone, in case you missed it here is Jonathan

341

Ross. Well, what's left of him." She panned the phone back to her; her nude body was covered in blood.

"Ok, I want to thank all of you that watched Brandy's last live stream. I'm sorry if any of you are hurt by my actions taken against her, but she was in the wrong. She happened to do it on the wrong day. I am going to get cleaned up before the police get here. Thank you all again and I will see you all later. Byyyyeeee…"

Claire stopped the live stream, and went and showered. She had finished getting dressed as the police were knocking on her front door.

"Ok. Here we go."

Claire was arrested by the Sheriff's deputies shortly after they arrived. They took her to the station, fingerprinted, swabbed her DNA and photographed her. The only thing she said to them during the whole process, was she would only talk with Lieutenant Nicole Walker with the Highway Patrol. They put her in an interview room and left her there.

Chapter 19

Nicole had gone home to relax and try to get some sleep for the night. That all came to a screeching stop when she got a phone call from the Sheriff's Department.

"Lieutenant Walker," she answered, half asleep.

"Lieutenant Walker, this is Sheriff Holly Jones from Jefferson County"

"Ok, what can I do for you Sheriff?" Nicole asked.

"We arrested Claire Ross earlier this afternoon; she will only talk with you. She won't talk with me or my deputies."

"Claire Ross? Why did you arrest her?"

"For murder."

Nicole shot up from the sofa. "You arrested her for murder?"

"Yes." Sheriff Jones didn't know what was so hard to understand.

"Sheriff Jones, have you talked with Prosecuting Attorney Meadows about this?"

"No. I haven't, why would I talk to her about that?"

"She is going to want to know why you jumped the gun in arresting her for the murder of Faith Ross!"

"Lieutenant Walker, I think you're confused. We did not arrest Claire Ross for the murder of Faith Ross, we arrested her for the murders of Jonathan Ross and Brandy Garcia."

Nicole felt like she'd been hit by a train. "Jonathan Ross is dead?"

"Yes, ma'am. The hairdresser, too, Ms. Brandy Garcia. They were killed earlier today while live-streaming. Now my problem is Claire is willing to talk but only with you, Lieutenant."

"I'm on my way down, Sheriff."

Nicole got down to the Sheriff's office about an hour after they called her. She had called Major Stephens and told him what was going on. Nicole found Sheriff Jones.

"Sheriff Jones, I'm Lieutenant Walker. Sorry about the confusion earlier."

"It's no problem. After our phone call I put a call into P.A. Meadows office. She is on her way down, too. I can only assume that means one thing, the Prosecuting Attorney and Highway Patrol have reopened the Faith Ross murder investigation."

"I can't comment on that Sheriff, you will have to talk with P.A. Meadows."

"Sure, I don't blame you all for reopening it, especially after that interview on television. Made you all look foolish."

"You know he confessed to killing her, not to mention, his DNA was at the crime scene, on the victim and had no solid alibi. What would you have thought?"

"Lieutenant, you're barking up the wrong tree. We are on the same team, that's why I called you."

Nicole was tired, frustrated, and now pissed off. "Let's forget it. I'm going to get a cup of coffee and wait for P.A. Meadows to get here before I go in there and talk with her." Nicole walked away before Sheriff Jones said anything. She was drinking her coffee when Rachel walked in, they caught each other.

"Lieutenant Walker, how is it going?" Rachel could tell Nicole was annoyed.

"Other than this Sheriff not knowing her ass from a hole in the ground, fine."

The Sheriff came over. "P.A. Meadows, how are you?"

"I'm good. How are you?" Rachel answered.

"I would be better if I was kept in the loop about open investigations in my county."

Rachel was in no mood for this. "First, there was no open investigation involving Claire Ross. Secondly, if you are referring to the Faith Ross case, that is a closed case, we were given new information, and Lieutenant Walker was examining that information. Before you ask, I gave the MSHP that information because they had to take the original case from the Sheriff's Department, because of all the mistakes that were made. Now I understand that it was under the old Sheriff, but the public still views it as the whole department. Let's work as a team and not have another blunder, so we can tell the public that their tax dollars are hard at work."

"That's fine. It's not my head on the chopping block," Sheriff Jones responded.

Rachel decided to drop it. She looked at Nicole, "Are you ready to go in there?"

Nicole finished her coffee with one last drink. "I'm ready."

"I will be watching from the room down the hall. There will be a deputy outside of the door."

Nicole nodded. "Have you talked with Major Stephens?" Nicole asked Rachel.

"I did. He told me that you could handle this, and to brief him in the morning," Rachel told her, smiling. Nicole grabbed her notes, gave Rachel a thumbs up.

Nicole opened the door; Claire was sitting at the table trying to occupy herself. They greeted each other as Nicole sat down.

"Claire, did they inform you of your rights?"

"Yes, they only read them to me twice," she laughed.

"Good." Nicole waited to see if Claire was going to say something. Claire didn't say a word. "What happened today?" Nicole asked.

"Karma. Karma is what happened today." Claire answered. She proceeded to tell Nicole that when she got home, she walked in on Jonathan and her hairdresser, Brandy, having sex in the salon room. Claire explained why she killed them, telling Nicole that a person can take so much until they explode and that's what happened.

"Why did you live stream the whole thing?"

"People needed to know why I did it. To be fair I did not live stream it, Brandy live streamed it. I guess she wanted to clear her soul," Claire said.

"Are we going to be serious with one another or did you bring me down here to waste my time?" Nicole asked.

Claire was caught off-guard by the question. "Why would you ask that? I wanted to talk with you because I feel there is no fakeness with you. You are who you are, like it or not. You don't give a shit what others think about you."

"Did you really not tell Brandy to start the live stream?"

Claire rolled her eyes, "Yes, I told her to get her phone and start a live stream video. When it came on, I told her to tell everyone what she did. In detail. I then asked her if she had ever had sex so good, that it felt like an out of body experience? She said she had, and I said that I hoped this would feel the same way and I shot her in the head."

Nicole was impressed, Claire was being honest. "Thank you, Claire."

"Why are you thanking me?"

"Because it will make this whole process easier for all of us."

"I guess you want to hear about Jonathan too?"

"Yes, Claire."

"He was such an asshole; it's not enough I play out every fantasy in the bedroom, I let him do whatever he wants with me, too me, and even with other women. The son of a bitch still has to cheat on me!"

"Was this the first time he cheated on you?"

"If I'm being honest, no. Jonathan would screw anything with a pulse. I know that doesn't say much about me. Guess Faith didn't have it all wrong."

Nicole asked her out right, "Claire, how did you kill Jonathan?"

"After I saw them together and how he reacted to me finding them, like it was no big deal. I was upset. I went upstairs, grabbed my stun gun and my .38 revolver out of my bedside table. I went back to the salon room; Brandy was already dressed and Jonathan had his underwear and pants on. He told me I had already ruined his day, could I at least let them finish. If I had not made up my mind by then, that sealed his fate. I walked up to him, hit him with a stun gun. He went down like a ton of bricks."

"Did he not see that you had weapons?"

"Nope."

Claire continued, "I zip tied his hands behind him, had Brandy help me get him to the couch. I saw he pissed himself, we took off his pants and underwear."

"We?" Nicole asked.

"I made Brandy help me. After we undressed him, I got the duct tape, taped his ankles together and then I put a ball gag in his mouth so he couldn't talk. He used to love using that stuff on women. Shit, I wouldn't call them women, they were young girls, eighteen and nineteen! Girl's that didn't know any better; they were naive. I thought he should know what it feels like to be humiliated and not be able to do anything about it."

"What happened next?"

"After I shot Brandy, he was screaming and begging for help. I told him that he was responsible for Brandy's death. I told him that it wasn't the first woman he killed."

"What did you mean by that, Claire?"

"I told him he killed Faith; he denied it, of course. I told him he killed Faith years before she actually died. He kills everything good in his life. His own children want nothing to do with him, it's sad. He started crying like a bitch, then out of nowhere he started screaming and yelling out who he is and our home address. I was tired of listening to him. I walked up, put the gun almost against his forehead but I guess it was lower and pulled the trigger until the gun didn't have any more bullets in it."

"Why do you say you guess the gun was lower than the forehead?"

"I blew off his face," Claire chuckled. "Let me put it this way, if I didn't know that's who I shot, I would not be able to identify him. Ask me, I did this world a favor."

Nicole felt good, she got Claire to admit to killing both Jonathan and Brandy, with her reasoning behind it.

"You mentioned Faith earlier, you want to talk about her?" Nicole probed.

"What about Faith?" Claire enjoyed this cat and mouse game.

"After the events of today, Claire, the public will make up their minds about the role you had with Faith regardless. I think it would be better for you to tell us, than find out later by DNA," Nicole told her.

Claire thought for a moment. "If I tell you everything and I mean everything, then what do I get for it?" Nicole was almost shocked, but realized it was Claire. This is how she is; she wants to tell us. She just wants to make a game out of it.

Nicole was going to use this as an opportunity. "If we are going to go that route, then you are going to need to talk with a lawyer. I will go out there and let them know what you're thinking and come back. Do you need anything to drink or to eat, Claire?"

"Green Tea if you have it."

"I'll check on that." Nicole gathered her notes and walked out of the room. Rachel was already standing out in the hallway, out of the line-of-sight Claire had. Nicole went straight to the bathroom, Rachel followed her in. Nicole had to pee; Rachel was pacing the floor.

"Lieutenant, do you have a plan?"

349

"Yeah, come out here to use the bathroom, check with you about making some kind of deal, then go back in there and listen to what she has to say." Nicole said, flushing the toilet. She washed her hands, all while looking at Rachel in the mirror, when she didn't say anything, Nicole said, "Oh! Prosecuting Attorney, how about it? Any deals you have to offer?"

Rachel jumped, "Oh, shit! Sorry. I have an offer already typed up just in case something like this was going to happen with her."

Nicole was surprised, "Damn, look at you! You're pretty slick, Meadows." She said smiling.

Rachel was a little embarrassed, "Stop. I will get it for you. It says that if she tells us everything and doesn't lie about one thing, we are willing to agree to life imprisonment without possibility of parole. But she lies about anything, the deal is gone, and we will go for the death penalty."

They walked to where Rachel was watching the interview. She gave Nicole the copy of the deal to let Claire read over it and sign if she wanted too.

"Walker." Nicole turned around, surprised to hear Rachel call her that. "You're doing a great job in there, you got this." Rachel said to her.

"Thank you, I appreciate it."

Nicole was a little flushed. *What the hell was that about?* She felt like that was something more than just her being nice. She told herself to get back in the game as she opened the door.

"Sorry Claire, no green tea. Can I interest you in coffee, soda or water?"

"No, thank you."

"As promised, I looked into whether the Prosecuting Attorney would be willing to make a deal. She is willing to make you an offer, you tell us everything and don't lie about one thing. You get life imprisonment, without possibility of parole. If you lie about anything or don't tell us something and we find out, the deal is off."

Claire looked it over. "If I sign this, will you send a copy to my lawyer? Making it official."

"We can do that. But it's official the moment you sign it," Nicole told her.

"Do you have a pen?" Claire asked. Nicole gave her a pen; she watched as Claire signed the paper. She handed it back to Nicole, "Can I get a copy of that, Nicole?"

"Absolutely. Let me go get that for you."

Nicole took it to Rachel, she made the copy, handing it to Nicole she said, "Why does this seem easy?"

"You have to put yourself in her shoes; she murdered two people today on live stream video. She sat in that room, told me everything that happened today. Then I mention Faith, now all of a sudden, she wants a deal. I think we are about to learn the truth of what happened to Faith."

"Yeah, but why now?"

"Because she wants to be in control of what story gets told. If she waits until the DNA comes back and it turns out to be a match. Then we fill in the blanks, making the narrative. Claire doesn't want that. It is all about control, she has kept all this in for ten years. She has not been able to talk about it, this is her chance." Nicole went back into the interview room.

"Ok, Claire. Here is your copy. Are you ready to talk?"

"Yes, let's talk."

"Let's talk about Faith Ross," Nicole said.

"Faith Ross. How long do you have?" Claire said, laughing.

"Don't worry about the time, I got all the time in the world."

"People didn't know the real Faith Ross; I had the extreme dishonor of that. She was a snake, a bitch and a cunt, down to her core. She treated people who had less than she had like they were garbage. Jonathan wanted to have a threesome; she would do whatever he wanted. The story goes, they both went to Douglas and told him to talk me into doing it. He basically told me I was his leverage over Jonathan and I needed to do whatever made Jonathan happy. I found out about this just hours before we were to meet up with them for dinner. I was a nervous wreck. As soon as I saw Faith, I grabbed her, we went to the bathroom, I told her the whole story. Faith calmed me down and told me that 'Jonathan and Douglas made this whole plan up and didn't include us in it. All we had to do was say no, not go along with it and everything would be peachy'. So, that puts me at ease. We ate dinner and had a few drinks, then we all went back to our house. What does that bitch do? She turns all that shit around on me, she tells me 'Go with the flow, that I was acting like we are in the 1800's'. I was shocked because we had just talked about it. Then she has the audacity to tell me 'This life comes at a price and she thought it was a small price to pay.' I got angry. I told her that just because her husband uses her like a whore, I should be ok with mine doing the same?"

"What did she say to that?" Nicole asked.

"Just what a slut would say, she told me, 'I thought you were going to be good with this, since everyone knows Douglas doesn't fuck you.' Then she tells me, 'You act like your vagina is trimmed in gold. You really need to get over yourself.' I was about to lose it right there with her, I wanted to smack the shit out of her."

"What did you do, Claire?"

"I made the decision that I was going to do whatever I had to do to get Jonathan's undivided attention that evening. It was so easy too. I did tell Faith before we walked into the house, I said, 'You may want to turn a blind eye when you go inside.' After that Faith did not stand a chance in hell with Jonathan. She may have been married to him, but after that Jonathan was screwing me instead of her."

"What happened at the end of the night?"

Claire rolled her eyes and threw her head back. "Jonathan and I are in the groove; he's dicking me down like a champ. I think by that point I orgasmed at least a few times. That is how good it was! She sat over on the other couch, until Jonathan told her to come over and suck his dick. We both took turns sucking it, then Jonathan told me to stand up and ride him. I rode Jonathan while Faith watched like a bump on a log. We ended up climaxing at the same time, just as Faith was getting her underwear off. Jonathan was supposed to finish with Faith, but he couldn't hold back any longer. He pushed me up and off of him, he told her 'Now use your mouth and clean this cock.' He liked dirty talk. Faith was upset because apparently that was not part of their master plan, her and Jonathan were bickering, I got tired of listening to it and I said, 'Jesus Faith! Go with flow, remember there is a price to pay for this life!' I hit that bitch back with her own words. Faith just ignored me, probably for the best. She did what she was told, as she finished cleaning him up, I leaned down and asked her, 'How do I taste?'"

Nicole was taking all of this in, while trying not to look disgusted. "What happened after that?"

"Faith got up, told me to fuck off and called me a nasty white-trash whore or something like that. Needless to say, they left for the evening. That's why Faith and I didn't talk."

They had been talking for three hours, Claire had to use the restroom. While officers went with Claire, Nicole ordered a pizza for them to share. Rachel came and found her, "Are you doing alright?"

"Yeah. This is just the tip of the iceberg I feel like. Claire wants to tell us everything, because she wants us to look at Faith the way she does."

"That it was Faith's fault," Rachel said.

"Yeah, Claire believes she had every right to kill Jonathan and Brandy. Shit, she felt like she was doing the world a service. But Faith is different, I think she is identifying with what Faith went through with Jonathan; now Claire knows the feeling," Nicole explained.

"How much of that story was true, you think?" Rachel asked.

"When I talked with Douglas, he told me the same story. The details were vague but the story is still the same."

Claire got done in the bathroom, she was escorted back to the room. She sat there alone for another twenty minutes until Nicole opened the door. Claire saw the pizza and two diet drinks.

"I thought you might be hungry; I know I am. I looked all over for green tea," Nicole said, setting down the pizza, two plates and the drinks.

"Thank you. I appreciate the gesture, Nicole," Claire said. Nicole put a slice on her plate and slid the box to Claire. Claire took a piece and opened the soda. They sat there eating in silence, but it was a comfortable silence.

"That was good, thank you," Claire said.

"I figured you had to be hungry. After that night with the Ross's, Faith and you didn't speak for how long?"

"I would say at least four months."

"When was the next time you two spoke?"

"It was in October. Faith asked me to lunch, I met her and we talked very little about our last encounter and more about how she found out that Jonathan and Douglas were having an affair with each other."

"How did that go?"

"Faith was pissed because she couldn't believe he would cheat on her with a man. As far as I was concerned, I knew that Douglas did his thing. I was pissed off that it was out in public, if Faith found out anyone could. He was playing a dangerous game with both of our reputations. It was at that lunch Faith first told me she was fooling around with someone."

"Did Faith say who she was fooling around with?"

"No."

"Ok, let's fast forward to lunch where Faith tells you about Adam. What was that conversation like?"

"That was late October if I remember correctly. At this lunch, Faith told me that she was pregnant, about eight weeks along. She told me that the baby was not Jonathan's and she needed my help."

"What did she need your help with?"

"She wanted me to deliver a letter she had written to Adam, her boy toy at the time."

"Did Faith say if Adam was the father of her unborn child?"

"She didn't come right out and say it, but she told me that it had to be his because she hasn't been with anyone else."

"Did you deliver the letter to Adam?"

"No, I never deliver it to him. I thought about it and decided not to. The fact was simple, even when she thought she was being nice, she was a complete bitch."

"How was she being a bitch?" Nicole asked, grabbing another slice of pizza.

"When Claire was upset or angry with you, she never came to you to talk or work it out. She would destroy you behind your back. Faith would spread rumors or tell your deepest secrets that you only told her, to everyone and turn them against you."

"Can you give me an example of what she told people?"

"When we weren't talking, she told people that I couldn't have children. She told people that Douglas and I were having money problems, that I was nothing but a white-trash whore and the reason I couldn't get pregnant was because I had an abortion when I was very young."

"Did you ever tell people the truth?"

"I tried, but when you're in that circle of people. The damage is already done once the words are uttered. Faith knew that; she didn't care. She has to learn lessons the hard way."

"What do you mean she learns lessons the hard way," Nicole asked.

Claire laughed and sat back in her chair. "I started hooking up with Jonathan almost every day. You want to know the funny thing about that?"

"What is that, Claire?"

"I know that Jonathan hooked up with Douglas and me on the same damn day. He just wanted to fuck, he didn't care who it was."

Nicole shrugged her shoulders, "Who am I to judge someone? Whatever makes them happy and if it's legal."

"Well, the funny thing is when Jonathan broke things off with Douglas, he broke them off with me too. Faith broke up with Adam and the Ross's went to Texas for a few weeks." Claire laughed, shaking her head.

"What's funny, Claire?"

"They went to Texas to work on their marriage. Apparently, everything was great down there, if they were good, why would you leave? I never understood that."

"Jonathan had to come back for work. That is what he told investigators."

"No, that's not the reason. Jonathan sat in an office all day, took meetings with investors. He could have done all that from laptop. Faith, she could have stayed down there too. But they didn't, they missed the lifestyle. They missed all the drama and sex."

"Did Faith or Jonathan ever tell you that?"

"No, but it was pretty obvious by the look on Faith's face when she came to the trailer that day and saw Adam with me. Which is interesting because Adam is the second man she watched finish inside of me, guess she couldn't handle seeing two men that she loved, do that to me."

"Faith saw you having sex with Adam, at his home?"

"I guess this is the moment you have been waiting for Nicole. I'm Lexi. When Faith saw us together, she flipped out. I saw her face through the window but I didn't give a shit by that point. There was some kind of crash outside, that got Adam's attention. He ran after her, I knew that he really loved her. But Faith uses people to get what she wants; she was just using him. I tried like hell to tell that dumbass how she was. But he didn't listen. I gathered my things and left."

"Claire, I just want to be clear, are you admitting that you are the woman that Mr. Lewis said he was with, who he remembers as Lexi?"

"Yes. That is correct."

"Where did you meet Mr. Lewis?"

"I was pissed off at Jonathan and Faith, they were in Texas trying to work their shit out, I wanted to get back at them. I went to Adam's house, but he wasn't there. I went to a couple of bars with no luck, then I went to the Main Street Bar, and found his ass three drinks deep already. I bought him a few more, and gave him some excuse to go back to his house. Didn't take much, we had sex and he passed out. I started coming over every 2-3 days to have sex, and told him I was Lexi."

"When you left Adam's trailer that day Faith saw you two having sex, where did you go afterwards?"

"I sat in my car in a parking lot for about half an hour, then I drove to Faith's house."

"Did you have a verbal argument with her?"

"Yes, we had a verbal exchange. Faith's problem was that she never knew when to shut up either. I tried to let her go, and gave her a chance to live. But she liked having the last word. She was good at tearing someone apart and making them feel like a piece of shit."

"Claire. What happened on the night of November 20th 2017?"

Claire took a drink of her soda, and began to tell Nicole the story.

Chapter 20

November 20, 2017

Monday

1:20 p.m.

Faith answered the front door to see Claire. "What the hell do you want?"

"Listen, let me explain, Faith! I went to see him that day we had lunch but I just couldn't give him that letter. He doesn't deserve to find out like that," Claire explained.

"That makes it alright to sleep with him? I get it if you didn't feel comfortable with giving him the letter. He doesn't deserve to find out like that. But come on, Claire, you are my best friend and you do that."

"What exactly did I do to you Faith? You said you were done with him. Then you started going about fixing your perfect little family! Which let me tell you, no one believes that bullshit for a minute. Everyone knows that you fuck anything with two legs!" Claire snapped.

Faith stepped outside and closed the door behind her so the kids would not over hear this conversation. "Claire, I know that this might come as a shock to you but normally when you have friends you don't sleep with their boyfriends. Those kinds of women are what we refer to as SLUTS and WHORES. I guess where you come from that is not the case. You need to remember that you are nothing in this town without the right connections."

Claire crossed her arms and shifted her weight to one side. "You really want to throw around words like slut and whore? Tell me something Faith, what do they call a married woman that got knocked up by someone other than their husband?"

"That is none of your business."

"Faith, you made it my business when you asked me to deliver that letter. Look, this is not what I wanted. I came over here because you are messing with Adam's head. We both know that you will never leave Jonathan. You care too much about what people will say and think about you."

Faith stood there a moment and thought about what Claire said. "I feel sorry for you, every time you think that you have gotten something ahead of me, you fall just a little short. When are you going to realize that you will never be as good as me?"

Faith turned around and was walking back into the house when Claire said, "I didn't want any of this to happen!"

"Fuck you," Faith said as she slammed the door.

4:15 p.m.

Faith was on her way to talk with Adam. She told him that she did not have a lot of time but was able to get away for an hour. Adam's place is just a few minutes down the road. Her head is spinning with everything she has to take into consideration when making this decision. She is thinking what to say to him, how and when to tell Jonathan, but trying to make sense of everything for herself. She was about half way to Adam's when she received a text message from Jonathan, trying to bring it up on her phone and not watching the road, she did not see the car in front of her slowing down, by the time she looked up and slammed on the brakes it was too late.

Faith hit the rear end of the car. "Shit! Just my luck!"

She followed the other driver's lead and pulled off to the side of the road. There is never much traffic on this road so Faith thought it was not necessary to pull off to the shoulder but did it anyway. Faith could see through the back window of the car that it is an older woman with gray hair. She got out and looked at her vehicle, there was no damage to her surprise. She looked at the back of the woman's car and there was no damage either.

"Thank God," she said, letting out a sigh of relief.

Faith realized that the woman was not getting out of the car. Faith started to walk up to the driver side window. She heard the woman talking to who she assumed was the police, hearing the woman give them their location.

"Ma'am, I don't think that is necessary. There is no damage," Faith said, standing at the back of the car. Faith saw the woman on the phone and was getting ready to repeat what she said when the woman cracked the window down just enough to say, "The police would like to speak with you, young lady."

Faith giggled to herself. The only person to call her that is her father. It made her think that she really needs to call him more often. She made a mental note to do that but then was interrupted by the old woman.

"Come around to the passenger side, so you don't get hit by a car, honey."

Faith shook her head, "There are no other cars, ma'am. It is literally just the two of us out here."

Without missing a beat, the old woman said, "Safety never takes a holiday."

"Of course, it doesn't," Faith said while rolling her eyes. She walked around to the passenger side.

Faith was waiting for the woman to roll down her window, "My window doesn't roll down, open the door." Faith opened the door, she extended her hand for the woman to hand her the phone, instead the woman tossed the phone into the seat.

"Seriously? That was rude," Faith said, trying to remember to be nice because she is old.

"Rude? Who hit who, honey?" the old woman snapped back.

"Whatever lady. Let's just get this over with."

Just as she picked up the phone, the old woman reached across, using a stun gun on Faith. She felt a huge jolt, then everything went dark.

Faith was coming out of it when she realized she was being pulled down into the ditch. She started resisting and the woman stopped.

"Good, I thought I was going to have to pull you the whole way. Sit up bitch!" she yelled at Faith.

Faith was trying to sit up when the woman walked up and kicked her in the ribs, sending a rush of pain through her body. Faith cried out in pain.

"Get up! Start walking and don't look at me!"

Faith managed to get to her feet and started to walk slowly towards the woods.

"What do you want? Money? I will give you anything you want, just don't hurt me; I have children!" Faith pleaded.

"Walk. Bitch," the old woman said.

Faith realized the woman's voice is different, it sounds like someone younger, and she moves like a younger person would, too. Faith continued to walk until they were about a hundred yards into the woods.

"Stop," the old woman ordered. Faith did as she was told. "Are you scared?"

"Yes."

"Why?"

Faith began to cry, "Because I don't want to die, I will do anything. Please."

The woman began to laugh. "Seriously? Ok. Let's test this out, I want you to piss in your pants."

This caught her off guard. She didn't know if the woman was serious or not, so she said the first thing that came to her mind, "What?"

"Yea, piss your pants, right now. Or die!"

Faith did what the woman said, she started to urinate. The woman laughed uncontrollably, watching Faith urinate on herself.

"You always do as you're told, don't you, Faith… Like a good little whore."

Faith thought she recognized the voice, but that is impossible. She turned around.

"Claire!"

She took off the wig. "Surprise!" she said, throwing it at Faith.

"I don't understand."

"I'm knocking you down a couple of pegs. Why should you always get what you want? You didn't want Adam until you saw him with me, then you are in love with him and that dumb shit thinks he actually has a chance at a life with you. Faith you can't even keep your current man happy. What makes you think you can keep Adam happy? Seriously, you can't keep Jonathan satisfied, and let's be honest all he wants is sex. It's not enough that you have everything, but now you are just being greedy. Adam was over you until you decided to come and ruin things. I am going to tell you something that you have probably never heard someone say to your face. You don't get to have everything you want and hurt people without there being consequences. I wish people could see you right now, they would give me a medal! This is a long time coming for you bitch." Claire pulled out a gun from her windbreaker she wore.

"Wait! Claire, don't do this. This isn't you. We can work this out together. Claire, please!"

Claire was expressionless listening to her pleas. "This is really boring, Faith." She brought the gun up and took aim. Faith closed her eyes as Claire pulled the trigger. *CLICK*. Nothing. Faith opened her eyes to see Claire standing there smiling and starting to laugh.

"God you're stupid. You should have seen the look on your face! Priceless!" Claire said as she took a step towards Faith. Her foot caught on a rock and she fell to the ground. Faith took off running in the opposite direction.

"Come back, I'm not done with you yet!!" Claire yelled as she stood, throwing the gun and running after her. Faith was running as fast as she could, her whole body was sore from getting hit with a stun gun. She got a glimpse of their vehicles on the road, just as Claire caught up and pushed her to the ground. "See, if you would have worked out more, instead of throwing your stupid parties, you might have gotten away, bitch," she said to Faith as she laid on the ground in a fetal position.

"You are pathetic! You are going to lay there and do nothing?"

"Claire, please! I have children!"

"Maybe you should try being a mother and not whoring around. Have you ever thought about that?"

"Please. Just let me go, I won't tell anyone," Faith said, tears coming down her face.

Claire started laughing and shook her head. "You really thought I would have wasted a bullet on you? I'm not going to kill you, Faith. Have I proven my point? Stay away from Adam. Understand?"

"Yes," Faith said.

Claire leaned down to be eye level with Faith. "Go home."

Faith got up and wiped her face. "Why are you letting me go?" she asked Claire with tears in her eyes.

Claire stood up. "You have never worked a day in your life, you have had everything handed to you on a silver platter. You tell me that I'm a whore and a slut! I can't wait for people to find out about the real you. That will be a hard and fast fall from your pedestal. People will see how selfish and pathetic you are."

"You did this for revenge against me because I called you a slut?" Faith muttered.

"Revenge? No. You have two beautiful children, a beautiful home, people just adore the ground you walk on and let's not forget a husband who if you weren't such a self-absorbed bitch probably would never have started screwing around. I'm done with you, go home."

Faith put her head down and started to walk away. She couldn't believe that Claire could do something like this to her. "I am sorry if I did something to hurt you. It was never my intention, Claire."

Claire shook her head in disbelief, "If you did something? Faith, you don't even realize it, do you? Let me be perfectly clear to you. You watched your husband go crazy for me and when you realized you could not compete with me you threw your hands up and went home. Then you get everything you want from Adam and you throw him away. I figure he is fair game and what do you do? BAM! You fill his head with lies and wishful thinking. Now he believes you and him are going to live this fairy tale life together and he drops me like I'm nothing. Well, he has to be taught a lesson too. You think it is alright to play with others' emotions; well, it's not. Is that clear enough for you?"

Faith stopped and faced Claire. "You dare say I'm the pathetic one? When you cannot see straight because of how insanely jealous you are of me. You want everything I have and know that you will never be good enough. Like you said I have a husband who loves me, everybody adores me, I have a beautiful home, two wonderful children and one on the way. That's the real issue, isn't it? You hate the fact that no matter what you do, I have something that you will never have. CHILDREN! That's why Douglas can't stand you, the only thing he wanted from you and you can't even do that."

Claire could feel her tears gathering in her eyes. She swallowed the lump in her throat, "You finished?"

"Yeah."

"Then go home, bitch!" Claire ordered.

Faith started walking back to the road, she could not believe this actually happened. As soon as she gets back, she is calling the police. She didn't care what she promised Claire. She could see the woods start to clear and knew she was getting close to the road. She heard the cracking of leaves and footsteps getting closer. She looked behind her, just as Claire tackled her.

"YOU JUST COULDN'T KEEP YOUR FUCKING MOUTH SHUT!! DON'T WORRY, I'M GOING TO FIX THAT FOR

YOU, CUNT!" Claire screamed, trying to get her hands around Faith's throat.

"Help me!" Faith screamed, fighting back. They were both rolling on the ground, when Faith finally got the upper hand on Claire. She was hitting her with everything she had until she saw the cell phone laying on the ground. She grabbed the phone and left Claire laying on the ground. Faith was trying to swipe the phone screen to make an emergency call.

Claire reached into her jacket pocket and pulled out the expandable baton, she shook her head, getting up to her feet. Faith's back was to her. She expanded the baton and before Faith knew anything, Claire struck her in the side of the head. Claire hit her again before she could react and continued to hit her as Faith fell to the ground.

"BITCH! BITCH! YOU WHITE TRASH WHORE! I HATE YOU! HOW DOES IT FEEL, FAITH? YOU CUNT!"

Claire beat her until she could no longer hold up the baton. She fell down to the ground exhausted and breathing heavily. She sat there looking at Faith's lifeless body and found it impressive that she did not feel bad at all. In fact, she wished that she would have done it more slowly. Claire got up and started kicking through the leaves.

"This will do," she said, picking up a medium size branch. Claire proceeded to remove Faith's shoes, socks and pants. She stopped when she saw Faith's underwear.

"Jesus Christ, Faith. No wonder you couldn't keep a man happy. You're wearing old lady underwear! What a waste of a decent ass. Oh, well. This is the last piece of wood you ever get!"

After she was done, she stood back to admire her work letting the full scope of brutality wash over her body. She inhaled the cool, crisp air and instantly felt a huge weight lifted from her shoulders. She felt amazing, "Damn Faith, if I knew that's how good it would feel, I would have done this a long time ago."

Claire felt exhausted, then the pain started. She realized that her ankle was throbbing, she looked down and saw it was starting to swell, it was definitely sprained. She felt a stinging sensation on her neck, she felt the spot, she noticed her fingers had a little bit of blood on them. The bitch scratched me, she thought. She started to limp away when she remembered. She reached into her pocket, pulled out a sandwich bag with a used condom inside. Claire laughed to herself as she put the contents of the condom on Faith's body and on the ground around her. She looked at Faith's life-less eyes, still open. "You brought all this on yourself! I promise I will take good care of the children; they will grow up with a loving mother." She said smiling at her, "I will also take good care of Jonathan too, but Adam needs to go!" She started to walk away when she stopped, "That's it, Faith! That's my only regret. I can't kill Adam, but the State of Missouri will."

Chapter 21

Present Time

Nicole was speechless for once; she was trying to keep her composure. She felt the tears coming; she excused herself with the excuse of needing to change her contact lenses. She walked out of the room and bolted to the restroom. She locked herself in a stall, the tears came down her face, she could not stop them.

Rachel came in, "Are you alright, Nicole?"

Nicole swallowed and dried her eyes. "Yes, just these damn contact lenses."

Rachel stayed with her until she came out of the stall. Rachel looked at her, "You don't wear contact lenses."

"You don't know that."

"Yes, because you would have had to change them a long time ago and you would be holding a little plastic case for them," Rachel said, smiling.

"I thought I was the investigator?" Nicole chuckled.

Rachel laughed, "Listen, you're doing great. This is not an easy case for any of us, it's alright to get emotional. You and I had nothing to do with this case in the beginning, but we had friends who were and have seen how hard it has been on them. You have been under a tremendous amount of pressure. Let it go."

"Thanks, I appreciate it."

"Now get in there, finish this up," Rachel told her.

"Yes, ma'am."

Nicole went back to the interview room feeling better, she was about to bring this to a conclusion.

"Sorry about that, I thought I would be able to wait, but it started scratching my eye."

"No, worries. I wasn't going anywhere," Claire laughed.

"Ok, so I have some questions for you. What happened to the car you used?"

"The car? I left it in a rest area parking lot. I bought it off of some old man, it didn't have a title to it. I remember I paid him cash for it."

"Do you remember who you bought it from?"

"No."

"Where is the baton that you used to kill Faith?"

"I threw it in the Mississippi river, there is a park with hiking trails and a lot of cliffs that overlook the river. I threw it from one of those cliffs."

"What happened to the clothes and wig that you were wearing that night?"

"I burned everything in our fire pit that night."

"Is that how you got those bumps and bruises Mr. Fulton saw on your body?"

"Yes. I didn't think I had as many until after I took a shower that night. I also twisted my ankle too when I tripped and fell."

"Did Mrs. Ross scratch you during the fight?"

"Yes, she did. Right below my collar bone."

"Enough to draw blood?"

"Yes."

"I want to be crystal clear; you are admitting that you planted Adam Lewis's semen at the crime scene and on the victim?"

"Yes, I did. I put it on and around her vagina, then some on the ground as well."

"How did you get Mr. Lewis's semen?"

"I made him wear a condom whenever we would have sex. I would pretend I was flushing it down the toilet, but I would put them in a sandwich bag and put them in the freezer downstairs in our basement."

"Why did you frame Mr. Lewis for killing Faith?"

"He made his choice; Faith was never going to leave Jonathan. He still chose her, he needed to be punished for how stupid he is."

"Do you remember how many times you hit Faith with the baton?"

"No, I don't. I went until my arm felt like it was going to fall off."

"Did you do anything else to her?"

"Is this to see if I'm the real killer? To see if I know a detail only the killer would know?"

Claire had a sinister look on her face. Nicole didn't say a thing.

"Ok. I found a nice size tree branch and put it to the side. I then removed Faith's socks, shoes, pants and her ridiculously ugly granny panties she had on. I grabbed the tree branch and I gave her the last piece of wood she would ever have." Claire said, grinning. "I had a hard time getting it in here. Imagine that, I thought she would have been all stretched out."

"Did Jonathan know that you killed Faith?"

"No."

"Did Jonathan ask, prompt, or pay you to kill her?"

"No," Claire rolled her eyes.

"What's wrong, Claire?" Nicole asked.

"If Jonathan didn't know that I killed her, why would he have asked me too?"

"These are questions I have to ask. Did you tell anyone that you killed Faith?'

"No, I didn't tell anyone."

"What were you thinking after you knew you had killed Faith?"

"It was a big sigh of relief; she had been a huge cunt to me and I thought she got what was coming to her."

"Do you feel any remorse for killing Brandy Garcia?"

"None whatsoever."

"Do you feel any remorse for killing Jonathan Ross?"

"Hell no! He got what he deserved."

Nicole nodded, "Ok, what about Faith, do you feel remorse for killing-"

"Let me stop you right there, Nicole. I don't feel remorse for anything I did, truth be told if I could go back to the day I killed Faith, I would. That way I could do it again but this time I would have a better plan."

There was silence between them. It was past midnight. They had been talking for nine hours, Nicole wrote down one final note, then closed her notebook.

"Well, that's it, that is everything in a nutshell. Now what?" Claire asked.

"I'm going home to get some sleep. You are going to a jail cell. I will come and check in with you in the morning," Nicole told her.

"I guess I will see you then. Good night, Nicole."

"Good night, Claire. Oh, I have one more question, do you still have the letter that Faith wanted you to give to Adam?

"Yes, I do."

"Where would that letter be?" Nicole asked.

"It's in my bedside table under everything."

Nicole closed the door; Rachel came walking out of the other room.

"I will go over and look for it, before I go home," Nicole told her.

"No need to do that, I already called Major Stephens. He is taking care of it. Go home, get some sleep. Come to my office first thing in the morning, we will read it then."

Nicole was tired. "Alright, I will see you in the morning."

Major Stephens arrived at Rachel's office; he could already see them waiting for him outside.

"I have not read it, I waited until we were all here together." He told them.

"Come up to my office," Rachel said. They all waited for the elevator in the lobby. It finally arrived; the ride up seems slow today too. They all were on pins and needles wanting to know what the letter said. The elevator doors opened; they went to Rachel's office.

"Take messages for me until I say otherwise, please," Rachel told her assistant.

They closed the door and stood there waiting for Major Stephens.

"Alright, I had them make three copies, one for each of us." He handed them their copy and each began to read.

Ronald is woken up by his phone ringing, he looks at the time. 5 a.m. on the dot. He checks his phone and does not recognize the number, "Hello?"

"Ronald?"

"Yes, who is this and what do you want at this time?"

"Ronald, this Rachel Meadows. I'm so sorry to call you this early, but it is rather urgent. I was hoping you would be able to come into my office as soon as possible."

"I can be there around 7:30 a.m."

"Is that the soonest you can get here?"

"Rachel, it's 5 o'clock in the morning, what is so urgent this call couldn't wait?"

"Turn on your television, watch the news. Then call me back!" she told him before hanging up.

He grabbed the remote, turned-on channel 8 news. He saw it was breaking news that Jonathan Ross and a female were killed at his home yesterday. That the police have someone in custody and will be holding a press conference later today. He was surprised by the news, he hurried, brushing his teeth and washing his face. He threw on some clothes and grabbed a suit for later if he needed it. He called his secretary and told her to cancel everything for this morning. He called Rachel back.

She answered, "Hello?"

"What the hell happened?"

"Ronald, I need you to come down to my office, I can tell you more when you get here."

"Is Claire dead?"

"Ronald, I will see you when you get here." She hung up, not giving him time to ask the question again.

The whole drive there, all he could think about was Claire being dead. If that happened Adam is not going to be getting out, neither will the truth. He was still tired and wish he would have made some coffee. It took him about 30 minutes to get to Rachel's office; she was waiting for him in the lobby, so security would let him in. There was media all over the place.

"Good morning, Rachel."

"Good morning, Ronald. I know you probably didn't have time for coffee. I took the liberty of getting you one. Let's go upstairs."

"Has it been like this very long?"

Rachel sighed, "I got here at 4:30am., they were here before me."

They walked into her office; her assistant wasn't in yet. They sat down and he started to prepare himself.

"Ronald. Claire killed Jonathan and a young woman yesterday."

His mouth dropped open. "Wow. I was not expecting you to say that, I thought Claire was the female victim."

"Well, that's not all of it. She was willing to talk but only to Lieutenant Walker. She of course went down there and talked with her; I was there too. We got a full confession, Ronald."

"That's good! We can get her DNA and run it against the unknown sample."

"We did that already, but it is not going to be necessary"

"Why the hell not?"

"Claire confessed to killing Faith."

"What? Just like that, she confessed?" Rachel nodded; she didn't say a word. She waited for him to take it all in. "What about Adam's DNA?

"She gave a full confession; she had detailed accounts that only the killer would have known and she admitted to planting Mr. Lewis's semen she told us how she got his semen."

"How?"

Rachel got a little embarrassed. "The way she explained it, was every time they would have sex, she would pretend to flush the condom, when she actually put it in a sandwich bag, took it home and put it in the freezer downstairs."

He was in a state of disbelief, he has worked on this for ten years and for it to end like this, he felt unsatisfied.

"Did she say why she framed him?"

"Claire admitted to being Lexi, she was there when Faith looked in from the window, like Adam said. Faith saw her, recognized her and the whole argument between her and Adam happened. When Adam went back to the trailer, that's when Claire let him have it. In her words, 'He made his choice. Faith was never going to leave Jonathan and he still chose her. He needed to be punished for how stupid he is.'"

"Are you kidding, how crazy is that!"

"I know, I couldn't believe listening to her tell this horrible story! There is something else I need to share with you."

He looked at her, she was trying not to let her emotions get the best of her. "Rachel, what is it?"

"Lieutenant Walker asked her about the letter that she was supposed to give to Adam, she still had it. We recovered it, I would like to give a copy of the letter to Adam, let him read it."

He took the letter. "Did you read it?"

"Yes. We read it this morning."

"We?"

"Major Stephens, Lieutenant Walker and myself."

"She just confessed, no deal?"

"We made a deal, life imprisonment without possibility of parole. In exchange for a full confession." Ronald shook his head; he couldn't believe they made that deal given the circumstances of this case.

"Look, without any question, Adam Lewis is innocent. I'm going to the judge right after this, show him everything."

Ronald was shocked to hear her say those words, he felt overwhelmed with emotions.

"Are you ok, Ronald?"

"Yes, I never thought we would be at this moment."

"I know, if I'm being honest, I thought he was guilty. We know different things now and we are going to tell everyone. We will be giving a press conference later today; you are more than welcomed to join us."

"No. I have to go talk with Adam first, he needs to know before everyone else finds out."

"I'm a step ahead of you, I put in a request to interview him up here. I have a friend at the prison that put it through. Adam is currently on his way to MSHP office, Major Stephens will hold him there. That way it keeps the Sheriff's Department out of it."

"Thanks, I appreciate it."

Ronald opened the letter, he needed to read it. When he finished, he was in tears. This was everything that Adam said happened and no one believed him.

"I'm sorry, Rachel. I don't know what has come over me."

"Don't apologize. This is ten years of your life!"

"I can't believe someone can ruin all those lives and get nothing in return!"

"She is going to prison for the rest of her natural life."

"Yeah, what a relief. I would rather have seen her go through a trial."

Rachel knew how he felt. "Listen, sit here as long as you need to. I'm going to talk with the judge. Let me know when you have told Adam." Rachel got her coat and closed the door behind her leaving Ronald to collect himself.

Adam was dragged out of bed at 4:30 a.m. They didn't tell him much, only that a prosecutor wanted to talk with him and he had to be up there at 7:30 a.m. He was now stuck in this cold van alone in the back wondering what the hell they wanted with him now.

He arrived an hour later; they stuck him in a little room. He was getting frustrated, no one was telling him anything. Suddenly there was a knock on the door and it opened, it was Ronald. Adam was happy to see him, "Ron, it's good to see you. What the hell is going on here? No one has told me shit! They dragged me out of bed at 4:30 this morning telling me some prosecutor wants to talk with me"

Ronald had to cut him off, "Adam! Stop!"

Adam stopped talking and waited for him to say something. Ronald was trying to find the best words to tell him. "Adam, Claire killed Jonathan and another woman named Brandy Garcia yesterday afternoon."

"What?"

"They took her into custody, she wanted to talk with the lead investigator for the case. Her name is Lieutenant Nicole Walker, she rushed down there to talk with her. Adam, Claire confessed to killing Jonathan, Brandy and Faith."

"Holy shit! Ronald, are you serious?"

"Hold on, Claire also admitted that she planted your semen at the crime scene and on Faith. She got your semen just like you thought, from a condom that she kept after you two had sex."

"Oh my God! Did she say why she did it?"

"She hated Faith, but it went over the edge for a few reasons. The first was when Faith spread a lot of rumors about her or some bullshit, then when Jonathan had tried to fix things with Faith when they went to Texas, he dumped Claire, she was pissed off about that. When you picked Faith over her that was the last straw."

"She framed me because of that?"

"Yes."

Adam was stunned, "I know I should be happy but I think I'm just shocked... Ron?"

"Yes, Adam."

"When the hell am I getting out of here!"

"P.A. Meadows is in front of a judge as we speak, showing him everything. Let's hope today, if not today, definitely soon because once the DNA comes back, there will be no denying it."

"Call Samantha González, tell her that exclusive is looking like a go."

Chapter 22

The Press Conference

There were reporters from all over, Major Stephens had to move the press conference to the main lobby of the building to hold everyone. It was Major Stephens, Rachel, Nicole and Sheriff Jones. The Sheriff was upset by the late notice she got about the press conference; her body language said it all.

"Are you alright, Sheriff?" Rachel asked.

"No, I'm not. I feel like I was kept completely out of the loop."

"Sheriff, there was no need for you to be a part of the investigation. It was the MSHP's case anyway."

"Yeah, ten years ago when they took it over because Sheriff Bennet couldn't keep his dick in his pants. If you haven't noticed, there is a new Sheriff and a better department."

"Sheriff Jones, I didn't keep you out of the loop to be an ass. This had to be kept in a small circle and not to keep beating a dead horse, but this case had nothing to do with the Sheriff's Department. Had we known what Claire was going to do, we would have warned you. But I'm here to tell you this, don't go out there with the attitude you have now."

"You can't talk to me like that!"

"Sheriff, I'm not trying to talk down to you. But if we go out there and they see we aren't united, that is going to be the story."

Sheriff Jones stood silent for a moment. "I know how to be a team player; in the future, please judge the department based on recent events. Not ancient history."

"Will do, Sheriff." Rachel putting out her hand. Sheriff Jones shook her hand and they buried the hatchet.

The four of them walked out together, Major Stephens walking to the podium, Nicole stood on his left, Rachel and Sheriff Jones to his right. The room got quiet, everyone waiting for Major Stephens to speak.

"A great miscarriage of justice has happened, we stood here ten years ago, with me telling you that the person responsible for the horrific rape and murder of Faith Ross was captured. I thought the right person was going to prison, we had a confession, case closed. That is not the case; we have arrested Claire Ross for three murders. She made the decision to cooperate with us, she has given a full confession. I will give some information regarding what led up to this. Mrs. Ross was brought in for questioning yesterday, as a result of new developments that had been made recently. We have been trying for several weeks to get Mr. and Mrs. Ross to talk with us. For one reason or another they would not cooperate. It finally reached a point where it was no longer a choice to talk, if she didn't come in to talk, we were going to arrest her. Mrs. Ross came in with her attorney and talked with the Lieutenant in charge of the case for about four hours. The interview was ended abruptly by Mrs. Ross and her attorney. She was taken home by her attorney; upon her arrival home she entered the residence. She caught Mr. Ross and Ms. Garcia engaged in sexual acts. Words were exchanged between Mr. and Mrs. Ross. Claire left the room to go to their bedroom to get her stun gun and a .38 revolver. She returned to where Mr. Ross and Ms. Garcia were. Mrs. Ross used the stun gun on Mr. Ross. She tied Mr. Ross up and had Ms. Garcia held at gunpoint.

After some back and forth between Mrs. Ross and Ms. Garcia, Mrs. Ross made her do a go live video, streaming the torment that was about to happen. Mrs. Ross made Ms. Garcia say many things against her will. Mrs. Ross asked her a question and she answered it. Mrs. Ross shot Ms. Garcia at point blank range, killing her instantly. She turned her attention to Mr. Ross, after a few minutes of talking with him. She turned the gun on him and executed him. She stayed live streaming for two more minutes, then told everyone bye, ending the video. We got several calls reporting the incident from people that watched the live stream, and Sheriff deputies were dispatched. When they arrived on the scene they were greeted by Mrs. Ross, who had taken a shower and changed her clothes. Deputies asked her what was going on, she took them downstairs where the bodies were. At that time, they placed Mrs. Ross under arrest and took her into custody. From that point, everything moved quickly. Mrs. Ross said she would only speak with one particular investigator; I would like to acknowledge her, Lieutenant Nicole Walker. Lieutenant Walker and Mrs. Ross talked for nine hours and during that time, Mrs. Ross admitted to the killings of Jonathan Ross, Brandy Garcia, and Faith Ross, the former wife of Jonathan. She also admitted to planting Mr. Lewis's DNA. I want to say very clearly, Mr. Lewis is one-hundred percent innocent. He was framed by Claire Ross, who killed Faith and planted his semen at the crime scene and on the victim. In the coming days and weeks, we will be releasing more information but for right now that is all we are prepared to say. We will take questions."

The reporters erupted with questions, "Folks! Folks! One at a time and we will go in order," Major Stephens ordered.

"Was Mr. Lewis notified of what happened?"

"Yes, his lawyer was called early this morning and informed. He then told Mr. Lewis this morning."

"What was Mr. Lewis's reaction to this development?"

"I would think it's good news for him, but you will have to ask his attorney."

"What about the Ross children, where are they?"

"The children were not home at the time of the killings; they are currently with relatives."

"Did Claire say why she did it?"

"Yes. She did tell us her reasoning, we will not be disclosing that right now."

"How did Brandy Garcia know Jonathan Ross?"

"Ms. Garcia was a hairdresser; both Claire and Jonathan were clients of hers. It was not abnormal for Ms. Garcia to be at the residence."

"How many times was Jonathan shot?"

"Mr. Ross was shot four times in the head and face."

"Have any of you seen the live stream?"

"None of us have seen it yet, we are working with the company to try and get it."

"Did Claire try to fight deputies when they arrested her?"

"No, just the opposite, she was very cooperative. Offered deputies something to drink, she did take them to the bodies. Deputies asked her where the firearm was, she pointed at it on the floor. They placed her under arrest without any incident."

"Major Stephens! Why did she only want to speak with Lieutenant Walker?"

"I don't know. I can only speculate that because she got to know the Lieutenant from earlier in the day. That she may have felt comfortable with her."

"Did the interview spark this investigation?"

"No. Ronald Hartz, who is Mr. Lewis's attorney, found new information. Mr. Hartz took what they had to Prosecuting Attorney Meadows, and she came to me."

"Did you reopen the case then?"

"No. We never reopened the case; we followed up on new leads. That led us to wanting to talk with Claire and Jonathan. Claire talked with us first, unfortunately we will never hear what Jonathan Ross had to say."

"Was Claire Ross, Lexi, the missing female that Mr. Lewis talked about?"

"Yes. Claire Ross did admit she had a sexual relationship with Mr. Lewis, under the fake name of Lexi. She admitted that she lied to Mr. Lewis about her name."

"Does Mr. Lewis know that she admitted to that as well?"

"Mr. Lewis is aware of everything Claire Ross said, but again you will have to reach out to him and his attorney for a comment."

"Will they be talking with us today too?"

"Again, I would direct your question to Ronald Hartz office."

"Was Jonathan Ross involved with the killing of Faith?"

"No. At this time we do not believe Mr. Ross had anything to do with the killing of his wife Faith. Mr. Ross cooperated with the investigation ten years ago and we wanted to talk with him now because of questions that came up about contract fraud, it had nothing to do with his wife's case."

"Contract fraud? What was this about?"

"It came to our attention that Mr. Ross may have allowed bid rigging with his construction company."

"How did this information come out?"

"I'm not speaking on that investigation any further."

"What is going to happen with Mr. Lewis?"

"I will let P.A. Meadows addresses that." Major Stephens stepped aside.

Rachel stepped to the podium. "Mr. Lewis was granted an emergency hearing. I presented all the new evidence to the judge, answered a few questions that he had. The judge will make his decision within 48 hours. By that time, we will have Claire Ross's DNA back as well, that will help verify her story. If everything goes smoothly Mr. Lewis will walk out of here tomorrow or the next day."

"Isn't that unfair? The man has spent the last ten years in prison for a crime he didn't commit. Then you come out here telling us he is innocent but you don't let him out of prison because of paperwork basically?"

"I don't make the laws, if you think it's unfair, I would tell you to call your state level representative and tell them to change the law. Ok? Next question."

"Will Mr. Lewis be entitled to compensation for being in prison for ten years, for a crime he did not commit?"

"Missouri does have a compensation law but it is pretty strict. If a person is exonerated by DNA testing, then yes, they are entitled to compensation. If they're not exonerated by DNA then they are not entitled to anything."

Rachel waited for the next question; everyone was silent. "Is there anything else?"

"Will the funeral be private or public for Jonathan Ross?"

"That's a good question, that will be up to the family to decide." Rachel decided that was a good place to end it. "Ok folks, thank you for coming. We will have more in the coming days and weeks."

They all walked back upstairs together to Rachel's office. Once upstairs they sat down and discussed what was really going to happen when Adam got out.

"I never knew that you had to be exonerated by DNA, in order to be compensated," Sheriff Jones said.

"Me either, that's crazy," Lieutenant Walker seconded.

Rachel shook her head, "I know Ronald, he is going to sue everyone."

"What do you mean sue everyone. You just said he isn't entitled to anything."

"I mean Ronald will sue your department, Sheriff, the MSHP, my office, definitely the Ross's estate, the county and the State of Missouri. I can say with almost certainty all of them will settle because it would be a public relations nightmare in and out of court." Rachel looked at Major Stephens, "You think they will want someone to fall on the sword?" she asked him.

"No. Everyone that fouled up back then is gone. We took the case over from Sheriff Bennet's department. Once we got it, we followed the DNA evidence which led us to Adam Lewis. Bo Carver, then the Prosecuting Attorney, was adamant about not going to trial, that he made a deal too sweet to pass up. Especially if you're looking at life in prison versus twenty or twenty-five years. Put yourself in Adam's shoes, the evidence in the case against him was overwhelming. If he would have gone to trial, he would have gotten the death penalty. He took the deal and signed a confession, deciding to have a chance at life, rather than nothing at all."

"How much do you think he will get?" Lieutenant Walker asked Rachel.

"All together I would say, a million, maybe two if he is lucky."

388

"Nowhere near enough for ten years in prison, if you ask me," Sheriff Jones said.

"Well, the fact of the matter is, we all will be eating some shit for a while in the press."

They sat there another ten minutes talking, until Rachel was needed on a call. They said their good-byes and left her office. Nicole was getting ready to walk out when Rachel stopped her. "Lieutenant Walker, can I have a quick minute?"

"Sure." Nicole closed the door.

"Lieutenant, can we be less formal for a moment?"

"Yes."

"Nicole, I was wondering if you would like to get dinner sometime with me?"

Nicole was not expecting that, before she could get anything out, Rachel said, "I'm sorry if I stepped over a line. I didn't mean to make you feel-"

"Rachel, stop. I would love to go to dinner with you. I didn't know if it was just me feeling those vibes."

"Oh, no. I felt them too. I can call you tonight."

"That would be great."

Nicole turned around, "Talk with you later." She left with a grin on her face.

Rachel went to her desk and picked the line on hold. "Ronald, what can I do for you?"

"For starters, have you heard anything from the judge yet?"

"No. I have not heard anything from him, to be honest I don't see him making his decision until we get the DNA back and we get that match from her DNA, helps to verify her story more."

"Are you kidding me! What more does he want!"

"Ronald, you know how this works. There is a process and it's in the works."

"Why did you talk about compensation?"

"The question was asked, 'is Mr. Lewis entitled to any compensation?' I answered it. Under the law no he is not."

"How can you say that, Rachel, after everything my client has been through. You tell the world he isn't entitled to anything!"

"Ronald, I don't know why you're pissed off at me. I didn't ask the question, I answered it."

"Because if we decide to sue, you're going to try and make it look like we are being sue happy!"

"Ronald. Listen to me, I never said Mr. Lewis wasn't entitled to something, but in accordance with Missouri statutes he is not entitled because he isn't going to be exonerated by DNA testing. You want to file a lawsuit then do it, I'm sure a jury would agree that someone who spent ten years behind bars for a crime they didn't commit is entitled to a little money! But don't call me with a nasty attitude when I have done nothing but go the extra mile for you. I hope you have a good rest of your day, Mr. Hartz!" She hung up on him.

Ronald was on his way back to the interview room they put Adam in this morning. He was tired, hungry, and fed up with people. He opened the door; Adam was sitting at the table with an assortment of food. There was a large pizza with everything on it, garlic bread, BBQ wings, salad, a 2-liter of soda and for dessert extra-fudge brownies.

"Where the hell did this all come from?"

"I don't know, a trooper came in, said it was for us. He went to get us plates, cups and napkins." The trooper came back with the items, Ronald asked, "Who did all this?"

The trooper handed him a note that came with the food. Ronald opened it, and read it aloud, "Hey Ron, I thought you guys could use some food. I will call you the moment I hear from the judge. Rachel." He got done reading it and felt like a complete ass. "Son of a bitch! I'm an asshole."

Adam looked at him, not knowing what he had just done, "What is it?"

"I literally just got off the phone with her, I was rude and totally out of line."

"This gives you the perfect excuse to call her back and apologize."

"You don't know Rachel, if I called her back right now, she would rip my head off and feed it to me for lunch. I'm going to let her cool down."

Ronald was wrestling with the idea of whether or not to give the letter to Adam. He needed Adam to stay mentally strong until he was out of here, but Ronald prided himself with always being truthful and honest with his clients. Adam wasn't a client anymore, he looked at Adam as being his friend, his colleague. Adam was always telling Ronald about some new statute the Missouri legislative passed. Ronald has grown close to Adam in the last ten years.

"Adam, before we eat, I need to talk with you about a few things."

"Alright. Go for it, Ron."

"I talked to Rachel; she says the judge hasn't made a decision yet. She said it could take up to 48 hours."

"I have been in prison for ten years. You think a couple more days is going to kill me? I will be fine... I do have a question though, where am I staying tonight?"

"Major Stephens has talked with the prison, he has taken custody of you, until your release. That means this is your home for at least the night, maybe a couple more."

"What is the plan going forward with compensation? Since I won't be entitled to any."

Ronald smiled, "Good old fashion lawsuits."

"Lawsuits. As in plural?"

"Yes. We are going to sue everyone that was involved for the prosecution."

"Everyone?"

"We will start with the Sheriff's Department, Prosecuting Attorney's Office, Missouri State Highway Patrol, the Federal Bureau of Investigation, Department of Corrections, State of Missouri and the Ross's estate."

"Do you think they will settle?"

"I think they will. I feel we should go after individuals, like: former Prosecuting Attorney Bo Carver, former Sheriff Thomas Bennett, and Major Stephens."

"Sounds good to me, Ron. Have you heard back from Samantha González?"

"Yes, her flight leaves in about an hour. She will be here later tonight."

"Did you talk with the network about paying me for this one?

"I did talk with them; they are not happy because you told Samantha that you would give her the exclusive. They made sure to tell me that the keyword was give. I told them other networks have already offered $75,000."

Adam looked at him, "You think that will work?"

"They will offer something; we have to take the highest offer. You are going to need the money, Adam. I suspect that a few of the defendants we sue will settle with us fast, while others will take longer."

Ronald and Adam started talking about what he could possibly see financially. Adam wanted to make enough to get him through until he found a job. Adam knew that Ronald had been working for free on his case for the last ten years. They needed to come up with an agreement and have it in a contract. Adam came up with an offer for Ron.

"You have helped me for the last ten years for free. How does this sound - whatever offer the network gives, we take. You take a third of it, after that any money I get from interviews, lawsuits, speaking engagements, books, whatever it is. If it's under $100,000 you take 25%, anything over $100,000 you take 38%."

Ronald smiled at Adam, the way an older brother smiles at a younger brother when he is proud of him. "Where did you get that plan?"

"I figured a lot of people would be willing to represent me now, but I need to make some money to live off of until I figure things out."

Ronald laughed, "Adam, what if you apply to take the bar test, come work with me."

"What's the salary?"

"Starting at $60,000."

"What did your firm do last year?"

"$3 million."

Adam sat, thinking how crazy this was; he never thought he would be discussing a job offer with Ronald at his law firm. He couldn't believe it; his emotions were all over the place. He couldn't hold back any longer, tears flowed down his face. He turned away from Ronald, he felt ashamed.

Ronald didn't say a word, he let Adam have his moment. Ronald got up, moved his chair closer to Adam, he put his arm around his shoulder, Ronald sat there with his friend as he wept. Adam wept for the life he was about to begin; it took him coming to prison to make something of himself. He also wept for the turmoil that was left behind, from Claire's path. He wept for Faith and his unborn child, the life that could have been, but will never know. Adam couldn't stop, everything he had been feeling for the last ten years was coming out, he never expected this to happen.

"I'm sorry, Ron."

"Don't apologize, Adam. This is a long time coming."

"I'm terrified that they are going to tell me there is some kind of mistake, then send me back."

"Adam, there is no mistake. You are innocent.

Adam wiped his eyes, feeling awkward for crying in front of Ronald. Neither man talked, it was just silence. Ronald thought now was as good as any time to tell Adam.

"Adam, there is something else I need to tell you."

"Ok."

"The police asked Claire if she ever delivered the letter that Faith wrote to you. She originally told them no, but they asked her again after she signed her deal. She told them that she never delivered the letter, but that she kept it."

"Wait!! They gave that bitch a deal!"

"Yes. They offered her life imprisonment without possibility of parole. She will never see outside of a prison again."

Adam shook his head; he couldn't believe it. "She is not going to stand trial for what she did to me and everyone else."

"Adam, you know better than anyone else about deals. It's the way things get done quickly around here."

"Yeah, it is what got them in trouble last time."

"Adam, what I'm telling you is I have the letter Faith wrote to you. Do you want to read it?"

Adam thought about it, "No."

Ronald was surprised. "No? This is the letter we've been waiting for; don't you want to read it?"

"Not right now. Not here. I want that to be the last thing I do, after all this is over, I want the letter to be the last thing I have to deal with regarding this case. That way I can properly mourn whatever the letter says."

Ronald saw how much it was hurting Adam, it wasn't enough they put him in prison for a crime he didn't commit, but by Adam not reading this letter right away it felt like another great injustice was being done to him. He couldn't mourn yet; he wasn't allowing himself that process.

"They will answer for what they have done to you, believe me Adam."

"I seriously hope they do; I just want to start my life. Put all this shit in my rearview mirror." They ate together that afternoon, Adam finally letting go of a small portion of emotions. The rest would come in time.

Samantha's flight was late getting into St. Louis, she should have arrived at around 7pm. but ended up landing and by the time she got her bag it was 9:30 p.m. She checked her phone; she had a missed called from her editor; they could not find any hotel rooms because they had already been booked up. They told her she would have to find a place and they would reimburse her.

"Great!" She called Ronald because she had a text from him asking her to call.

"Hello?"

"Hey Ronald, it's Samantha González. I'm just going to rent a car now; my flight was late."

"Oh no, I'm sorry to hear that. I hope it's not a long drive to your hotel."

"That's the funny part, I don't have one, they were all booked up apparently, there is some kind of convention in town and with Adam's news coming out a bunch of reporters already got them. So, I am going to drive until I see a motel, check if they have availability."

"Listen, we have a guest bedroom that literally only gets used when my mother-in-law comes to visit. It has its own bathroom, it's on the opposite side of the house, complete privacy. If you don't mind a couple of noisy kids getting ready for school in the morning, my wife and I would be happy for you to stay here."

"Are you sure? I don't want to put you or your wife out."

"Please stop, my wife will be thrilled that someone else is using it."

"Ok, that sounds great. Just send me the address and I will be on my way."

She arrived at Ronald's home forty minutes later, to both him and his wife standing at the front door. She started to grab her bag from the trunk.

"Go help with her bag, where are your manners?" Ronald came running over.

"Here let me grab that for you, Samantha."

"It's no problem."

"Samantha González, this is my lovely wife, Robin Hartz."

"Nice to meet you, Robin."

"Nice to meet you, Samantha. Welcome to our home, please come in." They showed her to the bedroom. "Here it is, we put fresh sheets on the bed and linens in the bathroom," Ronald said, setting her bag in the corner of the room. "There are hangers in the closet, shampoo and soap in the bathroom. Have you eaten?"

"No, but I'm ok. Seriously."

"Nonsense, I won't hear it. Follow me," Robin told her. They went to the kitchen, "We have some leftover spaghetti and cheese bread. You sit right there; I will heat some up for you."

"Thank you. You are too kind. I will only be here for a couple of days." She told Robin.

The phone rang, "I got it!" Ronald yelled from the other room.

"Here you go, Samantha. What would you like to drink?"

"Do you have bottled water?" Robin handed her a bottle of water; Ronald came out to the kitchen.

"That was Rachel Meadows on the phone."

Samantha finished chewing. "What did she want?"

"The judge called, he made his decision to release Adam in the morning, after a public hearing at the courthouse. He told her that he is going to allow the press in the courtroom."

"That's great news, babe," Robin said.

"Yes, it is. I will have to be up there early in the morning. Samantha, you are welcome to come along in the morning. Adam will be coming back here afterwards; he will be staying with us for the time being."

"I will follow you tomorrow to the courthouse. Then come back here, if that's alright."

"That would be fine, Adam is dealing with a lot right now. I don't know if he will feel up to talking right away, but I know he is excited to get his feelings out."

"I understand, Ronald. I will be up and ready."

"Samantha, just leave your dishes in the sink when you're done. I will handle it in the morning, if you need anything please let us know; our room is right down the hall."

"Thank you for opening your home to me and the great food."

"It's my pleasure. Good night."

"Good night."

The Hartz's retired to their bedroom, Samantha finished her meal and went to her room. She took a quick shower, set

398

her alarm for 5 a.m. and climbed into bed. Tomorrow was going to be a full day.

The courthouse was crowded, there wasn't an empty seat. The bailiffs were turning people away. Ronald sat up front with Adam on the defense side, Rachel was sitting at the prosecutor's table. Samantha sat behind Ronald; everyone was waiting for the judge to appear. As Samantha looked around the courtroom, she didn't see any of the Ross children. Not that she was expecting to, but she didn't see Major Stephens or Lieutenant Walker. It was 8:59 a.m. when the judge walked into the courtroom. He sat, took a drink of his coffee and looked at the court reporter. She gave him a nod.

"Ok, ladies and gentlemen. This is a hearing to decide whether Mr. Adam Lewis should be granted an immediate release from the Department of Corrections. Based on the confession of Claire Ross. Mrs. Ross, who's name at the time of the incident was Mrs. Fulton, admitted to killing Faith Ross on November 20, 2017. She also admitted to planting Mr. Lewis's semen at the crime scene and on the victim, giving details only the true killer would know. Is that correct, Ms. Meadows?"

"Yes, your honor."

"It also says here that there was DNA from underneath the victim's fingernails that did not match Mr. Lewis's, is that correct?"

"Yes, your honor."

"Is it true that Mr. Ronald Hartz, Mr. Lewis's attorney, came to you and gave you a name of who the missing woman Mr. Lewis had been with?"

"Yes, your honor."

"Does that sound like a job for a defense attorney?"

"No, your honor."

"Ms. Meadows, I know that this was way before you took over as Prosecuting Attorney. Please do not take offense with what I'm about to say. I have a brief statement to make before I render my ruling. This case against Mr. Lewis is the greatest miscarriage of justice I have ever seen while being on the bench. Mr. Lewis, you spent ten years in prison, that is 120 months, that is 520 weeks and that is 3,620 days in prison for a crime you did not commit! If procedures would have been completed correctly, this may have never happened. It seems to this court that a failure occurred. The Sheriff's Department, Missouri State Highway Patrol, and the Prosecuting Attorney's Office failed for ten years. It not only failed Mr. Lewis but also Faith Ross. Evidence was overlooked and people rushed to judgment. I would like to apologize to Mr. Lewis who bore the greatest punishment by being incarcerated. I understand that Claire Ross had physical injuries on her person as a result of the killing of Faith Ross. I can only imagine how investigators would have talked with her ten years ago, what would have happened. This in my opinion is a great injustice to this community, the family of Faith Ross, Mr. Lewis and the legal system. The systems we have in place to help protect individual's rights failed you, I would like to tell you Mr. Lewis that I know you earned an education while in prison, I can only hope that you take advantage of that degree. I would be honored to have you practice law in my courtroom. Now, Mr. Lewis would stand please?"

Adam and Ronald both stood.

"Mr. Lewis, it is my pleasure to tell you that you are hereby released from the Department of Corrections. I and this court wish you the best of luck with all of your future endeavors."

"Thank you, your honor."

Adam wanted Chinese food for lunch; they went to this small Chinese restaurant that Ronald would always talk about.

Adam, Ronald and his wife, and Samantha sat in the back room for extra privacy. They all laughed and talked about the movies and shows that Adam needed to watch, things he missed out on. Adam was sitting quietly; he watched the others converse.

Samantha finally asked, "What are you thinking about?"

He smiled at her. "When am I going to wake up? Because this has to be a dream."

"Why do you say it has to be a dream?"

"I'm sitting here with my best friend, well my only friend. I'm eating a wonderful meal, I have a job lined up, I'm sitting across from a beautiful young woman and I'm out of prison."

Samantha blushed. "Thank you, for the compliment. You have a job already? Doing what?"

"Is the interview starting?"

She looked at him indignantly. "No. This is me asking and caring. Trying to have a conversation with you, Adam."

"Oh. I'm sorry, I'm used to everyone but Ron having a hidden agenda with me. Ron is going to hire me as a legal assistant until I get my license to practice."

"What kind of law would you like to practice?"

"Criminal Defense. I would like to help people that are in similar circumstances as I was. They don't have a voice unless someone is willing to speak for them. Like Ron did for me."

"That would be tremendous. You would be able to relate to them, tell them exactly what they are going to face. It would also give you that voice that you desperately wanted but didn't have because no one would listen but Ron."

"May I ask you a question, Samantha?"

"Absolutely," she said, smiling.

"Do you ever miss living here?"

She thought for a moment, "Yes. I miss my family of course, but I also miss midwestern men."

Adam chuckled, "Midwestern men? Are we that different from men in New York?"

"Oh, yes! Midwestern men are more charming, polite, definitely more rugged and nothing beats the way you all talk with that accent."

"Accent!" he said laughing, "We don't have an accent."

"No, seriously. When I first moved up there, I thought that too. After living up there for a while now, I hear it. Don't worry, it's very sexy! Trust me."

"Now I want to hear what it sounds like."

She laughed, "It's hard dating up there for me because I haven't found anyone that fits that profile."

"Goodness, it has been a long time since I have been on a date. I think it would be a terrible date."

"I'm willing to bet that's a lie! You would be an interesting date; we would have lots to talk about."

"Yeah. That's definitely true," he said, smiling.

"You shouldn't cut yourself down. You have a lot to offer someone, plus your easy on the eyes!"

He was blushing now. "Sorry, I didn't mean to make you blush, Mr. Lewis."

"No, I really appreciate it. It's been a long time since I have felt those feelings. But you're too nice, I'm already giving you the exclusive."

Samantha leaned closer to him. "Adam, first I'm getting that exclusive because we paid $60,000 for it. Secondly, I said it because I meant it, stop thinking you're not good enough."

By this time Ronald had overheard some of their conversation, "She's right, Adam. It will take time for you to adjust but you need to learn that you are an amazing person with an inspiring story of survival."

The waitress brought the ticket over, Samantha grabbed it. "Lunch is on me."

"No, give that here," Ronald said from the other end of the table.

"No, I'm paying. You and Robin were so wonderful to open your lovely home to me. This is the least I can do to repay your kindness."

"Thank you, Samantha," Ronald said. Robin thanked her as well.

Adam grinned at her and said, "Well, this is different."

"What do you mean?" she asked.

"A beautiful woman paying for me, on the first date too."

"In your dreams, Adam," she said, smiling back at him.

"We already established that I'm not dreaming, but thank you so much. That's very kind of you. I will pick up the next one."

"It's no big deal. Who said there was even going to be a next one? You haven't asked anything yet."

They were all so full from lunch, they just had snacks for dinner, and hung out in the living room, drinking wine and listening to how Ronald and Robin met. Adam of course drank just water; he was not about to start that habit back up. Ronald was feeling pretty good from the wine and it was getting late. Robin took him to bed; it had been a full day for everyone.

"I guess, I will see you two in the morning. If you need anything, you know where we are," Robin told them.

"Thank you, Robin," Samantha said.

"Thank you, Mrs. Hartz," Adam replied.

She gave him a look, "Sorry, Robin," he corrected himself.

Samantha and Adam sat together in comfortable silence until Adam spoke, "Do you want to get this over with?"

"Get what over with?"

"The interview."

She felt foolish. "Yes, if that's what you want."

"I thought now is a good time, it's just us."

"Let me go get my things."

She sat everything down on the table. "Is it alright if we sit here?"

"Of course."

"Adam, are you sure you're good at doing this? We can wait."

"No, I'm good. I am ready to talk."

She placed her recorder in the middle of them, and had her notebook opened.

"Interviewing Adam Lewis, on the day he was released from prison for a crime he did not commit. How are you doing tonight, Adam?"

"I'm doing good, still doesn't seem real. I'm waiting for the bottom to fall out."

"Understandable. The first thing you did today after being released was go to a Chinese restaurant, why?"

"When Ronald would come and visit me, somehow, we always talked about this place. He told me when I get out, we would have to go there. I thought today would be a great day to try it."

"Was it worth it?"

"Yes. It was pretty good. My first-time trying sushi!"

"And?"

"It's different, but I can see the appeal."

"The top three reasons for wrongful convictions are: eyewitness misidentification, false confessions and police and prosecutorial misconduct. Other than false confessions, do you think the other two apply to your case?"

"Yes. I believe police and prosecutorial misconduct."

"Why?"

"The police had all the evidence ten years ago; they didn't finish the investigation thoroughly. Once they had their target set on me, they only focused on me. They had unknown DNA under Faith's fingernails. Yes, they had mine too at the scene and on her, but a separate unknown sample of DNA.

If nothing else, that could have meant there were two killers and they didn't bother looking very hard."

"When you found out that Claire Ross had killed her husband and Ms. Brandy Garcia, what went through your mind?"

"I was shocked. I heard about it on the news first and thought that maybe it was her that was killed, because all they said was Jonathan Ross and a female. So, I thought she was dead and that was my chance to get out of prison."

"When did you find out the truth of what happened?"

"The next morning. It was weird, the guards came and got me out of bed at 4:30 a.m., told me to get dressed and that I had to go up to the MSHP office, P.A. Meadows wanted to interview me. I tried asking them what was going on, but they didn't know anything. We drove the two hours there; they stuck me in a small interview room. Still haven't told me what is going on, I'm trying to tell them I want my attorney present, I was scared. About ten minutes goes by and there is a knock at the door. Ronald opened the door and I have never been so happy to see him, I told him what was going on. I must have been rambling on because I remember him telling me to 'shut up'. We sat down and that's when he told me that Claire had killed Jonathan and Ms. Garcia. Then, he told me that she also confessed to killing Faith and planting my DNA as well."

"What was your reaction?"

"I couldn't believe it, I was overwhelmed. I remember asking him if they got her DNA sample. He said that they did but I was missing the point, she admitted to everything. Even about being Lexi."

"Lexi was the woman you were with right before Faith was murdered, you told the police about her but they could never find her and just assumed that you were lying, correct?"

"Yes, even though they had unknown DNA again from my bedroom sheets, they didn't bother to run that sample. If they would have, they would have seen the sample from my bed sheet and from underneath Faith's fingernails would have matched. Just goes to prove my point of police misconduct."

"After the shock was gone, did you ask Mr. Hartz about getting released?"

"I did. He told me that they had to do it in front of a judge and see what he says, it was very nerve wracking. Ronald told me 'It could take up to 48 hours' I know he was mad, but the way I thought about it was, I already spent ten years in prison, what's another two days going to hurt?"

"How long before you got released?"

"I went in front of the judge the next morning and she released me."

"How did that moment feel?"

"I felt vindicated. The judge told me that my case was a great miscarriage of justice and that the system failed me. I have been dreaming for ten years to have those words spoken to me."

"Were there ever moments where you doubted your own innocence or that you deserved to be where you were?"

"I definitely had low moments inside, especially when I first got there. I remember I was so depressed that I literally didn't care if I lived or died. Then one morning I was eating breakfast and this old guy sat down by me and he said, 'Wasn't that sunrise just beautiful this morning?' I looked at him and said, 'I didn't see that my cell doesn't have a window'. He looked me dead in the eyes and said, 'neither does mine, learn to meditate because they can only keep your body behind these walls. Your mind can go anywhere.'

That stuck with me, and from that day on I learned everything I could about meditation. Now I meditate every morning and night."

"How did your entire roller coaster experience affect your thoughts on a higher power?"

"I absolutely believe in a higher power; I won't get into what higher power I believe in, because I believe everyone is entitled to their own beliefs. I know for me, if not for meditation and prayer, I would not be sitting here today."

"Why is that, Adam?"

"I would have probably taken my own life. I was that depressed, and thought my life was over."

"What was the usual response you would get from other prisoners or guards even, when you professed your innocence?"

"Most people don't care! That's first. Then the people that will listen, they ask you 'If you're innocent, why did you confess?' Prison life is very different from life on the outside. Prison life is very primal, so you only really talk to people that you are friends with. I didn't have a lot of friends. Now I talked with a lot of guys, but that's because I started teaching classes about writing, reading and history. I had a lot of guys come talk with me, but I didn't have that kind of relationship where there was someone over me that I could talk with."

"Do you believe there are others that are wrongfully convicted?"

"Yes, I do. I would have other prisoners come to me because they knew I got a degree in law. I would sit down with them and go through their court papers. I know for a fact there is one gentleman that we were going through his papers. The police wrote out a confession letter and had this gentleman put an X on it, he had to put an X because he could not read or write. They never read it or told him what he was signing. In his trial, the prosecution told jurors that the defendant wrote that letter then refused to sign his name and only put an X."

"Is he going to be your first client, Adam?"

"Oh no, I wish he could be. That gentleman died while in prison."

"I'm sorry to hear that. Is there anything positive you were able to take away from this experience?

"Yes. Believe it or not, I became my best self in prison."

"Tell me, what do you mean by that?"

"I learned that I was strong willed, I learned to have patience because anybody that says prison is easy or that we get too much, tell them to go spend a month in prison. I found out that I am not a waste of life, I am intelligent, I ended up getting my degree in law and plan on getting my license to practice here in the coming months. I learned to be a better human being towards others. The thing about prison is, most of us grew up the same, having to take care of ourselves at an early age. But most of the guys in prison suffered a traumatic event at an early age too. I learned don't judge a person until you have walked the same path in their shoes."

"Are there good people in prison?"

"Yes, just because someone is in prison, doesn't mean they are a horrible criminal. Some people are in there because of drug addiction, literally they are in prison because they were caught with drugs. They never committed a violent act towards anyone but they are in prison with murderers. The vast majority of men in prison are nice guys, they just made mistakes. They understand that they have to pay for their mistakes but that doesn't mean they should be treated like dogs."

"How has the State of Missouri compensated you for their mistakes?"

"The State of Missouri has not and will not compensate me for anything. The law is narrow when it comes to compensating wrongfully convicted prisoners. If a prisoner is exonerated through DNA testing, then he is entitled to compensation, but if not then they are entitled to nothing."

"According to the Missouri statute, you are not entitled to anything. Even though ten years of your life were taken away from you, you are not entitled to any compensation, correct?"

"Under the law right now, that is correct."

"Doesn't seem fair, there isn't anything you can do?"

"There are options that can be explored, they have the tendency to be unsuccessful."

"Are you talking about lawsuits?"

"Yes. But that is all I'm saying about that."

"What is the biggest challenge you think you will face while re-acclimating to normal life?"

"My biggest challenge is myself. I have to stop the negative voices in my head telling me I'm not good enough. That it doesn't matter what I do, I will always be a loser. The voice telling me I'm nothing but a trailer-trash piece of shit."

"Is that how you think of yourself?"

Adam didn't answer, he couldn't make eye contact with Samantha either. He felt the tears in his eyes, "I'm sorry, give me a moment."

410

"You don't have to answer the question, Adam. Everything is happening fast."

"No, I will answer it. I want people to know how I feel. Yes. That is how I think of myself. That is the most challenging thing to overcome."

"Adam? Look at me, Adam." He looked at her with tears in his eyes.

"You are not a loser; you are not a trailer-trash piece of shit. You are good enough and deserve to have great things happen in your life. You are a wonderful person," Samantha told him with tears coming down her face.

She took a moment, then settled back in, "Is there anything special you want to do, now that you're a free man?"

"I would like to travel. I want to go to Galveston, Faith loved going there. I have never been."

"Is that the only place?"

"No, I would definitely like to take a road trip. Just get in a car and drive. Whenever I end up is where I end up. And I want to buy my own house, so I can garden."

"Garden!?"

"Yes, it is something I picked up while in prison. It is relaxing and gives you a feeling of accomplishment."

"Ok, Mr. Greenthumb. I have trouble keeping a cactus alive, much less a whole garden."

"It is very easy and relaxing, when I get my garden up and going. I'm going to call you so you can come and help."

"Sounds good to me," she laughed, "What about dating, are you ready to get back out there?"

"No dating for me, I won't say never. But for the foreseeable future, there is no love connection. I want to focus on getting my law license and other important things done first."

"I heard you were given a letter that Faith wrote to you a few weeks before she was killed, the police gave you a copy of it, is that correct?"

"Yes, that is correct."

"Have you read it?"

"No. I'm not going to read it until everything is done with this case."

"When everything is done, what do you mean?"

"I mean when everything has concluded, it will be the last thing I read regarding this case. Then I will be able to properly grieve."

Samantha smiled, "That sounds like a good idea. Adam, thank you for opening up with me. It means a lot to me that you chose me first. Is there anything you want to add?"

"Yes. You don't have to use it, but I feel like no one ever asks me about it. I truly did love Faith; she has been the only woman I have ever loved. When you asked me about dating, it wouldn't be fair to the woman because I would be comparing her to Faith. That's a tall order to beat."

Samantha nodded, "That is certainly understandable right now. Maybe in the future you'll feel different when you meet someone."

Samantha turned off her recorder; they told each other goodnight. She went to her room feeling conflicted, she knew that he had demons to deal with and he could use a friend to help. But she also needed to stay professional, being professional meant doing to job and nothing else. She went back out to the kitchen; he had already gone downstairs to his bedroom. She felt that was fate stepping in, stopping her from doing something she should not have been doing in the first place. Samantha went back to her bedroom, took a shower and she laid in bed trying to get to sleep, but she couldn't fall asleep. Samantha decided to write up the article now and send it to her editor. She made the decision to leave first thing in the morning. If she didn't, she was going to do something she would possibly regret later.

Robin came out early in the morning to start getting things ready for the kids, she saw Samantha sitting in the kitchen. "Is everything alright, Samantha?"

"Yes, I have to get back. My flight is an early one, I wanted to thank you again for allowing me to stay in your home."

"Oh, no. I know the boys will be disappointed they weren't able to say goodbye. You are always welcomed here." Robin gave her a hug and walked her to the door. "Samantha?"

"Yes."

"You know men have to be painted a picture, don't take offense to it. Give him some time to clear his head, he will come around."

Samantha gave her another hug. "Thank you, but seriously if I don't go, I may never leave."

"You be safe and don't be a stranger now, you come and see us again."

"Bye," Samantha yelled, getting into her car.

Chapter 23

A Year Later

Adam is sitting in his office going through some papers, he is used to working 70 or more hours a week now. Since getting his law license, it has been non-stop for him. He was supposed to be on vacation this week, but had to change it because he had one last mediation and they called with another offer. He had settled all the other ones, at least the ones the court didn't throw out. But it wasn't all bad; Samantha was in town. They had been talking ever since she left without saying goodbye. When he woke up that morning and Robin told him that she had left, he was upset. He called her that same day, and they ended up talking for hours that night. He remembers they talked about silly stuff, things that don't matter in the real world but mean the world when you're getting to know someone. After that phone call, they talked to each other every night. Sometimes Samantha would fall asleep talking to him. He would tell her goodnight and hang up. They had become good friends and talked about everything. But this was the first time Samantha was coming back to town since she interviewed him after his release. Adam was excited to see her, he had invited her over for dinner to show her the new house, and of course the garden. She has seen pictures but he felt the pictures didn't give the full scope of it. There was a knock on his office door.

"I'm not here."

"Then why are you here?" Ronald asked, opening his door.

"I came in to review some notes that I left here."

"Adam, we talked about this, yesterday was your free day of coming in because of the mediation. You are on vacation for the next week."

"Was this your only reason for coming into my office?"

"No, I was going to call you, but something told me I would find you here."

"What's up?" Adam asked.

"The Ross's estate came in with a counter offer; they feel it is fair."

"They feel it is fair? Right, because they spent ten years in prison. Let's hear this counter offer."

"$10 million, one lump sum. They can have the funds available as early as tomorrow morning. Adam, I think this is a reasonable offer. But I do believe we could get them for a couple more million."

"Let's accept the offer. I have everything I need, that money will help us expand the practice."

Ronald laughed, "I'm glad you're thinking about our practice, but this is about you. Is this good for you?"

"Yes, I just want to be done with it. I want to move on."

"Ok, I will let them know. You know what that means?"

"What?"

"Adam, that's the last lawsuit that we needed to get settled. Before you leave, come by my office, you can take the letter out of the safe."

"Yeah, sounds good. I'm leaving shortly anyway; I have to run to the store to pick up some things for tonight."

"That's right, Samantha is in town. Are you ready to see her?" Ron asked mischievously.

"It's not like that, Ron. We are just friends; she doesn't see me like that."

"Let me tell you something Adam. That girl is crazy for you, she has been since the first time you two locked eyes."

"How would you know? You weren't even there!"

"Since Samantha stayed at our house last year, her and Robin have become friends. They talk sometimes."

"Really? Samantha likes me, like that?"

"Yes, you fool!"

"But, I'm more than just a few years older than her."

"What the hell does that have to do with anything?"

"Ron, you don't understand. She deserves someone better than me."

"Adam. We are good friends, right?"

"Yeah."

"Can I tell you something without you taking it wrong? Because you know I say it out of love."

"Dammit, Ron! Just say it!"

"Samantha is a great girl; we both agree she is intelligent as well. Most guys would kill to have a woman like her. You are wrapped up so tight in your own bullshit from the past, that you're going to sabotage what could be a great future! She likes you for you, if you can't let the past go, you never should have left that prison cell!"

"Ron, I'm twelve years older than her!"

"Big deal! Age is just a number, what's your next excuse?"

"What is her family going to think, with her getting involved with someone that has been to prison?"

"Are you kidding me? Adam you were wrongfully convicted, you should have never been in prison, in the first place. You know that in the year you've been out of prison how much you have accomplished?"

"Yeah, I just feel like I don't deserve all of this."

"Well, you do. I'll get you the letter, then take your ass home or wherever, but not here."

Ron was in his office when Adam knocked on the door. Ron waved him in and handed Adam the letter. "Listen, Adam. I just want to see you happy; you are like a brother to me and it kills me to see in so much pain. You are wrong, too."

"About what?" Adam asked.

"You deserve everything good that comes to you. It kills me to hear you say anything else. I never told you this, but when we were working on your case Robin and I were in a bad spot in our marriage. She kicked me out until I could get my priorities straight, I had to sleep in my car because I was working just on your case. I was running out of money and not spending time with my kids. Do you want to know what kept me going through all of that? It was the fact I knew you were innocent and I felt if you had to be in hell, I should too. Even though that's not true, that's how I felt. So, when you say shit like that and you let your life pass by without going after what makes you happy, it's a slap in the face to me and makes me feel like what I did was for nothing."

"Ron, I didn't know."

"How could you have known? I just wanted to let you know."

"I'm sorry, Ron. You know, without you, I would have never been able to get this far."

"Yeah. I said my peace. Go get ready for your dinner. I love you."

"I love you too," he said, giving Ron a hug.

Adam got dinner done just as Samantha arrived. Adam opened the door before she even got out of her car.

"Hey! Look at you, looking all cleaned up for me. In your suit. I feel underdressed," she told him, walking up the driveway. They hugged each other.

"Nonsense, you look wonderful in your black dress. Look at those legs! I love the shoes."

"Ok, I didn't even think you would notice."

He took her coat from her. "Would you like a tour?"

"Of course, I would."

He showed her the house, it was a story and a half, very modern; she could tell he was a bachelor. He showed her the garden, his tomatoes, potatoes and strawberry plants.

"Adam, this is beautiful. I really love it. Congratulations, you deserve it."

"Thanks. Are you hungry?"

"Seriously, I'm starving, it smells so good."

They had a great conversation while eating dinner. When they finished, they went into the living room where he had started a fire and sat with a glass of apple cider.

"I have something to tell you."

"Out with it," she said smiling.

"We settled the last lawsuit today."

"Really?"

"Yes, we did."

She didn't say anything for a moment. "I'm happy for you. That's great news."

"Yeah. I thought I would feel differently."

"It's alright, it's a lot to process, Adam. Did you get your letter?"

"Yes, I got it. But that's not the reason. I'm ok that it's over."

"Ok, was it the letter that upset you?"

"I haven't read it yet, I waited."

Samantha's eyes were focused on his. "Why?"

"I wanted to read it with you, because you are important to me. I wanted to share this moment with someone I love and trust, and that is you, Sam."

She got tears in her eyes and started to cry, "Are you serious?"

"I have been blind and caught in my own bullshit in my head. You are an amazing woman, you are my best friend Sam. You are the first person I think of when I wake up in the morning and the last person I think of before I close my eyes. When my phone rings I hope that it's you calling. When I found out you were coming back, I started getting butterflies in my stomach. I'm in love with you Sam. I have been for a long time, I have been too scared to say it, I thought I wasn't good enough for you. I know different now. No matter what this letter says, I want you and no one else. I'm ready for the past to be done and my future to begin. Sam, I want you to be my future. I'm willing to burn this letter without opening it to prove it's over, if that's what it would take."

"You are enough for me, I love you."

419

They embraced, both with tears in their eyes. They shared their first kiss, something Adam will never forget. The only way he can describe it was like watching fireworks in the night sky, pure beauty.

"Open it, Adam. No matter what, I'm here for good," she said, kissing him again.

He opened the letter and they read it together.

Adam,

I'm writing this letter because I don't have the self-control to do this in person. You are the love of my life. We've been through a lot these last nine months and I wouldn't have changed one minute of it. You mean everything to me, I'm thankful that you came into my life at the most perfect time. You've taught me so much. When I'm with you I feel like I can do anything. You make me feel loved, cared about; you make life worth living as much as my kids do. You allow me to act anyway with you, I can be myself and you love me for it. You never make me feel worthless, stupid or like a failure. I never question how you feel about me or how I look to you. Every time we are together, you tell me how much you love me, how beautiful I am. You tell me you even like my feet, when I think they are the ugliest feet I have ever seen. You tell me that I'm smart, that you like to have conversations with me. Even though I think I'm always the one doing all the talking. You make me feel more alive in five minutes with you, than Jonathan has our entire marriage. I don't regret my marriage because it gave me two beautiful babies. They are my everything, you need to know that in order to love me, you have to love them. The crazy thing is I know you do! We talk about them all the time! You make everything feel simple, there is nothing too difficult for you. I don't know how you can love me unconditionally; my hope is that you can teach me that. How you look, pass all my flaws and only see my beauty as you call it. There will be a learning period for us but I'm alright with that, it will be worth it. I know this is crazy and seems unrealistic but just don't give up on me yet,

420

I'm starting to take the necessary steps in preparing to leave Jonathan. I know it will be hard with him being the way he is; just stick with me, though. It is a lot to ask of you, but I ask you because I choose you, Adam! I would choose a life with you for one day, rather than years with him. I hope you're ready for all of this, I hope you know what you're getting yourself into, and get ready because all four of us are coming. That's right, four. Pearl, Weston, myself, and the baby. We are pregnant, Adam. I know this is a horrible way to tell you but if I told you in person, I would leave Jonathan that very moment and I can't do that just yet. But soon, my love. I am going to stop because the kids are going crazy. But know this, I love you. For everything that you are, for everything that you're not, and everything that you will become. I can't wait to spend the rest of my life with you and be able to wake up every morning next to you.

Your girl,

Faith

Zachary Hicks graduated University of Missouri Saint Louis with a degree in criminology and criminal justice. Zachary is from Jefferson County, Missouri, where his first novel, *Have a Little Faith,* takes place. When not writing, Zachary enjoys spending time with his wife of seven years, enjoying the outdoors, and looking for items for complete his ever-growing Batman collection. He currently resides in near St. Louis with his wife, and their cat, Henrietta. You can follow him on Instagram @zhicks318.

Made in the USA
Monee, IL
19 April 2024

57179950R00243